FIRST
INSTINCT

What Reviewers Say About BOLD STROKES Authors

∾

KIM BALDWIN

"*A riveting novel of suspense* seems to be a very overworked phrase. However, it is extremely apt when discussing Kim Baldwin's [*Hunter's Pursuit*]. An exciting page turner [features] Katarzyna Demetrious, a bounty hunter…with a million dollar price on her head. Look for this excellent novel of suspense…" – **R. Lynne Watson**, *MegaScene*

"*Force of Nature* is an exciting and substantial reading experience which will long remain with the reader. Likeable characters with plausible problems and concerns, imaginative settings, engrossing events, and a well-tailored writing style all contribute to an exceptional novel. Baldwin's characterization is acutely and meticulously circumscribed and expansive. It is indeed gratifying to see a new author attempt and succeed in expanding her literary technique and writing style. Kim Baldwin is an author who has achieved both." – **Arlene Germain**, reviewer for the *Lambda Book Report* and the *Midwest Book Review*

∾

ROSE BEECHAM

"…her characters seem fully capable of walking away from the particulars of whodunit and engaging the reader in other aspects of their lives." – *Lambda Book Report*

"When Jennifer Fulton writes mysteries, she writes them as Rose Beecham. And since Jennifer Fulton is a very fine writer, you might expect that Rose Beecham is a fine writer too. You're right…On the way to a remarkable, and thoroughly convincing climax, Beecham creates believable characters in compelling situations, with enough humor to provide effective counterpoint to the work of detecting." – *Bay Area Reporter*

RONICA BLACK

"Black juggles the assorted elements of her first book with assured pacing and estimable panache...[including]...the relative depth—for genre fiction—of the central characters: Erin, the married-but-separated detective who comes to her lesbian senses; loner Patricia, the policewoman-mentor who finds herself falling for Erin; and sultry club owner Elizabeth, the sexually predatory suspect who discards women like Kleenex...until she meets Erin." – **Richard Labonte**, Book Marks, Q Syndicate, 2005

"Black's characterization is skillful, and the sexual chemistry surrounding the three major characters is palpable and definitely hot-hot-hot. If you're looking for a more traditional murder mystery, *In Too Deep* might not be entirely your cup of Earl. On the other hand, if you're looking for a solid read with ample amounts of eroticism and a red herring or two, you're sure to find *In Too Deep* a satisfying read." –**Lynne Jamneck**, L-Word.com Literature

GUN BROOKE

"*Course of Action* is a romance...populated with a host of captivating and amiable characters. The glimpses into the lifestyles of the rich and beautiful people are rather like guilty pleasures....[A] most satisfying and entertaining reading experience." – **Arlene Germain**, reviewer for the *Lambda Book Report* and the *Midwest Book Review*

"*Protector of the Realm* has it all; sabotage, corruption, erotic love and exhilarating space fights. Gun Brooke's second novel is forceful with a winning combination of solid characters and a brilliant plot." – **Kathi Isserman**, *JustAboutWrite*

JANE FLETCHER

"*The Walls of Westernfort* is not only a highly engaging and fast-paced adventure novel, it provides the reader with an interesting framework for examining the same questions of loyalty, faith, family and love that [the characters] must face." – **M. J. Lowe**, *Midwest Book Review*

Lee Lynch

"There's a heady sense of '60s back-to-the-land communal idealism and '70s woman-power feminism (with hints of lesbian separatism) to this spirited novel—even though it's set in contemporary rural Oregon. Partners Donny (she's black and blue-collar) and Chick (she's plus-sized and motherly) are both in their 50s, owners of the dyke-centric Natural Woman Foods store, a homey nexus for *Sweet Creek*'s expansive cast of characters....Lynch, with a dozen novels to her credit dating back to the early days of Naiad Press, has earned her stripes as a writerly elder; she was contributing stories to the lesbian magazine *The Ladder* four decades ago. But this latest is sublimely in tune with the times."
– **Richard Labonte**, Book Marks, Q Syndicate, 2005

RADCLY*f*FE

"...well-honed storytelling skills...solid prose and sure-handedness of the narrative..." – **Elizabeth Flynn**, *Lambda Book Report*

"...well-plotted...lovely romance...I couldn't turn the pages fast enough!" – **Ann Bannon**, author of *The Beebo Brinker Chronicles*

Ali Vali

"Rich in character portrayal, *The Devil Inside* by Ali Vali is an unusual, unpredictable, and thought-provoking love story that will have the reader questioning the definition of right and wrong long after she finishes the book....*The Devil Inside*'s strength is that it is unlike most romance novels. Nothing about the story and its characters is conventional. We do not know what the future holds for Emma and Cain, but Vali tempts us with every word so we want to find out. I am very much looking forward to the sequel *The Devil Unleashed*."
– **Kathi Isserman**, *JustAboutWrite*

Visit us at www.boldstrokesbooks.com

FIRST
INSTINCT

by

JLee Meyer

2006

ISBN 1-933110-59-7

This Trade Paperback Original Is Published By
Bold Strokes Books, Inc.,
New York, USA

First Printing: November 2006

Credits
Editors: Shelley Thrasher and Stacia Seaman
Production Design: Stacia Seaman
Cover Design By Sheri (GRAPHICARTIST2020@HOTMAIL.COM)
Photo: Sheri

By the Author

Forever Found

Acknowledgments

Shelley Thrasher—for your unending patience and keen eye for details. You systematically (not my style) led me through a process that produced a far better book than we started with. Thank you.

Radclyffe—for vision and high expectations, not just for yourself or the Bold Strokes authors, but for lesbian fiction as a genre. It also didn't hurt to have your input on one scene in particular. Thank you.

Stacia Seaman—it's always a pleasure to work with you.

Kali's Kafe—a finer group of friends you couldn't ask for.

Cheryl—thanks for being such a fan of my writing. It wouldn't be on the page if not for you.

Dedication

For Cheryl and Bolero the Wonder Dog.
Our family is complete.

CHAPTER ONE

"That bastard! How dare he treat me like this?" Leigh Grove muttered, staring into her bathroom mirror. She shook off the memory of her ex-fiancé Peter's recent infidelity and hastily applied fresh pink lipstick with a trembling hand, careful of her healing lip. She checked her makeup. She had covered the bruises well, but her cheek was still puffy.

Running late, she left her third-floor apartment and hailed a passing cab to the Pacific Heights Diner on Union Street. It was upscale and hip, just right for the kind of snotty nouveau millionaires Peter liked to be around.

Her stomach knotted as the pretentious maître d' greeted her and showed her to Peter's table. She followed him through the mirrored bar into the dark and dreary dining area, where Peter Cheney sat at his usual table in the middle of the room. The better to see and be seen by his buddies. He was sipping what she guessed was his first or second Grey Goose martini. Leigh had never liked this place, primarily because of the phony clientele.

"Darling! I was worried when you were late." Peter rose and held the chair for her, waving off the waiter. He sat, rubbing the back of his neck, and immediately took another slug of the martini. "What can I order for you? A glass of wine? A cocktail?"

Leigh stared at him, then busied herself with the wine menu. He seemed nervous, solicitous to the point of fawning. He hadn't tried male manners on her since their first date. "A glass of the Wilson Zinfandel, please." She was surprised to see him order another round. He was perspiring, too. He was definitely nervous and maybe even guilty about something. Leaning back in her chair, she waited for him to speak.

Peter winked at her, as though they were sharing a secret. "I've ordered the oysters. They've just come in from the Chesapeake Bay."

Leigh fought the urge to slap him.

When the waiter arrived with their drinks, Leigh ordered a Caesar salad. The appetizers in the restaurant all tasted the same. She took a sip of her wine and watched Peter toss back more of his cocktail. He was jittery, but she wondered if it was because she'd left him. *Not likely. He hasn't even noticed the bruises on my lip.*

"Peter, I can't believe you'd treat me so shabbily."

He reddened slightly under his tan. "Leigh, I've already apologized for that little indiscretion. Can't we just forget it? I'll see that my 'mistake' is fired. Would that satisfy you?"

"My God. Does she work at the brokerage? What are you trying to do, set up a harem?"

He gave her his best hurt-puppy expression. "Now, Leigh."

Leigh leaned closer. "Don't 'now, Leigh' me, Peter. I walked in on you two in bed having sex. And the drugs, was that cocaine? Do you blame me for being upset? You're my—correction, you *were* my fiancé, for God's sake!" Leigh was feeling more the fool by the minute. How could she have been so blind?

The oysters and salad arrived, and they fell silent. Peter ordered yet another martini and sloshed down the rest of his current one. "It was a mistake. A misjudgment. I'll never do it again."

Leigh took a sip of wine, then tried to have a bite of her salad to calm down. This evening was turning out to be just as miserable as she'd thought it would. And Peter was smugly slurping down oysters and drinks without a care in the world.

"The only reason I came over to your condo was that I was worried about you. You hadn't answered my calls in over twenty-four hours. And your front door was ajar. I thought something had happened to you. Then I discover you rutting away in the bed that we'd shared. How *could* you?"

She pushed her plate away and reached for her wine. Willing her hand to stop shaking wasn't working, so she concentrated on not throwing her drink on Peter's hand-tailored suit. Why waste good wine?

Peter seemed to reluctantly turn his attention away from his plate.

"Leigh, I'm sorry. I...wasn't thinking. Let's put all this behind us. Darling?"

She was willing to bet his apology was fueled by vodka. Disgusted, she said, "Eat your oysters, Peter."

He instantly returned to his food.

❖

In a corner booth of the main dining room, Jen Stryker watched Leigh and Peter. They seemed to be arguing. Her attention diverted to the tall redhead who was walking in her direction, Jen grinned in welcome as the blue eyes that were so like her own sparkled in recognition.

Her niece slid in next to her and gave her a hug. "Hey, Aunt Jen. It's been a while."

Jen returned the affection. "Yes, Constantina, it has been a long time." Watching Conn flinch at the use of her full name made her silently vow not to tease her sensitive niece so often.

"Aunt Jen, you know I hate that name. I only let Marina call me that because she's Greek. I have no idea what Mother was thinking when she came up with it." Conn studied her menu. "I know, I know, it's been too long. But at least this assignment has brought us together. Please forgive me and call me Conn."

"I'm sorry. I like to tease you, and it *has* been too long. Hell, I would have accepted any excuse to get you here. To that point, our possible informant is having dinner with her fiancé right here in this restaurant." She nodded in the direction of Leigh Grove and Peter Cheney. "Lucky us."

Conn appeared to be looking for the waiter, but Jen knew she was studying her quarry. Jen poured her a glass of Pinot Noir from a bottle she'd ordered earlier. Conn Stryker had grown into a beautiful woman. No longer the gawky thirteen-year-old who used to spend her summers with Jen in California, she was now the CEO of a large software firm that provided forensic software to not only financial institutions, but to the government as well. And Conn was not just the CEO, either. She was a trained field operative and had enlisted Jen's help in a case she was working on.

Conn picked up her wineglass. "Well, she's just as gorgeous as her photographs. Can't say too much for her choice in men. Now the question is, will she turn against her own fiancé."

"I have a hard time believing she's involved in this scam. She's been nothing but intelligent, fair, and informative with me." Jen shrugged. "Maybe a touch naïve, but I don't know her very well. She could be one of those women who just does what her man tells her to do."

Conn eyed Leigh Grove noncommittally. "What has she told you about herself?"

"Well, let's see. She got a Wharton MBA in finance and was a sorority girl at Harvard before that. Popular, I would guess. She's very outgoing. But you probably know more than I do, Conn. What did the background check say?"

"She's from a moneyed Boston family. Wealth from her mother's side of the family. Mom is very socially connected. Daddy is a well-known attorney in Boston. I'm sure the social connections haven't hurt his career. Little Miss Debutante, though, did make over a 3.5 grade point average. She's no dummy. But I'm sure her parents thought an MBA wasn't necessary. After all, she could meet Mr. Right at one of their soirees, right?" Conn took another sip of her wine.

"Anyway, I bet she went against their plans for her when she split for California. But then she was swept off her feet by Peter Cheney. Ten years older, some would call him handsome, has his own investment firm. Probably fits the bill as acceptable to the folks. I don't know what kind of person she is, other than the kind I usually avoid like the plague." She turned her attention to the menu. "How about some fried artichoke hearts? I'm hungry."

"None for me, sweetie. I've been here before, and their fried food takes two days to digest. And don't eat too much. I'm making dinner later. I think I'll go over and interrupt the happy couple, see if I can get a read on them."

"Okay. Hey, how did you know they'd be here tonight?"

"She once told me this was his favorite place. When she called to reschedule our appointment she said something about meeting him for dinner. I connected the dots and we got lucky." Jen scooted out of the booth. "Be right back."

She walked straight to their table. "Hello, Leigh. I thought I recognized you."

As Leigh automatically smiled at Jen, surprise and embarrassment written on her face, Jen tried not to stare at the subtle bruises on her face and her healing lip.

"Ms. Stryker! What a pleasant surprise. Have you met my...Peter Cheney? Peter, have you met Jennifer Stryker? She's a large investor in some of your funds and a wonderful client."

Peter Cheney was struggling to his feet to greet her. To Jen's practiced eye he was drunk, or getting there. His expression was close to a smirk before he sat down abruptly, and Leigh seemed upset.

Jen reached over the table to shake Peter's offered hand. "Careful, Mr. Cheney. These chairs can be a little precarious. You must be so proud of Leigh. She's been a terrific help to me. Beauty and brains. You're a very lucky man."

Gazing hazily at Leigh, Peter said, "Yes, she is a beauty."

Jen noticed with interest that Leigh colored at the comment and diverted her eyes.

"Well, I won't keep you from your meal. I just thought I'd say hello. Nice to run into you, Leigh. See you soon." She waved and returned to her table.

As Jen settled into the booth, Conn said, "Seems our Ms. Grove isn't having as good a time as her fiancé is. She won't look at him, and her jaw muscles are working overtime. Interesting."

"I saw bruises on her face. And her lip's been injured recently. I'm concerned about her. Cheney is drunk and was barely able to be polite. I don't blame her for being upset."

Conn's gaze drifted back to the silent couple in the middle of the room. "Bruises and a split lip. Not something I would envision for a sorority girl and a debutante. Guess she hadn't planned on real life having a few bumps along the way."

"A little cynical, aren't we? If she agrees to go along with this, how are you going to work with her? You're going to have to keep your opinions to yourself."

"It's part of the job." Conn shrugged slightly and returned to her now-delivered appetizer. "If she agrees, I'll have to tolerate her plastic insincerity. Big deal. I've put up with worse."

She glanced at Leigh Grove again. "I'll say one thing for her. She *is* a knockout. Those magazine covers didn't do her justice. She's just about got it all. But those gregarious types, the ones that seem perfect, are usually only skin deep. Eye candy. Evidently that's what Cheney wanted, and that's what he got. And she got her perfect match."

Spearing one of the fried artichoke hearts, Jen caught the surprise on Conn's face and grinned, unapologetic. "Well, I'm hungry. You know, you might be underestimating Ms. Grove. Keep in mind, Conn, that she was raised to be gracious and politically correct. She probably says all the right things and makes small talk automatically. That isn't much of an indicator as to who she really is. Just my humble opinion, of course." She realized that, typically, her favorite and only niece wasn't listening but still studying Ms. Grove.

Jen sighed. Conn had always been a loner, courtesy of a brilliant mind, height developed too early, and an alcoholic mother. Only once had she confessed that she was afraid to bring anyone home during her childhood for fear of finding her mother passed out, naked, on the floor. Evidently the one time it had happened was enough for Conn.

Conn had spent every summer with her from the time she was thirteen until after undergraduate school. Jen loved her as her own and treasured every moment of watching her grow into an accomplished, strong woman.

But Conn never let anyone too close. Jen and Marina were thrilled when Conn came out to them, then saddened that she had yet to bring a woman home to meet them. Marina even wondered how Conn had figured out she was a lesbian. It seemed like all she did was work. So they practiced patience. And practiced, and practiced, and practiced.

Marina! Jen glanced at her watch. "Hey, I have to go. Marina should be calling from wherever in the world she is, and I want to be home to talk and get dinner going. Are you ready?"

Conn seemed a million miles away. "Huh? What? Oh, um, no. I'll finish my food and wine and be out shortly. Give my love to Auntie M."

Jen stared at her for a moment, wondering what had Conn so distracted. But now was not the time or place to ask. She gathered her things to leave. "Okay, see you in a bit."

Leigh had given up on her salad and the evening. Peter kept repeating himself about the offer to fire the woman with whom he'd been caught. He clearly thought that was all she was concerned about. Either that or his martini-soaked brain could only concentrate on one topic. That topic would, of course, be him.

"Peter, I am *not* interested in you firing the woman you had sex with. I doubt she even knew you were engaged." She watched him register vague surprise and perhaps even a trace of guilt. On second thought, the guilt was probably in her imagination.

"I *am* concerned about my clients' portfolios. The companies you're pushing don't have sound financials. We both know that. It's smoke and mirrors. Some of them are okay, but you're moving more and more into really risky investments. The clients you assigned to me are single older women who live on the income generated by their portfolios. Most of them can't recover if their investments bomb out."

Peter sloppily dropped his fork on the tablecloth and set his jaw. "I'll worry about what stocks they should invest in. I'm the expert. What exactly do you want, Leigh?"

Somewhat surprised by the shift, she pushed on. "I want more discretion in handling their money. I want to be included in deciding what funds they should invest in."

When he shook his head she continued. "Look, Peter, I may not have a lot of experience, but I do have a good education. I know how to do my research, and I know how to read financials. These aren't the right choices for my demographic. I want a say in how they're invested."

He stared at her blankly, then his eyes narrowed. "Leigh, the other members of the strategic committee won't go along. You don't have the chops to even sit on it. Don't be upset. There are just other people to consider."

"Strategic *committee*? When was this committee formed? Who's on it, and why am I *not* on it? What's going on here? My business ethics prof had plenty to say about the type of activities I've been noticing at the office."

When several of the diners around them stopped their conversations, Leigh realized that her voice must have grown louder. Peter was noticeably sweating, his eyes darting over her shoulder in the direction of the bar. She lowered her volume.

"Listen. I've tolerated your patronizing attitude, your buddies hitting on me, and you putting me off about my concerns. But I will *not* tolerate being told to advise my clients based on a mysterious committee that needs to decide if I can be a member!"

By the time she took a breath she felt as though her face was on fire. Peter sat back heavily in his chair, evidently surprised by her words.

The silence between them was palpable, and Peter regarded her with increasingly cold eyes. "Leigh, listen to me carefully. The strategic committee is my own concept. I recently decided to ask Bradley and Dieter and Scott to be advisors to the business. You may call them my buddies, but they're all wildly successful fund managers and have a lot of power in this market. They can make companies or break them, and they've decided to allow the brokerage, me in particular, to be a part of their success." He drained his martini, dribbling some on his chin and swiping at it.

"Anyway, I can't just go in there and tell them what to do. I won't say, 'Leigh says she wants to be in on the decisions.'" He regarded her evenly. The smugness had returned.

"You're serious, aren't you? You really are going to turn over your clients and your reputation to these guys. Peter, what do you know about them? They aren't 'wildly successful.' They're middle managers who've ridden the success of a few stocks, but how long have they been around? What's their track record?"

She tried to get through to him. "It's not just your money you're risking! Many of the firm's clients, like Jen Stryker, the woman you just met, rely on their portfolios for credit, income, and retirement. Others have cashed in bonds or borrowed against their homes to be able to buy more, all because they trust you. And me. I'm guilty of taking your word on most of this. Now you tell me that the foxes are in the henhouse. When were you going to let me in on that piece of information? If I hadn't caught you with that woman, would you have even mentioned it?"

The waiter hesitantly approached with their entrées, and Leigh busied herself with her napkin until he had served them, poured a glass of wine for Peter and refreshed her glass, and quickly left.

Peter took a few gulps of wine and cut a large bite of his porterhouse steak, cooked rare. After stuffing it into his mouth, he stared at her belligerently while he chewed. He washed it down with more wine and said, "Leigh, I've made all of the investors a lot of money recently, including you and your parents. One of the perks of my success is meeting and doing business with the movers and shakers of Wall Street. They want me to be one of them. It's something I've always dreamt of doing. Now it's here, and I intend to be a part of it, all of it. I may be a midlevel fund manager now, but the big time is just a few months away."

His voice took on a patronizing tone. "You were going to be part of it because of our personal relationship. You could have a cozy setup with plenty of time off to coddle your rich lady clients like that Jen Whatshername, who just wants someone to go to lunch with and hold her hand.

"If you stick with your choice to end it, you are just another employee. The fund will continue to be managed the way I want it to be, with the advice of the committee. You will take direction from me, or you will not be with this company. Am I clear?"

Peter was different than Leigh had ever seen him. Her stomach was in knots as she put her fork down. "I guess I have to think about this." She placed her napkin on the table. "We'll talk in the morning."

Peter took her hand as she started to rise and squeezed it a little too firmly. "I'm not finished. Please sit down."

His expression and the ache that was approaching pain in her hand made her sit. When he released her, she resisted the urge to rub it, not wanting to let him think he had intimidated her.

"If you decide to leave, don't even think about contacting any of your clients to give them your opinion about how their money is being handled. Those clients are mine, and any information comes from me alone. And one other thing—I gave you the names of the committee members in confidence. You are not to mention them or the existence of the committee to anyone. Not one soul. Understand?"

His tone was menacing and his eyes flat. "Tell me you understand, Leigh. Tell me now."

Leigh was dumbfounded. Who *was* this man?

"You really are an ass, Peter. I'm fed up with your patronizing attitude and pretentious lifestyle. I'm out of here."

He took a breath and leaned back, all smiles. "What, no dessert? You've always loved their Grand Marnier soufflé."

She grabbed her purse and stood up. "Correction. *You've* always loved their Grand Marnier soufflé. No, thank you."

Chapter Two

Though Leigh wanted to run, she forced herself to walk away from the table slowly. Passing through the bar, she picked up speed. She couldn't get out of there fast enough.

Once outside she discovered that a storm had rolled in while she was in the restaurant. Since she hadn't paid any attention to the weather or news for several days, she didn't have a raincoat or umbrella. Numbly standing in the parking lot, getting drenched, she was searching for her keys in her purse when someone roughly grabbed her arm and spun her around. It was the man who had ransacked her apartment and roughed her up earlier in the week. She started to scream, but he flashed a long, thin knife and held the point under her chin.

"Shut up."

She stared at him and froze. His eyes were like black marbles, and he had that same awful breath.

"I told you to behave, didn't I?" His eyes narrowed menacingly. "Now I'm going to have to teach you something about obeying."

"Excuse me, are you okay?" The voice was female, a rich contralto that commanded attention. Leigh craned, but could only make out a figure behind them in a long trench coat, backlit by the lights of the restaurant.

The man slipped the knife into his jacket, gave Leigh a warning squeeze, and turned, holding her tightly to him. "She's just had too much to drink. I'm helping her to her car."

The woman was tall, with long, thick hair, but it was impossible to make out her features. She stood her ground. "She doesn't appear drunk. Are you okay? Do you need help? I can call the police on my cell phone. Just the press of a button." She held up the phone.

The man squeezed Leigh's arm harder, the pain making her wince.

The tall woman growled, "Release her now or I call the cops."

Other diners came out of the restaurant, and some stopped to watch.

The man glared at the stranger, then bent until his mouth was almost touching Leigh's ear and whispered, "I'll see you later." With that, he let go of her and strode out of the parking lot.

Leigh felt her knees give out and knew she was going to fall, but suddenly strong arms supported her. She was able to right herself but was unsteady, and the taller woman held on to her. When one of the other diners asked if they needed help, the stranger said Leigh seemed to be fine and that she would make sure she got home. She walked Leigh over to a dark-colored Audi and propped her against it. The rain had turned to mist.

"Are you all right? Did he hurt you?"

Leigh took an inventory. Other than a sore arm, being soaked to the skin and scared to death, she was okay. "I'm fine, I think. Thank you. I don't know what would have happened if you…hadn't been there."

The woman surveyed the area before speaking. "Where is your car?"

Leigh glanced around. Then it dawned on her. "I took a cab." She ran a trembling hand through her wet hair. "My God. I could have been avoided all this if I'd just ordered a cab before I left and had it waiting for me. How stupid!"

The woman put a hand on her damp shoulder. "You left in a hurry and seemed upset. That's why I followed you out. That man appeared to be waiting for you. Some jerks will take advantage of a woman in distress. What did he say to you?"

Leigh tried not to hyperventilate. "That I wasn't behaving and he was going to teach me about obeying." His words were beginning to sink in. Her hands were trembling harder, and she hugged herself to try to stop the reaction.

The stranger was insistent. "What did he whisper to you before let go of your arm?"

Leigh struggled to get any words to come out. "He told me he'd see me later. Oh, God. I know him. He broke into my apartment a couple of days ago. He knows where I live!"

The woman kept her hand on Leigh's shoulder. The pressure served to steady her nerves, and after a few seconds she was able to drop her arms to her sides, take a deep breath, and stand up, away from the car. Her rescuer removed her hand.

"I should be going. I'll call a cab from the restaurant. I'm Leigh Grove, by the way. Thank you for all of your help, uh—"

"Conn. This is my car. Let me take you to your apartment. You probably shouldn't be alone just yet. As a precaution."

Leigh was suddenly exhausted. Tears came, unbidden. "When he broke into my apartment Monday he threatened me. Tonight I think he was going to make good on the threat."

She covered her face with both hands, trying to hold herself together. After a brief moment the same strong arms that had kept her upright a few minutes before wrapped around her again, holding her close. The events of the last few days landed on her, and a sob tore from her throat. She was embarrassed to be breaking down in front of a total stranger, yet had never felt safer in her life. She focused on trying to remember her rescuer's name.

After a few moments the woman—Conn—released Leigh and slowly walked her around to the passenger side of the car. Leigh heard the door unlock automatically and was aware of being helped into the seat. She sat, motionless, as the tall woman leaned over her to buckle her in. Soft hair smelling fresh and clean, misted with rain, brushed her face, and for a moment their faces were inches apart. Conn's eyes were light in color, but that was all Leigh could discern. Then, just as quickly, the door shut and the stranger was getting in on the driver's side.

As the car started to move, Leigh concentrated on calming down. She was freezing, then her back and thighs felt warmth. *Ah, heated seats.* Her trembling started to subside. Safety. "What if I short out your seats? I'm dripping wet."

"Don't worry about it. Where do you live?" Conn kept her eyes on the streets in front of her.

Giving her the address and a few landmarks to help find it, Leigh realized the effort was exhausting.

They wound around the streets of San Francisco and headed toward the Marina. As they entered the street where Leigh lived, she was about to point out her building when the car picked up speed and passed it.

Surprised, Leigh said, "That was it on the left back there."

Conn turned at the next corner and continued down the street. "Have you noticed that white van in front of your building? Has it been there for long?"

Alerted by something in Conn's tone, Leigh marshaled her forces and thought about the question. "A day or two. Why?"

"When did you say that guy broke into your apartment?"

"Two days ago. *Why?*" Leigh was wide-awake and worried.

Conn didn't answer right away. After a few exasperating minutes she said, "Two things. One, vans like that can be used for surveillance. Assuming that you could be the target of that surveillance, you might want to reconsider going in just now. Second, the ape in the parking lot knows your address and could be planning on paying you a visit after I drop you off. As a matter of fact, I think we have company."

She was checking the rearview mirror, and Leigh started to turn in her seat.

Somehow anticipating the reaction, Conn quickly said, "There's a vanity mirror in the sun visor. Flip the visor down and slide the cover to the left." She reached up to press a button. At Leigh's questioning look she explained, "I turned off the light on the mirror."

Leigh did as instructed and saw the headlights of a large car about a block away. Conn was making some turns, not speeding, perhaps appearing lost. The headlights maintained the distance, but stayed behind them.

"This is impossible," Leigh said. "I got mugged. I haven't stolen a state secret! Surveillance, being followed—this can't be happening!"

Conn didn't appear ruffled in the least. "Well, I don't know why they want you, but someone definitely does. Hold on, let's see how far they're willing to go to keep tabs on you."

With that, she sped up and skipped through the end of a yellow traffic light. The car behind them ran the red light and started to gain on the Audi.

Conn pursed her lips and chided, "Oh, no, you will not touch my babycar." The Audi nimbly jumped ahead, moving down Marina Boulevard toward Doyle Drive, the approach to the Golden Gate Bridge. The headlights fell behind, but paced with them.

As they were nearing the bridge, Conn abruptly exited down into the Presidio, made several hairpin turns, and came up almost at the tollbooths, continuing north across the span. The car behind them jerked and fishtailed once, but still followed.

The two cars drove across the bridge at the speed limit. The bridge was so heavily patrolled, Leigh could understand why the larger car wouldn't want to attract attention. What she didn't know was why *they* wouldn't want to. That thought was fleeting as the chase began in earnest the instant they came off the bridge and headed up Highway 101.

The Audi leapt ahead and up the Waldo Grade with a force that kept Leigh's head pinned to the headrest. As they came over the grade and headed down, the banks and curves would have made Leigh brake hard, but Conn accelerated into them and gained even more ground. Leigh glimpsed Conn's profile and saw that she was smiling.

They were in the fast lane when she cut across four lanes of traffic and took the exit that Leigh knew headed to the beaches. The larger car tried to execute the same maneuver, but missed the exit. Leigh let out a whoop of victory and raised her fist in the air. The driver, whom Leigh now thought of as either her new best friend or her worst nightmare, eased to the right so that they could go into Mill Valley.

Conn blew out a breath. "Maybe we should find a place to stop and talk this over. We need a strategy."

Just then a set of headlights appeared right behind them. Conn's jaw tightened as she threw the car into a lower gear.

"Hold on." She took off like a bullet, slipping around a corner with a funky old bar on it, then snaked up into the hills so rapidly that what little Leigh had eaten for dinner now had the very real possibility of ending up in her lap. She closed her eyes and hung on to the handle above the door that Audi had so thoughtfully provided. *Probably for just such an occasion.*

A few moments later the car slowed a bit, and she dared to open her eyes and check the mirror. Nothing. She took a deep breath.

As they rode along in silence for a while, Leigh had no idea where they were. They weren't on Highway 1 but continued to climb. The road was narrow and heavily forested. The headlights were very bright and the scenery flashed by rapidly, almost hypnotizing her. Leigh was vaguely aware that this situation could be more dangerous than taking her chances in the city. She knew nothing of this person. She had come almost out of nowhere, seemingly to help, but…

Though Leigh realized she should be on guard, she was simply too tired to care. The adrenaline rush had worn off. She silently prayed that she had made the right choice and drifted off toward sleep. It had begun to rain again, the windshield wipers making a steady metronome sound that only made her groggier as the car continued up and over the mountain and headed toward the coast. After about half an hour Leigh felt it slow down and stop briefly, then roll a few more feet and stop.

Leigh roused herself and opened her eyes. To her amazement, a familiar person stood at the door of the house and waved at them. She twisted in her seat to face the mysterious stranger who had rescued her.

The woman smiled and extended her hand. "My name is Conn Stryker."

Leigh stared at her in wonder and took her hand: "As in Jen Stryker?"

CHAPTER THREE

L eigh did some mental calculations. *This must be Jen's house in Bolinas.* Jen had described it as sitting on a bluff. Leigh had offered to visit her when they were getting to know each other, but Jen had always declined, asking instead to meet at one of the local coffee houses in the village. That was fine with Leigh because it was always a challenge to even find the town.

She couldn't make out a thing about the house because it was raining and dark. Jen came out and escorted her inside what appeared to be a large mudroom.

She studied Leigh for a moment and frowned. "Let's get you into something warm and dry. Wait here."

With that she and Conn left the room, and Leigh stood in the middle of the small mudroom, dripping and feeling like something very large and pitiful that a cat had dragged in. She hugged herself to try and stop shivering from the cold and fear, starting to think maybe this wasn't a good idea. Jen was a client, after all, and the fact that her stunning—what?—daughter had helped her only made the situation more confusing and humiliating. Leigh should be solving the problem *for* Jen. She needed to think.

Jen reappeared with a large towel. "Here. Take your shoes and clothes off and wrap yourself in this. Then come on down to the kitchen. Out the door and on the left. I'm going to finish making dinner. How about linguini with pesto, garlic bread, and a nice salad? Maybe a good glass of wine. Something to warm our stomachs and put some meat on those scrawny bones of yours."

Leigh quickly put her thoughts aside. "That sounds too good to be true. Be right there."

Jen flipped a switch on her way out, flooding the room in florescent light.

Leigh blinked a few times as her eyes adjusted, then took in her surroundings. Washer, dryer, large sink, cupboards full of household and outdoor things. She kicked off her ruined shoes. Next, her designer jeans, then everything else. She wrapped the soft, clean beach towel around her and opened the door into a hallway.

Hearing noise, she followed it and found Jen busy in the kitchen, putting pans on the stove and getting food from the refrigerator. Leigh cleared her throat softly, feeling awkward and vulnerable without her clothes.

Jen glanced at her and grinned. "Okay, let's get you fixed up." She checked the stove, adjusted a burner, and motioned for Leigh to follow.

Leigh let out a quiet sigh of relief as she trailed after her. She felt cold to the bone as they walked out of the kitchen, through a room with a large fireplace that was cheerfully snapping and roaring, to another hallway. At the second door on the left Jen stopped, flipped the wall switch, and stepped back so Leigh could go inside. The lights were soft, making the room warm and cozy. A queen-size bed with a fluffy down comforter occupied most of it. Leigh had the urge to take a leap and land in the middle of the bed, burrow under the covers, and sleep for two days. Jen seemed to read her mind.

"I know, it's inviting. If you'd like, you can just shower, eat, and go to bed. You must be exhausted. We can talk in the morning, if you still want to. But I won't let you leave. I'm going to finish making dinner. I'll dig up some clothes for you while you shower." With that, she closed the door and left Leigh to her thoughts.

The offer of shelter without strings attached just about did it for Leigh. She fought back tears as she dragged herself into the bathroom.

The water was tepid by the time she got out of the shower. There was a hairdryer in the vanity and even a tube of antibiotic ointment in the medicine cabinet above the sink that she applied to her lip gingerly. She felt well scrubbed, her lip and face tended, by the time she went into the bedroom. On the bed lay a pair of thick, warm navy blue sweats and a much-worn white T-shirt that said M.I.T. on it. The clothes were a bit baggy but wonderfully soft. She guessed they belonged to Conn Stryker. Something about that thought made Leigh suddenly feel shy and she felt her face heat. Strange.

Before she dressed she noticed her naked reflection in a full-length mirror on the wall. There was a well-formed bruise around her right breast from when that monster had twisted it so hard during the initial attack. Finger marks were already forming on her arm from tonight's run-in. She noticed the rest of her body and was surprised to see her ribs so visible. She really had lost weight. *What was it Jen said? Scrawny bones?* She shook her head. How the the hell had she gotten herself into this mess? What had she done that had brought that horrible man from the apartment after her? In the past few days her life—the one she thought she should have—had dissolved into terror and chaos.

Leigh sighed and stuffed her feet into a pair of heavy socks and some fuzzy slippers. It felt so good to be dry and clean. She concentrated on shuffling down the hall, smelling something delicious. Suddenly she was starving. She would search for answers tomorrow. Right now, she was safe and warm. She just needed to proceed with caution.

When she walked into the kitchen Jen had her back to her and was stirring something on the stove. Without turning around she said, "All better?"

Leigh leaned against the door frame as Conn entered from another direction, dusting off her hands. Staring at Conn, Leigh was struck by her beauty. The woman had thick auburn hair that fell past her shoulders in gentle curls. She seemed strong and confident. Leigh envied her.

Emerging from her daze, Leigh realized that she had been asked a question and they were both waiting for the answer, so she said the first thing that popped into her mind. "Better than I have for quite a while, actually. Thank you, Jen, Conn. You two saved my life."

Jen laughed. "Can't take that much credit. Let me put you to work. Conn? Is the fire going? Open that bottle of Chianti for me and, Leigh, you get the garlic bread out of the oven. We're almost ready to eat."

Conn immediately located a wine opener and tossed her some oven mitts.

Performing such a simple task was immensely comforting. She and Peter had always been with a group, rarely alone. They had never cooked together or shared anything that resembled housework. She realized with surprise that she hadn't laughed for a while, either.

The three of them sat at the table and ate and drank and talked about the weather, which had gotten worse and was raging at the windows, rattling the doors, and making Leigh very grateful to be inside.

"Storms out here can come in quickly and violently, like this one," said Jen. "But by tomorrow morning it will be gone and the world will seem clear and pristine. I get high just hiking the trails around here after a good storm."

"You love it out here, don't you?" Leigh said wistfully.

Jen sat back in the chair. "Bolinas is a sleepy little town populated with a mix of old hippies, new yuppies, and townies who have been here for generations. We can agree to disagree on just about every subject but one: the love of privacy. A popular joke in Marin County is that every time the state transportation department puts up a highway sign to direct outsiders to the town, it mysteriously disappears within twenty-four hours. Possession of one of those signs is a badge of honor around here."

Her description sounded so comfortable, so easy. Leigh had never known that kind of life; hers had been all about appearances, striving for success, competition. She felt her chest tighten and knew the emotion was longing. She'd felt it before.

Leigh studied the woman across from her, suspecting there was more to the story. "How many signs do you have?"

Jen let out a full-throated laugh and blushed.

Conn grinned. "Go on, tell her."

Startled by the warm burr of Conn's voice, Leigh realized that those were the first words she had uttered since they had come to Jen's home.

"Hah! Busted. Well, um, two, actually. But I can't take all the credit. I, uh, had some help." Jen's eyes twinkled as she glanced at Conn but softened as she regarded Leigh again.

"Seriously? To me, Bolinas is the most peaceful place on the planet. I wouldn't trade it for anything."

An awkward silence followed. Leigh, acutely aware of Conn's presence and the fact that she had been frankly watching her for most of dinner, wondered why Conn had been so quiet since arriving at Jen's. Leigh was no stranger to being stared at or studied, mostly by men. Usually she ignored such attention, but something about Conn made her feel like a bug under a microscope. Leigh shifted in her seat, trying not to squirm.

Finally, Jen came to the rescue. "Let's take the wine in by the fire."

They cleared the dishes and went to the living room where Leigh met Tippy, Jen's large black-and-white cat. He was occupying as much as he could of one of the overstuffed chairs in front of the fire, which were angled to allow the occupants to enjoy it and conversation at the same time. When Jen introduced Tippy to Leigh, he yawned and displayed an ample belly, which apparently needed to be rubbed. Leigh obliged and was rewarded with a loud purr before he jumped down.

"Wow. You must be special. Tippy doesn't yield his chair to just anyone. As a matter of fact, there are only three people in the world he would willingly do that for. I'm one of them, and I feed him. Conn is another, and she found him." Jen chuckled. "I guess you make four. Consider that a compliment. He can be quite fierce if he doesn't like you."

Leigh watched him saunter off to the kitchen, unable to imagine him as anything other than the big ball of fluff that he appeared to be. She was glad he liked her because it made her feel included. Though she wanted to ask who the third person was, she thought it would be impolite. Was it Jen's boyfriend? She knew Jen wasn't married because of all the forms she had filled out for the company. Maybe it was Conn's boyfriend or fiancé. That thought was oddly deflating, probably because it would exclude any chance she might have to get to know these women. Leigh chose not to dwell on it.

Jen went back to the table for the wineglasses and Chianti, and Conn was already in the kitchen feeding the cat. As Leigh busied herself adding more logs to the fire, she could hear Conn and Jen talking quietly and suspected she was the subject of the conversation, but was too tired to react.

Then Jen came back alone. "Conn is going to finish doing the dishes and go to bed. She just got in from the East Coast and is beat. We'll catch up to her in the morning."

"Okay." Leigh settled in her chair, relieved that Conn wasn't going to be there to witness her miserable story. She felt shy about confiding in someone she really didn't know that well, yet she trusted Jen—and perhaps even Conn—more than anyone else at that moment.

Jen gazed at her steadily. "Let me tell you one more time. You have no obligation to me. I enjoy your friendship, and we all have hard times. You're our guest tonight. Other than that—"

"Actually, yes, I do. Part of this has to do with you. Your money."

Jen's blue eyes revealed nothing. In that moment Leigh realized Jen and Conn had the same color of eyes exactly. Very clear blue.

Leigh took a breath and continued. "Maybe I overstated that. As far as your account is concerned, Peter is making money for you. Most of the stocks are doing well. Part of our problem—his and mine— according to him, is that I don't trust him enough to know when this run will end, and I don't trust some of the companies he's put my clients' money into." Leigh stopped to compose her thoughts.

"My demographic, because of my interests and his apparent lack of interest, I suppose, are mostly women, forty and older, with substantial portfolios that they rely on for income. He wants me to service the accounts and encourage them to sell the old reliable stocks in favor of high-tech, Internet, and energy industries. All volatile in terms of return of investment."

"They've done very well. What's the problem?"

Leigh could barely hear her own voice. "With the stocks? Perhaps nothing. Peter is adamant that the sky's the limit. He says the problem is with me. I started worrying about when this circus will end, but he said he would know and to just stick with him. After all, we are… were…engaged, right?"

Leigh felt her eyes well with tears. She hesitated, then pushed on, trying to control her shaky voice. Now was not the time to cry. "But I couldn't do that. I started my own technical analysis of stocks. Read books and newsletters, talked to some of the brokers I met at meetings who had been around for a long time. I believe the markets, especially those segments, are going to take a deep dive soon. All the signs are there. I also think some of the companies are built on sand, with questionable accounting practices. The world economies are already in a downturn, and I think we'll follow. No matter what some politicians say, we're a global economy."

Leigh caught herself and sat back heavily in the chair, staring into the fire. "Anyway, Peter didn't want to hear any of this. The more success he's had, the more his way of doing business has changed. He's started hanging around with a new set of friends. He and his buddies are getting into more and more deals involving what I would consider shady practices. Insider information, stock manipulation. He won't…

wouldn't…listen to my concerns about it. He's become more distant, irritable, and angry. We barely saw each other before our breakup. His new friends occupy most of his time."

Leigh sat forward, the words tumbling out of her mouth, and clasped her hands together. "Jen, his new friends are high rollers. They have a lot of cash and they like to party. I don't trust them. There are always a lot of women around them, and by that I don't mean colleagues." She listened to the wind buffet the windows with rain. "Peter loves all of it. The women, the drinking, his new best friends. He doesn't even react when these buddies of his hit on me, which is constantly. He tells me they don't mean it, they're just kidding. But they're not kidding. And the way they treat women… It makes me sick. Excuse me for sounding cynical, Jen. You can tell I have a lot of anger about this."

Jen was watching her intently, seemingly absorbed in her words. Leigh pushed on, needing to get the whole story out.

"Monday, I decided that Peter and I had to talk about this. I hadn't even seen him all weekend. He said he was tied up with clients. I called and left a message that he didn't return. I thought about it a lot. I even called my parents, who think he's wonderful. Sometimes I wonder who likes him more, my parents or me." Leigh studied her fingernails, fighting more tears. "Ouch. I've never said that to anyone before." She sighed. "But I've thought it."

She took a deep breath. "Anyway, my parents, while telling me about poor Peter and the pressure he's under to make everyone rich, encouraged me to go over and talk with him." As she listened to her own words, she was dumbfounded that she hadn't caught on sooner. She had blindly followed her parents' urging, like some ten-year-old.

"It seemed like a good idea at the time. I called him and got his machine again so I decided to just go over. If he was there we could talk. If not, I would let myself in and leave a note. I *had* to do it then, before my courage failed." *And so I could tell my parents I'd tried.*

For some reason Leigh really needed Jen to understand her state of mind. "So there I was, standing outside his apartment. The first thing I noticed was his door slightly open. Well, that scared me. What if someone had broken in? What if he was hurt? Should I call the police? I thought about that, but decided against it. Peter would be furious if it was a false alarm. So I decided to check it out for myself before I called anyone.

"I pushed the door open and stepped inside. The place was kind of a mess. There were wineglasses on the table, and the pillows from the sofa were on the floor. Then I heard sounds coming from the bedroom. Thinking back, I should have recognized the sounds. But…I kept moving toward his bedroom door. I stood in the hall and pushed the door open a bit so I could see." Her voice faltered.

"There, on the bed, was my fiancé and some woman I had never seen before, having sex. I stood there like some voyeur, and they didn't even notice me. On the nightstand was Peter's prize antique hand mirror with a pile of white powder on it. I could guess what the powder was."

Jen slid out of her chair and sat on the floor. She refilled both wineglasses, and Leigh joined her on the thick throw rug in front of the fire. Sitting side by side, both stared into the flames.

"You know, Jen, at that moment I think I snapped. I walked into the room and stood next to the nightstand. As I did, the woman focused on me for the first time. Or rather, focused on the diamond in my engagement ring. Peter was still pumping away. I took the mirror and held it up to my lips and blew on the powder. It went into the air, snowing on the happy couple. The woman's eyes got bigger, and she stopped her gyrating, but Peter didn't notice.

"I did it again. He slowed down and seemed to finally notice she wasn't moving. Then he followed her eyes. We stared at each other and he said, 'Ah, shit. Leigh. What are you doing here?'"

Leigh felt trapped in the memory. "So I held the mirror over his head and dumped the rest of the powder on him. I took off my engagement ring, grabbed the woman's hand, and jammed it on one of her fingers. Then I told Peter, 'Here, she needs this more than I do. Oh, and Peter? I quit.' He was staring at me with his mouth hanging open. I said, 'One more thing. Fuck you.' And I slammed the door behind me."

They sat in silence for a moment.

Jen started to laugh. A chuckle at first, then with more gusto. Leigh smiled tentatively and began to giggle. Soon they were both guffawing, holding their sides, tears rolling down their faces, gasping for air.

When they'd recovered, Jen said, "But that doesn't explain your lip or cheek. They're obvious, you know, even though your makeup hides the worst. What happened then?"

Leigh studied her hands. "I got the hell out of there and drove to my apartment. Next, I tried to call my friend Pat in Boston to tell him what had happened. Pat's the only one who's never liked Peter, has always been suspicious of him. But I couldn't reach him, only his voicemail. I left a message and was trying to figure out what to do next when my buzzer sounded. I thought about not answering it, but a man said, 'Flower delivery,' so I thought, 'Now the apology begins,' and I buzzed him in."

Leigh tried to relax her fingers, which were tightly laced together. "When he knocked I looked through the peephole and could only see the flowers. I started to unchain the door, but before I could even open it he shoved it and I went flying across the room. I tried to sit up, but he was on me and yanked me up by my hair. He had horrible breath, and his face was about an inch from mine. He said, 'You'd better behave, bitch. Keep your mouth shut and do as you're told, or I'll be back. You won't like it if I come back, bitch. But I will.'"

Leigh heard her voice come out in a flat monotone. It was the only way she could keep talking. "Then he ground his...pelvis into me and twisted my breast and nipple so hard I almost passed out. Before I knew it he pushed me back and slapped me, then stood over me for a few seconds. I was hoping he would think he'd knocked me out. He laughed after a minute and said, 'Oh, yeah, and don't even think about the police, cunt, because that would really piss me off.' Then he walked out the door."

Leigh's tears finally fell as the magnitude of what had happened both Monday and tonight settled in. Jen put an arm around her and held her as she quietly sobbed. When she wound down, Jen helped her up and led her to the spare room, turned down the bed, and tucked her in. Leigh was asleep before her head hit the pillow.

Silently closing the door to Leigh's room, Jen tiptoed to the next room and softly knocked on the door. Conn immediately ushered her inside.

Jen sat on the chair next to the bed. "Did you hear any of that?"

"Most of it. From all appearances, Ms. Grove is innocent. Just a bad judge of character."

"I like her, Conn. I think she's a good person."

"She likes you, too." Conn shrugged. "That will go a long way to getting her help in planting the program. Good work."

She was surprised when Jen snapped at her.

"Constantina Stryker, are you really sitting there and trying to tell me you don't have the slightest qualm about sending this young woman into that place? Someone sees her as a danger. She's been threatened, and if we hadn't been there, God knows what might have happened to her."

Conn chose to ignore the tightening in her gut at the thought of what might have happened to Leigh Grove if that goon had gotten his hands on her. She held up her hands in surrender. "Aunt Jen, okay, she seems nice. But that doesn't change the fact that now is the perfect time to ask her to plant the software. I thought you were all hot to trot to nail these guys who are defrauding so many older women of their life savings. I'd go myself, but if they discovered a break-in, the whole operation goes up in smoke. They fade away and pop up somewhere else to run the same scheme all over again. I just don't know a safer way."

Seeing the expression on Jen's face, Conn finally admitted, "And I feel shitty about it. Are you happy now?"

Jen's features softened. "Conn, it's just that sometimes you sound so tough, so hard. That's not the way Marina and I raised you."

A scratching sound at the door made Conn get up to let the cat in, glad for the moment to think. Tippy ran over and hopped into Jen's lap, and Conn finally met her aunt's eyes. "No, you didn't. Mom took care of that for you. At least I'm not out robbing banks. So you must have done something good. Right?"

At that moment in time Conn felt like the gawky, unsure teenager who so desperately wanted her aunt to love her. She was relieved when Jen reached over and took her hand.

"You are a wonderful, brave woman. I'm always proud of you. I'm just...concerned for Leigh's safety."

Her aunt always was a soft touch. "I'll take care of Ms. Grove, Jen. I promise." Stretching and yawning, Conn added, "Listen, I have to take care of some business early tomorrow. Why don't you show Leigh around and talk to her. Hell, if you're really worried, invite her to live out here. We're pretty secure and off the grid."

Jen gave her a hug good night and left, Tippy in tow. After Conn shed her robe and climbed into bed, she closed her eyes and examined the day. There was something about Leigh Grove. And not just her beauty. Something that made Conn want to keep her safe. *How ridiculous. I barely know the woman.*

She turned over and fluffed up the pillow. Tomorrow would be an early one.

CHAPTER FOUR

Leigh stirred from her sleep, moving for the first time in many hours. Something heavy was on her chest, and she struggled to open her eyes, which seemed like a monumental task.

Then she heard it. A low, purring sound. She jerked awake to find serene green eyes regarding her. Tippy, the large black-and-white cat from the previous night, had claimed her for his mattress. Since the door was still closed, how had he gotten there? *Must have been in here when I went to bed. Went to bed. I don't even remember how I managed that.* She peeked under the covers and saw she was still wearing the warm-ups that Jen had provided.

Tippy started kneading her chest with his front paws and, yes, drooling. *Just like a man, drooling over breasts.* The cat did indeed seem to be in heaven, and he was so cute. Her body, with long, well-shaped legs, a small waist and rib cage, and larger breasts, had attracted a lot of attention from men since she was an early teen. Even some of her father's friends had eyed her lasciviously, which had always made her very uncomfortable. But Tippy? He got a free pass.

After the cat left, Leigh found her watch next to the bed on the nightstand. Eight a.m. What time had they gone to bed? Then the smell of coffee and some kind of yeasty bread made her stomach growl and her mouth start to water. *I'm starving again.*

That was unusual for Leigh, at least recently. She supposed she'd been under such stress she hadn't wanted to eat. That and all the years of training from her mother watching every calorie of her own and her daughter's. Then in college, working as a model—well, half of them were afraid of food. She thought again about her image in the mirror last night. No wonder she was hungry.

She stumbled into the bathroom, accomplishing her morning tasks on automatic pilot. As she was brushing her teeth, she focused on her face in the bathroom mirror. *Ohmygawd!* Her eyes were red and swollen, with the shiner starting to fade on the right. Her short, thick blond hair was currently standing straight out from her head, like she'd had a run-in with an electrical outlet. She was pale and drawn, but the swelling on her cheek was almost gone. Her lip was better, too. *That's good. Now I only look like half a train wreck, since I don't have any makeup to put on.* She was so astonished at the sight that she forgot to keep brushing and dribbled down her chin onto the front of the sweatshirt. *Great. Completes the picture nicely.* She wouldn't have been so concerned if it were only Jen she would be facing, but the mysterious niece, Conn, was also around. She would have felt better with some makeup and her own clothes.

She closed her eyes, then took a big breath and released it, managing to pepper the mirror with toothpaste. Croaking "Crap," she bent to rinse her mouth and splash water on her hair to try to get it to lie down, but her efforts to wipe the toothpaste from the mirror only succeeded in smearing it. Vowing to clean it properly later, she aimed in the direction of the delicious smells and found the kitchen without banging into too many walls or pieces of furniture. She still felt a little out of it from the past few days.

A note lay on the table.

Morning, Leigh, hope you slept well. Coffee on the counter, mugs in the cupboard, bread will be ready about 8:30. I've gone for a walk, see you soon. Jen.

Leigh searched the cabinet for a large cup, grabbed a tall one with some sort of company logo on it, and filled it to the top with a very fragrant and strong coffee. Wrapping both hands around the cup for the warmth, she really noticed the large, cheery kitchen for the first time. Her parents' home had two kitchens—one for the caterers and one for show. It was *Architectural Digest* perfectly put together, but cold and sterile. This place was cozier, but still could support some serious cooking.

What did Jen say she did? Leigh always assumed she had family money and didn't work. She had thought Jen lived alone and was divorced or widowed. For all of their conversations, she actually knew very little about the woman. She had had a million dollars to invest, and that was all Peter had cared about.

Now that Leigh's head was clearing, she walked through the doorway nearest the windows into a dining room with a long country table and benches. A sturdy sideboard on the right wall held plates, flatware, and various serving dishes. The dishes were brightly colored and matched the rural atmosphere of the house. Again, Leigh compared it to the formal dining room in her parents' home. There, they would be served. This place was one where a group of friends could pass dishes to each other and help themselves amid raucous, friendly banter. Leigh liked it.

Once inside the living room, she stopped abruptly. There, before her, spread the Pacific Ocean. Not just a glimpse or an inlet. She walked over to one of the windows and gazed out. She could sit here for hours and just watch. *The entire Pacific Ocean is right in front of me! Miles and miles of blue. Wow!* A ship on the horizon seemed a million miles from her. This was an amazing view, one that soothed her, made her feel insignificant but real. This entire house was *lived* in, not just occupied. Leigh had often felt like an occupant in her own life.

Just below and surrounding the house was a lovely garden, roses everywhere, and paths going through them. Beyond that were cliffs and, beyond that, nothing but ocean. To the left about a hundred feet from the main house stood a cottage. *Older, but what does it look like inside? Does someone live in it?*

Leigh was lost in thought when she heard the back door open and someone stomp around. The oven timer went off, and Leigh returned to the kitchen, where Jen greeted her.

"Well, you look like you just might make it. How are you?"

Jen acted genuinely interested in the answer. No one but her friend Pat had asked her that question and cared about the answer for a long time. Maybe her mother, way back when.

"Better. Other than a severe case of bedhead and no makeup to hide the bruises, I'm okay. Thanks for the toothbrush, by the way. I don't think my finger would have done the job."

Meowing plaintively, Tippy wrapped around Jen's legs. "Where have you been? I couldn't find you this morning." When she picked him up the big furball, he nuzzled her chin.

Leigh smiled affectionately at him. "I can solve that mystery. I woke up with him on my chest, staring at me."

"I'll bet he was scratching at your door when Conn left this morning, and she let him in. He's always had an eye for beautiful women."

Leigh felt her cheeks warm at the compliment. "Well, I'm not so sure about that. He had to see through a lot of damage to find the beauty."

"That's never been a problem for the old Tipper." Jen scratched Tippy's head before putting him down.

"So, Conn isn't here?"

Jen was busy opening a can of food for the cat. "Nope. She had some business to attend to early this morning."

With Tippy fed, Jen washed her hands and effortlessly prepared scrambled eggs with scallions and goat cheese for their breakfast. Leigh set the table in the dining area and made fresh coffee, humming contentedly and thinking how pleasant and peaceful she was feeling. Maybe she liked the rural life. Or maybe she just liked *this* rural life. She quickly decided to not spin any deeper. She had no real ties to these women.

Between the eggs and the fresh hot bread with butter, Leigh ate like the farmhands she had imagined would sit at the long table in the dining room. After two helpings of everything, including rhubarb marmalade (which she had never had before and decided was her new favorite), she finally pushed her plate away and sighed contentedly. "Jen, you're a marvelous cook. Have you ever done this professionally?"

Jen's eyes twinkled. "I used to. In another lifetime. I still enjoy it, but just for friends and family." Her remarkable blue eyes became a shade darker. "Leigh, maybe we should talk about a game plan for you. I have some ideas, but I need to know your thinking."

Leigh abruptly stood and started clearing the table. "Let me do the dishes. I, uh, need the time."

"That's a deal," Jen replied easily. "I'll show you where everything goes, and we'll be finished in no time. Then I can give you the grand tour."

Leigh was grateful for the reprieve. She was not looking forward to facing either Peter or her apartment again. She didn't have a plan and had never felt more alone in her life.

As the women busied themselves with the dishes and then started through the house, Leigh found herself curious about all of it. She noticed how comfortable the place was, how warm the energy. So different from what she had grown up with. In the back of her mind, she knew that as soon as her parents found out about the break-in, they would insist she move back to Boston. Yet this home and Jen felt more like a safe haven in the one day she'd spent with them than her parents' house had ever felt. And Conn was, well, maybe a friend in the future. Leigh knew nothing about the woman, really, but somehow she felt a connection to her. Maybe it was her eyes, so much like Jen's. *That must be it.*

In the living room, Leigh stopped in front of the large rock fireplace with its one-piece carved oak mantel, obviously crafted by an artisan. She was admiring it when she noticed the pictures resting on it.

Several pictures showed Jen's family and friends, and one featured a younger Jen in chef's whites, her arm around the shoulders of a diminutive, attractive, and familiar-looking woman, both grinning into the camera.

Leigh was drawn to another picture, of Jen with a young girl. Then another with the same girl, only older, a tall, gangly teen with dark red hair. One close-up showed the same striking blue eyes. *Remarkable. This has to be Conn. I wonder when she's coming back.* Feeling a bit odd asking directly about Conn, but not knowing why, she kept her comments general.

"Wonderful pictures, Jen. Tell me about them."

Jen's eyes lit up. "That one is me, my brother, and sister with our parents. We were pretty close at the time. We've had our differences over the years, particularly my sis and I. I'm still close with my brother. These are my good friends, most of whom live in the area. Some are artists, craftswomen, a few authors. We get together on a regular basis. Maybe you'll meet them."

Leigh thought that would be nice, since she didn't have any close women friends and never had. Being good-looking had its drawbacks, especially when she so easily attracted men. The irony was that she had never consciously tried to attract them. But she'd been accused several times of trying to steal a boyfriend from a girl. She'd learned to stay away from both men and women.

She pointed to the picture of Jen in chef's whites with the attractive woman.

"That's me in Paris. I was a chef over there for several years. In fact, I met that woman in the restaurant where I worked. Remind me to tell you the story sometime."

Turning to the pictures of her and the young girl, she spoke with obvious pride. "And this is Conn." She didn't immediately speak, instead gazed lovingly at the picture.

Leigh couldn't contain her curiosity. "How old was she then?"

"In that picture she must have been sixteen. She used to spend all of her summers out here with us." Jen's grin faded. "But she's grown up now and busy with a career in D.C. I think she had to leave early this morning to take care of some business in L.A. We don't see as much of each other as we would like, though we e-mail several times a week when she's in Washington. She's very special. In fact, I think of her as my own. She's my brother's kid."

The affection in her voice was obvious. Leigh found she envied their relationship and was surprised she felt that way. After all, Conn was Jen's niece. Of course they were close. But Leigh had no older female relatives that she could confide in. Her mother certainly didn't qualify.

The tour continued. The next room was an office, complete with the latest-model computer, fax, scanner, printer, copier, and a multiline phone. Jen explained that Conn had assembled the equipment and that she was slowly getting used to everything.

"All of this is state of the art," said Leigh. "I'm surprised she didn't make the system wireless."

Looking out the door, Jen replied, "Well, Conn said something about wireless being too easy to hack. I think she's working on that. I leave all that stuff to her."

Jen smoothly shifted the conversation back to the mundane, about how she loved e-mailing Conn and her friends, surfing the Web for information, and doing some writing. She assumed the machines could do a lot more, but that was all she needed. Conn had told her that when she visited she would be able use the office for work , and that prospect had made Jen relent.

Jen passed the guest room where Leigh had slept and past a door that remained closed. "This is Conn's room," she said. "You two were neighbors last night."

Leigh found herself studying the closed door intently as she followed Jen down the hall. She wanted to thank Conn properly for rescuing her last night. She had been too scattered to think straight during dinner, and then Conn had just vanished.

Next was the large master bedroom with a picture window facing the ocean and providing the same spectacular views as most of the house. Beside the window, at an angle, was another fireplace.

The bed had a huge down comforter like the one in Leigh's room. She decided she *liked* down comforters a lot. "How do you get out of bed in the morning? I'd never want to get up!"

"Well, let's just say it depends on where your interests lie."

On one of the nightstands stood a picture of Conn and a headshot of a darkly attractive woman, the same person as the one in the picture of Paris. More than that, she was familiar in a celebrity kind of way. Leigh wanted to ask about her, but Jen was almost to the mudroom.

"Come on, slowpoke, there's more to see."

As they walked Leigh noticed how peaceful the setting was. Most of the garden contained mature plants, but several areas appeared to be works in progress.

"Between the wind and rain from the ocean, the soil that contains a lot of salt and can disappear with a good storm, and the general size of the place, these gardens are a full-time project. There aren't a lot of tall trees up here. A strong wind will uproot the saplings before they can grab hold of the soil. You have to be careful what you plant."

Suddenly Leigh became aware of some high-pitched chittering. As she and Jen toured the grounds, little creatures zoomed past them and zipped through the flowers and shrubs. Lots of little creatures. Leigh stood still, watching as Jen continued. They were hummingbirds, and Jen appeared to be the focus of their activity—Jen and the myriad of flowers throughout the gardens.

"Jen, you have escorts." They watched as twenty or more of the tiny birds swarmed the yard, buzzing and chittering.

"Oh, the hummers. Yes, we've become pals over the years.

Generations have been raised around here. I've planted flowers they like, and in the winter I feed them. Hungry little buggers. I don't even notice them anymore, except if they're quiet. Then I know something's wrong—probably a stranger on the property. If the person is with me they don't mind, as you probably noticed."

"Doesn't Tippy bother them?"

"He used to try. But they must have had a talk because now he'll sit out here in a sunbeam and watch them for long periods. So do I, for that matter. They're wonderful entertainment."

Leigh had never known the sound of a hummingbird. She was enchanted.

When they came to the cottage and stopped, Jen explained that the cottage was the original building on the lot. Her grandparents had owned the place for many years, and when her grandmother had passed away twenty years earlier, she had left it to Jen. She'd lived in the cottage and slowly transformed the property to its present state.

"Actually, Conn and I planned the new house. She would help me in the summers, and my friends were all involved. Out here, you find a lot of women in nontraditional roles. We had a wonderful time creating it. Some of my most precious memories happened in this cottage. Sometimes I miss it."

The cottage needed updating, and there were stains in the ceiling where the roof was probably leaking, but Leigh felt immediately at home in the one-bedroom dollhouse.

"This is great! So cozy and inviting. The whole place is like that, Jen. You've done an amazing job creating it. It's so peaceful and healing."

Again, Leigh felt pangs of something she couldn't put into words. Her life was the opposite of this world and had been since she could remember. A familiar fatigue dropped over her like a blanket. She knew it was time to return to the real world.

Jen was studying the ceiling and turned to say something, but stopped. "Hey, are you okay? You look like all the air just went out of you."

Leigh sighed. "I guess it's time to figure out how I'm going to deal with my life. Just the thought makes me tired." It also made her nauseous, but she kept quiet about that fact.

As Jen put an arm around her shoulder and gently squeezed, Leigh soaked up the strength and support from her new friend.

"Let's go back to the main house and talk. Over the years I've learned there's always a solution. Sometimes it's just not the one we had in mind."

They walked back and settled in with some tea, a fire in the fireplace, and Tippy firmly ensconced on Leigh's lap.

"Have you checked your messages at home?"

"No!" Leigh was startled by the fear in her voice. She took a breath and tried again. "No, I haven't. I'm totally through with Peter. The woman was bad enough, but the drugs are just as bad. I've been exposed to enough of them and enough people on them to realize how profoundly they can affect you and everyone around you. I refuse to let them be a part of my life."

Stroking Tippy, she added quietly, "Not to mention I still don't know who that goon was last night, just that I'm certain that he was the same one who roughed me up Monday. And I don't know if Peter is somehow involved with him. That thought really scares me."

"Hon, I don't mean to pry, but may I ask you a few questions?"

The kindness and lack of judgment in her voice allowed Leigh to nod her head.

"You and Peter were...engaged, right?"

A nod.

"Do you love him?"

Silence.

"Now, here's the big one. Are you *in* love with him?"

Leigh felt her eyes widen. "No, I don't think I am."

That answer hung in the air for a while. Tippy got up and rearranged himself in her lap and started purring as she absently scratched his ears.

"Well, that's a place to start," said Jen. "But I'll ask you something else. Do you think he's in love with you?"

"Actually, I don't think he is, Jen. He's in love with himself. I fit the bill as far as someone who has the right papers for him to marry. I come from the right family and have the right education, and he never failed to mention that I've been a model. I'm ten years younger, so he likes that, too. Now, thinking back, I'd bet he actually enjoyed it when his friends hit on me."

"And you?"

"Excuse me?"

"Did you enjoy his friends hitting on you?"

Leigh looked away, embarrassed. "Wow. No one's ever asked that question before. To tell the truth, no. I didn't enjoy it. Especially from those men. But I'm accustomed to it and have been trained to expect it. I know how to dress to attract it, too. So I guess Peter and I were perfect for each other. I don't know if that's the answer you wanted, but that's all I've got."

Quietly, Jen said, "Don't be too hard on yourself."

Leigh studied the cat. "He even gave me a job and put me in charge of clients that, to him, weren't as exciting as his. I'm sure he thought he could control me that way." She had been containing her anger for too long, and now the words spilled out without her bidding.

"Our arguments started when I began to think for myself. Then I questioned him about his new friends and really irritated him. We grew apart but kept up appearances. He's big on appearances. Hell, I was *raised* on appearances, so it was probably second nature for me to go along with what he expected." Tippy abruptly got down, his tail switching as he disappeared into the kitchen. *God, now I've upset the cat.* The realization made her misplaced anger dissipate but allowed other thoughts to intrude.

"You know, I'm as much to blame as he is. I should never have let it go this far. Now I just want to run away. I told myself I could make it work, but I think I was afraid to disappoint my parents. There wasn't much about the relationship that was…satisfying."

Leigh glanced at Jen, embarrassed that she had shared those thoughts. She concentrated on brushing fur off her lap for a few moments before continuing. "I must be such a loser. I'm supposed to be having the time of my life with the perfect everything. Now…" She leaned back and let her head drop onto the back of the chair. She wasn't sure she could even get up.

After a silent moment Jen said, "I have another question for you."

Leigh nodded.

"Do you think Peter is purposefully trying to deceive his investors? Do you think he's dishonest, or just so full of himself right now that he's making choices based on greed and ego?"

"I'd go with greed and ego. He has made so much money so quickly, he thinks he can do no wrong. These guys he's hanging out with are all like that. They sought him out. Swaggering, driving their

Porsches, smoking Cuban cigars. And the drugs. That all started with them, too. Except for one man—Dieter. He doesn't do any of that. They all defer to him, too. To tell you the truth, he's the one that scares me. His eyes are so, I don't know, dead. And I think Peter and his buddies are afraid of him, too." She rubbed her forehead. "I'm sorry. This probably all sounds melodramatic to you."

"Do you really think there's some connection between Peter and that guy who assaulted you?"

"Well, the timing was sure good. He got in the downstairs door by saying he had flowers. That seems a little too coincidental. But Peter has never done anything like that before. He yells and can be a manipulative ass, but he's never hit me. I don't know what to believe, Jen. But I'm scared."

"Hon, it's probably best not to jump to conclusions. You need to make some decisions, sure, but you should base those decisions on more information. Check your messages and talk to Peter again."

"I guess you're right." Leigh sighed. "I have to go back sometime. I'm being a pest at this point. Thank you so much for your time and patience." She started to get up from her chair, but Jen leaned forward and put a hand on her knee.

"Wait, Leigh, that's not what I meant. You're always welcome here. I've enjoyed your company tremendously. You remind me of Conn, as a matter of fact, in the way that you always try to be honest. But she's always gone before I even realize she's here. If you spent some time with her outside of a speeding car, you two would probably become friends. I was even going to…ah…well, never mind. It's too soon to think beyond the rest of the day for you."

"What?"

"Well, I've been thinking recently that this place is too much to handle by myself. I used to have help, and Conn was always here in the summers, but right now it's mostly me, and sometimes it ties me down. I've thought of advertising for a caretaker to live in the cottage and oversee the place, finish the gardens, fix up some things, whatever. I haven't done it yet because I'm very careful about who I invite on the property. I want, and don't laugh, someone to have the right *energy* for it. Now that you've seen it, I think you understand what I mean."

Jen hesitated. "Anyway, I was thinking that I would offer it to you. If not as the caretaker, perhaps as a new place to live. But I realize that you have a lot to handle before that can happen, and I don't even know if it would appeal to you in the least. So, that's it." She grinned. "Remember, you asked."

Leigh broke into a huge smile. "Phew! I thought you were trying to politely get rid of me. I didn't want to leave and was wondering what could I do to be invited back. At least we're on the same page. Thank you!"

Tippy meowed from the kitchen doorway, probably concerning food.

"You know, if I could, I'd never go back to San Francisco. But I know I can't do that. If I do decide to chuck it all, or even part of it, I want to do it honestly. I need to go back and sort out this mess."

Afraid Jen might interpret her answer as a turn-down, she hastily added, "But, Jen? You have no idea what that offer has done for me. To know there's a place like this with a friend like you really helps. I can't thank you enough." Leigh's eyes were misty as the words tumbled out. She quickly stood.

Jen rose with her. "You know the offer is there. And you're always welcome to visit. You don't have to live here. I'll drive you back to your apartment now, if that's what you want. Do you think you'll be safe there? Why don't you think about spending the weekend with us just to be careful?"

Leigh sighed. "I should be fine. That guy who's after me would be pretty stupid to hang around in broad daylight. It's something I have to deal with." She knew her words sounded braver than she felt.

Jen gave her a big bear hug. "You're a friend now. Let me help you get your things together, and I'll make you a basket of food. And, Leigh? When you're in the middle of all of this, remember to be true to yourself. This is *your* life, not your parents' or your friends' or Peter's. Do what you know is right in your heart. Always."

"I'll try. No, I *will*. It's time."

CHAPTER FIVE

Leigh and Jen were almost to Highway 101 before a cloud of apprehension settled over Leigh's shoulders. After spending just one night away, she was struck by how she had come to accept her life. Even the sight of the Golden Gate Bridge as they rolled out of the Marin headlands couldn't lift her spirits.

By the time they reached her apartment in the Marina District, she was determined to face whatever was in front of her and make some changes so that she would feel better about herself. Unfortunately, she had no idea what those changes would be. She'd assured Jen that she didn't need her to come with her to the apartment, thanked her for the ride, and sent her on her way, forcing herself not to notice the white van still parked across the street.

The closer she got to her third-floor apartment, however, the more she wished she'd accepted Jen's offer. She was terrified when she pushed her door open and peeked in.

Nothing except water stains on the hardwood floor from the flowers that her assailant had used to obscure his face on Monday. She stopped. Not hearing anything, she removed her shoes and tiptoed through the apartment, warily checking every room. She even peeked under the bed. It took another five minutes to gut up enough to fling back the shower curtain and make sure Norman Bates wasn't standing there with a big knife.

She laughed nervously. "Girl, you are really losing it."

When she was satisfied the place was empty, she examined the living room closely and found a few spots of dried blood under the couch. Her blood. Her clean-up efforts had missed them. She didn't see any cameras or microphones, but still wondered about that van.

Before they had left Bolinas, Jen had questioned her about calling the police and repeated her offer to have Leigh spend the weekend. Leigh had replied vaguely because her assailant had warned her not to call the cops. Besides, it was too late now. She knew she was rationalizing but couldn't force herself to make the call.

For the first time she noticed that her answering machine light was blinking. Now she was tired again. She let out a big sigh and plopped down on the chair beside the machine. Five messages from Peter ("Sorry, I was drunk, you misunderstood, if you paid more attention to me this wouldn't have happened, let's give this one more chance."); one from her mother ("Dear? Are you there? Peter called to say that you two had a fight. I'm sure he has a good explanation for what happened. Now don't get all upset before you talk to him."); *Yes, Mother, it could never be Peter's fault;* one from Pat ("Hey, girlfriend, where the hell are you?"); and one from a telemarketer ("This message is for Mr. L. Grove..."). After seriously considering trying to call the telemarketer, she dialed Patrick.

Pat had been her best friend since college. He and Peter had never liked each other so she hadn't told Pat about her misgivings, thinking that she and Peter would work things out. Whenever Pat probed, she changed the subject and even avoided calling him. She owed him an apology.

After dialing his number, she got his voicemail. "Hi, Pat. Sorry I've been out of touch. My life is a mess. I'm thinking of running away to join the circus. Love you." She faltered when she said good-bye.

She sat for a few minutes to gain some composure. Then she pushed Peter's button on her speed dial, and he answered on the first ring. "So this is my fault again? Excuse me, but I wasn't boinking someone behind your back, taking drugs, or warning someone that she better keep her mouth shut or else." *Well, that felt good.* She stopped and let it sink in. When there was no response, she let the silence grow.

Peter finally said, "Leigh? Are you still there?"

"Yes. I just don't have anything else to say. Your turn."

"I, uh, I...don't know what to say to you. Um, I am sorry, again. I feel awful and—"

"You're probably hung over. Anything else?" This was getting better. She waited. She could tell he was searching for a way to regain control of the situation.

"Are you really going to quit?" he asked.

Ah, there it is. Highest on his priority list—his wallet.

"I don't see how we can work together now. Even if we put the personal stuff aside, we disagree about how the business is run and how my clients in particular are being handled."

"Now, don't be so hasty, Leigh. I'm not that much of a jerk. We can sit down and talk about it one more time, can't we? Perhaps I've been too quick to discount your judgment and ideas. Please, just meet with me in my office. Please."

Peter knew her buttons. Reluctantly, she said, "You know my clients are important to me. But if this is just more lip service, I'm out of there. I mean it."

"Great, darling." Peter sounded relieved. "I really have some exciting plans for the company, and you can be a big part of them."

Leigh felt trapped. "Peter, is that all? You don't mind if we break our engagement as long as I still handle the clients for you? Thanks. And one more thing: did you send that thug to harass me the other night, and last night too, after I left the restaurant? Because if you did, that'll be the last time you'll ever see me. I mean it."

"What are you talking about?" He sounded genuinely confused.

"I tried to tell you at dinner last night, but since you didn't even notice my bruises and split lip, I decided not to bother. Some guy stormed into my apartment under the pretext of delivering flowers, which, considering the circumstances, I thought were from you. He threatened me, told me I'd better do as I'm told or he'd be back. He hit me, Peter. You don't know anything about this? And to make matters worse, he tried to grab me when I left the diner last night."

Peter hesitated a second before answering. "No, I don't. You know me, Leigh. I might be a lot of things, but I don't do stuff like that. Come by my office as soon as you can this morning and let me make sure you're okay. I wondered why you weren't here yet."

"I definitely can't come to work today. I'm exhausted and need some time to think. Let's make it tomorrow."

"Sure, sure. No problem."

She hung up. It felt good to take a day off and to realize that she had instinctively pushed Peter's offer of comfort away. She wondered if his offer was a new behavior for him or if she had routinely refused his overtures of emotional support.

Leigh scrutinized her apartment with disgust and decided that cleaning it would help her sort things out. She had to remove the blood spots and could always think best if everything was orderly.

As she tried to get the stains off the floor, she talked to herself. "Leigh, I'm so sorry. Leigh, I screwed up. Leigh, I love you more than money or drugs or my job. Leigh…Bullshitbullshitbullshit!"

She finished the floor and started on the kitchen and the rest of the apartment. When it was sparkling, she felt better. Removing all traces of the violence and scrubbing the dirt and grime from her living space helped scrub her mind as well.

In the evening, when she called Jen and filled her in on the conversation with Peter, Jen asked, "Hey, do you think you'll be safe going back to work?"

"Peter's selfish and manipulative, but he denied having anything to do with the assault, Jen. It really doesn't seem like his style. I should be fine. Don't worry."

"I've been thinking about it, Leigh. I want you to consider what we talked about earlier. Just consider it. When are you going to your office?"

"Tomorrow." After promising to call the next evening, Leigh hung up. Right now all she really wanted to do was zone out in front of the TV for a while and heat a frozen dinner.

Later that night, Leigh lay in bed and tried to feel betrayed, or heartbroken, or even terribly sad that Peter was cheating on her. She could only muster up embarrassment. That, and she dreaded telling her mother.

Realization hit her with an almost physical force. She was probably the last to find out about his infidelity. His new buddies considered that behavior part of doing business. They probably encouraged him. She decided to talk to Pat about it because he was always good for some perspective.

Her thoughts meandered to Conn. Those blue eyes. They were like looking out at the ocean from Jen's window. She'd always loved the ocean. With that vision on her mind, she drifted into a light sleep.

❖

As the apartment quieted, two men in the white commercial van parked across the street relaxed. Jeffrey Simpkin, the smaller of the two, started adjusting the equipment. He made copies of the phone calls they had recorded and reset the equipment to pick up anything new.

"Nice job of hiding the mikes, Hatch. Going back in after she left the other night was a stroke of genius. I was afraid she'd spot one when she was cleaning, but it's all coming in loud and clear. I'll see what I can find out about that last caller. The number didn't show up on the screen, and the conversation was hard to hear. We can usually override call-blocking."

Hatch blew smoke in his face.

Simpkin nervously cleared his throat, trying not to react to the man's godawful breath. "Um, the order I got didn't say anything about video. It means another break-in. Do you really want to place the cameras? She's pretty and all, but what if Dieter finds out?" He didn't know who made him more afraid, Hatch or his boss.

He tried to hide his uneasiness as he watched Hatch pick up the disk and stub out his unfiltered cigarette just short of one of the expensive machines that outfitted the van. As Hatch slid open the door to the van and vanished into the night, Simpkin let out his breath, adjusted his thick glasses, and left the door ajar for a few minutes to clear the air. He used a piece of paper to carefully sweep up the cigarette butt and ashes, trying not to touch them.

He was scared of Hatch, and Hatch knew it. Hell, Hatch loved it. Simpkin was paid well to do surveillance and keep his mouth shut. If Hatch wanted video, he wasn't going to raise a red flag. Dieter had never questioned his fees before, and Hatch would pulverize him if he reported the extra cameras. Screw it. It was healthier that way. A chill ran through him as he slid the van door closed and locked it.

Safe inside, he muttered, "Asshole."

About three in the morning, Leigh's phone rang. She sleepily picked it up.

"Hello?"

The line was open, but no one said anything.

Leigh croaked, "Pat? Is that you?"

Nothing.

She could hear somebody breathing. She hung up, turned over, and lay on her back, staring at the ceiling and shivering.

❖

Replacing the phone in its cradle, Dieter leaned back in his desk chair, clasped his hands behind his neck, and spun around to gaze at the San Francisco skyline, rocking back and forth in thought. Things were on schedule for the IPO; everyone was in place. The Grove woman was the only possible problem. He would just as soon make her disappear, but he had to be careful to stay unnoticed.

When his office door opened, he glanced over his shoulder to see a woman carrying two glasses and a bottle of Scotch, then resumed his contemplation. She quietly put them down on the desk and came around behind him. Placing her hands on his shoulders, she scraped long, bloodred lacquered nails down his chest until her mouth was next to his ear. "Who was on the phone?"

"Just a little call to instill uncertainty."

"Is everything okay?"

"Perhaps," he replied. She released him as he swung around to face her. "I spoke with Hatch a few hours ago. Peter's fiancée might cause trouble for us. I thought once he fucked her over, she would go away. Now I'm not so sure. That idiot Peter is trying to keep her around. Probably to deal with the old biddies and keep them in line. She seems to have brains *and* ethics. Unfortunate combination in one so beautiful."

Dieter watched the woman fidget slightly, enjoying her discomfort. "I'm glad you aren't bothered by such an inconvenient problem."

She handed him his drink.

"Here's to so much money we won't be able to spend it all."

"What do you want to do about her?"

He took a sip. "We have surveillance in place. Let's see what she intends to do. I won't let anything get in the way of our fortunes or purpose, especially some little piece of fluff from nowhere."

She nodded. "Are you going to tell Peter?"

"No. We need him to believe he's still in charge. But when the dust settles, he'll be left holding a sizeable empty bag. And he'll deserve it. Now, don't we have more important things to do?"

"What will you tell him if he asks about Hatch breaking into her apartment Monday and trying to grab her last night?"

"Simple. I know nothing about it." Dieter could tell his companion adored the way he dealt with his minions. It aroused her.

He crooked his finger, and she put her drink down, kissing him hard on his lips and letting her hands wander down his shirt to his belt buckle. He breathed heavier as she expertly unbuckled his belt and slid his fly open. When she got to her knees and massaged him slowly, then more urgently, he grabbed her hair and pulled her head back so he could see her face, then kissed and bit her neck, down to her breasts. He picked her up and carried her to his conference table, where he tore her panties off and climbed on top of her. She was wet, ready for him.

Chapter Six

L eigh really didn't want to go in to work the next day, but she
had already missed practically the entire week. Her bruises
were fading, and when she arrived at the office, everything seemed
fine. Perhaps *too* fine. Almost no eye contact. A few of the employees—
executive assistants, mail-room clerks, the receptionist—seemed to be
gathering in groups and furtively glancing at her as she went about
her business. *My, my, news travels fast around here.* Had they heard
something or noticed her ring was gone?

Some seemed to be smirking; others had a pitying expression. Still
others almost gave her the thumbs-up. *Ah, jeez.*

As Leigh headed to the copy room with her mind on her co-
workers, she almost ran over a short, buxom blonde. She began to
apologize for not paying attention, but stopped and stared.

The other woman. The boinkee.

The woman backed away, blushing and stammering. "Oh, uh,
excuse me. I was just copying these for Mr. Marks."

"You work here? You really *work* here?"

"I, um, I'm a temp from the Nelson Agency. To replace Sharon
Jones. She's out on pregnancy leave."

"Well, that explains everything, doesn't it?" Leigh said acidly.
"What's your name?"

"Karen…Phillips. I just started. Look, I'm sorry. I didn't know
Peter, um, Mr. Cheney, was engaged. I swear. He never said a word.
I…I feel terrible!"

Leigh sighed. "Assuming you aren't lying, Mr. Cheney—Peter—

owes you an apology, too. Be careful, though, because if he can lie to me, he can lie to you. But do me a favor. Stay away from me, okay?"

Karen smiled nervously and leaned as if to give Leigh a hug, but stopped abruptly and hurried out of the room.

She passed Mary Lyle, Leigh's assistant, who was standing in the doorway, and Mary seemed embarrassed by having heard the conversation. She was blushing and looking anywhere but at Leigh.

"So now you know," said Leigh. "Does this little display match the rumors going around here today?"

Mary blushed furiously. "Yes, the rumor is you caught Mr. Cheney doing, um, *it*, and you quit, and he begged to get you back. Is that close?"

Mary, her matronly assistant, was a staunch Catholic, devoted to her church and her family, and Leigh didn't want to offend her. *Ah, what the hell.*

"Pretty close. Except I told him to fuck off."

At that, Mary blushed more deeply and grinned shyly. "Hah! Good for you!" She hurried on. "Leigh, are you really quitting? I don't think I can stand it around here without you. Too many arrogant young boys issuing orders. Please don't. Mrs. Tuttle will be devastated. She can't change brokers again at the age of ninety-two. She *loves* you. All your clients do."

Leigh's shoulders sagged. She knew Mary was right. She had gotten them into this, and until she could figure a way to make sure their money was safe, she had to make the best of it.

"Don't worry. I'm staying, at least for a while. I have to meet with Peter this morning so we can figure out how to work together without me killing him. To tell you the truth, the relationship was in trouble anyway. I just hadn't faced the truth about it. Come on, we have work to do."

Two hours later Leigh marched down the hall toward Peter's office. As she entered she saw Georgia Johnson, Peter's executive assistant, fiddling with a machine under her desk. She cleared her throat and Georgia popped up, tossing a small digital audiotape into a desk drawer.

Leigh had never liked Georgia. No one liked Georgia. Six months ago, Peter had surprised everyone by bringing her in and announcing he had a new executive assistant. The woman she replaced, a sweet young mother of two, was fired with two weeks' severance. Georgia kept to herself, and no one trusted her. When she did talk, it was to make sure everyone knew how superior her talents were to theirs.

Cold hazel eyes appraised Leigh and lingered on her face. Without a doubt, she hadn't missed one bit of the damage done by the man who'd attacked Leigh.

Georgia made no comment on Leigh's appearance. "You can go in, *Miss* Grove."

Suddenly Leigh realized that Georgia had just not-so-subtly acknowledged her new status as not engaged to Peter. Now she was a spinster and employee. Striding past Georgia, she quickly closed the door once inside.

Peter was just getting off the phone. "Leigh! How are you?"

"Aren't you a little late in asking that question? I'm better now than at the restaurant, Peter. But you were too blasted to notice."

"I've apologized for that, Leigh. We shouldn't dwell on it." Peter was drumming his fingers on the desk impatiently, a habit that indicated he wanted the subject dropped. She wasn't surprised.

"Yes, let's. What do you want from me, Peter? Forgiveness? Do you still want to get married? What?"

His tone softened, but Leigh saw no affection in his eyes. "Leigh, we look good together, and your parents love me. I made a mistake, that's all. Besides, I'm still free to do what I want. We're not married yet."

His comment about her parents stung. He was right; they thought Peter was perfect.

"So you still want to get married? Or are you more interested in my clients, Peter? Who would handle the old women who are over half of the net worth of your funds if I left? Would you do it? Maybe someone on your *committee*?"

Peter's voice hardened. "Leigh, it's true they'd miss you. But we've been over that. You just keep them happy, and I'll take care of the investment end. I don't care what school you graduated from, you're still a rookie. The committee and I know what's best for you and your clients."

That did it. Leigh could feel her face beginning to flush. "You're just like my father! Like my *parents*! You think it's a waste of time for a girl like me to get a fancy MBA when all I really need to do is find some rich man to take care of me, then raise his children and entertain his clients, maybe even let some of them fawn over me. That makes you a big man, right?"

A blue vein on Peter's forehead started to pulse.

"Peter, I am *not* a girl. I am a woman. An intelligent, fully capable woman. Let's get this straight. You and I are over. You are free to screw whomever you wish and snort as much crap as you like. I'm staying here because of my clients, because I am *responsible* to them. Am I clear?" Leigh was afraid she would hyperventilate.

Peter's face had turned a darker shade of tan during Leigh's tirade. He splayed his hands on the desk and ground out, "Perfectly. You were too confining anyway. Just be sure you keep your clients in line while I make them even *wealthier* than they are. Then you are free to leave and take your precious parents with you."

Leigh glowered at him for a moment before she stormed out of his office, leaving the door open. She caught a smirk on Georgia's face and resisted the urge to snarl at her.

Back in her office she fumbled in her purse for her PDA and searched for Jen's phone number. "Jen? Hi, it's Leigh. No, no, I'm fine. I just had a meeting with Peter and it was… Listen, is the offer still good to spend the weekend with you? I just have to get out of town. I don't mean to impose."

"Great!" Jen responded. "Hey, Conn is going to be coming through the city on her way back tonight. Care for a lift?"

Leigh let out a big sigh of relief. "That sounds wonderful. What time? I think she knows my home address. I'll be waiting."

After hanging up, Leigh collapsed in her chair and swiveled to face the window. She was upset about her conversation with Peter, but inordinately pleased that she would be spending the weekend with Jen. However, what really pleased her was that Conn would be picking her up and possibly spending the weekend, too. She noticed her cheeks warming at the thought and was puzzled by her reaction.

CHAPTER SEVEN

When Leigh awoke the next morning at 7:15, Tippy the cat was nowhere around. The house was quiet. She got out of bed and slipped on her warm-ups, intent on locating a cup of coffee and Conn. After they had arrived the night before, Jen had taken her over as soon as she walked in the door and bundled her down the hall to the guest bedroom. Conn had disappeared, as seemed to be her habit.

Ignoring the empty kitchen, Leigh walked through the mudroom and out the back door. The Audi was in place, but Jen's truck wasn't there. She headed toward the front, admiring the decking that surrounded most of the house.

As she rounded the corner to the front door, she stopped, dead still. Before her stood Constantina Stryker, tall and striking from the back. Her hair was shoulder length and blew gently in the morning breeze, the dawn light bouncing off deep auburn curls. She did to a pair of designer jeans things a fashion photographer would drool over. Her cowboy boots placed her at over six feet, and her thumbs were hooked in the belt loops as she leaned on the support beam of the front steps, gazing at the ocean.

The sky was getting lighter. After what seemed like a long time, Conn slowly turned to meet her eyes. "It's not polite to stare."

The front of her was as stunning as the back. High cheekbones, a strong chin, and a perfectly straight nose. Robin's-egg blue eyes under eyebrows that matched her hair regarded Leigh evenly. The corners of her mouth notched slightly up, as if she were amused.

Leigh quickly recovered. "Oh. Good morning." Conn's gaze held hers a moment longer, then returned to the ocean.

"Good morning to you, too." The smooth contralto that was her first memory of Conn.

Afraid to ask what might be considered stupid questions, Leigh cleared her throat and stood beside Conn. This was going to be an interesting day.

"Where's Jen?"

Before Conn could answer, the automatic gate opened and Jen drove through in her truck, its bed loaded with groceries.

Leigh's awkwardness was relieved as they hurried toward the truck. "By the way," she asked, "how did you learn to drive like that? The other night I almost lost what little dinner I'd eaten on a few of those curves. I wouldn't have been surprised to read that the car chasing us ended up in a ravine."

Conn kept walking. "Oh, just a little thing I picked up. Let's help Jen unload the groceries. I'm hungry!"

Could you be more obtuse? Leigh consciously thought about the delicious food that came from Jen's kitchen and picked up her pace. She had to lengthen her stride to keep up with Conn, but managed to arrive at almost the same time.

After the grocery bags were inside, Leigh set the table and made coffee while Conn put the groceries away and gathered pots and pans for Jen. Leigh thought that, without really trying, they made a pretty good team. They moved in concert with each other. When Peter had spent the night, he had always waited to be fed. And never cleaned up. She hadn't noticed because they rarely ate at her apartment or his. But it didn't matter; there had been nothing about them that suggested partnership.

Ginger pecan scones went in the oven to bake, and Jen whipped up a frittata. After they all got fresh coffee, they went to the long dining table to wait for the food.

"It was so nice to be greeted by you two this morning," said Jen. "It can be lonely around here. Now I have two of my favorite people. Speaking of which, Conn, any idea how much longer you can stay?"

As Conn studied her coffee, Leigh was betting she'd reply in five words or less.

"Well, I have that thing on Monday. Other than that, I hate to be vague, but the answer depends on Ms. Grove." She smiled at Leigh, who reflexively reciprocated, although she saw no warmth in Conn's eyes. Leigh cocked her head to one side, questioningly.

"I think I can clear some of it up for you, Leigh. Conn, may I?"

Leigh faced Jen, aware that Conn was still watching her.

"You see, Conn, uh, works for a company that develops software for the financial services industry. The Securities and Exchange Commission is one of their clients. When I explained your difficulties, she said she was already aware of Peter's company, and she did some further checking. She, uh…Conn, you explain this better than I do. Your turn."

Conn talked to Jen when she spoke.

Why doesn't she speak directly to me?

Conn's voice cut through Leigh's musings to bring her back to the conversation. "Some of the software I have developed analyzes trading patterns in the markets, searching for patterns. Originally it was marketed as helping companies predict trends in individual sectors. It was…is…still successful, but I have built on the basics and developed other parts to it.

"We're beta testing a new program that can track suspicious patterns of trading. You know the routine. Fund managers take stocks that really aren't that sound and buy them cheaply. They then start rumors of impending success to run up the price. When they get them up to a prearranged point, they sell and make a bundle. The program can trace such transactions back to the specific trades and traders. That's the one the SEC is interested in, for obvious reasons."

She finally spoke to Leigh directly. "Last year, Aunt Jen mentioned she was changing brokerages. A few months later she said she had a new broker with Cheney's firm and that she was putting a lot of her funds into an upcoming IPO. I confess I hadn't paid too much attention up to that point, but when she said that, my antennae went up. I ran the program with your company profile, and red flags popped up everywhere. We suspect these people are bilking innocent people out of millions of dollars. My aunt might be next."

Conn seemed to be assessing her.

Leigh lowered her eyes, embarrassed to be under scrutiny. *Why shouldn't she be suspicious of me? I must have made a great first impression. And Peter warned me not talk about the investments. Well, to hell with that. If I lose my job, the account, and even the friendship, I have to make things right.*

She leaned toward Conn. "Look, I know now that I've been a fool. I took Peter at his word and chose to do nothing when he started hanging out with some questionable associates. I don't know what Jen has told you, Conn, but I was only naïve, not dishonest. I'll do what I can to help. It's not just Jen. I have several clients in the same situation."

She added, "I still can't believe my argument with Peter and breaking the engagement would lead to being physically assaulted and spied on. Couldn't he just fire me? He threatened to do that Wednesday night. And today we went around again. It's so confusing."

She caught Conn and Jen exchanging a look and sat up straight in her chair. "What? What else don't I know?"

Just then the oven timer beeped and Jen hurriedly excused herself.

"Your ex-fiancé might be the tip of the iceberg." Conn appeared to be weighing her words. "He seems to have involved himself with some very bad individuals. From the information we have, he's a relatively new and insignificant player. He might just be greedy, Leigh. We noticed him when he started his overseas trips. This is an international operation. So, if you're still interested in getting back together with him, maybe I can help."

"No! I mean, I'm not interested. Our relationship was a mistake from the beginning." Surprised at her own outburst, she clasped her hands together under the table to try to calm down.

Conn's gaze was noncommittal. "Here's where you come in. The internal network at your office is probably monitored. There could even be listening devices in various rooms, but the obvious and easy thing to do is watch what the employees do on the Internet. You mentioned to Jen that you've been doing your own research and technical analysis regarding some of the companies your firm has been pushing to investors."

Leigh nodded.

"You also said you and Cheney had been arguing about his business practices and choices. The people who are influencing him are probably keeping a close eye on you. Perhaps with his knowledge, perhaps without. Think about it, Leigh, millions of dollars. If there's even a chance that you could interfere with their operation, what's one life? Especially a woman's."

Leigh slowly absorbed the information. Ever since moving to San Francisco— hell, her whole life—she had been used for other people's purposes. The dutiful daughter, the graceful debutante, the perfect model, the gorgeous girlfriend, the compliant shill for her fiancé's schemes. No one had ever considered who she was or what she felt about anything. And she had gone along with them.

Feeling her jaw start to ache, she realized she was clenching her teeth. It was going to end here. She had made her decision. "Well, they picked the wrong woman to mess with. What do I need to do?"

Conn studied her fingers and continued, a smile playing at the corners of her mouth. "All right. Peter, then. According to Aunt Jen, you said he's into drugs and, evidently, women. I'm sure his new friends are encouraging much of the recreational fun. Are you, as his fiancée, included at most of these client functions?"

Conn's focus was intense, her questions short and to the point. She didn't seem to miss a nuance of behavior or a word, and the blue eyes that had reminded Leigh so much of Jen's turned to granite. By the time Jen arrived with food, Leigh had been debriefed thoroughly and professionally. She felt a chill and was relieved to be out from under the microscope.

"Okay, you two. Let's forget all this for a while and enjoy breakfast. I've been slaving over a hot stove, you know."

As soon as Jen spoke, Conn's whole manner became much warmer.

Leigh dove into the feast, eating like she hadn't seen food in days, and noticed that Conn seemed to be as hungry as she was. Maybe the interrogation had helped her work up an appetite. As far as Leigh was concerned, the food was a welcome distraction from answering questions. Her brain hurt from dredging up so many facts. And she *really* didn't want to think about what conclusions the beautiful woman across from her had drawn from her story. Conn was unreadable.

When Jen commented that she was glad she hadn't gotten her hand in the way or she might have ended up short a finger, Conn gave them both an embarrassed grin and Leigh relaxed.

As they ate, Leigh gathered her thoughts and questions, then refused any help clearing the dishes. "No, my turn. You two sit and enjoy the morning. Then we can talk some more."

Both women nodded and drank their coffee. As Leigh worked she kept an eye on them, noticing the family resemblance, similar mannerisms, and obvious love they shared. She had never had that kind of relationship with an older adult, least of all her mother. The transformation in Conn when she was talking only to her aunt was amazing. Perhaps Conn was just shy. Although the thought seemed ridiculous, given her drop-dead gorgeous appearance and obvious success in her career, Leigh couldn't rule it out. The only other explanation made Leigh uncomfortable. Maybe Conn simply didn't like her. Who could blame her? Conn probably thought that Leigh was either in on the scam or a complete idiot.

Self-absorbed, she didn't hear Conn come up behind her. She turned suddenly and bumped squarely into that same softness and strength she had felt the night Conn had rescued her at the restaurant. "Oh! Excuse me, I was...I was just..."

Conn stepped back, sputtering also. "I didn't mean to startle you. I was bringing our coffee cups in."

Leigh laughed nervously, instantly shy. She felt her face heat and couldn't figure out why. Trying *not* to blush only made things worse, so she took the cups, spun back to rinse them without a word, and tried to get a grip.

❖

Giving Conn a shrug and a wink, Jen said she needed to do some work in her office, though Conn suspected she was going to call Marina and abandon her to Leigh Grove. She was surprised to realize that the prospect of being alone with Leigh was exciting rather than irritating.

Leigh had seemed honest and forthright during Conn's questioning, her answers matching what Conn had been able to research about Peter Cheney's company. But Conn found herself constantly distracted by the woman. Her voice had a gentle quality to it, and her eyes seemed to change color depending on what she wore or the background. She was very animated and smiled so easily. Disconcerted, Conn had to force herself to withdraw behind her well-constructed wall in order to complete the interview. Jen and breakfast had been welcome diversions.

Then Jen made that comment about losing a finger and, without thought, Conn glanced first at Leigh, as if to see a co-conspirator. Her wall, her dependable wall, dissolved. To top it all off, they had touched. That was a cardinal rule she tried not to break. And it was the second time, too.

In the parking lot Ms. Grove had almost fainted, and Conn had no choice but to help. Then she had started to cry and, well, Conn needed to get her settled down, so she'd put her arms around her. All part of the job. But in the kitchen just now, the inadvertent run-in, that was different. It had caused a strong heat to run through Conn's body, like a jolt of electricity. Not part of the job, and she didn't know what to do with it.

Conn was accustomed to others reacting to her height, her appearance, her intellect. Most people wanted something from her, and some were afraid of her, with good reason. Her employer had taught her well.

However, Leigh showed none of those reactions, which threw Conn off balance. Since Leigh had finished in the kitchen and was headed in her direction, and Jen had disappeared, Conn didn't have any place to direct her attention except to the stunning blonde, so she busied herself with the file she had printed out that morning. And she ignored the stir of anticipation in her belly. It was a new sensation, or at least one she hadn't felt in a long while.

Leigh cleared her throat. "Does that file have to do with me?"

"Yeah. From what I can tell, not only is your computer being monitored, but that van we saw outside of your place is meant for you. I ran some diagnostics and made a few phone calls. Your phone is tapped."

Leigh's eyes grew wide with surprise and shock. "Damnit! This is unreal."

Conn inexplicably felt the need to somehow distract Leigh from the question she most wanted to ask. Maybe the timing wasn't right. She was fishing for something to say when her eyes landed on the local paper sitting on the counter. *Perfect.*

"Leigh, have you ever been to Point Reyes Station? They are having Founders' Days this weekend. Want to go over and walk through it? There are always lots of colorful characters, art, and great food. You don't have to go back to your apartment today, right?"

Leigh's eyes lit up, truly a remarkable sight. "Well, let me see. *Okay*! I'm not anxious to go back there, and I'd love to escape for a day. Thanks for the invitation! Um, will Jen come with us?"

"I'll ask." Conn slid her gaze to the closed office door. "But will it be okay if she doesn't want to?" She knew she made most people nervous and would prefer for Jen to come. But she had to give Leigh an excuse if Jen couldn't. Leigh needed to know she might be stuck with her.

"Sure. Either way is fine."

Conn tried on a smile, which she suspected appeared half-hearted at best. "Okay, let's meet at my car in twenty minutes."

Chapter Eight

They were showered and changed, ready to head down the road right on time. Leigh wore the clothes she had been wearing the night Conn had rescued her outside the Pacific Heights Diner. When she'd awakened that first morning, she'd found them neatly laundered and folded on the dresser in the bedroom, but she'd absentmindedly left them in the mudroom when she returned to San Francisco.

A client had given her favorite jeans to her years before, after a shoot for the product. He told her they seemed made just for her, so she could keep them. He was flirting, but the jeans were comfortable, so she accepted them. Over the years they had faded and gotten softer. They still hugged her body just right, and she was glad to see them. She knew she looked good in them today and needed a bit of confidence. Alone with Conn Stryker, she needed all the courage she could muster. So jeans, sneakers, and a sweater over a tank top helped. She was excited and hesitant all at the same time.

Conn wore much the same, except her pale denim shirt rolled up at the sleeves was tied to reveal a lightly muscled, flat abdomen. She stopped a few paces out the door to join Leigh, who continued walking around the Audi, inspecting it and Conn. "So, nice wheels. That explains a lot. Quite a hot little number. What size are the tires?"

"Eighteen-inch racers," Conn answered noncommittally. "That's why the wheel wells are channeled. I, um, ordered it from Germany. You like it?"

"Oh, I like it. I like it a lot."

Conn's usual neutral expression was in place as she pressed the keyless entry button. She probably wondered how such an obviously privileged woman would even know to ask about tires.

They rode in silence. Conn didn't say much, and though Leigh had a million questions, she chose to let Conn set the tone. Conn had her at a disadvantage in that she was the investigator and was suspicious of Leigh. Because Leigh needed to know more about Conn, she decided to just observe her for a while. But she had to admit, it could be a long afternoon. She might just learn that Conn was impossible to communicate with. That thought made her sad for a moment, though the sadness was for Conn.

After Conn parked on the road that led into the small town of Point Reyes Station, they walked the few blocks to the festivities, Leigh trailing slightly behind Conn, who seemed lost in thought. Leigh found herself wondering why she had even agreed to come along in the first place. More than that, why had Conn suggested it? Her frustration was growing.

Leigh heard the festival long before she saw it, and when they arrived, she immediately began browsing, admiring some of the work of the residents of the coastal small town. She tried to make small talk and engage Conn in conversation, noticing that while Conn ignored most of the craft and clothing tables, she was willing to sample the wines and cheeses. Okay, maybe a conversation topic.

Leigh bought things she thought Jen would like. She joked that maybe these gifts could cajole Jen into making another fabulous meal, but Conn seemed oblivious, as though she thought her aunt would do that automatically. The frustration of getting more than two words out of Conn was mounting. Leigh again wondered why on earth Conn had even invited her. At this point she suspected it was to get her out of the house and grill her some more about Peter. Or maybe to give Jen a break. The woman was a mystery.

Occasionally, Conn would meet someone, presumably an old friend, and say hello. She appeared happy to see them and introduced them to Leigh, but only if they made it obvious they wanted an introduction. They all seemed inordinately happy to meet her. Since the women were mostly Jen's age, Leigh speculated that Conn rarely was with anyone else, especially someone in her age range.

And another thing. Conn seemed to be *tolerating* Leigh's habit of stopping at almost every stand and store, admiring items and talking to the vendors. She appeared to be resigned to a long afternoon and placed herself behind and to the side of Leigh. Almost like she was keeping a vigil behind her sunglasses, constantly scanning the crowd. Leigh was going to confront her about it and suggest they just go back to Jen's, since Conn was obviously miserable. But she caught sight of something at an artist's display and asked about it, determined to confront Conn soon.

In the middle of her transaction, Leigh felt Conn's absence and turned to see her slowly move away, focused on something or someone in the crowd. She couldn't take her eyes off Conn and excused herself and followed. The people parted a bit so that no one was between Conn and the object of her attention, an older Japanese man. They stood a few feet apart, regarding each other for perhaps fifteen seconds, and Leigh tensed, worried about what was going to happen next.

Slowly, Conn brought one hand up in a fist in front of her and covered it with the other hand. He did the same. They then bowed deeply to each other and broke into large grins before opening their arms and covering the distance between them to exchange hugs.

Leigh stood silently and observed in amazement while they spoke Japanese, a language in which Conn appeared to be fluent. She wryly wondered if Conn was more talkative in Japanese. She had to admit this woman was intriguing. After a moment Conn noticed her, then motioned for her to come over.

"Leigh, this is Mr. Odo, my master teacher. He's taught me T'ai Chi and Aikido since I was a kid." Conn seemed relaxed and happy.

Mr. Odo bowed to Leigh, then took her outstretched hand and smiled at her. His eyes were warm and intelligent, with just a hint of mischief. "It is so nice to meet a friend of Conn's. I haven't seen her in a very long time. But our hearts are always in the presence of each other. She is one of my best students."

Leigh liked him instantly. "It's very nice to meet you, Mr. Odo."

Leigh noticed Conn was coloring from her teacher's compliment. Surprised, she wondered what prompted the display of emotion. Was it that her respected teacher had praised her? Or was it that she didn't want Leigh to know that much about her? She chose to believe the former, because that explanation made Conn have more texture, more depth. It made her more likable. And, for whatever reason, she wanted to like Conn Stryker.

Leigh glanced at Mr. Odo and was met with an amused expression. Caught staring at Conn, she quickly said, her cheeks burning, "Um, you'll have to excuse me. I left that table over there in the middle of haggling over the price of something. Be right back."

❖

After Conn watched Leigh walk back to the vendor's table, she noticed Mr. Odo grinning. "What?"

"Oh, nothing. I was just admiring your friend. She has soft but powerful energy. Don't underestimate her, my friend. She likes you, I think."

Conn made an effort to not stare at Leigh and instead studied the sky. "Well, she's really Jen's friend. I mean, I flew out to help her when… I like her too, of course, but we've really just met. I thought she might enjoy seeing West Marin, and this festival was on, so I—um, anyway." *God, Conn, could you at least complete a sentence? What's wrong with you?*

"So she doesn't work with you?"

"Oh, no. That is, she might help with something, but no." A gentle hand touched her arm.

"It's okay to have a friend, Conn. Of any variety. I am honored to have met her. And to see you again. I must go now, but come by and visit sometime. I'm not that far away, you know."

He started to leave, but stopped to say something to her and glance in Leigh's direction. They bowed to each other, and he was gone.

Conn smiled, grateful for being let off the hook, then turned to find Leigh standing a few feet from her, observing. She shoved her hands into her pockets. "I, um, haven't seen Mr. Odo for a long time. It was good to catch up."

"Tell me about him. He seems very nice."

Conn kept her eyes on a table full of silver jewelry while she considered what to say. "The first summer I stayed with Aunt Jen, I was thirteen, almost this tall, and very clumsy. Jen and Mr. Odo had been friends for years, and she put me in classes at his dojo. I was lucky because he took me under his wing. From then until I stopped spending the summers here, I was his student. He taught me a lot about myself and about life in general. In fact, he lives just down the way from us." She stopped and finally met Leigh's eyes. "Of all of my instructors, he is my only teacher."

Conn was surprised that she had told Leigh so much and even more surprised when Leigh seemed interested. "I studied Aikido for a while in college. My best friend is Japanese, and I convinced him to take it with me. I'm a bit rusty, but perhaps I can join the dojo and brush up. What level are you?"

"Black." Conn hated it when people asked questions. She should have known Leigh would want more; the woman was a bottomless pit of curiosity. Personal questions always made her uneasy. Not wanting anyone to discover the covert side of her life was reasonable. But she had hated talking about herself and her background since she was a kid, afraid someone would want to know about her mother. Her fear seemed irrational now, but there it was. Restless, Conn spotted a booth with sandwiches for sale and directed her attention there.

The brush-off seemed to work because Leigh's next comment was only, "Hungry?"

Leigh's eyes were a new shade of teal, matching the clinging V-necked sweater that revealed just a hint of cleavage. The overall effect caused a visceral reaction in Conn, though she chose to ignore it. "Yeah. Let's go eat something really bad for us. How about a sausage sandwich?"

Leigh put her hand on Conn's arm and joked good-naturedly. "Only if they have sauerkraut and mustard and onions and relish." She walked ahead of Conn to the food booths.

When Leigh had just touched her, Conn wanted to return the touch. But she didn't. She didn't push it away, either, and she should have. Over the years she had learned to keep her emotions under control, because emotions caused mistakes. And mistakes could get you and others killed.

With relief, Conn filed away the fact that when Leigh mentioned food, she quit asking questions. She couldn't tell if Leigh was just easily distracted or had consciously let her curiosity slide. Within minutes they were sitting at an outdoor table, munching on sausages.

The day had warmed up, and Leigh was roasting in her sweater. Yanking it off to leave only the tank, she caught Conn watching her, then quickly averting her eyes. Leigh was surprised to find herself pleased with the attention. *Now, that's different. I usually don't like to be noticed in that way.*

"Phew! Hot out here."

A brief nod was Conn's only response.

After a few hours of eating and browsing and buying, Leigh heard music and nudged Conn toward where people were dancing with each other, their children, and their friends. When several men invited each of them to dance, Conn refused them, and after Leigh obliged a few, she politely declined the rest.

She joined Conn at a table where she sat, guarding several bottles of water for them, and downed a long swallow. "Thanks for the water. It's hot out there. Want to dance?"

"I—what? Oh, no thanks. I'm not that good anyway."

"Are you shy about dancing with a woman? It's just fast stuff."

Conn wouldn't meet her eyes. "I'm not in the mood."

The curt rebuff stung. Leigh had tried her damnedest to become friends with Conn, but one step forward always ended with two steps back. *Two can play that game, missy.* "Yeah. Me, too. Would you mind if we called it a festival and left?"

Conn's expression was unreadable. "Do you want to go to Jen's now?"

Leigh struggled to keep her voice even. "Conn, what would *you* like to do? You've been polite all day, but never really seemed to enjoy yourself. So, consider yourself off-duty from babysitting me. If you want to go back to Jen's, fine. Somewhere else? Just *tell* me." She held her breath. Conn's response would tell her a lot about why she'd extended the invitation in the first place.

Conn's eyes tightened, then she met her gaze evenly. "To tell the truth, I'd rather be someplace that isn't so noisy. I don't like crowds. How about a walk on the beach?"

Finally, something we can agree on. "Let's go."

Just then a handsome, slightly inebriated man came up to the table and zeroed in on Leigh. "Good afternoon, ladies. Are you alone today?"

Without missing a beat, Leigh graciously said, "Of course not. We're together. Buh-bye." She stood and sauntered off in the direction of the car.

Glancing over her shoulder she saw Conn stand, wink at him, put on her sunglasses, and follow her. The man muttered, "Jesus. I can't tell. I just can't tell!"

When Conn caught up to her, they grinned at each other and kept walking.

"You know," Conn said casually, "that he thinks we're lesbians."

"I don't care what he thinks. I get tired of men seeing two women together and saying such stupid things. Like your friends don't matter when there's a man around." Leigh stopped. "Oh! I'm sorry! Did that embarrass you? I shouldn't have assumed you'd think the same thing."

Without breaking stride Conn said, "That's exactly what I would have said, but not quite so diplomatically. Well done."

Leigh was stunned at the compliment and ridiculously pleased. Pleased that Conn had wanted to continue their day and pleased that Conn approved of what she had said. She hid her smile, though, as they loaded the car. She was afraid that Conn might catch herself being nice and withdraw again. The woman was very confusing.

Conn drove to one of her favorite beaches, where not many tourists ventured and waves crashed magnificently onto the sand. The tide was coming in, and Leigh became occupied with trying not to get her clothes wet as she raced the waves onshore. Conn watched her, envying the obvious fun she was having. *When did you stop enjoying the waves, Conn? When did everything get so damned serious?*

"Constantina? Yoo-hoo, hello!" Conn was surprised to find Leigh standing beside her, grinning. She matched it and even felt her eyes relax, which seemed to please Leigh, and they continued down the beach, side by side.

Finally, Conn decided, *this is a good a time to ask Leigh a few questions*. "Leigh, may I ask about your fiancé?"

"You mean my *ex*-fiancé? Sure, go ahead."

Before Conn could continue, Leigh ran after another wave and whooped as she tried to outrun it, returning to Conn's side a little soggy. "Sorry. What do you want to know?"

Conn was a caught between the need to know and the temptation to join her. "Um, yes, where were we? Did you love him?" *Where did that come from? Why do you care?*

Leigh kept an eye on the waves as they walked. "Well, I actually think the answer to that question is no. But since we were engaged, I feel like an idiot saying it. It sounds more acceptable to say my heart is broken. Truthfully, I was relieved to find out he'd done all the work for me. I do wish he hadn't turned out to be such a scumbag, because of my clients. Until the second attack and that van you pointed out, I was committed to staying until I could figure out a way to get their money out of there. Now, I'm not so sure I can."

Conn listened, mentally registering and filing the information, barely admitting her relief when Leigh said she didn't love him. She knew she was skipping a perfect opportunity to bring up planting the software, but the words just came out by themselves. "Why do you think you fell for him?" At least she was able to keep her tone neutral.

"Well, aside from everyone else telling me how lucky I was, I liked the fact that he could dance." Leigh seemed tempted to chase a wave, but stayed by Conn's side.

"I'd been in San Francisco for about six months. Apartment in the Marina with all the other yuppies, trying out the life. You know, rollerblading, volleyball on the Marina green, sailing, hanging in the bars to meet guys."

Conn refused to mention she had no idea what that was about, or what she thought of those who did.

"But most guys I meet don't dance very well. I guess they don't think it's important. My friend Pat is great, and we used to go to clubs all the time in college. But he doesn't get out here very often. I really missed it.

"Peter, though, could dance. I don't mean the kind that was going on back at the festival. He could samba, cha-cha, a lot of the Latin and Caribbean stuff. And he could actually lead. I loved it. That and the fact that he was older and seemed more sophisticated than my peers, I bought the package. Although—"

"Although what?"

"He turned out to be technically good, but without the heart and soul for that kind of music." Leigh smiled ruefully. "I guess it's just a stupid fantasy of mine, but I always thought that my true love and I would just fit together perfectly. Move like one, with the music."

Leigh slowly lifted her liquid eyes, and the setting sun did a dance of its own off the blond highlights in her hair. "Do you dance? Really?"

Conn struggled to focus on the question and not the mesmerizing beauty of the woman before her. "Yes, I...but you'd have to ask Aunt Jen about it." She forced herself to break the connection and headed toward the car, calling over her shoulder, "We'd better get going or Jen won't fix us dinner. As much as I've eaten today, I still love her cooking whenever I can get it."

Conn knew she was being obtuse. Leigh was still standing in the sand, so Conn stopped and faced her and waited. Leigh straightened her shoulders, marched up to her, and placed a hand on her arm. Looking directly into Conn's eyes, she said, "Okay, have it your way. But I have another question for you. What was Mr. Odo asking you before you said good-bye to him? Because he was staring at me when he said it."

"He was… just kidding me." Conn stiffened slightly. "He told me he liked your energy and thought we fit well together." She glanced everywhere but in Leigh's direction. "He, um, that's all." Leigh's hand was still on her arm. Conn's skin tingled.

Leigh hesitated, then stammered, "Oh, that's nice. I liked him too."

With that, they hurried to the car. Once inside, Conn turned on the heated seats and let the engine idle a minute to warm up.

"I, um, bought something at the festival for you," Leigh said. "You know, while you were talking to Mr. Odo. As a…thank you, for everything."

She reached into the backseat and produced a small, flat rectangular package and shyly handed it to Conn.

Conn unwrapped a photograph of a single, vibrantly red rose in a bud vase. "You don't owe me anything."

"I know. But I saw it and thought of you. So I bought it."

"It's beautiful. Thank you."

Leigh gave her a luminous smile, one that Conn couldn't help but return.

That night after a dinner filled with a recounting of the day, when Conn began clearing the dishes, she refused Leigh's offer to help. "No, sit. My turn. Enjoy."

Jen laughed as Leigh chanted in a loud, singsong voice, "Okay, I guess that'll give me a chance to ask Jen questions about you when you were a child."

She watched in amazement as Conn went with the tease, cringing, then ducking into the kitchen. And as she and Leigh walked into the living room and the fire, Conn noisily banged around in the kitchen, much as she had done when Jen and Marina used to make her do the dishes and she made a show out of it. When she was happy and relaxed and it was just the three of them.

Tippy gallantly offered Leigh his favorite chair, which he had personally warmed for her. As soon as she sat, he jumped up and kneaded her lap into the proper shape for napping.

Jen settled in her own chair. "You know, not everyone would be able to tease Conn like that. I'm glad you two are becoming friends. I hope you're glad too." She said the words lightly but held her breath as she waited for the reply.

Leigh sighed and stroked a loudly purring Tippy before saying, "I'm glad too. I've never really connected with anyone like Conn. She's so intelligent and unique. I'm glad to have the two of you in my life. And that doesn't even include her saving my life at that restaurant. She's a very special individual."

Leigh was speaking with such candor that Jen had to fight her tears. Leigh's refusal to edit herself or shade her words in any way worried Jen. *Young woman, I hope you're careful.* She well knew how her niece avoided personal involvement.

When Conn reappeared, she brought them some small glasses of late harvest wine and sat down on a few floor cushions, studying a blissed-out Tippy. "Should I be jealous? Usually I'm the only lap that gets blessed with a Tippynap. Obviously I've been usurped." *I also don't know who to be more jealous of, the cat or Leigh. The cat. Definitely the cat. Stop it, Conn.*

Conn glanced at her aunt and found knowing eyes regarding her. *Ah, shit.*

Finishing her wine in one gulp, she blurted out, "Leigh, you said you wanted to help with the situation at work. Given all that's happened, is that still what you want?"

The air in the room chilled with the change of subject. She felt rather than saw Jen's annoyance.

Leigh hesitated, then evenly replied, "Yes, I do. Do you have a suggestion?"

More in control yet guilty at the same time, Conn plowed on. "I'd like for you to install a disk on your computer when you go in on

Monday. It'll allow me access to their intranet, and I can run diagnostics from here. You probably should think about it before you say yes or no."

The silence almost deafened her.

"Well, it's been a long day. I'm going to turn in." Conn got up, kissed Jen, and scratched Tippy's head as he sat in Leigh's lap, meeting Leigh's eyes as she did, then said good night.

❖

After Conn left, Leigh excused herself, too. She lifted the protesting cat off her lap and placed him in his chair, said good night to Jen, and started for the bedroom. At the hall entrance she hesitated.

"Jen, today I asked Conn if she could dance. She said yes, but that I would have to ask you about it. Why the mystery?"

Jen took a moment. "Well, actually, Conn is a very good dancer. We used to have music and parties over here a lot when she was growing up. Only one thing I can think of, though. Conn never could get the hang of following. She was always the lead."

"Oh."

"Good night, hon. See you in the morning."

Quietly making her way down the hall to her bedroom, Leigh stopped in front of her door. Then she slid down to the next door and knocked quietly.

Conn opened the door after a few seconds, wearing a large T-shirt and apparently nothing else. She looked surprised to see her, and Leigh thought she'd probably expected Jen. She ignored her nerves.

"Thank you for a wonderful day," Leigh said softly. "I really don't remember when I've had such a good time."

Conn paused. "I had fun, too. Well, good night. I'll, um, see you tomorrow."

Before she could shut the door, Leigh put her arms around Conn's waist and gave her a hug, then quickly kissed her cheek and walked to her own door. "Good night, Conn. Thanks again."

As she disappeared, she watched as Conn touched her cheek where the kiss had been. She seemed thoughtful, but Leigh was too busy dealing with her own physical reaction to the impulsive action to analyze Conn's reaction. She was tingling in every part of her body.

Leigh stared at the ceiling for a long while before sleep claimed her. She didn't know why she had hugged and kissed Conn, perhaps gratitude for the rescue. But her mind repeatedly replayed how Conn felt. Her soft skin, her strong but feminine curves. So different from touching a man.

Of course, the fact that Conn was stunningly attractive and completely mysterious had nothing to do with it. *Are you attracted to her?* Leigh decided to table those thoughts for later. She barely knew Conn and damned sure was no judge of character, considering her choice of Peter Cheney. *Besides, this woman could be married or engaged. In other words, just as straight as you are. You're obviously extremely grateful and confusing that with attraction.* But Leigh had felt gratitude before, and if this was gratitude, she was registering it in some new and different places.

One thing she was sure of, though. She didn't want another relationship or friendship where one person always led and insisted that the other follow. From now on, those duties were going to be shared.

CHAPTER NINE

Time to head back to reality, Leigh thought the next morning as she sat on the steps of the back deck, coffee in hand, and stared at the ocean. The air was cool and crisp.

She hated the idea of returning to her apartment and whatever horrors awaited her. She would have to move because she didn't feel safe there, dreaded even opening the front door. She muttered to herself, trying to gird up for the day.

"Leigh, just deal with it. Get a Sunday paper and start searching— nice way to spend a day. You can't rely on the kindness of these people forever. They're a family, and you have to take care of yourself." She sounded like her mother. *Great.*

Out of the blue, Conn lightly dropped down beside her with a carafe of fresh coffee and her own steaming mug. Leigh jumped slightly, but smiled when she saw her. Conn refilled Leigh's cup, and Leigh was silent.

"You're quite a conversationalist," Conn teasingly commented.

Leigh was embarrassed, then irritated. "Look, I'm trying to get the courage to go back to my apartment. This might be easy for you, Miss Black Belt, but I've never been in a situation like this. So back off."

Conn seemed stunned. She colored and studied her coffee, then quietly said, "Sorry."

Leigh put her cup down, hugging herself. Wanting to change the subject, she asked, "Is that a path going down to the beach over there?" She pointed to the far end of the property at a break in the green of the grass and shrubbery.

Conn looked in the direction Leigh pointed to and nodded. "Yeah. It's a bit steep, but I can do it blindfolded." She hastily added, "Well, I mean in the dark. One summer I made it my project to know every nook and cranny of this area. That's when I started shore swimming."

Leigh still didn't respond. She wanted more.

Conn twitched her mouth as if a little exasperated, but she continued. "When you shore swim you go out beyond the waves and undertow, then swim parallel to the shore. No wet suit because then you might resemble a seal, and the sharks really like seals for lunch. It's wonderful exercise, and it gives a whole new perspective to see this area from the ocean side. From there I went on to scuba diving, anything on or under the water."

Leigh was intrigued. "Did all your friends do the same thing?"

Conn glanced away and seemed interested in something in the yard.

"Conn?"

"My friends were usually Jen and Marina's. Not that many kids around and, besides, I was too busy."

"Learning every nook and cranny."

"Yeah. I think breakfast is ready. I should go help Aunt Jen."

Leigh realized she had hit a nerve and felt awful. "Conn, please sit. Jen will call us when she needs us." When Conn hesitated, Leigh added, "Please?"

She sat down again, a bit farther from Leigh,

For the first time Leigh noticed that Conn's hair was wet. She must have been swimming that morning. Leigh instantly had an image of Conn in a swimsuit and forced the picture from her mind just as quickly. But she had already started to talk.

"Your hair. So that's where you were this morning. I was wondering." Catching herself, she quickly added, "I mean, I noticed you weren't around, and the Audi was here and, and..." She studied her coffee intently and fought a blush that she felt beginning to warm her face.

"I almost knocked on your door before I left," Conn blurted out, "to see if you wanted to come along, but I thought you probably needed some rest."

Leigh grinned, relieved that Conn was extending an olive branch, which probably wasn't easy for her. "Yeah, I was pretty tired. But ask me again sometime. I'd enjoy going with you."

"Okay, um, we need a plan for returning to your apartment." Conn cleared her throat. "I will, of course, drive you. And I'd like to go with you when you enter your place. I have some experience with surveillance and am pretty good at spotting bugs and the like. Once we've assessed the situation, we can decide where to go from there. What do you say?"

Leigh hesitated. On the one hand she felt like hugging Conn. On the other, this was her problem. "Do you always take over the planning for everyone in your life? You don't have to, Conn. I can ask the police to go back in with me."

A moment of hurt crossed Conn's eyes and vanished. "Whatever you say."

Leigh sensed she'd wounded Conn and quickly added, "But if you want to, I'd be very grateful. You and Jen are the only people I trust, and," touching Conn's arm, "I need someone to trust. Thank you."

That sentiment had come out with more emotion than she would have liked. *But it's so true*, she thought.

Leigh took Conn's hand and squeezed it, and Conn returned the pressure.

Standing abruptly, Conn said, "Well, I'd better get showered and changed before we leave." Her eyes were darting everywhere except at Leigh, and she seemed distracted.

Just then Jen leaned out the door. "Hey, you two. Nobody goes anywhere before breakfast. Come and get it!"

Conn knew the small talk at breakfast was a bit stilted, but still could manage to speak only when spoken to. She watched as Leigh easily directed most of the conversation to Jen. Leigh seemed able to read her discomfort and didn't try to force her into the conversation. Marina was like that with Jen and Conn, too, but Conn could never figure out how they did it. Suddenly Leigh got up and left the table.

"Where's she going?" Jen asked.

Conn was watching the direction in which Leigh had gone, staring at the empty doorway. "Beats me."

When her gaze drifted to her aunt, she quickly checked her watch, and Jen didn't say a word. Conn groused, "What?"

"Why are you so quiet, Conn?"

She shrugged. "She's just so…different. One minute I think we're friends, and the next she bites my head off."

"About what?"

"I don't know. All I did was offer to help her secure her apartment, and you'd think I was going to rob it or something."

"Did you tell her what the plan would be and how you would take care of it for her?"

Conn nodded, still trying to analyze Leigh's response.

Jen was silent, then said, "Well, honey, you're so accustomed to being able to handle every situation, I can see where Leigh might think you're taking over. Remember her background. She's trying to break away from men and family controlling her, and here comes Conn to the rescue. Give her some room."

"She's the one with all the friends, the one who knows all the right things to say." Conn was mystified. "Why would she think I'm trying to control her?"

"Perhaps you came across like most of the men in her life. No expectation that she can handle things herself."

Conn felt her mouth form an *O* as Jen's words struck home.

At that moment Leigh came hustling back into the room, carrying a photograph. "They had one of those get-your-picture-to-remember-the-day places. Look!"

And there, in living color, was a picture of Conn and Leigh staring at the camera, arms loosely around each other's waists, smiling broadly.

Jen studied it for a long while. "I love it. May I put it on the mantel?"

Conn glanced at Leigh and saw uncertainty. She nodded slightly.

Leigh grinned. "Well, sure. If you want to."

In the great room, Jen elaborately placed the photo with all of her most precious pictures and said, "There, you're officially family, Leigh. And I got to update my picture of you, Conn. Now scat. I'll do the dishes. You have some work to do."

Leigh beamed. She gave Jen a big hug and thanks, then turned to hug Conn but seemed to catch herself. Instead she just smiled shyly and excused herself to get ready.

As Conn started to follow, Jen called out to Conn, "Take care of her, sweetie. These guys sound rough."

"I intend to, Aunt Jen." Gazing after Leigh she muttered, "If she'll let me."

❖

They were quiet on the way to the city. Leigh was nervous, and Conn seemed to be in her own world. Their few attempts at small talk were just that—attempts. As they crossed the Golden Gate Bridge, Conn got down to business.

"Okay, let's have a plan. We'll park a few blocks away. Is there a back way into the building?"

When Leigh nodded, Conn continued. "Good. We go in, we search for bugs and cameras. But if we find them, what then? Do we disable them and call the cops? Do we pretend we haven't found them? Do we disable all but one, then be careful about what is said near that bug?" She left the questions hanging in the air. "This is your call, Leigh. What do you want to do?"

Leigh thought about the options. She appreciated the fact that Conn was leaving the decision in her hands. That said, she was starting to feel like a lab rat. These people apparently thought they could use, manipulate, or even kill her with no consequence to them.

"How I handle this situation depends on who's responsible. The logical candidates are my dear ex-fiancé and his buddies. If they're the culprits, I can either a) destroy the bugs and yell 'fuck you' as I'm doing so, then try to disappear off the face of the earth and hope they don't come after me; b) pretend I don't see them and go back to work, try to find out more before I call the cops, and hope I don't get killed in the meantime; or c) buy an AK-47 and go gunning for them myself. Not very appetizing choices."

Conn was quiet for a moment. "You left out d) none of the above." She kept her eyes on the road as she navigated the narrow side streets of San Francisco and had Leigh's full attention.

"Let's assume the worst, Leigh. So far we're only sure of your phone being tapped, but if they're sophisticated enough and the prize is big enough, they can set up in an apartment across from or close to yours, and you'll never know they're there. Well, that's not entirely true. I would know because I'm kind of a freak with equipment and gadgets and I believe in privacy. Believe me, I've been bugged by some of the best. You'd be surprised how lucrative corporate espionage is and how resourceful the agents can be. Every time I develop a new program, I'm amazed at how many people will try to pirate it and beat me out of my own material. Greed, Leigh. It's all about greed."

Leigh considered all of this information, but said nothing.

Conn continued. "However, no one's ever succeeded. If they do get something, it's because it's my choice. And payback is a bitch, Leigh."

Conn had a gleam in her eye that both frightened and thrilled Leigh, who hoped her new friend was for real and that she never had to go against her.

"I think it's time for a little payback, if you're game. I have a plan. Want to hear it?"

All her life someone else had taken care of her—made her decisions, guided her on a safe and comfortable path. Leigh was grateful. But she was an adult, and she knew it was time she directed her own life. Right or wrong, she had to choose, and live with whatever happened because of her choices.

Conn parked about three blocks away from Leigh's apartment and sat back in the seat, waiting.

Leigh didn't hesitate. "I'm in." She knew her life had changed in a way that would be permanent, whatever happened, and she was ready to rumble.

Conn gave her a hard look. With a slight nod she tugged a large hooded sweatshirt from the backseat and handed it to Leigh, sighing when Leigh sniffed it tentatively. "It's clean, Leigh. Put it on."

Embarrassed, Leigh grinned and complied.

Conn's hair was up in a ponytail, and she wore a black ball cap and an old peacoat. Both had dressed in jeans and sneakers. Next, Conn rubbed dirt on Leigh's new cross-trainers. She'd almost had to chase her down to get her to agree, but the reasoning was sound. Finally, she yanked a scruffy-looking bag out of the trunk and slung it over her shoulder, then set the car alarm remotely as they walked in the direction of the apartment.

"You are now officially practicing invisibility," said Conn. As they walked, she instructed Leigh to not make direct eye contact with people on the street, but to be completely aware of her surroundings. Leigh did as she was told and was amazed to realize that no one paid attention to either of them. That type of anonymity was rare for Leigh. She was always turning heads or getting whistles or comments from men. She decided she would practice this "invisibility" stuff more often.

Leigh guided them to a service entrance, happy to be contributing for a change. After they checked for anyone watching the door, they entered and took the back stairs to her floor. Leigh had used them only once and was surprised how grimy they were compared to the elevator she habitually took.

After Conn eased the door open and saw the empty hallway, they walked down the familiar hall to her apartment. Leigh had her key ready and was about to shove it in the lock when a hand covered her own. Conn bent down and examined the lock, explaining that it had been picked, expertly.

Conn also explained that to some extent that was good news. Whoever had been in Leigh's apartment hadn't wanted her to know and probably wouldn't be around to greet them. The intruders had had plenty of time to search since Monday night.

She nodded for Leigh to unlock the door and, before going in, motioned for Leigh to push back her hood. She then stood in front of Leigh and pushed the door open.

Peeking over Conn's shoulder, Leigh then skirted around her and walked into the middle of the living room. Conn remained at the door scrutinizing the room and its contents.

As Leigh scanned the kitchen, bedroom, and bathroom, she immediately knew someone had been there. A lampshade was slightly tilted, a refrigerator food drawer slightly open, the medicine chest door over the bathroom sink left ajar. In her zeal to clean only a few days before, she remembered it all being just so. A stranger had touched her clothes, her personal items.

The violation made her blood boil. Her face felt hot with anger, and she whirled around as Conn came up behind her. Conn quickly closed the distance between them, covering Leigh's mouth with her hand, her gaze locked on Leigh's. Leigh immediately calmed, concentrating instead on the compelling blue eyes.

As they parted, Leigh suddenly felt excited about starting the search with Conn. Of the options they'd discussed while driving in, she had chosen disabling all but one device. The listeners would still think they had control and hadn't been detected. Conn pulled something out of the bag she'd brought, a device that detected the presence and location of listening devices, and they began.

Conn located the cameras first—in the living room, bedroom, and bathroom. When she pointed out the one in the bathroom, Leigh almost lost it. Conn quickly tore it down, gestured for the lens, and smashed it with her foot, while Leigh did a rather sexy victory dance. Next, they proceeded into the bedroom to make a show out of examining the device and checking for more. After a faux search they found and destroyed the one in there. Last, the living room.

"Well, if they had one of those things in the bedroom and one in the bathroom, the little voyeurs that they are, there must be one in here," said Conn. After another elaborate hunt, they identified a few audio bugs, remarked how they were different, and eventually located the video and disabled it.

Conn slipped the last camera into a plastic bag, along with one of the audio bugs, and slid it into her pocket. From what Leigh understood, they had effectively blinded whoever was maintaining the surveillance, but given them limited ability to hear. Conn cursorily examined the telephones, pronounced them okay, and left them alone.

Leigh sat down on the sofa, deflated at the idea of staying where those creeps in the van could listen to her. "I guess I have some shopping to do. I'll never wear that underwear again."

"Well, come on, then, let's go," said Conn. "The stores aren't open very long on Sundays."

As Hatch listened to and watched the destruction of his carefully placed and expensive surveillance equipment, he found the cramped quarters of the van even more uncomfortable. He had been anticipating watching the woman without her knowledge. Invading a woman's privacy was arousing and made his fantasies of rape and torture all the more vivid.

He knew Dieter would be angry if he found out about the cameras, so he wouldn't report this incident. He never did. Now the bitch and her Amazon friend from the other night had stolen some of his fun. He could get enough information from the telephone tap and the remaining device, but he wouldn't forget them. For now, he had to call in and receive orders. His mood was dark when he picked up the phone. Simpkin had gone to get something to eat or he would have made him place the call.

❖

Conn drove Leigh to Union Square in downtown San Francisco. Though she usually detested shopping, she found herself thinking it might not be so bad with Leigh. *It's been a while since I've wanted to be in anybody's company except a computer's. Just stick to business, Conn. You're helping her because you need her in place tomorrow. That's all. And you don't need her freaking out because of the clothes she's wearing. This trip is a necessary evil.*

Leigh bought a few things at Macy's, but Conn steered her to Neiman Marcus to find a business suit because she knew one of the sales consultants there. The woman would ransack the store for clothing for Conn whenever she came into town. She had hinted that she would like to be friends with Conn, but Conn kept it strictly business. No ties, no distractions.

Having phoned ahead to confirm that the saleswoman was available, Conn steered Leigh toward the designer section of the store.

Leigh hesitated. "Conn, I don't usually shop in this section. At least not since I've been supporting myself."

Conn was surprised that Leigh, from such a wealthy family, wouldn't still indulge in the finest clothes, so she had to scramble to justify bringing Leigh here. "Hey, you agreed you'd go back in there tomorrow to plant the program. You definitely need a power suit. Come on."

The moment they set foot in the area, everyone began catering to them. The staff, practically salivating, offered them cappuccino, croissants, bottled water, wine, champagne. Conn had to admit she had spent some money there in the past.

The impeccably dressed consultant, Ann, a striking woman of about forty with dark hair and light hazel eyes, greeted them and went right to work appraising Leigh. She asked her a few questions about her size and color preference, told them to enjoy their coffee, and went to gather a selection.

Within twenty minutes a fashion show was underway with Leigh as the model and Conn as the audience. Before they started,

Conn suggested champagne to celebrate "the new Leigh." Actually, she thought alcohol might help her survive the shopping experience. Each time Leigh tried another suit, they toasted, and soon they were pleasantly buzzed.

After one or two outfits, Ann asked Leigh if she had modeling experience, and Leigh admitted she'd done some in college. Suddenly the two were chatting away, Ann having been in the business for years herself. When Leigh went back to the changing room, Conn could hear them giggling and chatting about clothes, designers, and experiences and was surprised that she was sitting and listening to them rather tolerantly. Usually, waiting made her irritable and jumpy. Probably the champagne helped. She tried to overhear as much of the banter as she could; maybe she could pick up some pointers that would come in handy for a job.

Small talk didn't come easily to Conn. She had to know a person for a long time before more than perfunctory words came out. *Except Leigh. With her it's easier.*

Just then, Leigh appeared in an exquisite cobalt blue suit that made her eyes shine. The soft drape of the light gabardine hinted at the lovely figure underneath. The hemline revealed shapely long legs leading down to simple, elegant pumps. A pale oyster silk shell under the jacket completed the picture. Everything was perfect, and Conn was speechless.

Leigh had come out of the room laughing and joking, but as soon as she saw Conn, she stopped and held her breath, suddenly awkward. For an experienced runway and print model, that was weird.

After a few seconds Ann cleared her throat. "Well, I guess that settles it. I'll wrap the suit. Do you want to keep the shoes and accessories we picked out too?"

Leigh managed to mumble, "Okay." She self-consciously smoothed the front of the skirt, then meekly asked, "Do you like it?"

Without taking her eyes from her, Conn said, "I think you ar— look stunning."

Leigh tried to make light of the confusing emotions running through her. "I've never been so nervous about showing friends clothes before. You'd think it was a prom dress. I must be jittery about tomorrow."

Ann poked her head out of the dressing room. "What about the lingerie, Leigh? What do you want to keep?"

Leigh started to shake her head, but was interrupted by Conn. "All of it. Put it all on my account." Ann disappeared immediately, and Leigh began to protest before Conn held up a hand.

"You can pay me, Leigh. They have all the information on me, which means we get to go eat that much sooner. Besides, you need that stuff if you give the rest away to charity. You can't live in my old warm-up suit and your jeans forever. No matter how cute you look in them." Leigh noticed Conn's cheeks turn pink as she hurried on. "So, did you find some pants and a sweater to wear? I can't take you to one of my favorite restaurants until you do." Her eyes said she was enjoying herself.

Leigh went with it. "Yup. Ann has great taste. I'll be out in a minute."

As Leigh changed into the casual outfit, Ann reappeared. "Does she do that often? Put things on her bill for her friends?"

"Conn's never been in here with anyone before. We've all voted you luckiest girl of the year. She's quite something." Ann winked and went to write up the ticket.

Left alone in the dressing room to consider the remark and her own red face in the mirror, Leigh decided to ignore it. But it was hard to ignore the fact that the emotion she felt was not embarrassment, but distinct pleasure.

❖

"I want that bill. I'll write a check as soon as we get to the car," Leigh said as they left the department loaded down with bags. She wouldn't take no for an answer, and Conn finally nodded.

Passing Tiffany's on their way to the parking garage, Leigh slowed and shared that her secret tradition was to ogle every window each time she walked by the store.

"We can do better than that," Conn casually said. "Let's ogle all the display cases in the entire store. Come on!" She headed for the door and was inside before Leigh could protest.

Inside the quiet, sedate store—the jewelry tastefully displayed with a myriad of overhead lights—one of the clerks asked if he could take their packages so they could browse unencumbered. They admired various pieces, and Leigh talked about what piece to wear to which occasion.

Although Conn had an account there for business purposes and an occasional gift, she had always let the sales people decide or just called them and had something sent. She'd never thought about the whats and wherefores of the jewelry itself.

Now she listened attentively, not quite sure why the information interested her.

Leigh seemed to be having a ball, and eventually they stopped in front of an exquisite pair of diamond, tanzanite, and blue chalcedony earrings.

Noticing how taken Leigh was with the earrings, Conn asked to examine them. She tried them on, then gave them to Leigh to try. *Lovely.* Conn told the clerk, "Wrap them."

Now Leigh's eyes sparkled the color of the tanzanite. "Conn, they're striking! I hope you wear them all the time, because I love seeing them on you." Then she blushed, as though embarrassed at assuming that they were friends.

Conn was fascinated that Leigh might be shy about wanting to be friends, but dumbfounded that Leigh would feel that way. After all, it was Conn who was so clumsy with people, Conn who wanted to be friends and didn't know how to go about it. But she just nodded and quickly said, "Excuse me. I forgot to give the clerk my charge information." She strode to the back of the store, grinning at the memory of Leigh's words. *She wants to see me again. She thinks I look good in those earrings.*

She found herself chatting with the clerk for a bit before signing her sales slip, something she rarely did. She got his business card, then popped the small turquoise box into her purse and rejoined Leigh. Gathering their packages they left, determined to make it all the way to the garage this time.

Leigh scooted into her seat on the red leather bench in the booth of the restaurant on Market Street, advertised as Asian Fusion food. Sounded intriguing. Conn had asked for a particular booth, slightly elevated, with a good view of the restaurant and the street outside.

After perusing the menu and asking Leigh if she could order for them, Conn ordered two lemonades with ginger in them and enough appetizers and entrees to feed a small army. Then she dug around in her purse until she found a small, sleek cell phone, pressed a button, and whispered to Leigh, "I'll call Jen and see if she wants me to bring anything home."

Leigh nodded, but her heart sank. *Oh, God, I have to go back to my apartment. Maybe after Conn leaves I can call a cab and go to a hotel.* She busied herself with arranging the flatware, slightly nauseous and trying to shake it off when she heard what Conn was saying.

"She is? That's wonderful! Uh-huh, yeah, are you sure? I could just stay in the city if..." Her voice trailed off as she glanced at Leigh. She quickly added, "I mean, I could stay at the Four Seasons or..." Then her face lit up. "Well, I don't know, but I could ask. Is that okay with M? Hold on." She turned to Leigh.

"Jen wants to know if you'll spend the night with us one more time. She has someone she wants you to meet." Conn hesitated a beat, then added, "I'd like that too. Just until we're sure you're up to going back to your place. If you'd like to."

Leigh almost leapt across the table. "Yes! I'd love to meet your friend and stay. Thank you!" She felt her eyes well and didn't care if she was a wimp. She'd had enough bravery for one day.

Conn smiled into the phone. "That's a go, Jen. We'll gather up all the goodies and be there in about ninety minutes. And Jen? Give Auntie M a kiss for me."

They added to their order, then chomped on some delightful potstickers and other treats as they sipped their lemonade and waited for the order to be boxed up. Their waitress helped them load the Audi and was still grinning at her tip as they pulled away from the curb.

Conn drove Leigh to her apartment and waited for her to pick up her car. Leigh was nervous about claiming it, even though it was parked underground and Conn was there. Conn carefully examined the vehicle for any kind of transmitter, using a flashlight to check underneath, then pronounced it clean and they were on their way.

Leigh kept Conn directly in front of her, feeling silly because she wished they were in the same car. She repeatedly checked the rearview mirror, hoping she would be able to spot a tail if there was one.

She had enjoyed Conn's company, even though the reason they were together terrified her. Conn's ability to handle the situation went a long way toward allying her fear. Conn was unusual—kind of klutzy, frustrating, and dense sometimes, ill at ease in social situations, and even shy. But instead of being annoyed by these traits, Leigh found them endearing. It was good to know Conn had a not-so-perfect side. In that respect they complemented each other, and that thought pleased Leigh. The fact that it pleased her so much was something that she would have to think about some more.

Conn had warned Leigh that they were going to take a circuitous route to make sure they weren't followed, but within the promised ninety minutes they arrived at Jen's property. Loaded with armfuls of packages and food, they struggled into the house.

The first thing Leigh noticed was music—Nat "King" Cole and his daughter Natalie singing "Unforgettable." Conn seemed delighted. As they put down their parcels and took the food containers into the kitchen, the music played on. The great room was unlit, although Leigh caught the flickering of a fire in the fireplace.

Conn whispered to Leigh, "Be right back," then removed her shoes and tiptoed in the direction of the music.

Leigh followed just to the edge of the room and peeked in, thinking she would wave at Jen, but stopped abruptly as she saw Jen and another, smaller woman dancing together in a tight embrace. The tenderness between them filled the room and was intensely romantic. Leigh felt like a voyeur but stayed still for fear of breaking the spell.

When Conn went up to the smaller woman and leaned down to kiss the top of her head, the woman seemed delighted, and they all hugged and kept on dancing, the three of them. The song was just ending, and as they separated and started talking, Leigh tried to step back into the kitchen before she was seen.

"Leigh, come meet someone," called Jen.

She walked over and recognized the woman whose picture graced the end table beside Jen's bed, the one from the picture in Paris. One of the most recognizable and famous faces in the world of journalism.

Jen smiled. "Marina, this is Leigh Grove. Leigh, meet Marina Kouros, Conn's Auntie M."

CHAPTER TEN

The previous night had been so much fun! Leigh leaned back in her desk chair, yawning and stretching. She didn't care that she was exhausted; the excitement had given her energy to spare. And today her new suit, and especially the earrings she was wearing, had garnered many compliments from the troops.

Conn had knocked on her door early that morning, just after Leigh rolled out of the shower. Her hair was slightly tousled from bed and she was dressed in her sweats, presumably getting ready to go swimming at the beach. Beautiful. Although a moment of warm greeting was in her eyes, she quickly got down to business.

"I have a few items for you." She gave Leigh a slim cell phone, just like the one Leigh had noticed the night before at the restaurant. "Your phones, including your cell, are being monitored. This one is off their screen. If they do somehow try to eavesdrop, they'll find the voices scrambled. Push this button, and this phone will find me no matter where I am. This button is to contact Jen. I can program other numbers for you later. It's not just for emergencies and not just for contacting me. Use it for personal calls or ones that might give them any clue as to what you're up to. Try not to let anyone else see you use it, but don't act concerned if they do."

Next, she produced a disk from her other pocket, but hesitated. "Are you sure you want to do this? It could be dangerous. Very dangerous."

Leigh took a moment to run through her choices again and reminded herself that she had made a commitment. Then, before she chickened out, she said, "I'm sure."

Conn handed her the disk. "When no one is around, install this on your hard drive at work. Bring the disk back with you. Don't put it in a drawer. They might search periodically. It will allow me to tap into the network and see who's doing what to whom. It will help to assess the extent of involvement of others at your company. For now, assume they're all in on it."

Leigh was a bit overwhelmed, but also excited to finally be part of the solution to the mess that this had become.

Conn was standing a bit awkwardly, shifting her weight between feet. She finally looked directly into Leigh's eyes. "Be careful, Leigh. I don't know about your ex, but the ones in charge of this operation are professional and serious. Don't take chances. And, um, one more thing." She handed Leigh the Tiffany box and said, "Here, these are for you."

Leigh opened the box to see the earrings Conn had purchased the day before. "Oh, Conn, but these are yours! I couldn't—"

"They're perfect with your new suit. Just until you get back to your stuff. They'll protect you."

Leigh started to laugh at the last comment, thinking it was a little joke, but the expression on Conn's face stopped her. "Why will they protect me?"

Conn's face colored. "Because they're from me." Leigh was speechless. Her heart strarted thudding in her chest, and she felt her breath catch. What did that mean?

After a moment, Leigh managed, "When are you going back to D.C.?" She wasn't sure why, but she relished every second with Conn.

Conn studied the earring box. "I'll be here for a few days. I have a meeting and can work from Jen's office, and with Marina here and all…"

Leigh was remembering how she had resisted the urge to hug Conn, instead settling for what was probably a ridiculously large smile, when her assistant, Mary, pulled her from her daydream by announcing a visitor. Leigh glanced at her work calendar and saw no appointments scheduled for 11:30.

She was about to have Mary send the person away when someone pounded on her door. She got up and marched over to it, ready to tell whoever the rude idiot was to go away, but there, smiling at her, was her best friend Pat Hideo, all five foot three inches of him.

"Pat! Yay! Pat!" She grabbed him and they danced around, Mary smiling at them. "What are you doing here? Why didn't you call? How long are you staying? I'm so glad to see you!" She hugged him fiercely and introduced him to Mary.

When they settled down Pat said, "Well, I just found out yesterday that I was coming. One of our other agents is sick, and there's a conference here this week that costs a fortune to attend, so I volunteered! I'm here for four days. The conference starts tomorrow and ends Friday at noon. So, gorgeous, are you free for lunch?"

"You bet I am! Come on. Mary, do I have any afternoon meetings? I may not be back. Oh, wait. Change Johnson to three…"

Mary nodded and gave her a thumbs-up sign. She was searching for the phone number as they bustled out of the office.

Leigh and Pat strolled arm in arm down the busy streets of the financial district in San Francisco, covering the few blocks to Rubicon within a few minutes. After being seated upstairs and ordering some tea, they started munching the fresh, warm sourdough rolls for which the restaurant was known.

Leigh had asked for a table in a far corner, with a view of the room and away from the wait staff, so she could keep an eye on anyone possibly interested in their conversation. *Hmm. Paranoia and caution are quickly learned.* She had installed that disk right after she had gotten to the office that morning and felt jumpy. The disk was in her purse.

"Pat, I'm so happy to see you! It's been a helluva past few weeks. I broke up with Peter. That sleazeball. Caught him doing it with a temp at our office. Turns out his new business associates and he are into cocaine and women. Evidently, the joke is on me." She nervously ran her hand through her hair.

Pat's expression was not one of surprise, but anger. "I knew that asshole was up to something. It was more than just bigotry or jealousy of our friendship. Listen, sweetie, can I help? I'm only here for a short time, but you know you can always come back to Boston and live with me."

Leigh reached for his hand and squeezed it, grateful for his support.

"But I must say, for having been through so much so recently, you look absolutely gorgeous. Not just your clothes, although where have you been shopping? But it's more than that. What's up?" Leigh could feel a blush start to creep up her neck.

"Have you met someone? Someone special?" He leaned back in his chair and grinned. "You have! Get *out*! Come on, give. Tell me all about him." With that he leaned closer, his warm brown eyes alive with curiosity.

Leigh stared at Pat. *What?* "Oh, it's not that, Pat. I have a new friend. At least I think we're going to be friends. A woman who's helped me through all this, practically saved my life, in fact. Her name is Conn, and her aunt is one of my clients. They've been so kind!"

She related the story, including the rescue from the man in the parking lot of the restaurant, but omitting the part about meeting Marina Kouros. That part was private.

"What does your new friend do for a living? She seems familiar with your business. Is she a broker?"

"No. She works for a company that develops software for the financial services industry, though. She mentioned something about the SEC using their programs for fraud detection, and that was why she knew about Peter. She's developing more tools in that line and is in town for a meeting or something related to her business. Your company probably uses some of the software. It would seem a natural for a forensic accounting firm."

Leigh felt Pat watch her as she buttered her roll. Then his eyes grew wide. "Oh. My. God. This woman. Describe her."

Leigh was only too happy to oblige. "Pat, she's an absolute knockout. Taller than I am, probably six feet, with long auburn hair that falls in natural curls and the bluest eyes I've ever seen. She has a terrific figure and long legs and her nose is—"

"Her last name wouldn't happen to be Stryker, would it?"

Leigh almost dropped the roll. "How did you know?"

"Girlfriend, do you have any idea who she is?" Pat clapped her on the shoulder.

"Obviously I don't and you're going to tell me." What if he knew something bad about Conn? She braced herself because she didn't want to hear anything negative about her.

"If Conn stands for Constantina, she doesn't work *for* that software company. She *is* the company. Stryker Software, Inc. She is a god—

excuse me, goddess in our field. She doesn't merely develop programs, she innovates. Her forensic accounting software is the benchmark for all others. Government contracts, overseas contracts, you name it. She's cutting edge in designing ways to reduce fraud. Very ethical and very, very rich. She has got to be a millionaire many times over."

Leigh opened her mouth, but no words came out.

"And something else, Leigh. I've seen videotapes of some of her talks but never seen her live. She's supposedly remote and unapproachable. Very mysterious. Everyone wants to know more about her. And most people call her *Doctor* Stryker."

How could that be? Conn is a little shy, but she's generous, warm, humorous, lovely...

Pat brought her back into the room. "So anyway, that's who I think your friend Conn is. And she's the keynote speaker at the conference tomorrow. Want to go with me?"

Leigh jumped at the invitation. She enjoyed being with Conn, but the opportunity to see her in her work environment was too good to pass up. And Pat's description of her as "mysterious and remote" was fascinating. She would, of course, ask Conn if it was okay. Besides, it was a good excuse to call her. She'd been trying to think up a reason without sounding like a whiny thing. Installing the software had left her goosey, and she could use a little hand-holding. Well, maybe that was the wrong way to say it, although her touch was very warm and... *Wait. Just call her later.*

She steered the conversation to Pat as they ordered and ate. He told her he'd met someone a few weeks before, a banker based in San Francisco specializing in international finance, and casually mentioned he hoped to see him while he was visiting.

"You dawg!" exclaimed Leigh. "I knew you weren't just volunteering and coming to see me. Tell me about him."

Now it was Pat's turn to blush. "Well, he's about six feet two and has huge chocolate brown eyes and a really good build and—"

"No shit, you interested in a good build?"

He ignored her. "He was in Boston to interview our firm. They want us to analyze their international division and make sure everything is running according to standards. He and I just clicked. We had a wonderful two days together, and I'm afraid I'm hooked. I can't stop thinking about him, Leigh."

The expression on his face spoke volumes. Leigh immediately became protective, but since she'd never seen Pat so smitten, she opted to tread gently. "Do you think he feels the same way about you, Patty?" It had been years since she'd used the endearment with Pat, but it just popped out.

"He says he does, but we've only been around each other two days. He's rich, worldly, and handsome, Leigh, and probably has guys in every port. He says I'm special, but how do I know?"

"Pat, the relationship is new." Leigh touched his arm. "You have to spend time together and go through a few things together. I recently met two women who've been together for eighteen years. One of them, who's pretty famous, travels and is gone for her work. I asked her if it's hard for her. She must have a lot of opportunities and temptations."

Pat nodded miserably.

"She said that before she met her partner, she accepted some of those invitations."

She squeezed his arm. "But when she met Jen, they just didn't seem important anymore. They both said to be yourself and never settle. So if this man really cares, he won't want the others. Give it some time, hon."

The waitress brought their entrees, and they busied themselves with lunch.

"By the way, when do I meet him? No one gets my boy's heart without passing my inspection."

Pat's eyes softened. "Thanks for being my big sister and wanting to protect me. He flies in today from Hong Kong. But I won't see him until tomorrow because of my damned client meetings and the conference. Do you want to have dinner tomorrow with us? We can see Dr. Stryker's speech at noon. Later we could duck out of the gross conference dinner and go to a nice place. He actually invited you after I told him you're my best friend."

When she hesitated, he added, "Bring Conn if she can get away. I'd love to meet her, professionally and personally. I have to inspect your new friend too. We have standards, you know. It'll be fun!"

The hesitation disappeared, but for a second she worried that Conn wouldn't want to have anything to do with her friends. *Oh well, can't hurt to ask. Much.* "I'll see. If she can't come, I will. At least for dinner."

After Pat walked her back to her office building, Leigh stopped off a few floors before her own to find a quiet place to use the special cell phone. Pushing the magic button, she listened to a lot of clicking.

Conn answered the phone after one ring. "Hi, stranger. Where have you—uh, how's the day going?"

"My best friend surprised me and dropped by the office. He's in town for a conference, and we went out to lunch. Have I ever told you about Pat? He's the one I talked into taking Aikido with me. He's still living in Boston, and guess what he does for a living?"

"Okay. What does he do for a living, Leigh?"

"He works for a forensic accounting firm."

Silence on the other end, then, "Oh."

"You know what else?"

"No, what else?"

"You are so busted! Why didn't you tell me you own the company and you're famous and they're your programs? He said you are, and I quote, 'a goddess in the industry.' So what do you think about that?"

There was a lengthy, uncomfortable pause. Leigh couldn't stand it. She laughed and said, "You're blushing, aren't you. I'm sorry, Conn. I didn't mean to embarrass you. In fact, I think all the more of you because you didn't say anything. But I do have two questions. Conn? Are you there?"

Conn coughed. "Yes, I'm here. I would have said something if I'd known your friend was in that field. Most people have never even heard the term 'forensic accounting' before. And as soon as the word 'accounting' is mentioned their eyes glaze over. As to the goddess thing, your friend is very kind, but it's just software, and I'm just a geek. Um, you said you had two questions. What are they?"

"Oh, I have a lot of questions, Conn, but for now, just two. Come to think of it, three."

"Okay, fire away." Conn sounded resigned at this point.

"First, is it okay if I attend your speech with Pat tomorrow? Second, would you like to come to dinner afterward with me and Pat and a new friend of his? And third, do you have a problem if someone is gay?"

Leigh heard some noise, then swearing on the other end. "Conn? Are you okay? Conn?"

"I'm fine…just dropped something." She cleared her throat a few times. "Well, I guess it's okay to come to the speech, if you don't mind being bored. Second question, sure, I'd like to meet your friend. Third, why would you think I would have a problem with someone being gay? You did meet Jen and Marina last night, right? Two of the most important people in my life?"

"Because Pat is gay, and it would break my heart to…to have my best friend and my new friend not like each other because of that."

The silence that followed made Leigh fidget.

Quietly, Conn said, "I would be glad to meet your friend Pat. And anyone else in your life who is gay, straight, or whatever. The fact that you love him is all the reference I need. So, yes, I'll come with you. Besides, I needed an excuse to not have that hotel banquet food twice in one day. You've rescued me."

Conn paused for a moment. "On a different note, the program you installed came up on my screen and is in working order. I won't start running diagnostics until early in the morning, around two a.m. Although the program is virtually undetectable, no sense in taking chances. Um, I was wondering if you would mind spending one more night out at Jen's. I could meet you at your place after work and we could grab a bite, then head on out. I might need your input on some of the files that show up."

"I'd like that. Six o'clock?"

Leigh agreed and they ended the call.

Seeing Conn again so soon elated Leigh. She paused and thought about that word, "elated." Was that right? *Yes, Leigh, "elated."* That was going to require some more consideration, but she was too excited to do it now.

Deciding to take the stairs up to her floor, she realized she would have to pass by Peter's office. *Why not talk with him? Maybe I'll have more to report to Conn.*

She stuck her head in the reception area and saw Georgia talking on the phone, evidently so engrossed she didn't hear the door open.

"I don't know. I didn't recognize the name. Short, Asian. Is this really impor—" When she saw Leigh leaning in the door, she quickly said, "I'll get back to you on that quote, Mr. Jones. Good-bye." She hung up and gave Leigh a hard stare. "Leigh. You surprised me. How long have you been standing there?"

"I just wanted to know if Peter's in."

"He's at a meeting. Do you want to schedule something?" Georgia's tone was dismissive. That was obviously another of her ways of acknowledging the change in Leigh's status from fiancée to employee, which was fine with Leigh, though the nervousness in Georgia's voice caught her attention.

"Yes. Anything tomorrow morning?"

Leigh left the office thinking that the proverbial plot was getting thicker by the minute, and back at her office she found Mary searching through her own desk distractedly.

"Hi. Lose something?"

"The extra key to your office. I had it right here in my drawer, and now I can't find it. I must be getting old. This is driving me crazy."

"Why do you need it?" Leigh was instantly alert.

"Well, Georgia was saying that some of the office keys were missing and Peter was worried about it. I showed her I had all of our keys accounted for. At lunch I thought about it and decided to put them in a more secure place, but when I returned, they were gone." Mary looked worried and guilty, and Leigh decided the day had been long enough.

"Mary, go home and don't worry about it. I'll see if I can find them. I didn't realize you and Georgia talked that much. Are you friends?"

"Not really." Mary shrugged. "She never comes in here." Then her expression changed. "Do you think she took them?"

"It doesn't matter. I'm sure they're just misplaced. Why would she take them? Peter has a master set. All she has to do is ask him for them. You're tired. Go on home. I'm sure they'll turn up."

Leigh closed the door behind Mary and started to casually scan her office, ostensibly for the keys. Spotting and leaving in place an audio bug, she packed her briefcase, glad beyond measure she had kept the disk with her in her purse. She hoped she didn't have to wait too long before Conn got to her apartment. She was spooked.

CHAPTER ELEVEN

As Leigh circled the block and saw the white van, her stomach clenched, but she stuck to the plan. Per Conn's instructions, she drove into her underground garage, stopping just on the other side of the gate to make sure no one slipped in behind her before it closed again.

After parking, she checked the garage for anyone she didn't recognize. It seemed vacant. As she walked toward the elevator a tall shadow appeared to her right, and she jumped and almost screamed before she recognized the figure as Conn, who noiselessly joined her as they kept pace together.

Once the elevator door closed, Leigh sighed in relief, resisting the impulse to reach over and touch Conn. "I am so glad to see you! I was really dreading going into the apartment. I saw the van. Guess they haven't given up."

Conn quickly pushed the button for the floor below Leigh's. When the doors opened, they got off and walked to the stairwell. Once there, Conn kept her voice low and moved close to Leigh's ear. The effect on Leigh was immediate and intense; she could barely hear Conn's voice over the pounding of her heart.

"We'll keep the conversation light when we go in. Throw some clothes for tomorrow in a grocery sack as we talk about where to go for dinner. Mention some place across town. We'll stow the bag in my car and walk to Mio's for pizza. I'll bring you back to your car in the morning. Is that okay?"

Leigh leaned back a bit to look into Conn's eyes, and they stayed that way, several inches apart. For a second or ten minutes, Leigh couldn't have guessed which, they gazed at each other. Suddenly a door several floors below them banged open and she could hear hurried steps. A man in his midthirties, with briefcase and hanging bag in tow, bounded up the stairs, then screeched to a halt. He was taller than Conn and ruggedly handsome, his brown eyes sparkling with good humor.

"Whoa. You two are gorgeous. Want to come watch me play rugby? I have about ten good-looking blokes who would love to meet you."

Feeling Conn tense, Leigh smoothly took the lead. "You guys play over in the Marina, right? We have a late appointment, but will try to drop by later. Okay?"

"It's a date." He smiled broadly. "M'name's Teddy. You'd better show up, or my mates will never believe that you two exist. See you later!" He opened the door and was gone.

"Those Aussies aren't shy."

"Evidently." Conn shrugged and started up the stairs, Leigh trailing behind.

After checking to see if any new eavesdropping devices were around, they chatted as Leigh changed into jeans and sweatshirt and threw some clothes and makeup for the next day in a shopping bag. She noticed with amusement that Conn made a point of walking into the other room when she changed her clothes. After choosing a suit from the dry cleaning she had just picked up, she was ready and suggested dinner at a small French restaurant in the Golden Gateway Center, for the benefit of their listeners. Ten minutes later they were out the door.

Conn helped Leigh stow her bag and suit in the trunk of Conn's car, and they sauntered toward Mio's, a wonderful Italian and pizza joint that she had frequented for several years when she was in town. Leigh hadn't followed her instructions about the grocery bag to the letter, but it didn't make much difference. She just hoped that if it ever *did* make a difference, Leigh would listen.

Chestnut Street had many trendy restaurants that served the Marina, but this one had the best pizza and the most crowd noise. She assured Leigh that even if they were followed, no one would be able to overhear them.

They snagged a small table in the back corner of the little bistro and ordered pizza, salad, and a bottle of Sangiovese. As Leigh told her about Georgia and the overheard bit of conversation and the mystery of her assistant's missing keys, Conn listened intently.

"Interesting. My guess is she doesn't want Peter to know. Peter probably isn't as much a part of this as he would like to believe. In these kinds of schemes they usually play to the ego and greed of the head guy, then leave him holding a very empty, very illegal bag. They're out, free and rich, to do it again."

"You're saying this isn't just a one-shot deal."

Conn nodded.

"But why? They could make more money than anyone could spend. Why keep doing it? They're bound to get caught eventually."

Conn felt a smile form on her lips. Leigh was so refreshing, so genuine. *So don't go there.* She sighed.

"Well, some get themselves into trouble financially and see it as a way out, such as compulsive gamblers. They're amateurs and eventually get caught. Others are genuine con artists with their own compulsions—the art of deception, the thrill of success. They would, and do, cheat the very people they love. Some still try to run a scheme even in prison, where, if you cheat those guys, they know where to find you."

Their wine arrived, and they toasted to success.

"None of those sound like Peter, unless he's a gambler or something," said Leigh.

"The third type is the most dangerous. They're the real professionals, who do it repeatedly and don't get caught. They have an organization behind them and are deadly serious about staying in business. Some use their profits to buy influence and build their organizations. You see that every day in our government. Many of our esteemed elected representatives are for sale to the highest bidder. Some want the power, others have other, more sinister agendas."

Conn stopped and leaned toward Leigh, who was following every word. "Believe me when I say that some of these people want nothing less than to destroy this country, brick by brick."

Leigh took Conn's hand, and Conn held it and sat for a minute, allowing herself to relish the contact. "Let's change the subject. The problem will still be there after we demolish our food and wine, and I don't intend to leave one scrap on my plate. I know you won't." She grinned.

Leigh snorted, glad for a respite from the intense topic. "Got that right."

❖

Leigh noticed a spirited rugby match taking place under blazing lights as they walked back to the car. Spotting her neighbor, she remembered her promise to Ted and tugged Conn over to the sideline. They watched for a while until Ted saw them, waved, and a member of the opposing team promptly broadsided him. But he bounced back up and grinned as he continued playing.

During a time-out, he ran over and invited them to join him and his team at the Wet Whistle Brewpub after the game. Leigh thanked him but declined the invitation.

As they started to walk away he called after them. "We play a couple of times a week, and you're always welcome!"

Leigh yelled, "Thanks! See you soon!"

Conn strode quickly down the street, and Leigh nudged her playfully a few times, but got no response. "Hey! What's up?" Leigh had to work to keep up with her.

Conn's tone was neutral. "Teddy's cute. I think he likes you. He might be a nice guy to date. If you want to join him at the pub, you should."

Leigh stopped. Her mind had been anywhere but there. Conn kept going, shoulders hunched, hands stuffed in her pockets, and Leigh quickened her pace and caught up with her. She slipped her arm into Conn's and walked beside her in silence. Then she tugged on her to stop and stepped in front of her so they were facing each other. She waited to make sure she had Conn's total attention, which wasn't easy because Conn's eyes were everywhere but on her.

"Teddy is cute. And nice. But other than being tall, dark, and handsome, that's where it ends. I thought it might be fun to join them sometime, that's all. Besides, I prefer blue eyes."

Conn's mouth opened and closed like she was gulping air.

"Now don't we have some criminals to catch? Can't catch 'em without a smile on your kisser." With that she chucked Conn gently on the chin.

Conn wondered if Leigh was out of her mind or just clueless. Leigh seemed not to have registered her remark as anything out of the ordinary and didn't act aware that her words could be taken as flirting.

But at that moment in time, under the street light in the narrow streets of San Francisco, Conn realized she was beginning to like Leigh. She liked her because she stood up to her and because she was taking chances for what seemed like a sense of honor. She admired her gentle way of putting people at ease, of putting *her* at ease. Conn had to admit that maybe her assumptions about Leigh were wrong. What if Leigh Grove was the real thing?

As they strolled together, Conn felt a swirl of emotions coursing through her. She easily identified confusion and caution, but there was something else, something new. Perhaps a bit of hope.

❖

The lights were out at Jen's house when they arrived, except for the one by the back door. They entered quietly, made some tea, and tiptoed into the office. After Conn booted up the computer, Leigh clinked her cup excitedly against Conn's. "Here's to finding something."

Conn studied the screen and put down her tea to start issuing commands on the keyboard.

"Don't we have to wait until later?"

"I'm going to open the program and connect to the office system. If anyone is still online we'll wait, but we can see what they're doing."

Leigh was shocked that of the several workstations still running at ten o'clock, one was connected to a porn site. "Why, that sanctimonious prig. All day long that man tells people how to lead more Christian lives. Including how to dress, how to behave. You should hear him! I have half a mind to make a comment about glass houses."

"Absolutely not. He might wonder if you know his secret, and that could be a red flag. Think 'under the radar.' We have bigger fish to fry than that guy."

"Okay, okay," Leigh groused. "But it's tempting."

At the other workstation was a woman Leigh didn't know, who

seemed to be checking out vacation spots. Within twenty minutes both stations went dark.

After explaining her procedure to Leigh, Conn launched the program, which quickly scanned through each workstation for content. Then she opened the database and started a search for any programs that might be used for identifying investment parameters for the committee.

Leigh, relaxing in a big soft chair next to the computer, sat up straight when Conn said, "You've been doing your own research. What have you found?"

She got up and hauled the large chair a bit closer to the monitor. It was the only other chair in the room, but it scooted pretty easily on the hardwood floor. "I've mostly been doing analysis of the companies in which Peter has invested. You know, the usual—balance sheet, cash versus debts, fixed assets. At least half check out just fine, but some of them are good on paper until you dig a bit deeper. The fixed asset category, for instance. One of them sells toys, but has an inordinate amount of fixed assets in fancy company cars and property in the Bahamas. There are several like that. Recently I've been investigating the backgrounds of some senior executives of the companies that I thought were hinky."

Conn arched an auburn eyebrow. "Hinky?"

Leigh tried for a knowing expression and, hearing some scratching at the office door, got up to let Tippy in. He ran toward Conn and jumped.

She grabbed him midair, before he landed in the middle of the keyboard. "Oh, no, you don't! This is off limits for you, mister." She gave him a hug and scratches and handed him to Leigh, who resigned herself to that fact that her jeans were soon going to be covered in cat fur.

"Let me help you find out more about those senior executives. My programs can link to each company and identify and gather data about the names in question. I have access to a database of background information and can quickly match anyone who's ever had a complaint filed or been suspected of being 'hinky.' We'll just flag the executives who interest you."

❖

Conn glanced at Leigh and Tippy, who were deeply engrossed in each other. He had his front paws on her chest and was purring and kneading her, rubbing his head on her chin and drooling. Conn shook her head. *Lucky damned cat.*

She returned to the program, swiftly going through, downloading and tagging areas for further investigation or ones she wanted to link elsewhere later, when she was not directly tied into the system. Several hours passed before she realized it.

Finally, she decided it was time to quit. Leigh and Tippy were curled up together in the chair, sound asleep. *You are lovely.* She disconnected from the database and shut the computer down.

Leaning over Leigh, she picked up a protesting Tippy and put him on one of the many nests he had throughout the house. She gently shook Leigh, who made a pouty face and mumbled, "No way, I won't do it."

Conn shook her shoulder again and gently said, "Leigh, time to go to bed. Come on, I'll tuck you in."

Leigh smiled without opening her eyes and grabbed the hand that had shaken her as she rolled to her side and resettled into the chair. She evidently intended to use the nice warm hand as a pillow, because she took Conn with her when she rolled. Now Conn was precariously balanced between lying on top of her or dropping to her knees.

She managed to sit on the arm of the chair and lean over Leigh, whose face lay cradled in her hand. Sitting like that, loving the warmth of Leigh's touch, she eventually had to maneuver her up to a sitting position. "Come on, I'll get you to bed."

"'Kay." Leigh allowed Conn to get her to her feet, and they walked slowly to Leigh's bedroom, where Conn yanked back the covers before Leigh sat heavily on the bed and landed, face half buried in the pillow, feet still on the floor. Conn took her sneakers off and thought about what else to do.

She herself could never sleep well in jeans and hoped Leigh felt the same.

"All right, I'm probably going to rot in hell for enjoying this, but your jeans are coming off."

Grabbing the top snap she popped it, then pulled down the zipper. That done, she carefully peeled the pants off, then tucked Leigh under the covers with her sweatshirt still on. *No way am I going any further. There's only so much a person can stand.*

CHAPTER TWELVE

Before dawn Leigh's door opened and closed, and two seconds later, with a big *whump,* a purring furball sat on her chest, nuzzling her face. Struggling to open her eyes, she stared into the darkness for a few minutes, willing herself out of a lovely dream of being kissed and nuzzled by a tall, decidedly feminine lover and into reality. She firmly placed Tippy aside and got up. After stretching, she aimed directly for the bathroom and shower.

As she toweled off she smelled coffee and saw a steaming cup sitting on the nightstand, and she silently thanked the coffee goddess. The clothes she had thrown in the bag had been hung up so they were passable for work. *I don't even remember getting to bed. When does that woman sleep?* Within twenty minutes she was dressed, ready, and down the hall to the kitchen.

Conn sat sipping coffee and munching on a scone, her makeup understated, her mane of auburn curls held back at her neck by a clip to fully reveal her face. Her suit was Armani, and the soft Italian leather shoes perfect. Leigh was dazzled.

Picking up Conn's cup, she poured more coffee for them and sat down in companionable silence. *Seems both of us like a little quiet time in the morning. Nice.* After they finished eating, Leigh cleared the table and cleaned up while Conn made some coffee to take with them, then started a fresh pot for Jen and Marina when they awoke.

They gathered their briefcases and bags and headed out the door, and when they were well on their way Leigh finally broke the reverie.

"Um, I wanted to thank you for putting me to bed last night. I don't remember much about it, but…and thanks for helping me out of my jeans. I hate to sleep in my clothes."

Conn watched the road. "Same here. And did you appreciate your alarm clock this morning?"

"Well, let's just say that my really nice dream was interrupted by a furry-faced drooling thing and leave it at that."

After a few minutes, Conn glanced at her. "Dream?"

A coughing fit, evidently caused by sudden inhalation of coffee, ended the conversation. It was all Leigh could do to not get it all over herself and the car.

As they passed through the Golden Gate Bridge tollgate, Leigh ventured a glance at Conn, whose profile revealed a small smile.

Leigh cleared her throat. "You look like you're ready to give your speech. What will you do until lunchtime? You can use my apartment if you like. Might give our snoopers something to do."

"Thanks for the offer, but I have to go talk to my headhunter about finding some new employees. A few more client visits, then to the Omni for the speech."

Conn seemed distant and preoccupied.

"Do you get nervous giving speeches?"

"No, actually that's probably the one time I don't mind." Conn gave her a wry grin. "I've had coaching. As long as there's distance between the audience and me, I can think of them as my best friends. It's when they want to get personal I draw the line, most of the time."

Leigh was pleased that Conn had said "most of the time," and hoped the comment was for her because of her next request. "Well, I can't wait to introduce you to Pat. You two will like each other, I know it. And I'm really looking forward to tonight. I'll have to go back to my place to change. Mind meeting me there? We could take a cab to meet Pat and his mystery friend. Or I could drive. I have the parking spot, and it'll be late when we get back. Could you spend the night at my place, rather than drive all that way back to Bolinas? I know it's not ideal with the bugs and all, but as long as we keep the conversation neutral it should be okay."

Leigh was breathless after spitting that whole piece out at once. She had been forced to, or she would have lost her nerve. She could see Conn start to object.

"Just think about it. The invitation is there." She finally took a breath.

Conn was silent, remote as they drove to the apartment building and used Leigh's key card to get into the garage. Conn checked the surroundings to be sure they were alone, then they transferred Leigh's things to her car. Before Leigh exited the garage, she gave Conn her extra access card for guest parking.

As Leigh drove to work she wondered if she had presumed too much by extending the offer to stay at her place. But it was the only polite thing to do, rather than have Conn have to drive to Bolinas and back after a long day. Still, she hoped she hadn't overstepped and made Conn nervous. The woman was maddening. *I mean, friends extend those invitations all the time.* Then she realized that Conn might not have that much experience in the "friends" department. Well, Conn had a friend now, so she could just learn.

Conn waited to see if Leigh was followed, then drove in the same general direction. Her meetings were of a much different nature than she had described to Leigh. She was going to the Federal Building.

Driving during morning rush hour in downtown San Francisco always reminded Conn of trying to park before a 49ers football game— slow and tedious. She crept down the canyons of the city toward her destination, her mood matching the fog and chill of the morning despite the seat heater. Whatever positive effects the coffee might have had on her had disappeared the moment Leigh had stepped from the car. *I miss her. Worse, I worry when she's not with me. This isn't good.*

Conn was irritated. She didn't like involving an innocent person in an operation. The fact that Leigh had volunteered didn't count. She hadn't known the full scope of it and didn't understand how dangerous these people could be. Worst of all, Conn hated lying to Leigh. Lying by omission was still deceit.

Conn was tired of the carefully constructed fabric of half-truths her life had become. It was bad enough that Marina and Jen were sometimes involved, even on the periphery. They knew the risks. Their position was dangerous, but Leigh could get killed. Her friend. Hell, it was more than that, and she knew it. She really cared about her. *Crap.* It was her own damn fault. She could have stuck to the original plan all those years ago, but, no, she got into the cloak-and-dagger end and dragged everyone with her. *If anything happens to Leigh...*

As she had done so many times before, she parked and took a circuitous route to her meeting, making sure she wasn't followed. Her radar was finely tuned, down to the unconscious level. Her striking appearance often turned heads, but she had developed the ability to be invisible. Mr. Odo had taught her to pull her energy in and disappear, and amazingly it always worked. She had walked down some of most dangerous streets in the world and been ignored.

When she reached the Federal Building, she relaxed. As soon as the elevator doors opened on her floor, a young woman about the age that Conn had been when this all began was waiting to show her to a meeting room, where she asked her to wait. Alone, Conn walked over to the window and surveyed the streets of the financial district.

Soon Maggie Cunningham and Jim Frellen entered the room. Conn had first met them during her initial interview, when she was only nineteen and graduating from Stanford. Over the years Jim had been her main contact with the FBI, and Colonel Cunningham had acted as liaison between her and the covert operations in which she was sometimes involved. They quickly got to the business at hand.

"So you're in. Good," Jim said. "Any problems so far? Does anyone suspect your contact?"

Conn knew only too well what could happen if something went wrong. "Calm down, Jim. She hasn't been compromised. But, actually, I'd be more comfortable if she got the hell out of there now that the software has been installed. I don't like for an innocent person to be this close to an operation. Too many things could go wrong. She's not trained for this."

"You've never minded before, Conn," Jim offhandedly replied. "Besides, she needs to stay until we're through with the analysis. It's always better to have someone on the inside. She's been cooperating, hasn't she?"

"She's made it clear she'll stick tight until we have what we need. Do you have a line on who's watching her?" Conn was irritated at Jim's cavalier approach to Leigh.

He checked his notes. "Yes. One's a techie, Jeffrey Simpkin, who seems to be in it for the money. He drives the van and runs the machines. We think the other is Günter Schmidt, aka Hatch. He's done jobs for Dieter before and isn't a nice guy. Very mean and very lethal. He's served as an enforcer for the outfit, in addition to being an all-around asshole. He enjoys his work—takes it above and beyond the call of duty, so to speak. Be careful, Conn. I'm sure he didn't like getting shown up at the restaurant the other night."

"I can handle him," Conn said tersely. She showed him the plastic bag containing the disabled surveillance devices. "I got these from Ms. Grove's apartment. We left one audio bug and the phone tap. You might be able to get something from them." She leaned back to indicate the meeting was over.

❖

"Thanks Jim. See you later." Maggie didn't take her eyes off Conn as Jim gathered up the bag and his notes and was gone.

"What's going on, Conn? You seem a little tightly wound around this project. What's different?"

"Nothing's different," Conn snapped. "You know I don't like it when Jen's involved. That's all."

Maggie said nothing, hoping Conn would say more. As Conn's handler, she had run interference for Conn before and always told her the truth, and over the years they had developed a trust of sorts. Maggie's years of experience in the military always helped her identify signs of stress from her young operative. That experience had also taught her patience, so she waited.

Finally Conn said, "I'm just tired of *projects*. Tired of dragging innocent people into them, destroying whatever pitiful illusions they have about justice and fair play. Maybe I'm burned out. I don't know." Conn wouldn't meet Maggie's eyes and shifted slightly away from her.

Maggie was surprised. She hadn't seen this coming. Then it dawned on her. She had read the complete dossier on Leigh Grove, seen the pictures of her. The woman was a knockout and, from what she could tell, the genuine article. *She cares about her. My God. Constantina Stryker cares about her. Uh-oh.*

She chose her words carefully. "Are you worried about the Grove woman? Is there something you haven't mentioned?"

The way Conn tried not to look at her told her all she needed to know. *This must be so hard for you. It's not something you can control, probably for one of the first times in your life.* Maggie touched Conn's arm to get her attention, and Conn stiffened but didn't pull away.

"It's okay, you know. It's okay to like someone, to have feelings for her. How do you think Jim met that wife of his? The one he talks nonstop about if you let him. A lot of us have stories like that."

"I do *not* 'like' her." Conn used her fingers to put quotation marks around the word, and her tone was defensive.

Maggie knew she was walking on ground filled with landmines, but she tried again. "Hey, we'll watch over her when you go back to D.C. Promise. Does that help?"

Conn let out a sigh and nodded.

"Does she know? I mean, that you…like her?"

Conn stared at her with wide eyes. "God, no! I don't even know if she…no. I can't have a relationship. That's like painting a target on someone's back. I can't do it, no way." Conn's voice was rough with emotion.

Maggie knew that Conn hated any appearance of weakness in front of her cohorts. She just hoped that her operative would view her differently.

"Conn, you've always been in pretty deep cover. Your legitimate businesses more than explain your travels and contacts. You could care about someone. If it's that important, quit the covert side and stick with your original purpose for joining. Just develop software. I'll help on this end, I promise."

Conn seemed wary.

"In the meantime, watch her back and yours. These guys are playing hardball. Let's get this one put to bed, and then you can re-evaluate your future. Okay?" Maggie tried for a reassuring tone.

Conn had more than paid her dues. Maggie hoped Leigh Grove returned the affection, because she doubted Conn would ever try again if this didn't work.

Meantime, she needed to think about taking care of things from her end. "Are you seeing her today?"

"She's coming to my speech, and we're going to dinner with her best friend from college and his friend this evening. Pat Hideo is her best friend's name. He's a forensic accountant from Boston, probably with Marley-Willams. Check him out, okay? More thoroughly, I mean."

She got up to leave but paused and gazed at Maggie, her tone unsure. "Maggie, I, um, thanks. I mean it. She's just so…different." They shook hands.

"Good luck. Ms. Grove sounds like a very nice woman."

The meeting was over.

❖

Leigh drove to work on automatic pilot. Needing some high octane before her meeting with Peter, she stopped at Sally's Coffee across from her building,

Ling, a young Chinese girl who worked the counter and machines in the shop, greeted her with her usual smile, in spite of the fact that she had dark circles under her eyes. They had grown to be friendly over the past year, with Leigh coming in almost every morning.

Since there was a brief lull in the shop, they took a moment to chat. "How are you, Ling?"

"I'm fine."

"How's your mother? Is she well?"

Ling's mother was a cleaning woman in Leigh's building. They had met once when Leigh was arriving at work and needed coffee, and Ling's mother was just coming off shift and had dropped by to see her daughter.

"I think so," said Ling. "She never complains."

Must run in the family. Leigh knew from previous conversations that Ling worked this full-time job, went to high school, and helped out with her younger siblings.

"Sometimes we talk about the people we work for," said Ling. "In this job you hear all sorts of crazy things from the customers, but in my mother's job, she gets to see them, too. She and I talk because the others are too young. Hoo! Some of the stories!" Her eyes were wide, and they both laughed.

"Haven't the workers gone by the time your mother gets there?"

"Most of the time, but sometimes, she'll open a door and have to close it fast, for decency's sake. You'd be surprised." Ling was blushing now.

It was probably nothing, but Leigh was curious. "No! Really?" Leigh glanced around to see if they were still alone, then leaned over the counter conspiratorially. "What did she see?"

"My mother came into a conference room up on the sixteenth floor, "Ling whispered, "and there were two people, ah, well, doing you-know-what on the table!"

Ling and Leigh simultaneously covered their mouths and giggled.

"Did your mom know the people?" Leigh worked on the sixteenth floor and wondered just how low Peter had sunk.

"Just that she'd seen them before, meeting after hours. They were always rude to her. Sent her away like she didn't exist. She told me to see them doing such things didn't surprise her. They are both people of low degree. She said she has seen people who have romance before, but not these two. No romance, just *it*."

"Did they see her?"

"No, too busy!" They laughed again.

Ling handed Leigh her latte and took her money. After Leigh put her usual dollar tip in the jar beside the register and got ready to leave, she thought of one more question.

"Ling, did your mother happen to describe them? I won't get anyone in trouble, and I have a reason for asking." That seemed to be enough for Ling because she didn't hesitate.

"She said the woman worked on that floor. She had short brown hair and long red fingernails. Mom said she's not a boss, but thinks she is. She didn't know if the man worked there or not. She's only seen him at those late meetings. He has light hair and cold eyes. Mom said that man is scary. She was glad to leave before they saw her."

More customers arrived, and Leigh winked at Ling and waved good-bye. She inched her way past the line and out of the small shop, holding her drink above her head to make sure it didn't spill. The description didn't match Peter, and she felt a small sense of relief.

Her meeting with Peter was scheduled for ten o'clock. She shoveled through her in-box and returned phone calls, and it seemed like only a few minutes later that Mary buzzed to remind her.

Georgia was there, ensconced at her desk, guarding the door. She ignored Leigh, instead talking on the phone for a good five minutes. While on the phone she unconsciously examined her manicure for flaws, which gave Leigh time to observe her. *Hmm. Short brown hair, long red fingernails, not a boss but thinks she is. Bingo*. Leigh felt her eyes narrow in concentration. *But who's the guy? No one in the office fits that description. But "scary" only fits one that I know of. Dieter.* She almost laughed out loud at her brilliant conclusions.

When Leigh was finally announced, she walked past Georgia's desk and gave her best wide-eyed innocent look. "Have a nice day, Georgia." She could feel eyes boring into her back as she closed the door firmly.

Peter was on the phone too, apparently arguing with someone. He quickly ended the call, but his face was flushed and he seemed upset. A short time ago she would have been concerned; now she was just relieved that he wasn't her problem anymore.

"Are you okay, Peter? You look a little frazzled." Her curiosity was genuine.

"Well, I *am* tired. It's been frantic around here, what with putting together these portfolios and meeting with clients. You'd think they'd be more appreciative of getting in on the ground floor of these IPO's."

Leigh was silent. This was one of the main points that they argued about. It was one thing to be in on an initial public offering of stock that actually had a future, but these… The potential for fraud and lawsuits far outweighed the possible gains. The pressure on him was building. Or maybe it was just one too many late-night meetings.

He seemed to understand her silence and changed the subject. "Well, to what do I owe the honor of your presence?"

"Let's cut to the chase, Peter. Did you have anything to do with my apartment being broken into after I caught you with Karen Phillips?"

"What? No! I told you I don't do stuff like that. Why would I?" While he seemed genuine, perspiration was starting on his brow.

"The man who assaulted me ordered me to do what I was told. He was nasty, Peter. And then when he tried to abduct me in the restaurant parking lot, we had just had our conversation in the restaurant. I haven't pressed it because I didn't want to think you were connected in any way, but who else but you would want me to do what I was told? And the timing of both attacks is suspicious, at the very least." As she talked, his perspiration became sweat. His face turned red, but of most interest was the fear in his eyes. She'd seen something like it at the restaurant.

"Look, Leigh. I don't know who in the hell he is or why he came after you. Maybe he mistook you for someone else, or maybe he's some psycho who's stalking you. You're a beautiful woman. Some guys get off trying to scare women. Have you, um, gone to the police?"

Leigh was silent.

He cleared his throat. "By the way, how did you get rid of him?"

Leigh decided to end the meeting. As she got up from her chair she said, as casually as she could, "A friend." She didn't take a breath until she closed her office door.

❖

Peter stared blindly at the door to his office for a while after Leigh left. What she had said was unsettling as hell. After he buzzed for Georgia and ordered her into his office, she entered with an irritated expression already in place.

"Do you know anything about Leigh being mugged last week?"

Georgia regarded him coldly. "Why would I know anything about something like that?"

He fought the urge to squirm.

"Look, Leigh's not involved in anything about our deal. We've broken our engagement and she's just an employee. I need her to hold her clients in place until after the IPO, that's all. I didn't sign on for any rough stuff. So if you do know something about it, stop it."

Georgia came across the room and leaned on his desk, her eyes full of contempt. She was almost nose to nose with him. He could smell garlic on her breath when she spoke.

"You will do exactly as you are told, when you are told to do it. You're in this up to your egotistical little neck and in no position to issue orders about anything. Your involvement is more than well documented, Peter. If you so much as sneeze in the wrong direction, your career will be over. And it won't be just a slap on the wrist and a fine. You'll be in prison, a criminal. I'm told they don't play tennis every day there, either. Think about it."

She stood up and folded her arms, glaring at him. "Will there be anything else, *sir*?" The sarcasm dripping from her voice made him queasy. She whirled around to leave and, when she reached the door, asked, "Would you like me to order lunch for you, *sir*?"

"No, thank you. I'm going out to my tennis club."

"Good luck."

He watched the door close and swiveled his chair to stare out the window. He had a magnificent view of the bay, Alcatraz, the bridges. His gaze returned to Alcatraz. Leaning back in his chair, he steepled his fingers under his chin.

"What have I done?"

CHAPTER THIRTEEN

Pat looked like the cat that had swallowed a rather large, tasty canary when he appeared at Leigh's door at 11:30 sharp. She scooped up her purse and nearly ran out the door, delighted to get out for a while and eager to see Conn.

As they walked to the hotel she nudged him and said, "Okay, give. What's that silly grin on your face about?"

Pat was attempting to play coy, but she could tell he was bursting to tell her. "I met my friend last night, Leigh. We hadn't seen each other since he left Boston three long weeks ago. And I wasn't free until late because of my client meetings. He was waiting in the lobby with flowers and champagne. I was afraid that he would forget me, but he didn't! If anything, it was better than before. I am so hooked, I can't believe I'm even able to put a sentence together!"

He stopped, taking both of her hands, and people in the street had to flow around them. "I love him, Leigh. More than that, I'm *in* love with him." His eyes were shining, and Leigh felt her eyes tear as well.

"Oh, Pat, I'm so glad to hear that! He must be an exceptional man. What's his name?"

Her playmate returned. "No way. You have to meet the whole package first. Tonight, at dinner. Until then, my lips are sealed."

"You rat! Now I'll be crazy all day. And you know it! Just remember, you can't do anything permanent unless he meets my approval. That's the rule. Agreed?"

Pat laughed and nodded. "Oh, I think you'll approve. He's gorgeous and kind and funny and—"

Leigh held up her hands in surrender. "Okay, I get the picture.

Now I get to at least go and listen to *my* gorgeous new friend." As she stepped to one side to avoid a piece of gum on the sidewalk she thought she caught a look from Pat.

Later, in the grand ballroom, the woman at the desk checked both of their names, located them on to a list, and said, "You two have been seated at one of the front tables at the request of our keynote speaker."

"Well," said Pat, "since I don't even know the woman, someone must be special. That would be you, girlfriend." He mimed licking his thumb and poking his tush, then made a sizzling sound. As he walked toward the entrance to the room he chanted, "Hot, hot, hot!"

Leigh ducked her head when she realized the woman at the door seemed to be appraising her, then scurried after Pat.

❖

Conn had checked the equipment and arranged the room the way she wanted it. Now she was literally prowling outside one of the service entrances to the ballroom. *Why are you nervous? You've given this talk or something like it a dozen times.* She checked her watch again and peeked through the small pane of glass in the door.

Toward the back of the room she spotted Leigh moving to the front, her hands on the shoulders of a short, handsome Japanese man. They were laughing and seemed completely at ease with one another.

"That must be Pat. Seems nice."

Someone behind her cleared his throat, making her start and whirl around. A waiter stood there, a tray of water glasses balanced on one shoulder. As he smiled at her, she laughed. "I must be crazy, checking out the audience and talking to myself."

"Actually, most speakers do the same thing, no matter who they are. Why don't you go out and work the room?" When she didn't respond he suggested, "Or, if you know some people out there, go talk to them. Makes the time pass more quickly."

"Brilliant!" Conn knew this, but she'd never done it before because she'd never considered anyone worth talking to. Today was different. After holding the door for the waiter, she walked over to where Leigh and Pat were seating themselves.

Leigh was saying something to Pat when Conn placed her hand on her shoulder and gazed down into the bluest eyes she'd ever seen.

Conn's breath caught in her chest, and she matched Leigh's smile. The moment lasted until Conn realized that Leigh's friend had gotten up from his chair.

"Oh, hi," said Leigh. Then she turned a delightful shade of pink. "Um, this is my friend, Pat Hideo. Pat, this is Conn—Dr. Stryker."

"It's a real pleasure to meet you, Dr. Stryker," Pat said as they shook hands. "I've admired your work for a long time and use your software every day. From what Leigh tells me, I also owe you a debt of gratitude for helping her the other night. Thank you. Anytime you need anything from me, you've got it. She's my best friend."

Conn was touched by the sincerity of his words. "I didn't do much. Just happened to be in the right place at the right time. But it's nice to meet you too. Leigh speaks so highly of you. Any friend of hers is a fr—ah—well, you know what I mean. And, please, call me Conn." *Well, that's a sentence you rarely say.* Leigh covered her hand and held it in place on her shoulder.

"Will you join us for the rubber chicken portion of the meeting?" asked Pat.

Leigh looked at Conn reassuringly and saw her relax. *God, I hope what she said about speaking is true. She seems so nervous.*

"I'd love to. But I have to sit up on the dais with the head cheeses. I'll have to content myself with knowing I have a friend—friends—in the audience and look forward to dinner this evening. Speaking of which, I'd better get up there. Nice to meet you, Pat. See you after this is over."

Feeling a gentle tug from Conn, Leigh realized she'd been holding her hand the entire time they'd been talking. She released it, and Conn winked at her and made her way over to the dais with the other VIPs.

Pat leaned over and whispered in Leigh's ear, "She's spectacular. Even more so in person. She seems to think you are, too. You did good, girl."

Leigh stared at him for a long moment before being distracted by a waiter putting food in front of her.

The waiter had evidently heard his comment because as he set her plate down he said, "I'll say. She's really nice, too."

Leigh immediately dove into her food as though it were the most delicious meal she had ever eaten, and Pat blessedly didn't say anything else. But his comments were swirling in her head. Of course, Conn was spectacular. In every way. Now that Leigh thought she understood her shyness and her stoic ways, she didn't even notice them. The Conn that she was getting to know was amazing. So, why did Pat's remark make her feel shy and vulnerable? And the waiter, what was *that* all about?

After dessert, Leigh watched the chairperson of the event, a rather square woman with nondescript hair, glasses, and a really bad suit, get up and make some announcements in a monotone, then give the mike to the president of the Conference Association. He introduced Conn with such a long list of credentials and accomplishments that Leigh was in awe. When, at last, Conn took the podium and flipped on the microphone attached to her lapel, Leigh was riveted to her.

Conn cut an imposing figure. Height, clothes, long auburn curls, and clear blue eyes made a stunning package. She stood quietly behind the lectern, apparently waiting for the flatware to stop clinking and the voices to dissipate, seemingly in complete control of the room. All eyes were on her.

Conn made the obligatory thanks and joked that with such an impressive introduction, she'd found herself waiting for the speaker to stand up. Everyone laughed and seemed to relax.

As she spoke, Leigh was mesmerized. During the talk, several times Conn seemed to look directly at her and smile. Once, Leigh swore Conn lost her place and had to take a sip of water to refocus. Leigh took a sip of water, too, her face warming with pleasure.

Leigh occasionally glanced at Pat, and he appeared as enthralled as she was. Once or twice she caught him staring at her, though, even winking. She was too engrossed in Conn to be rude and ask why, but she would later.

Finally, Conn closed her talk by warning the audience, "You must all remember that 'the price of freedom is eternal vigilance.' Vigilance over the accounting practices of your clients; vigilance about taking the word of your counterparts in the companies you work for; vigilance over your own laziness and even greed. Don't *ever* lull yourselves into believing that because they are your biggest clients, they aren't capable of outright swindling. Last of all, take care of yourselves. Truth and honesty can be dangerous at times. Thank you for your time."

The audience rose instantly, cheering, clapping, even giving a few whoops and whistles. Leigh and Pat were among the first on their feet. Conn was magnificent—so poised and full of commitment and passion. Leigh had never been so moved by a speaker before. More than that were the brief seconds that they shared during the talk. Leigh could only use the word "intimate," if she had to describe them. Leigh was in awe of how she did that and wondered if others felt the same way.

Conn seemed surprised and embarrassed by the extended applause, and finally she waved to quiet them and said, "Dismissed!"

As the audience good-naturedly began to drift away, Conn unhooked herself from the microphone and spent a few minutes shaking hands before she made her way over to Pat and Leigh.

Leigh impulsively gave her a hug, unable to resist the closeness she craved. "That was great! You were the best speaker I've ever heard."

"You were terrific, Dr. Stryker." Pat shook her hand warmly.

"Thanks. And, again, please call me Conn."

Leigh realized there was a long line of people behind Conn, patiently waiting, so she reluctantly said, "I know you need to talk to these people. Do you want to meet at the apartment later?"

"I have a seminar that starts in a few minutes," Pat interjected. "We'll see you at the Carnelian Room at seven for drinks, okay? You girls dress up, now. We're celebrating!" He gathered his coat and briefcase.

In a voice that only Leigh could hear, Conn said, "Hang on a minute. Then I'll walk you back to your office."

Leigh nodded, thrilled to have Conn want to be with her. She touched Pat's arm. "I'll walk out with you in a minute."

As Conn greeted her admirers, Leigh watched people shake Conn's hand, give her their cards, and ask her questions. There was even a fair amount of flirting, although Conn appeared oblivious to the subtle invitations. But for some reason, Leigh was alert to every nuance.

One attractive woman talked to Conn, then headed in Leigh's direction. As the woman passed her she smiled and nodded, making Leigh feel confused and self-satisfied. *Back burner. Bring it out later. And no smirking.* That part was hard.

Pat interrupted her thoughts. "I really have to go. You stay. But tell you what, I didn't know who to watch during her talk, you or Conn."

"Why?" Leigh held her breath. Pat knew her so well.

He leaned in to talk quietly. "When she met your eyes, she lost her concentration. And you could barely tear yourself away for a second. I even wondered if anyone else noticed." Checking his watch, he kissed her on the cheek. "See you tonight."

Leigh was stunned. Now the nod the woman had just given her made some sense. She didn't know how she was *supposed* to feel, but the warmth spreading through her body was a new experience and not unpleasant at all.

As they made their way back to Leigh's office, Leigh filled Conn in on her conversation with Peter. "He seemed surprised when I connected the apartment break-in and the restaurant jerk, then was sweating by the time our meeting was over. He said he didn't know anything, but he's lying, and he's scared. From what you've said, he could be in over his head and can't figure a way out."

"His office is probably monitored, too. Whether or not he acknowledges it, he's on guard. Any ideas about who's in on it besides him?"

"Not that I can think of."

As they neared her office, she automatically glanced at the coffee kiosk, then slapped her forehead and exclaimed, "Oh! I forgot the best thing!" She related Ling's story and how she'd connected it to Georgia and a mystery man.

"None of the guys in the office fits the description, but according to Ling, her mom had seen them in there before. Late at night, for meetings. This meeting was just a wee bit more personal. Now that I think of it, it does kind of match one of the committee members. The scary one, Dieter."

"Good bit of sleuthing there, my friend."

Pleased at the compliment, Leigh raced on. "Yeah. I could get into this. Maybe I should try to sneak in late at night and go through Georgia's desk. I could get all sorts of—"

Conn abruptly grabbed her arm to face her. "Don't ever say that! Don't even think it. These people are dangerous and wouldn't think twice about killing you. If they even get a sniff that you're anything less than innocent—" Conn seemed to catch herself, then released Leigh's arm and backed away a few steps. "I'm...sorry. I didn't mean to hurt you. It's just that…"

The pain and fear in Conn's eyes made Leigh's heart ache. She started toward her and said, "I was just joking. I wouldn't do anything without telling you. Really. Don't worry."

Conn seemed embarrassed by her actions and wouldn't meet Leigh's eyes. Then she straightened her shoulders. "Okay. Just so we understand each other. I'd better go. I, uh, have some shopping to do if I'm going to meet Pat's expectation of 'dress up.' See you at the apartment later." She walked briskly back toward the hotel.

As Leigh watched her go, suddenly she remembered something and yelled, "Conn! Wait!" She hurried to catch up to her and almost skidded to a halt, nervously smiling.

"I almost forgot. Here's a key, in case you get there early and want to shower or anything. You know where everything is, including the bugs. Help yourself! See you about five thirty. Deal?"

"Deal." Conn's voice was noncommittal, but she took the key. Thinking about what had just happened as she entered her building and waited for the elevator, Leigh wondered about Conn's sudden reaction. But what most unsettled Leigh was the fact that the fear in Conn's eyes was for her.

❖

Out of sorts all afternoon, Leigh felt terrible for upsetting Conn. *I should have gone after her and made her talk. What if she just chucks it and drives back to Bolinas?* She thought of calling on the cell phone, but didn't want to further antagonize her. *Why didn't I keep my big fat mouth shut?*

The traffic oozed like molasses in winter all the way home. As she approached her building and passed the white van, she had the urge to flip them off but stopped short, remembering Conn's instructions to not acknowledge them in any way. She swiped her key card, craning her neck to check if the Audi was there yet, but couldn't see. Zooming in, she almost hit Rugby Ted as he walked to the elevator.

"Whoa!" He glared in her direction, then broke into grin. "Well, g'day, pretty lady. You trying to knock off Aussies these days?"

Leigh quickly lowered her window. "I'm so sorry, Ted. I was in a hurry and wasn't paying attention."

"No problem. You didn't actually break anything. Why don't you finish parking and I'll get the elevator for us."

Leigh nodded gratefully, and when she reached her spot she saw Conn's car in one of the guest parking places and sighed. *Thank God.* She hurried to the elevator, where Ted was waiting.

"Thank you so much. Again, sorry for almost running you down." She punched her floor button with a lot of zeal.

"Got a hot date tonight?"

Leigh studied her feet. "Yeah, I guess so. How about you?"

They had reached his floor, and he was on his way down the hall when he yelled back, "The hottest!" He waved as the elevator door closed.

As soon as the door opened on her floor, she practically ran to the apartment, fumbling with the key and swearing under her breath. Bursting into the room and finding no one there, she momentarily panicked before she heard someone singing in the shower.

Leigh closed the door and leaned on it, listening. The Oleta Adams tune, "Get Here," was one of her favorites, but she was so excited she was damned if she could remember any of the words except the reoccurring "get here." It didn't matter. Conn's voice was soft and seductive and the tune recognizable. *Nice.*

When the shower and the singing stopped, she decided to make some noise so she wouldn't startle Conn—and for the benefit of the pricks, as she had charitably come to think of them. She dropped her briefcase and went into the kitchen. Banging open the refrigerator door, she took out two bottles of water and stomped through the apartment to the bathroom door, which she pounded on.

"Hi there. Want some bottled water? I'm afraid that's all I have!" The door burst open and there stood Conn, wrapped in a bath towel, hair dripping, smiling at her. Her knees almost buckled.

Leigh managed what must have been a goofy expression and squeaked out something like, "Hi." She was sure that the hayseeds must have been sticking out of her hair a mile. *Yessir, it doesn't get much better than this.* She stuck the water bottle out, almost punching Conn in the chest. Her beautiful chest.

With no warning Conn dragged her into the bathroom and closed the door. She put both bottles on the vanity and her finger to her lips, then turned on the faucet. Then she leaned in to whisper in her ear.

"Nice attempt at subtlety. This is the only room where I'm certain we can't be overheard on a listening device, even an outside wand from across the street. I, um, I wanted to apologize for grabbing you and yelling today." She leaned back. Her eyes matched the apology.

Conn was just inches from Leigh, whose ear was still tingling from the contact. *What did she say?* She squeezed her eyes shut and tried to clear her mind, swaying a fraction before gathering her wits.

"Um, then you have to accept my apology too. I was just mouthing off. I didn't mean to upset you. I would...never...okay?" She registered terry cloth and that heady mixture of strength and softness emanating from Conn's body. She forced herself to step back a bit, gazed at her another second, and took a breath.

Leigh felt flushed. *Is this what it's like to have a hot flash?* She managed to sputter something about needing to find something to wear.

Conn shrugged, and her towel slipped a bit. "Okay. The bathroom'll be all yours in about ten minutes."

Leigh swept the length of Conn's body, then stumbled into the bedroom. When she closed the door, she had to lean on it because she was trembling. *Okay, not self-conscious about herself or nudity. Definitely a California girl. My God, what a body.*

Leigh was accustomed to female nudity. The sorority house, modeling—all involved naked women. But she was pretty sure Conn was in a class by herself, because Leigh was in overdrive.

She fumbled her closet open, barely noticing the bags and packages from Neiman's. With difficulty she focused on the evening ahead.

All the van picked up was buzzing, much to Simpkin's consternation. "Shit. Why am I doing this? I haven't heard a damn thing since we started this operation."

When the cameras were put out of service, he figured the women hadn't found the other devices. Now, he wasn't so sure. Hatch was going to be pissed. Dieter had told him to lay off the rough stuff, and Hatch had been in a lousy mood every time he had checked in at the van. All Simpkin could do was keep a log of activity and try to avoid his wrath.

After the chase through Marin County, they tried to trace the license plates of the mysterious Audi, and it came back as registered to a Lottie Sommers in Noe Valley. A check of that address yielded nothing but a furnished, empty house. Like the owner wasn't there. Dieter ordered them to stick to the Grove woman for now. But here was the Audi again. And she got there before Grove. Must have had a key. Then the shower running.

"Pretty cozy, girls." He checked the equipment and turned up the dials to try and grab any bits of conversation that would feed his imagination.

❖

Conn sat on the sofa, pretending to read the newspaper as she waited. It might as well have been upside down. Being that close to Leigh in the bathroom had unnerved her. She was turning one of the pages when a tag dropped out of her sleeve and hung there.

"How many of these things can there possibly be on one piece of clothing?" After finding a pair of scissors in the kitchen, Conn was inspecting the outfit for further offenders as she walked back into the living room.

There, standing in the bedroom doorway, was Leigh, wearing a short black dress cut to hug her curves. Her legs were spectacular, and the strappy high heels revealed lovely feet. Two panels joined behind the neck, baring her back and the middle of her front down to her waist. The gentle cleft between her breasts, barely suggested, was definitely there. There was a shortage of oxygen in the room.

Conn was dumbstruck. Suddenly her cell phone mercifully rang. Tearing her eyes away from the vision in front of her, she tersely answered and said a few words before folding it.

Leigh continued to stare at Conn for so long, Conn was afraid another tag had appeared in an embarrassing place.

Finally, Leigh said, "That's the most gorgeous tuxedo I've ever seen on a woman. And the vest reminds me of the color of dark blue Venetian glass. It fits you perfectly. Conn, you look amazing."

Conn knew she was blushing furiously and said, "Ah, it seems our chariot is here to escort us." Smiling, she pointed to the window, where a black stretch limo was waiting outside the front entrance to the building.

Leigh's eyes were sparkling, and she hugged Conn. "What a treat! Let me get my jacket and let's go!"

Desperate for something to say, Conn gave a theatrical sigh of relief and said, "Thank God. I was wondering if you were going to freeze to death tonight. By the way, you look spectacular, Leigh. But, if you don't mind my asking, what's to prevent, uh, you know, an, uh, accident from happening…if you shift too quickly?" Conn felt her face reddening as she asked, but couldn't contain her curiosity.

Leigh extracted a short jacket that matched her dress from from its hanger and gave it to Conn to hold while she slipped it on. Turning, she gave Conn a very sexy look. "Well, I guess I'll just have to be careful, won't I?"

CHAPTER FOURTEEN

As the limo left the entrance to Leigh's building, Conn glanced back briefly to watch a dark sedan fall in behind them. She wasn't surprised.

Twenty minutes later they arrived at the Bank of America Building. Pat was waiting outside, and Leigh immediately went over to say hello, while Conn stayed for a moment to speak to the driver.

"Did you spot the tail? Keep an eye on them. Thanks, Jess."

Jess, a colleague of Conn's who was dressed in full livery for her stint as a chauffeur, nodded. "Wouldn't be surprised to have people watching you inside tonight. You might want to think of a cover story." She closed the limo door and tipped her hat.

When Conn joined them, Pat put Leigh on one arm and offered her his other, and they walked to the express elevators with every eye in the place on them. Pat had a grin plastered on his face that couldn't have been sanded off.

"So where is this mystery man of yours, Pat?" Leigh teased. "I'm beginning to think he's just a figment of your imagination."

"He went up to get a table by the window for us. He's a banker, and it's a banker's club. Besides, I wasn't going to miss giving these lovely people around us the opportunity to envy me. Not in a million years."

Conn and Leigh regarded each other over Pat's head, and Leigh winked. She started fawning over him—brushing imaginary lint off his shoulder, straightening his tie. Then she snuggled close to him and kissed his cheek. Pat was bright red by the time the elevator doors opened, and Conn was laughing at the two.

"Ooh, Mr. Hideo, this is a real classy place," Leigh exclaimed. "I like it!"

Pat rolled his eyes and said, "Okay, okay. I give up!"

The woman at the reception desk showed them to their table, where a man was seated, staring out the window at the spectacular view of the city. He turned when he heard Pat's voice.

Leigh gasped, "Rugby Ted?"

Ted seemed equally surprised. "You two! My beauties from the building! I don't believe it."

As they sat down they explained to Pat how they knew each other.

Leigh chuckled. "We thought you were hitting on us, Ted. It didn't occur to us that you might have been trolling for your teammates."

"I wasn't. The whole team is gay. I thought you made a cracker couple and would enjoy watching us play."

Conn was exchanging a confused look with Leigh when what Ted was saying sank in, and she quickly broke eye contact. Leigh immediately began studying the view, so Conn suspected she understood as well. She could only hope that Leigh would rise to the occasion and not blurt out something that might be overheard.

Movement in Conn's peripheral vision brought her attention to two men being seated at the table closest to them. *The room isn't full. Why there?* A well-trained alarm went off in her head, so she excused herself and headed toward the restrooms, which were past the maître d' station. After talking to the hostess a moment, then continuing to the restroom, she was back a few minutes later.

She smiled pleasantly as she sat down and tenderly put a hand on Leigh's chin, then turned her so they were facing each other.

Quietly she said, "I think these fellows at the table to your left are following us. They specifically requested that table, and you may *not* look at them. Play along with me tonight. We need to give them a reason for being together. I'll explain more later."

❖

Leigh momentarily froze, resisting the urge to stare openly at the men. The rest of Conn's words computed, and she imperceptibly nodded in agreement. At that moment Conn leaned in and lightly kissed her lips.

Leigh pretended to cough into her napkin, about to jump out of her skin with the adrenaline rush. Between the danger of being followed and the excitement of the kiss, her head was spinning.

Then her eyes settled on Pat. His eyes bulged and he started to say something, but she put her foot on his and applied pressure, giving him a meaningful look. He didn't say a word, but quickly asked Ted how his day had been.

"Let's order a drink, shall we?" said Conn. They all agreed so quickly and wholeheartedly that Ted probably wondered what in the hell he had missed.

After ordering a bottle of Perrier-Jouët champagne they chatted amiably; then at eight o'clock Pat suggested they proceed to dinner. All four shared Conn's limo, and by eight thirty they were seated in a private booth at the Fifth Floor ordering appetizers.

The food was fabulous and Leigh was thrilled. The four of them were having a wonderful time joking and talking, and Conn seemed more at ease in this social situation than Leigh could have hoped for.

They discussed Ted's rugby team, and then Conn and Leigh wanted to know how Pat and he had met. Leigh enjoyed seeing the sparkle in both men's eyes as they retold their story. Ted laughed at just about anything Pat said, and the two were sitting with shoulders touching. Leigh was delighted that Ted seemed to be just as much into the relationship as Pat.

After Leigh explained that she and Pat had met in college and had been best friends since, Conn couldn't help herself and fished for information. "Didn't your dates get jealous?" Despite the circumstances, she realized this must be what it would be like to be out to dinner with friends. She soaked in the experience, but told herself it was just part of the cover story.

Pat regarded Leigh and spoke softly. "Well…Leigh and I both complained that we didn't really enjoy anyone else like we enjoyed each other. As a matter of fact, we decided that if we hadn't married by the time we were thirty, we'd marry each other. But then I told Leigh I was gay. And we're still best friends."

"We always knew we wouldn't marry," Leigh added. "But we agreed that whomever the other chose, we had final approval. I realize now that I broke that promise, Pat. I apologize. You never liked Peter. I was so stupid." She felt Conn covering her hand and tried to hide her delight and surprise.

"We all make mistakes, Leigh. Right, Pat?"

"Right. You won't do it again. In fact, you're already improving."

Once the dishes had been cleared from the table, Ted said, "I'm stuffed! Let's get the check and go have some more fun."

After arguing about who would pay for dinner and Ted winning, Pat said, "Let's go someplace and dance."

Ted agreed. "There's a gay dance club south of Market Street."

Conn hesitated, but offered the limo and silently got Leigh's permission before they gave the word to the driver. As they left the restaurant she'd spotted the two men at the bar and knew they would have company.

The club was bone-jarringly loud and full of an eclectic crowd. After Conn slipped the bouncer a fifty-dollar bill, they were shown to one of the booths that surrounded the dance floor. Big-screen monitors were strategically placed around the large dark room, some of which showed the dancers; others showed dance videos. In addition, roving spotlights illuminated the dancers. Most were early twenties, pierced, buzzed, and a lot were stoned. Male or female couples were the majority, with a smattering of mixed. Since talking was out of the question, Conn ordered Irish coffees for the table, and they watched the dancers.

Leigh yelled, "Seems like all of the dance clubs I've been to."

Conn nodded, "Yeah! I was in a few in Europe, but it was business." What she didn't say was that those clubs had always made her extremely uncomfortable, and it wasn't just her assignment's inherent danger. She hated crowds of strangers.

But here, with this group, she felt oddly calm. She refused to entertain the idea that it was due to Leigh sitting so closely beside her, holding her hand. *Holding my hand.*

A bit later when an older song with a Latin beat started up, Pat tapped Leigh and they both whooped.

Pat yelled, "Come *on,* C.G., let's go!"

Both Leigh and Pat had natural grace and rhythm, and their moves reflected their familiarity with each other. Conn was mesmerized by Leigh. When others cast appraising eyes on Leigh and Pat as they danced, Conn found herself feeling territorial. Although she'd been vaguely aware of something similar at the Point Reyes celebration, she was surprised at the intensity.

She told herself it was because she knew Leigh better now; they were being followed, after all. She needed to protect her asset. Wait, that was too harsh a word. Her charge—that was better. Perhaps friend would be more accurate. But the fact that women were hungrily staring at Leigh bothered her. She felt unsettled.

Leigh and Pat danced for a while as Ted and Conn watched, but when the music slowed, Ted grasped Conn's arm and said, "I don't know about you, but I'm going to dance with my man!"

Conn almost did a double-take, because evidently Ted had read her mind. She grinned at the realization that he probably didn't appreciate the way men were appraising Pat. "Let's go!" she said. They made their way to the couple and each tapped the shoulder of their date.

Leigh was surprised and delighted to see Conn approach her. While she and Pat had been dancing, she'd noticed that Conn had not taken her eyes off her. Conn had leaned back in her chair, watching her as if she were the only woman on the dance floor.

Without much thought, she'd thrust her hips more suggestively, touched and teased Pat, dancing around him seductively. Then she realized she was dancing for Conn. Pat immediately matched her style, and Leigh wondered if Ted was watching.

When the music ended and the slow, sexy beat of a samba began, she watched Conn stride toward her, eyes never leaving her own. She held Leigh's hands in hers, then slowly spread them apart and stepped between them to bring her close. Leigh stopped breathing when Conn's hand settled on the small of her bare back.

Conn gazed deeply into Leigh's eyes and said, "Only look at me and listen to the music. Nothing else exists, just you and me and the music."

In that moment, Leigh knew she was right. Nothing else existed. The lights dimmed as the borders between them slowly melted, and Leigh entered a world she knew only from her dreams. She glided effortlessly in Conn's arms, nearly overwhelmed by the sensation. Peter would have instructed her as to the proper movements for whatever the dance was. There was no need for words or instruction with Conn; they fit together perfectly.

Conn made her feel things she'd thought impossible. Conn seemed to be touching her everywhere, inside and out, stirring so many sensations at once, Leigh's mind overloaded trying to identify them all. Then she didn't think at all. When Conn's arms encircled her, Leigh felt safe. When Conn effortlessly spun her to the sensual drum beat, her front brushed across the delicate material covering Leigh's breasts, making her nipples pucker and ache. Their hands together created a current that raced through her, making her breathless and wet.

Leigh felt at once dangerous and protected, breathless and serene. And completely turned on. She was thankful that the lights were low because she knew her body was flushed with heat, from the top of her head to her toes. Every erogenous zone she knew of and a few she had no idea could produce pleasure were on full alert. Every action, every turn awakened something more in her—newer, fresher, more exciting. It was happening so quickly she was almost dizzy with the possibilities.

Suddenly, she wondered about being with Conn as more than just a friend. Her lips so close to Conn's, she wanted nothing more than to taste them. She felt the warmth of Conn's breath. The heat from Conn's body seemed to match her own. Could this be what she'd always dreamt of having in a partner? Someone to make love to endlessly?

Leigh focused on the clear blue eyes, darker now, plumbing the depths of her soul with such ease, and wondered how Conn could do so much to her with just a simple glance. They swayed to the rhythm of percussion and guitar. They moved as one, Leigh a natural counter to Conn's strong lead. Their hips never separated as the beat slowed and the song ended. They never broke eye contact, and Leigh never wanted to let her go.

Leigh was only vaguely aware that an area had been cleared around them and people were watching. A few couples clapped, and others nodded their approval.

When the music started again, loud and raucous, Leigh reluctantly pulled away, taking Conn's hand as they made their way back to the table, aware only of her tether to this world, Conn's touch. She'd never before danced that way with anyone and recognized this was a beginning. Of what she didn't know.

Pat was beaming. "Where in hell did you learn to dance like that,

Conn? You're marvelous. Leigh, let's face it, hon. You and I are good, but you and Conn? Spectacular. Like you were born to dance together." Ted was vigorously nodding in agreement as Pat spoke, but they became absorbed in each other within minutes.

Leigh tried to make sense out of what had just happened. She'd just experienced something she'd thought impossible for her. And the person who'd made that happen was Conn. Perhaps it was because Conn accepted her for who she was—not the debutante, not the model, not the eye candy. Maybe Conn wanted the woman who was Leigh. And Leigh wanted her back, wanted to know every detail, shadow, and light of this woman who had danced into her heart and claimed it. Leigh tried to memorize every touch and emotion, every second. Perhaps this was the person she could trust with her love.

Conn studied Leigh, who seemed to be still catching her breath. *I'd better explain before she never speaks to me again.* "Well, I guess we've given them something to report to their boss, huh?"

Leigh seemed momentarily confused, then looked like she had been slapped. "Oh. Yes, I guess so." She stared at her lap.

What did I do? Conn fumbled for something to say.

There was silence between them for a few minutes. Then Leigh, eyes shining, said, "I think I'd like to go now. Tomorrow is a long day." She fumbled for her jacket, which Conn helped her with, then stood and started making her way to the door. Conn trailed after her, motioning for Pat and Ted to follow. They seemed mystified too, but didn't argue.

Outside, the fog had settled over the city. Conn phoned for the car, and as they waited for it to arrive, Leigh stood hugging the light jacket to her, shivering. Conn couldn't stand it and took the risk of being rejected when she stood behind her, wrapped her arms around Leigh, and pulled her back into a warm embrace. She stiffened slightly, but then accepted it. The limo arrived in minutes and they got in. The silence in the car was awkward.

"Ted, do you want to be dropped at the B of A building to get your car?" said Conn.

Conn noticed Pat squeeze his hand. "No, thanks. I'm sure the garage is closed. Since Pat has an early meeting, you can drop us at the Hyatt. I can walk tomorrow to pick up the car."

Conn scrambled again for something to say. Small talk was so difficult. "Pat, what did you call Leigh as you went to the dance floor? G.G.?"

Pat seemed to understand what Conn was trying to do. He tried to get Leigh's attention, maybe asking permission to tell, but she was staring out the window.

"I called her C.G.. It's left over from college. Stands for 'cover girl.' Leigh paid for most of her own college tuition and all of her expenses by modeling. She was on the cover of *Glamour* and *Seventeen* and even got an offer from *Sports Illustrated* for their swimsuit edition. But she turned that one down. Right, C.G.?"

The warmth in Pat's voice seemed to get through to Leigh. "Right, Patty. My rule was no nudity or swimsuits. I don't even know where that offer came from." She managed a half-hearted smile.

"Oh, I think I know," Ted chimed in. "You're spectacular, Leigh. The *SI* blokes figured they'd give their subscribers a good ogle. Good for you, turning them down." His enthusiasm and sincerity were infectious, and the mood in the car felt more relaxed to Conn. But she knew something she'd done had hurt Leigh, and that knowledge made her heart ache.

When they arrived at the hotel they said good night to Pat and Ted. The ride to the Marina was silent.

Conn couldn't stand it any longer, so she took Leigh's hand. Leigh kept her eyes averted, but let her hand remain. "Leigh? We need to talk. Mind if I ask the driver to take the scenic route home?"

Leigh shrugged, and Conn gave instructions to the driver, asking her to raise the modesty shield. With that in place, Conn faced Leigh and waited until Leigh met her eyes. "I said something that hurt you. I didn't intend to. I was trying to reassure you that I wasn't going to do anything that you...wouldn't... Crap. Leigh, I just wanted you to know that I'd never do something to upset you. I'm not very good at this, am I? I did the one thing I tried not to do. I'm sorry." *I can't do this! What am I thinking?*

She plowed ahead into unfamiliar waters. She wasn't accustomed to having to explain her actions. "Look, I said I would explain. We've been shadowed all evening. My face, at least in some circles, is fairly well known. If the people behind this scam know me, you could be in danger. My whole company is based on detecting irregularities in stock transactions and accounting procedures. If they see us together, and they certainly did if one of them was at the conference today, it wouldn't take long to figure out my purpose here. But if we throw them a curve, put us in a personal relationship, that might at least confuse them."

Leigh was silent.

"I think you should quit that job as soon as possible. I talked to Aunt Jen, and she told me she offered to have you live out there. I want you to seriously consider the possibility. Okay?"

No response.

"Please?"

Leigh nodded. "All right. But I still think that Georgia and Peter's desks are a trove of important information. Maybe the two of us…" The words died on her lips at Conn's expression.

Conn struggled to maintain her composure. "Leigh, no. Listen, you've done more than enough already. We aren't trained to do that type of thing." *Well, you aren't.* "It's illegal and dangerous. If the analysis of the database yields enough information, I can turn it over to the proper authorities. Then they can handle it. For now, I just want you out. Please. I, uh, I need to know you are safe." *That was true enough.* "Besides, Marina is on her way to Pakistan on assignment as of tomorrow, so Jen will be alone again. It would be wonderful knowing you two are taking care of each other. Will you do that? Will you agree?"

Leigh smiled and was about to say something when Conn's words sank in. "Take care of each other? Where will you be? I mean, aren't you here for a while longer?"

Conn couldn't meet her eyes. "I have to head back to D.C. tomorrow. Things have come up that need my attention. I can have further analysis of the program done from there."

As miserable as Leigh had felt earlier, Conn now seemed just as miserable. Leigh watched her. *You are such an enigma, Constantina Stryker. What are you really thinking? More important, what is your heart saying?* But anger immediately overrode any concern for Conn's feelings, and she said, "Tomorrow. When were you going to tell me? Never mind. I'll get out to Jen's as soon as possible. We can 'take care of each other.'" *Why is this so upsetting? Why do I care?* But she did care. She cared quite a bit.

"You'd better call a lot."

That elicited a sigh of relief. "I promise." With that, Conn pressed the button that signaled the driver to lower the shield, and they drove to the apartment.

"Well, if you and I are an item, you'd better come on up." Leigh knew her eyes conveyed that this request was not negotiable. They got out of the limo, and Leigh dragged Conn along by her hand to the door. She let them in, and they walked to the elevator with arms around each other's waists. In the elevator Leigh made no effort to shift away from Conn, because every molecule of her body craved her. Conn didn't resist either; if anything she held her closer.

When Conn had embraced her while waiting for the limousine, Leigh was helpless to resist. Then Conn had explained that she didn't want Leigh to do anything against her will. Did that mean that Conn was a lesbian? That Conn had cared for her as more than just a friend? Leigh had been on an emotional rollercoaster since the evening had begun and had to do something about it.

After they entered the apartment, Conn checked the tiny motion detector that she'd engaged before they left. She seemed satisfied and reset it for the night.

Signaling the all-clear, Leigh took her by the hand again. She walked them over to the window, where only the sheer white liner was closed. Their silhouettes were easily visible from the street because of the lamp she had left on.

Leigh positioned Conn in front of the window and slid her arms around her neck, under the auburn hair, registering her strong shoulders and the warmth of her body. She gave her a smile laced with irony and whispered, "Well, as Granny used to say, 'In for a penny, in for a pound.' Let's give them something to report back to their boss."

CHAPTER FIFTEEN

Conn had left before dawn, and for the first time in her life, Leigh knew what it was like to ache for someone, be incomplete without them. She sat listlessly behind her desk, rolling a pen around her fingers, and replayed the dance that had changed her life, but her longing only intensified. She didn't even remember getting to her office. So many emotions coursed through her, business was the absolute last thing on her mind.

She jerked back to reality when her intercom sounded and Mary told her Pat was in the outside office.

When Pat stuck his head in, he seemed to quickly register her mood. "What's up?"

Leigh shook her head. "Come on, let's get some air."

After they left the building and had walked a block or so, Pat ventured, "So, how was the rest of your evening? I was a little worried about you. Are you okay?"

She didn't answer, but concentrated on locating the first open restaurant she could. When they were seated, Leigh studied him intently. "Pat, are you sure you're in love with Ted?"

Pat seemed to give her question careful thought. "Yes, I am. More with every passing day. Why, hon? Are you having some feelings for Conn?"

Taken aback by Pat's directness, Leigh realized her expression told Pat most of the story. She was miserable.

She put her head in her hands, elbows on the table, and let out a slow breath. "That would be an understatement. I'm so confused, Pat. I've never thought about being with a woman before. It's never been an option. But as I think about it, except for you, I've never been particularly attracted to men. I was just *supposed* to be. When you came out to me I didn't think too much of it, other than wanting you to be happy, you know."

He nodded, but said nothing.

"I mean, it made sense. And I'll always be your best girl, so there's no downside, you know? I really like Ted. I did even before I knew he was the one. He's so…" Leigh stopped because Pat took her hand. She ducked her head. "I'm babbling, aren't I? Okay. One more question, Pat. How did you *know* he was the one?"

"Leigh, I just knew. And I think you know, too. What happened?"

They discussed the night before. Pat registered surprise to hear they'd been followed, but then his eyes glittered with understanding.

"Leigh, I really didn't understand how serious this situation is. Now the sudden change in Conn's behavior makes sense. She's right to want you out of there. You *are* leaving, right?"

She just stared at her fork.

"Oh, there's more. What else, hon?"

She felt tears form in her eyes. "She stayed the night. I made a show out of bringing her to the front window of my place and kissing her so that the jerks watching from outside would see it. But it backfired, Pat. I've never felt like that when I've kissed someone before. Never."

Pat squeezed her hand.

"She stayed. She offered to sleep on the couch, but I lied and said it wasn't a big deal to sleep in the bed. We were like two stiff boards. I finally fell asleep, and when I woke up I was sprawled practically on top of her. I had managed to snuggle right in. Pat, I've never felt so complete, so happy. I didn't want it to end." Just then the waiter brought their iced tea, and she was quiet until he left.

"But it did end. She's gone. Back to D.C. She left before dawn this morning."

"Did you talk about it? I mean, was it just for show from her end, or did she mean it?"

Leigh just shook her head. "I don't know. We didn't even acknowledge ending up in each other's arms. But before she left, I gave her a kiss that we'll both remember for a long time. I hope." She smiled wanly, holding tears back as best she could.

Pat leaned toward her and gently asked, "I want you to think about this before you answer. Did she return the kiss?"

"Yes. Absolutely." There was no hiding the passion in that kiss.

"Leigh, she didn't have to. It wasn't something that could be seen or heard by the surveillance. She returned it because she felt it. And something else. From where I sat last night, either she deserves an acting award, or she was just as much into you as you were her. Trust me, I know. Ted thought the same thing, has always thought of you two as a couple. He's not stupid, Leigh. None of us are. I think she cares, very much."

"Do you think so? Really?"

Pat started laughing. "You sound like Judy Garland just finding out Andy Rooney likes her in one of those old black-and-white movies we used to stay up all night watching in college. All that's missing is 'gee whiz!' Oh, you've got it bad, girl."

She felt her ears start to warm, then soberly said, "I don't know when or if I'll ever see her again. She didn't say more than two words this morning. If I hadn't pushed the kiss, I might never have known she felt anything. What if I never—"

A distinctive ring interrupted her train of thought, and it took a second for her to register that it was coming from the phone Conn had given her. She fumbled in her pocket for it, almost dropping it trying to flip it open.

"Hello?" She grinned into the phone, and Pat excused himself to the restroom.

By the time he returned Leigh was waiting impatiently.

"Well? What did she say?"

"She said she was sorry to not have told me sooner that she had to leave."

"And?"

"She said she would call as often as she could."

"And?"

"She said she wanted to dance with her cover girl again!"

Leigh cocked an eyebrow at her best friend.

"Okay, and?"

"She wanted your phone number."

❖

Conn stared out the window of the plane. Jess had picked her up at Jen's and driven her to the executive jet airport adjacent to San Francisco International, where they were quickly underway. The steward on board brought her coffee and the newspaper, then started preparing her breakfast, but she wasn't hungry.

When she had arrived at Jen's that morning, Marina was finishing packing. Watching them together reminded her of her brief experience with Leigh that morning.

As a child she had always wondered about the tears Jen and Marina shared whenever she left on assignment. Her mother had never cried when her father left for a business trip. In fact, she seemed relieved to see him go. But every time Marina and Jen separated, they were upset. Now she understood. She dismissed the errant emotion immediately as fatigue and too much fun the night before.

She'd absently offered to drop Marina at the airport, but Marina reminded her she had a rental car. Marina gave her a fierce hug and gazed up at her. "Follow your heart, sweetness, follow your heart." Conn had glanced at her watch, kissed Marina on the cheek, and excused herself to finish packing.

After Marina left, Jen had found her and leaned in the bedroom doorway, watching Conn pack. "Hey, stranger. Haven't seen you for a while. Marina and I thought maybe it was something we said. Did you see Leigh while you were in town?"

Conn kept packing. "Yeah. She came to my talk, and later we went out to dinner with her best friend and his friend—correction, lover. Then we went dancing at a gay club. It was late when we got to her place so I...stayed."

"Dinner, huh? Sounds like fun. Did you like her friend?"

"Yeah. He's a forensic accountant. That's how Leigh knew I would be giving a speech. He's a good guy. Turns out we had met his new love, a banker who actually lives in Leigh's building. Really nice men." She closed the bag and snapped the lock. "Well, I guess I'd better hit the road. The car should be here soon."

They walked down the hall toward the mudroom to leave her luggage, then to the kitchen for coffee, to wait for the car. Conn was quiet and remote.

"You care for her, don't you?"

Conn busied herself with finding a mug. "I...don't know."

"Talk to me, honey."

Conn couldn't resist telling Jen about the rest of evening. When she described the kiss in front of the window, she discovered her jaw was clenched so tightly she had to consciously think about relaxing it. "Then we shared her bed last night. I clung to my side for dear life, but when I woke up we were wrapped in each other's arms. Aunt Jen, I can't do this." Conn felt such a loss at her words, but she knew she had to make a break.

"Did you talk at all? How did you leave things?"

"Well, that's another problem." Conn sighed. "Before I left this morning, Leigh kissed me, I mean really kissed me. And I kissed her back." She felt like she had committed a capital crime.

"Is that so bad?" Jen took her hand. "Leigh is a wonderful girl. From your description, she seems to return your caring. Why are you so miserable?"

Conn abruptly stood, almost knocking the chair over behind her. "You don't understand. I can't *care* about anyone. Aunt Jen, look at me, my life. I could get her killed! I'm a *spook,* for God's sake! I've done things…I've hurt people. Even this operation is far deeper and more dangerous than we first thought. And I set her up. I *can't* care!"

Jen rounded the table to hold her. "Conn, it was bound to happen. Love is a wonderful thing, and Leigh can make her own decisions. She offered this information to me, if you recall. And she volunteered to install the disk. You can't beat yourself up about something over which you have no control."

Conn stiffened and pulled back. "You forget one very important thing, Jen. She doesn't *know* about me. What's she going to do when she finds out I've lied to her? Betrayed her like that idiot ex-fiancé of hers? No, it's better I end it now, before she gets hurt."

Jen studied her. "It might be too late for that, Conn. There are two of you involved here. Why don't you just see where it goes?"

Conn was quiet as she listened to the soft, assured voice of her aunt. Jen had always been there for her, no matter what. When Conn's mother had died after a horrendous binge of drinking, Jen and Marina had flown to be by her side and convinced Jen's brother to let them take her to live with them. She was sixteen. And they always, always insisted it wasn't her fault that her mother had died. Always.

Maybe what Jen said was true. Maybe. But what if something happened to Leigh? What if, because of Conn's past, she was hurt, or worse? The few who knew of her double life were either dead or on her side, but she dealt in forensics and had been openly involved in more than one operation that brought down some very influential people. If she allowed herself to care about Leigh, the consequences of that caring could be grim. Worse, what if her emotional involvement with this woman she had set up and used somehow backfired and endangered not only the entire operation, but the lives of other innocent people involved in it? That could include Jen and Marina. She simply couldn't indulge her unwelcome emotions for Leigh, which would probably pass quickly. Too much was at stake.

Jen interrupted her morose thoughts. "Conn, you can't live in a cocoon forever. You're a wonderful, warm, caring woman. You deserve the same."

Her aunt knew how to get to her, Conn thought, clinging to the faint ember of hope that Jen's words provoked. "Aunt Jen, I don't even know if she's gay. What if she wakes up and decides it was just the night and the music?"

"Well, why don't you let *her* decide?" Jen smiled at her. "You'll never know unless you try."

Conn was silent.

"Look, I'll invite Leigh out for the weekend again. She'll be safe here. And you said you liked her friend, and he's a forensic accountant. Why not see if he's interested in working for the company? You've been searching for good people. If he is, you'll have a friend around. A gay friend. You could use someone like him on the inside—a friend first, employee after."

Conn had started to protest, but Jen kept talking. "*Just* try it, please?"

The steward placed Conn's breakfast in front of her. Jen's idea was a good one. If Pat checked out and was interested, well, he was another tie to Leigh. Maybe she'd just have to see where it would go. For now.

After she'd eaten she checked her watch. A few phone calls later, she decided it was okay to call Leigh. After all, she had to find out Pat's phone number.

When she got off the phone she was smiling. The sound of Leigh's voice was like a soothing balm. She thought Leigh sounded happy to hear from her, and she didn't hesitate to give her Pat's number. Conn's expression must have confused the steward, because he came over to ask if she needed anything. Other than wanting to turn the plane around, she only needed to be left to her thoughts.

Even though memories of Leigh's beauty and their shared kisses intruded more often than she would admit to herself, after some time she forced herself to solve the unending list of problems she encountered as CEO of Stryker Software.

Chapter Sixteen

Jen helped Leigh carry her stuff into the house on Friday, then suggested a more extensive tour of the grounds and a hike down to the beach. After assembling a picnic backpack and water, they jammed some old hats on their heads and set out toward the cliffs.

The ocean side of the property was much less developed than the front half. The grasses were tall and wild; the paths were just beaten-down footpaths, the footing less sure.

At one point Jen, who was in front, turned to say something and yelled, "Freeze! Yellow-jacket nest!"

Leigh halted midstep, her right foot in the air, until Jen took her arm to steady and guide her away from the nest. When they were a safe distance away, Jen said, "I just recently found it. Those pesky things chase the hummers away from the feeders and attack poor old Tippy when he's trying to sun. I need to find a way to destroy it without poisoning the earth all around it. Then I have to remember to do it after they've returned to the nest at sunset, or before they leave at dawn. Until then, we avoid it."

Leigh assured her that the location was emblazoned on her mind, and they continued to the cliffs. When they got to the edge Leigh carefully peeked over at what appeared to be a sharp drop of several hundred feet to the sea below. As magnificent as the view was, the thought of hiking down to the water scared the crap out of her. Jen seemed to read her mind.

"Having second thoughts?"

"Uh, something like that. That seems straight down to me." Leigh's feet were sweating, and her breathing was shallow.

Jen assured her that she wouldn't let her fall and that the trip would be worth the risk. And since Leigh was desperate to not appear a wimp, she smiled reluctantly and said, "Oh, well, no pain, no pain."

As it turned out there was a trail of sorts, and the footholds Jen showed her were solid. A few times she slid on her rear end, and the scrawny plants that insisted on growing out of the cliffs were the worse for wear after she grabbed them to keep her balance. All in all, she thought she did well to get down the path in one piece.

Jen grinned. "Conn would be impressed."

In return, Leigh was sure she was grinning like an idiot at the praise, but she couldn't do much about it.

After the harrowing descent, they strolled along the rocky, sandy shore. It was low tide, so there was plenty of beach to explore. Just off shore lay large rocks that the waves crashed against with such force and beauty that Leigh stopped and stared.

"This is magnificent!" She realized that Jen was probably too far away to hear, but didn't care.

They picked their way between rocks, jumping over small streams of water running back to the ocean from tide pools and trying to avoid the giant tubers of seaweed that had washed ashore. Finding a place relatively free of obstacles, they stopped to set out their picnic lunch, and the conversation inevitably turned to Conn, Leigh hanging on every word.

"Conn would spend hours down here by herself. That was actually how *I* learned the cliff and beach by heart, in the dark." Jen stared at the ocean. "Scared the hell out of me. One summer, I had gone to the city to pick up Marina at the airport. Conn was about fifteen, and she decided to stay here by herself. I didn't think too much of it. Conn knew all the neighbors and had helped build the place. She said she would cook for us. It was all planned."

"Conn can cook?"

Jen's eyes were just short of twinkling. "Well, I don't know about now. She probably hasn't given much thought to it in years. Back then she could manage a pasta dish pretty well." Jen returned her gaze to the ocean. "Anyway, when Marina and I returned from the airport, Conn was nowhere around. We thought, at first, she was playing a joke. But it was getting dark, and we scoured the place. Dinner hadn't been started, and her hiking shoes and fanny pack were gone. We called at the cliffs, but the sound of the waves drowned out our voices."

Jen seemed lost in that moment. "Marina suggested we take flashlights and go to the edge of the cliff. Maybe we could see something or, if she was there, she could signal us with her flashlight. We always carry them in our fanny packs. You know, little ones."

"We went to the edge and started yelling and listening, shining the lights in arcs. We were both so anxious we were basically yelling at each other. Nothing. Then I told Marina to not use her flashlight, and I did the same. We stood there in the darkness, listening, watching." Leigh leaned closer, completely absorbed in the story.

"Suddenly Marina said, 'Over there!' Sure enough, there was a tiny light blinking. We flipped on our flashlights and tried to see her, but lost the penlight in the blaze of our own lights. Off they went again and we hiked toward the blinking light, in the dark."

Jen turned to her. "Trust me when I say that you can do anything if you love someone enough. Marina and I *felt* our way down the cliff, trying to get to that light. As we got closer we started yelling and could hear her calling back. When we finally reached her, we found she'd fallen, broken her arm and gotten her foot and ankle wedged between two rocks. We were able to work her foot free, but she was in shock. We put her between us and started back up the hill. Conn at the age of fifteen was as tall as she is now, and she was a handful because she was out of it. We used Marina's flashlight occasionally, to get our bearings, but that was about it. It took forever to get back to the house, sometimes on our hands and knees."

Leigh was spellbound. In that moment she knew that she wouldn't have hesitated to do the same thing for Conn. Anytime, anywhere. The realization surprised her. She really didn't know Conn well enough to have such a deep-seated certainty. But, with or without an explanation, it was true.

Jen laughed. "We never did get to eat that night. Between the emergency room and the emotional exhaustion, we all just came home and went to bed. What a night! Bottom line, all of us have no fear of the cliffs. You'll get that way, too. Just stick around."

"You know, my life was tame growing up, compared to your adventures," said Leigh. "I was pretty sheltered as a kid. About the most dangerous thing I did was fending off amorous photographers."

"Give yourself more credit, Leigh. Conn told me you paid for college by yourself, you left home and got your MBA, then struck out on your own to California. All that is not for the faint of heart.

And you've handled all that's happened recently with a lot of guts and courage. I admire you."

"Really? I hadn't thought about it like that. Those words mean a lot coming from you. Thank you."

Patting her on the shoulder, Jen said, "Well, think about it."

❖

After dinner that night, Jen and Leigh finally settled in front of the fire. Tippy added his girth to Leigh's now-familiar lap and seemed to think they should stay there for the rest of the night, because he was perfectly content.

Leigh was quiet.

"What do you want to know?" Jen asked gently.

Leigh was at first surprised, then relieved, and finally chagrined at Jen's ability to read her. She let out a big sigh and leaned her elbow on the chair, propping her head on her hand.

"Either you're a mind reader or I'm a lot less subtle than I thought."

"Maybe just on one particular subject. Go ahead. I'll answer if I can."

"Thank you. I was wondering how it came to be that Conn spent all summer, every summer out here."

"Well, that didn't start until she was eleven years old. I...was gone for several years."

The pain on Jen's face was obvious. "Oh, Jen, I didn't think the question would invade your privacy. Just forget I asked. I'm too—"

Jen held up her hand. "It's okay. It's just a part of my life I don't normally discuss. It was a long time ago." She sighed. "I ran away. I used to be married, and I ran away from him and the marriage. It's a long story, but the bottom line is that I stayed out of contact for five years. When I finally called my brother, he helped me get a divorce. Actually, my ex was already remarried, so it was fairly simple."

Leigh could think of nothing to say.

Jen's eyes were shining. "There's only one thing I regret during that time. That I wasn't there for my little niece, Constantina."

Concentrating on her hands, she continued. "During the time I was missing, my brother's wife, already a rather moody person, had started drinking pretty heavily. Conn was an only child, you can guess why. She and I were very close. I wouldn't have blamed her if she'd never spoken to me again, but as soon as she heard I'd resurfaced, we wrote or called each other almost every day. Leigh, I felt like I was throwing a lifeline to a drowning child. Dear God, that sweet baby."

Jen had tears in her eyes, and Leigh felt her throat catch at the thought of what Conn must have suffered.

Jen paused a moment. "Anyway, Conn's from a small town. She was always taller and smarter than her peers. From some of the things she's said over the years, I suspect she couldn't risk bringing friends home. Her father, my brother, said that if her mother had been drinking, she could be abusive and, well, you get the idea. Her dad did the best he could, but he had to travel in his work. Conn was alone. As soon as we reconnected, I asked if she could spend the summer with me, and the rest is history."

The fire crackled, and Tippy stretched in Leigh's lap.

"Wow. I wish I'd known her then. We'd have been great friends."

"Doesn't matter. You're great friends now. The timing is perfect."

❖

Leigh's eyes popped open before dawn. Wide-awake, she got up and wandered into the kitchen to put coffee on and feed a very insistent cat, then showered. When Jen mentioned that she had to run a few errands, she asked if she could tag along, and Jen seemed glad to have her company.

After their outing, as they walked in the door the phone was ringing. Jen plopped her bags down on the counter and picked up the receiver.

"Hey, Conn, I was wondering when you were going to call." There was definitely amusement in her voice. "Oh, I'm fine. Thanks for asking. What? You weren't asking? You want to talk to Leigh? Well, she must be around here somewhere. Oh! Here she is! Standing right beside me. Shall I put her on the phone? What? I can't hear you. Okay, okay! Jeez, what a grouch. Here she is." She laughed and gave the cordless to Leigh, pointing to the great room, where she could have some privacy.

Leigh's pulse had picked up when she heard the phone ringing. Realizing it was Conn, and she was asking for her, she almost let out a squeal of excitement. *Control yourself, Leigh, you're so strange. After all, it's only a call from a friend.*

Standing by the window in the great room, she stared at the ocean and could see Conn's eyes before her as she spoke. "Hi, stranger. How's D.C.?" was all she could manage to get out.

"Hi, yourself. Enjoying your weekend?" Leigh could hear the smile in Conn's voice.

"Yes! Jen and I hiked down the cliffs to the beach for a picnic, and I managed not to break any bones. Today we went into town for breakfast, and Jen introduced me to a lot of her friends. I heard a few stories about you, my friend. Ones that, were I to mention them to some of your peers, might give them a new perspective on you. Quite a little hellion, weren't you?"

"Those stories must remain with you. Promise?" Conn's voice was deadly serious.

"Okay, Conn. I was just teasing. I'd never say anything about you to anyone without your permission. Promise." The rebuke stung.

Conn was silent for a few seconds. When she continued, the warmth had returned to her voice, and she sounded contrite. "Sorry, I didn't mean to bite your head off. To tell you the truth, I'd prefer my colleagues not know much. It's easier." She cleared her throat. "So... will you keep my secret?"

Leigh heard apology in the request. "Of course. I understand the wisdom, believe me. If anything, I tend to err on the other side, and I'm not sure it's done me any good."

"Leigh, don't change. You're wonderful just as...I mean, um, I admire how friendly you are."

If Leigh could have levitated, she would have. She searched for something to say to keep the moment. "Well, I wouldn't want you to change either. I...I'll never tell." She felt her face heat and tried to think of something to fill the awkward silence.

"Well, I haven't had much luck at the office finding out about Peter's cohorts, Conn. People there know basically what Peter has said about them, and he really plays them up. I don't get the impression people know the committee even exists. It isn't in any legal or published papers about the company. As far as I know, there's no formal connection. Have you had any luck?"

"Yes and no. These guys do manage funds that have had success recently, like Peter. But they're average. They seem to be riding the crest of the bull market. And I'm guessing they're as caught up in themselves as Peter is. All but one check out that way. Guess who doesn't?"

"Dieter. He's number one on my skin-crawl meter." Leigh didn't have to work hard on that one. She got the creeps just at the mention of his name.

"Good intuition. As a matter of fact, confidentially, Dieter has attracted the interest of the SEC before. My software is used internationally and has picked him up in Germany and Britain. As a guess, something big is in the works, and I don't like the smell of it."

Leigh could hear a pencil tapping in the background.

Conn cleared her throat. "Listen, I still want you to immediately move out of your place and in with Jen. Her house isn't easy to find or watch, for a number of reasons."

Leigh considered her words. "Well, I—"

"She'd love to have you around. Both Jen and Marina. And we're all concerned about your safety."

"But the commute would be—"

"I want you to quit."

"Well, I haven't—"

"Please. You can take your time deciding what to do next once you're in Bolinas."

"But my clients—"

"I know all of your considerations, Leigh. I'll do what I can to protect their money. I can't say any more. Your safety is more important."

"I don't want them to know where I'm moving, Conn." Leigh's stomach was in knots.

"Don't tell them. You have underground parking. Load boxes and a bag or two and stuff them into your trunk. Small trips. Put your home phone on voicemail with the phone company. Don't have it forwarded. And don't mention Jen or me. We have to assume a few people know of our connection. From the other night, if nothing else."

Conn paused, then added, "If Georgia Johnson does a little

snooping and finds out my field of work, that could raise all sorts of alarms. Frankly, we'd be safer if they thought we were lovers than if they thought you knew about my work. If anything's mentioned, play along and play dumb. Let's keep a lid on it until we know more. How soon can you quit?"

"Wait a minute, back up. Are you saying you wouldn't mind if people spread it around that you're a lesbian? With me?"

"I could care less. Especially with…you." Pause. "I mean, I don't want them to find out you and I are working together, and if that's what it takes, who cares? Besides, it's not like those rumors aren't out there anyway. I'd think you'd be concerned about yourself. Are you?"

Leigh took a moment to think about it. "That's a good question. For some reason I'm not. Ha! I'm not! Wait until I tell Pat."

"Leigh, for now, make Pat the only one you tell, and talk to him only on the secure phone. It's safer for others to believe what they want. Assume you're being watched. Later, you can set them straight, so to speak."

Trying to keep her voice light, Leigh said, "So, lover, when do I see you?"

The comment got a nervous laugh at the other end of the line. "Hopefully, soon, but I'm tied up here with a project for a while. You work on getting to Jen's, and, um, I want you to check in every day. Call before you go to bed so I know you're safe and so we can update each other. And, Leigh?"

"Yes, Constantina." Leigh was surprised to hear her own voice drop and become slow and seductive.

"I, ah, be careful."

Chapter Seventeen

One afternoon the next week Pat Hideo sat waiting to be ushered into the office of the president of Stryker Software. The company was obviously sound and growing, its employees intelligent and creative, many with a rather good sense of humor. But what most intrigued Pat was the way they viewed their founder and leader, Constantina Lynn Stryker—with admiration, respect, and just a touch of awe.

One young software engineer had almost stuttered when he mentioned her name, blushing furiously. He had told Pat that he had met Dr. Stryker only once and didn't know who she was when he did. "I mean, she's so young and awesome. After she left the room someone told me I'd just met the CEO and I almost…I almost, well, I was really embarrassed."

Pat had already met with several vice presidents and visited every floor but the sixth. While in the elevator he had observed that a special key card was necessary to get to that floor.

He now sat in a plush chair in an outer office obviously designed to be warm and inviting. The receptionist was a young, quite attractive Japanese woman who politely announced his presence and returned to her work. Although there seemed to be a lot of activity, the sound treatment of the walls muffled everything.

Five minutes of waiting was broken by a soft tone that the receptionist, wearing a headset, responded to. She smiled into the space in front of her, then nodded to Pat.

"Mr. Hideo? Please come with me." Removing the headset, she rounded her desk and escorted him to the door. Impeccably dressed, she seemed to glide instead of walk. She opened the large door and held it for him to enter, nodded again slightly, then closed the door.

The large office was mostly window, overlooking the nation's capital. The desk in the middle of the windows, handcrafted and huge, held two flat computer monitors, both to Conn's left and discreetly secure from prying eyes. The desk was uncluttered and unadorned, and Pat could see no photographs anywhere in the office. The artwork on the walls appeared to be originals, ocean and mountain vistas. One smaller painting hung closest to the desk, within easy view of Conn. A single bloodred rose. Except for the rose, the office was professional and revealed nothing of the occupant.

A large overstuffed sofa and chair, a coffee table, and a table and chairs seemed new and rarely occupied. Closer to the desk stood a drafting table with whatever was being worked on covered by an intricately hand-woven piece of cloth. Again, warmth without revelation. Pat was sure the room had been purposefully designed that way.

When Pat first entered, Conn had her head down, reading something in front of her, so he had time to view his surroundings without feeling like he had to sneak a peek. He didn't know if she thoughtfully allowed him that leisure, but when he looked at her again, she was regarding him evenly, her eyes acknowledging nothing of their previous meeting or personal time spent together. He silently took a breath and tried to relax.

Conn greeted him with a firm, dry handshake, then took him over to the sofa and motioned for him to sit. He chose the chair since the huge sofa might force him to sit with his feet dangling like a child's. Conn took the sofa. Standing, she was a good nine inches taller than he, and she didn't slump. Yet she hadn't made him feel smaller with her presence. He wondered how she did that.

When they were seated, she pressed a button on the console on the end table next to the sofa and within minutes they were enjoying a wonderful cup of cappuccino. Pat waited for her lead.

"Well, what do you think? Do you like it here?" She put her coffee down and sat back. She evidently didn't mince words.

"Yes, I do. It's very impressive. Are you offering me a job?" Tit for tat.

She smiled for the first time. "As a matter of fact, I am. I want you to help in several areas. We have some projects that need a forensic accountant to oversee development and beta testing. You would be working directly with the engineers. You would also liaise with marketing and sales. I need someone to make sure everything we claim the programs do, they indeed can do. I don't like having to put out patches. We charge a lot, and I want clients to have confidence that their money is well spent."

"I can do that. But don't you already have that base covered? Your reputation in the industry is exactly that. Few, if any, bugs. What else? Do I get to go on the sixth floor?"

Pat returned Conn's steady gaze.

"First, these are new tools being developed specifically to allow companies to detect fraud among their employees and their internal and external accountants—your area of expertise. I want them to be integrated into the operating systems and databases. Second question: depends. That floor is classified. Government contracts. Security. Are you interested?"

"What do I have to do to work there? Is it so different than your general work? I know you've already interviewed down to my high-school teachers. I've signed enough nondisclosure agreements to cover even the locations of the bathrooms around here. Your security is tight to just enter the building."

"Those projects are classified, and the necessary clearance would make what you have been through to date seem like a stroll in the park. Everything, and I do mean *everything*, in your life would be under scrutiny. These people don't mess around."

She seemed to hesitate for a minute, then continued. "I know that Ted gave you the okay to have him checked out. So far, both of you pass. May I ask you a personal question, Pat?"

First time she had used his name. "Sure."

"Are you in love with Ted?"

Pat studied her for a moment. "Yes, I am."

"Are you monogamous? Both of you?"

"Why don't you ask something more personal?"

That remark garnered a small smile that didn't quite reach her eyes. She continued. "If you want this clearance, he will have to undergo more scrutiny too, because there's a danger you might confide too much in him. That could be a matter of national security."

He nodded agreement.

"There's a flip side to this, too. You might find out some things about each other you won't like. If you want to pursue this position, I suggest asking him again and, if he agrees, having some show-and-tell with each other before they dig up anything the least bit compromising. And they will, too."

He whistled. "My, my, the government has changed. You mean the fact that I'm openly gay wouldn't automatically cancel my chances?"

A corner of her mouth quirked. "Turns out that someone finally snapped to the fact that it wasn't being gay that was the problem. It was having to *hide* being gay that opened people up to blackmail. That, coupled with the fact that this is a private company and the owner will not tolerate discrimination. If they want the work done by my people, it has to be done on my terms. There you have it. Instant tolerance."

Pat gazed at the impressive woman across from him. She protected her employees. No wonder they all loved her—from a distance. "I'll talk to Ted. This sounds like a decision we should make together. If I don't go for the whole clearance, am I still being offered a job?"

"Yes. Definitely, yes. I want you to begin ASAP. We can discuss money if you like."

"No need. I'm sure what you offer will be more than fair. So I'm moving to D.C."

"Yes. We'll pay all of your expenses, and we have a company apartment that you can stay in until you find suitable digs. Is that all right?"

"Perfect. I'll give my notice tomorrow."

"All right, then." Conn started to rise, signaling the end of the interview.

Pat stayed seated. "Conn?"

She turned her head quickly toward him and sat back down, her expression guarded. Pat had used her first name, and he suspected she realized that it was a sign of something personal coming up.

"I, um, need to ask *you* a personal question."

"Depends on the question." Her eyes revealed nothing.

"Let me explain before I ask. You've probably guessed that I did some research of my own before I came here. I know your reputation in the field. What I'm trying to say is that you and your company have impeccable credentials."

She waited. He noticed her hands were tightly clasped together and surmised this was new territory for Conn. Answering a personal question.

Pat held her gaze. "My question is, do you care about Leigh?" He saw it. Her guard dropped for a second, and he saw surprise, then something more. Just as quickly, neutral was back in place.

"Why are you asking me, Pat?"

"No one knows anything about you personally. Because of that, and probably fueled by your beauty, you're rumored to be anything from a dominatrix to a woman who plays fuck 'em and chuck 'em on a regular basis."

"That's all they are. Rumors."

Okay, here goes. I hope Leigh doesn't kill me. "My point is this. Leigh really likes you. Really likes you. She's my best friend and I love her very much. I'm not trying to pry, but you should know that she hasn't, uh, had a lot of experience, and she could be easily hurt. With Leigh, what you see is what you get. You are a mystery."

Conn didn't reply. He watched as her jaw muscles clenched, but she was silent.

"You should also know that I couldn't work for someone who treated her badly. As much as I might want to, and I do, I couldn't. I won't."

Conn sat for a minute, her eyes diverted to the picture of the rose. Then she stared at him. "If you're asking if my intentions are honorable, I'll tell you that I respect her too much to ever consciously try to hurt her. If you're asking if I'm in love with her, all I can say is that I don't even know what that means."

She seemed sad, even a little lost, sitting in her large office. He wondered how many people ever saw that side of her.

"It's funny you should say that." Pat leaned toward her. "Those are almost the exact words Leigh used last week when I saw her. She asked how somebody would know if they were in love."

"And what was your answer?"

"I said, 'You just know.'"

Conn gazed back at the rose. "Are you going to tell Leigh about this conversation?"

"No. It really isn't my business. I needed to ask you because of the job offer."

Conn looked briefly relieved, then smiled. "I'm glad Leigh has such a good friend. That's the highest recommendation one can have. I envy her."

Pat was genuinely nonplussed. "Why? Any friend of Leigh's is my friend too. And, aside from Leigh, both Teddy and I really enjoyed our time together. I'll call as soon as I've given my resignation. I'm excited about working with you."

They shook hands and Pat let himself out, leaving Conn staring out the window.

❖

A friend. Now there's a concept. She went back to studying the contract on her desk, trying to concentrate.

A knock sounded at her door. "Come." She glanced up as Colonel Maggie Cunningham entered, then motioned her to a seat. She appeared tense, and the little hairs on the back of Conn's neck stood up.

"What can I do for you, Maggie?"

Colonel Cunningham held up a piece of paper. "We just got word from our people in Europe that the preliminary information we got from Ms. Grove is pointing to a large, well-organized terrorist cell. We'll need to get in there before they release that IPO. There might be some big fish to be netted."

Every nerve in Conn's body leaped to full alert. "Has Leigh been compromised?"

"I don't think so, but it won't be long."

Conn slowly straightened her back as Maggie handed her the report.

"That's it. She's out of there."

"Wait. Listen, we haven't been this close to nailing these bastards before. The higher-ups want her to stay. They figure we have some time before someone figures it out and she could—"

"No. We'll send someone else in."

Picking up her phone, she hit the number for Leigh's cell phone. Voicemail picked up and she paged her. The message: 9-1-1, Conn.

CHAPTER EIGHTEEN

L eigh was in the middle of a staff meeting when she felt the phone vibrate in her pocket. She didn't want to take it out because it might attract attention.

Peter was droning on about something, and she knew how he hated for people to leave in the middle of one of his pontifications, so she started coughing. A little at first, then more vigorously. Taking a sip of water she smiled apologetically to those who glanced at her. A few seconds later she started again, this time with gusto. She held her breath, scrunched up her face as she felt it flame, and managed during a few of the coughs to allow some spittle to fly. Those closest to her leaned away, probably irritated.

Finally, she waved her hand and got Peter's attention, pointing to her throat, then to the door. She held a tissue over her mouth and grabbed her pen and note tablet containing some very nice doodles of kittens and cats and fled the room.

Letting out a few coughs as she made her way toward the elevator and away from the conference room, she was almost laughing by the time she got to the floor below. She hurried to the bathroom, which was usually deserted because so few women worked on that floor. *Wait until I tell Conn how I got out of the meeting.* She dove for the phone in her pocket.

Her smile died as she read the message. "My God." Her hands trembled as the phone rang. Once. Twice.

"Stryker."

"Conn? Are you okay? What's wrong?" She was gripping the little phone so hard she had to think about easing her hold so it wouldn't break.

"I'm fine. I need you to do me a favor." Conn sounded stressed and all business.

What the hell? "Sure. What do you need?" She was beginning to wonder how Conn defined 911. Her dark thoughts were replaced by something much worse with the next sentence.

"They've traced some of the information from the program you installed."

Leigh sat down heavily on the toilet seat. "And?"

"It's pointing to being funded by a terrorist cell with ties to the Middle East."

"You're kidding! How could that possibly be?"

"It has happened before and will happen again. The important thing is for you to get out of there. Immediately."

"Won't that raise a red flag?"

"I…It could. But there's no telling when or if they'll discover they've been compromised. This is a major operation, and Peter and his friends are just a small part of it. They won't take chances."

Leigh was stunned. How could this be true?

"Leigh?"

"I'm thinking."

"Just leave. Go out to Jen's now. We'll talk there, okay?"

Leigh was stunned.

"For me. Please."

"Okay. I've already acted like I was sick, so I can leave for the day."

She could hear the sigh of relief at the other end of the line.

"Leigh? Thanks. I'll talk to you later."

Leigh started to reply, but realized the line had gone dead. She folded the phone, dropped it back into her pocket, and headed for the stairs.

After Conn disconnected, Maggie shook her head. "Conn."

"What?"

"Leigh has to stay in place until we're ready to move. Orders. This could be the biggest bust we've had in years. And it might be directly tied to national security. No options."

"No way. She's a civilian, she's out of there."

"This isn't your call, Conn. If she leaves before we're able to nail this down, it could blow the whole operation. You've already told her too much. She volunteered for this and she stays. She doesn't have to do anything more than occupy her chair and pretend to work. For a little while longer."

Conn glared at Maggie. She felt her jaw muscles tighten and tried unsuccessfully to relax.

"What has to happen for her to get out?"

"We need more data."

"My program should provide—"

"You told me yesterday you didn't think it would give you everything you needed. This is our chance."

"I'll work on it. I designed that program, and I can get more out of it than anyone."

"Good. But she still stays."

"Are we through? I have an appointment."

"I'm sure she'll be safe."

"I've heard that before." Conn turned in her chair.

Maggie let herself out of the office.

Forty-five minutes later Leigh rolled through the open front gate. "Good. Jen got my message."

Jen was waiting for her.

"Well, seems like things have picked up." She took Leigh's briefcase and purse, and they went into the kitchen.

"Yeah. I was shocked. Did Conn tell you what they found?"

"A little bit. Listen, I'll make us some dinner. Why don't you go rummage in Conn's room for some clothes to put on. She should be calling soon."

Dinner came and went with no word from Conn. Leigh was agitated, and Jen even seemed a bit frustrated with not hearing from her niece.

About eleven o'clock, Leigh finally decided to turn in.

"I'm sure she'll call as soon as she can, hon. She was so insistent to get you out here."

Leigh couldn't hide her disappointment. "I can't tell what's going on with her. One minute she seems to care, and the next minute she's ordering me around and refusing to call." She stood. "Good night, Jen."

Once in bed, she lay there for a long time. Suddenly, nothing seemed more important than talking to Conn, just hearing her voice. Leigh didn't even care if Conn didn't return her concern or caring. She *had* to talk to her. In the dark, she picked up the cell phone from its charger and pressed the number.

"Stryker." It was after three a.m. in Washington, and Conn sounded tired.

"Well, Jen's in bed. Tippy's with her. And I'm here, waiting to talk to you."

There was an awkward pause. "I wanted to call you. I…got so busy."

"You said you would explain more to me. Why didn't you call?"

"Well, a lot of it's classified. I can't talk about it."

"Wait. It's so dangerous that it's classified, but you just handed me a disk to install?" She heard a chair squeak over the phone.

"Shit. No, of course not. I had no idea this would lead to…these people. I'd never have asked you to do it if I'd known! You have to believe me, Leigh."

"Then talk to me, for God's sake! Tell me…just help me understand." The uncomfortable silence stretched out into the room.

"Conn? Are you still there?"

"Yes."

"I better go back to the office tomorrow. I'll set off too many alarms if I don't."

"Look…you may be right. If you disappear suddenly, the whole deal will be blown. It's a house of cards, Leigh, a labyrinth of financial dealings dependent upon each other. You inadvertently provided us with some key components."

Leigh listened with growing astonishment. "Did the program give you everything you needed?"

"Yes… no. Not yet, anyway. That's what I'm working on. But if we need anything else we'll get it later. You do need to stay for a while longer. I'm sorry."

Leigh sighed. "Listen, the reason I called…I wanted to say that I, um, that I…hell. I just wanted to hear your voice." She heard a slow release of breath.

"I miss you terribly, Conn. You're so far away. I wanted you to know that. It seemed important. I just want us to be together again soon, like we were that night we went out with Pat and Ted."

There was silence at the other end of the line, then, "I miss you, too, Leigh." The line hissed for a moment. "Um, on a lighter note, I saw Pat today. He sends his love."

"Is he going to work for you? I know he was excited about the interview."

"Yes, I think definitely. We're not sure of the exact projects yet, but he'll have a full plate, no matter what. We talked about you today. He's a good friend."

Leigh frowned. "Me? What did he say? No more embarrassing stories, I hope. I'll really have to hurt him if he did that."

She could hear the smile in Conn's voice. "No, nothing like that. He just wanted me to know he was your friend first, no matter what the job offer was. He's a bit protective of you."

"Oh. Well. I, we're best friends, and, you know." *What prompted that remark from him?*

"Yes, you're very lucky to have a best friend."

"Then I guess that means you're *really* lucky," Leigh said softly.

"What do you mean?"

"Because you have me."

"Oh. Because you're my friend. Like Pat."

"Like Pat. But so much more. Good night, Conn."

Chapter Nineteen

L eigh loaded another box into her trunk and closed it. For the
past two weeks she had slowly shifted her life to Bolinas.

Since Conn and Patrick had gone back East, Ted and Leigh had
started hanging out together more. Ted told her he had promised Pat he
would take care of her. He either dropped by or called every night, and
she had his number on speed dial on her magic phone. When she was
busy, she told him where she was going and when she would be home.
The nights she didn't see Ted, she drove out to Bolinas with the trunk
of her car full of her belongings. She hated being alone in her apartment
but knew she was close to getting out of there.

Work was quiet and boring. She did her best to not make any
waves, but time seemed to drag and rush by at once.

Weekends she stayed with Jen in the room she was accustomed
to in the main house. They visited Jen's friends, though she was most
comfortable with just Jen. It made her feel closer to Conn.

Leigh enrolled in weekend classes with Mr. Odo. Between exercise
after work at the Bay Club and the martial arts training on the weekend,
she was finally beginning to walk without every muscle in her body
protesting. And she thought she'd been in pretty good shape before.

So she kept busy. But no matter how much she did, the fact that she
heard from Conn only when she was with Jen hurt her, more than she
would admit. Although Conn had made her promise to call each night
before she went to bed, most often Leigh would just leave a message
on Conn's voicemail.

That night, Jen had invited her and Ted out to the house for dinner.

Ted also filled his SUV with her belongings, and they drove in tandem. Leigh was always careful to check to see if they were followed and didn't think they were.

❖

Georgia shifted in her chair, but Dieter chose to ignore her. He was not pleased. Something wasn't right. Dieter had run this scheme often enough to have a sense for it. They were close to the IPO, and he wanted no mistakes. He glared at the woman across from him.

She had been his lieutenant for several years and was efficient and ruthless. The fact that they were lovers meant little to him. He knew the day would come when he might have to dispose of her. A small sacrifice in his line of work. He suspected she felt that sleeping with him would ensure her safety. They always did. He turned his attention to her.

"Any new information on the Grove woman?"

Georgia gave him a sly look. "You mean other than discovering her new taste for women? We tagged her car with a transponder and discovered she's going out to some place in Bolinas about three times a week. We can locate her if we need her. She works out at the Bay Club after work and watches rugby matches a couple of times a week. Some guy walks her home afterward. Must be a friend because the bug isn't picking up any noise other than her in the apartment. Who knows?"

Dieter suspected she considered the subject boring and a waste of time. That was why she took orders from him.

"At work, she seems to be keeping her nose clean. The woman who was around for a few days, the one she was kissing? Gone. Maybe a brief fling."

"Who was that woman? Why can't you tell me who she is?"

Georgia reddened slightly. "The license plates on the car came back as belonging to a woman in Noe Valley. We checked. A house with nobody home. And she's not around. Probably her home in San Francisco. We're keeping an eye on it, Dieter."

He wasn't pleased. "When she shows up again, I want a picture of her. We're close to launching this thing. I want no mistakes, Georgia. And one more thing—find the exact address of the place in Bolinas. And who owns it."

❖

When Leigh and Ted walked into the mudroom loaded down with boxes and the wine Ted had brought for dinner, the first sensation that hit Leigh was the delicious smell wafting from the kitchen. And music with a Latin rhythm was drifting from the house.

Leigh was excited. Maybe Conn was on her way to California. She and Ted finished unloading the boxes, and Ted dug out the wine. As they entered she heard Jen humming.

"Hey, Jen. What's the occasion? All this just for us?"

She greeted them with a smile. "Leigh! I'm so glad you're here! And you must be Ted." He reached out to shake her hand, but instead she gave him a hearty hug. "Well, two things have happened, actually. Marina called and invited me to Paris! She's got two weeks off before going back to Pakistan."

Leigh dug around in a drawer and tossed the corkscrew to Ted. "That's wonderful! But you said two things. Is Conn coming home?" She hadn't meant to say that, but there it was. The fleeting look of compassion on Jen's face told her the answer was no.

"I'm sorry, sweetie. Conn wants to, but she's been working overtime trying to get this project completed."

Trying to recover from her revealing question, Leigh kept the conversation going. "Oh, sure. I know she's been really busy. So what's the second thing you mentioned?" She knew she wasn't terribly convincing.

"I'm offering you a job!" The expression on Leigh's face must have prompted more explanation. "I want you to oversee the renovation of the cottage! And when it's done, you can live there. Top to bottom, your call."

Leigh forced a smile. "Wow! That's great. Thank you, Jen. But I don't have any experience doing something like that. Are you sure?"

"Absolutely. You'll learn as you go. I want you to start as soon as you can and handle the whole thing. Ted? Break open that wine, would you? This calls for a celebration!"

Ted, standing with the corkscrew in one hand and the bottle in the other, said, "Straight away," then opened the bottle and filled their glasses.

All took rather hefty slugs of the wine and became silent.

Clearing her throat, Leigh asked, "Well, great news. When do you leave?"

"In two days. Leigh, is that all right?" Jen had turned her attention back to the stove. "Can you be be out here by then?"

Leigh checked with Ted, who shrugged. "I suppose so. We might have to ask one of your friends to feed Tippy for a few days. I have to wrap up some things in the city."

"That's fine. Mr. Odo and Tippy are great friends. I'm sure he can feed him for a while. From the weight he's put on, I'd say that's already happening."

"Jen, does Conn know about Paris and the...my new job?"

"Not yet. I just heard from Marina. I'll call her and tell her soon. Or maybe you wouldn't mind doing that for me?" She winked, making Leigh color with embarrassment at being so transparently needy.

"That's a good idea, Jen," said Ted. "Leigh, why don't you do that and I'll help Jen with dinner." After he raised his eyebrows and nodded toward the other room, she took the portable and walked into the great room.

Leigh was worried. Conn had been so removed from her, they had barely had any contact. She pressed the number on her phone.

"Hey, Aunt Jen."

Leigh kept her voice neutral. "Hello. It's me. Jen wanted me to call."

Conn's tone softened. "Oh. Hi. How are you?"

"I'm...fine. Jen said to tell you that Marina had called. She wants Jen to meet her in Paris for two weeks, and she's leaving in two days."

"Well, that's good news, isn't it? I'll bet Jen is really happy."

"Yeah. Ted and I came out for dinner, and she made a real feast. She offered me a job, too."

Conn hesitated. "Really? What kind of job?"

"She wants me to oversee the renovation of the cottage. The whole thing."

"Oh. Are you going to take it?"

"Probably. Sounds like a challenge. How are you, Conn?"

"I'm fine. Um, how are you?"

The fact that Conn wasn't trying to hang up as soon as possible was encouraging. "Let me see. I've been moving out slowly like we agreed upon. Ted followed me tonight and brought his SUV full of stuff." She walked a little farther away from the kitchen.

"Jen said she's leaving in two days. I'll give notice soon and be out here, I guess. Although being the mascot to a bunch of huge rugby players has been fun. I might have to go in for the last few games of the season."

"Oh, yeah? Have you been pounding down a few pints with yer mates after the games?"

Leigh sighed. "One pint is more like it. That stuff is lethal. Ted walks, or rather steers, me home and checks the apartment before saying good night. We've become friends since our, ah, since Pat and you left. He even is, well, I don't know."

"He's what?"

"Well, if I didn't know better I'd say he's being more than protective. I'd use the word 'territorial.' Whenever members of other teams try to strike up conversations, it's like he's there beside me doing this macho thing with the other guy. You know, sizing each other up, talking in a way that lets the other one know to back off. It's very cute, but I have no idea why he's doing it."

"Strike up conversations as in flirting?"

"Well, yeah. The guys have been very nice. No one has been obnoxious or anything. A couple of times he's even had private conversations with the more persistent ones. They know most of the team is gay, and the confusion on their faces is comical. It's almost like he's telling them I'm taken."

"He's probably just watching out for you. Maybe he knows these guys are players. Um, do you want to go out with any of them?"

Leigh thought about that. And the fact that Conn had asked. She'd never wanted to play games, and she wasn't going to start now. "As a matter of fact, no." She heard a slow exhale on the other end of the line.

"Oh, well, then, he's doing you a favor, right?" Conn sounded pleased.

"I guess so. I guess he thinks I'm spoken for."

Silence. "Oh."

Leigh didn't say anything. *Come on, Conn, throw me a crumb.*

Big sigh. "Um, yeah. I guess no one has the right to stake a claim on your heart."

Leigh's chest tightened. "Why don't you let me be the judge of that? I have to go. Dinner's almost ready. Oh, by the way, have you been able to get all of the information you needed from that program?"

"What? Oh, no. I'm still tweaking it, but so far we haven't been able to get everything we need. I'll probably need to copy his hard drive and search his office. Don't worry about it. You said you were giving your notice next week?"

"Yes. My contract specifies two weeks' notice."

"Um, Leigh? My guess is they want you out. Be prepared to leave the same day. They'll probably have all the codes and passwords changed before you leave the building. I just don't want you to be surprised."

"Oh. Of course. I hadn't thought about it. Well, good. I guess Mr. Odo won't have to feed Tippy too long, then, before I can take over." She took a breath and steeled herself. *Here goes.* "Any chance of ever seeing you again, Conn?"

"I...am so busy back here. I'll try to get out as soon as I can."

Feeling like she'd been slapped, Leigh ground out, "Well, don't hurry on my account. I wouldn't want to take up too much of your valuable time. Good night, Conn." She hung up and wanted to go somewhere and cry. As hot tears ran down her cheeks, she went directly to the bathroom and splashed water on her face and fought to compose herself before she went in to Ted and Jen.

They were laughing, but both fell silent when they saw her. Jen finally said, "So, how's my wayward niece?"

"Just fine, I guess. She wants you to have a good time in Paris. She wants me out of my job and out of my apartment and sitting with Tippy. And she's very busy so doesn't know when or if she'll ever be out here again. That about sums it up. Is dinner ready?" Leigh knew her voice sounded rough, but there was little she could do about it.

"Um, Leigh?" Ted put his arm around her shoulders, and she could see the concern in their eyes.

"Let's not talk about it, okay? It seems Dr. Stryker couldn't care less about me. My mistake for thinking otherwise. Let's eat." She hoped to get through the meal and out of there without breaking down again.

Jen got ready for bed and called Conn's number, which rolled over to a machine.

"Hey, Conn. It's Aunt Jen. I guess you heard I'm going to Paris. I'll give Marina a hug for you."

She waited. "Conn? You really upset Leigh. I can't tell you how to lead your life, hon, but I can tell you this. True love is hard to find.

If you love someone and you're lucky enough to have them love you back, don't waste time making noble excuses about how it can't work. You'll regret it for the rest of your life. Take a risk, Conn. Take a risk. I love you. Good night."

Conn played the message again and again, into the night. Her mind kept spinning. Images of Leigh. Her lips, her touch, her eyes. How it felt to hold Leigh in her arms. As quickly as she let herself drift down that path, she hauled her mind back to the rigid place of survival that had always worked. Detachment meant control. But it also meant loneliness and isolation. Leigh was different, harder to let go of. Harder to erase from her heart. As she drifted, Leigh's face was the only thing that existed. She finally slept.

After saying good night to Ted, Leigh went into her apartment and threw her purse on the coffee table, then to the refrigerator to grab some bottled water. Without turning on the lights, she went to the window and sat down in a chair facing it.

She stared into the darkness for a long time, and hurt slowly transformed into anger.

She started a monologue directed at Conn, then caught herself, glancing in the direction of the one listening device still active in the living room. She wanted to tear it from under the tabletop and stomp on it. Instead, she marched into the bathroom and closed the door. Twisting the faucet on full force, she stared into the mirror and watched her face transform into fury.

"So it's just business. You only care about nailing down my ex and his buddies. Well, if that's what will make you happy, I'm going to give it to you. You want the crap that's on Peter's hard drive? Let me serve it to you on a silver platter. As a swan song to you, *Doctor*. Once you have that, you can break this scam, and I can be on my way. Get the hell out of here. Maybe return to Boston. Jen can renovate that cottage without my help."

She washed her face and got ready for bed, a plan forming about how to go about making her gift a reality. She was the best choice to secure what Conn wanted from Peter's office. Stumbling over one of the few remaining boxes, she swore loud enough for the microphone to pick up.

CHAPTER TWENTY

L ing, I'm going to tell you something that you must not tell anyone else. Promise?" Leigh had arrived at her habitual coffee stop early, where Ling Fong had prepared her usual order while they chitchatted for a few moments. When they were alone, Leigh had decided to take a chance.

Ling studied her as if making a decision. Suddenly her eyes were much older than her years. "Promise."

Leigh knew she meant it.

"I'm going to be quitting my job soon. Some of the people there are doing things that are illegal, cheating my clients. You knew that I was engaged to the CEO of the company, but I ended that a short time ago, because—well, that's not important. Let's just say that he is not an honorable man."

Ling nodded in a way that suggested she had observed a difference in Leigh, but would never have mentioned it.

Leigh forged ahead. "I'm trying to protect my clients now. I need access to a particular office when no one else is around. Your mother cleans those floors late at night and has the new key card to get in." She saw fear cross Ling's eyes. "Your mother will be safe. She can clean while I work on the computer, then I disappear. No one will know."

"Won't they know the computer has been compromised? And at what time?"

"I know how to cover my tracks. Your mother won't be involved. I'd like to pay her for allowing me this access."

"I will ask my mother when she comes in," Ling said after a few moments' hesitation. "It must be her decision. Check with me at lunch. When do you need to do this?"

"As soon as possible. Tonight or tomorrow. I would follow your mother's advice about time." Leigh knew she had to act quickly, before she thought about it any longer.

Just then several customers came bustling into the shop, looking like they needed a caffeine fix. Ling wiped the counter. "Very well. I'll get that information and have it for you by noon today."

Leigh nodded her thanks. "See you then."

After she crossed the street to her office building and waved to the guard as she got into the elevator, she leaned heavily on the back wall as the doors closed. *Shit. The guard. You have to buzz to get in at night. And sign in and out. That means I can't leave. This is more complicated than I thought.*

The morning passed slowly. Leigh was a jumble of nerves, though trying to behave normally. After her conversation with Conn, she realized that she was probably being phased out of Peter's business. She no longer had access to any of the high-level meetings, and Peter barely spoke to her, the little prick. Mary was obviously aware of the change, and Leigh could tell she felt bad but needed the job. She was accepting work to do for other associates in addition to hers.

Leigh had been so absorbed in her other life she hadn't noticed that she was no longer part of the "in" group at the company. People avoided her. Now that it was obvious to her, she thought it was just as well. In her mind she was gone from the place anyway. *Just one more thing to do. What time is it?*

Eleven fifteen. Ling would have talked to her mom. *Get there before the lunch crowd.* Leigh had decided that if Ling's mother agreed to help her, she would figure out how to gain access and egress to the building herself. If not, Plan B.

There was no Plan B.

She walked into the shop as Ling was finishing with one of her regular coffee hounds. Afraid to look at Ling's eyes, she studied some packages of biscotti, wondering what scared her more, being turned down or having the request accepted. *Oh well, here goes.*

Ling was smiling at her expectantly. *Request granted.* "What did your mother say?"

"She was not surprised that these people are dishonest. She will help you. We could not accept your money."

Just like that. *My God, I'm a spy.* "When?" She had to fight the urge to toe-tap.

"Tonight. She suggests you meet her on your floor at two a.m. She will clean the office while you work. Can you get out of the building without being seen? Mom thinks you wouldn't pass for a cleaning worker. Too white."

They both acknowledged the truth of that racist statement.

"I'll be there and I'll get out."

"Good luck to you."

Ling was suddenly not the innocent teenager she had talked to all those mornings. Leigh was sure that she was completely aware of all of the risks that both her mother and Leigh would be taking. Crossing the street to her building, Leigh wondered what the hardworking family must have endured to get to America. What she would be attempting probably paled by comparison.

During lunch Leigh went to her apartment and packed her gym bag with a change of clothes, a pair of running shoes, and makeup. She also put in some energy bars and bottled water, along with a lightweight warm-up suit and T-shirt. *Ready.*

On her way back to work she stopped by the local UPS store and bought an envelope and transit bill. While there she wrote Conn's address and her own name with Jen's address in the return section and paid cash for the letter weight, next day delivery. It would weigh under a pound. As an afterthought she purchased a small pack of bubble wrap. Placing the items in her briefcase, she ran by her local computer shop and purchased a flash drive with a sixteen-gig memory. *That should be big enough.* Her next stop was her bank to withdraw three thousand dollars in cash.

Last, she stopped in a shop and purchased a thank-you card. In the parking garage she wrote a note inside the card: *I would be honored if you would accept this small gift of appreciation.* She signed her name, enclosed the cash, and sealed the envelope. This, too, went into her briefcase. *Set.*

Arriving at her office before Mary was back from lunch, Leigh stowed her gear in the closet. She returned phone calls and cleaned up paperwork to help make the time pass and was able to tie up some loose ends before she left the company. She didn't go anywhere near Peter's office.

At five o'clock Mary waved as she hurried out the door to catch her bus. Leigh then said good night to some people on her way out the door. She was free until seven, needing to be back in the building before the guards locked the doors and instituted the sign-in procedure. She went to the Bay Club, worked out and showered, reviewing her plan repeatedly. Afterward she wandered around downtown until settling on a small Italian restaurant where she had a quick dinner and a glass of Chianti. She desperately wanted to order another, but decided she needed her wits about her.

After walking back to the building, she waited across the street to see if the guard switched just before seven. Sure enough, a distinctively large, but younger, night guard replaced the ancient daytime guard. Several people were entering the building, so she hurried across the street to take advantage of the activity and slip in with them. They were all with the same company, apparently working late on a project. She got into one of the elevators with them. *Go.*

The others exited two floors before hers. Alone, she decided to go up one more, then take the stairs. Just as she opened the stair door to her floor, she heard loud clanging all the way up and down the stairwell. When her door closed behind her, it locked as well.

"Shit."

She realized that she was, indeed, locked on her floor unless she wanted to take the single elevator that was still turned on. That one would open in front of the guard, who would definitely notice her. *Okay. You planned for this. No going back. Calm down.*

Quietly she walked through the dim office. Most people had gone home, but she could hear a few keyboards clicking. Carefully making her way to her office, she quietly unlocked the door, entered, and closed it behind her, then let out a sigh of relief.

The blinds were open to let in sunshine during the day, and they provided a surprising amount of light from the surrounding office buildings—one advantage to a big city financial district. She allowed her eyes to become accustomed to the dark of her office. Now for the wait until two a.m.

Facing the window, she sat in her desk chair and idly watched the people who were working late and had chosen to keep their blinds open, had forgotten, or didn't have any. Most were on the phone or the computer.

A few of the windows showed several people either engaged in what could have been business or laughing and horsing around.

She envied them a little. Those days were long gone for her. Slowly, they finished for the night and turned out their lights as they left. She checked her watch. Eight thirty. She could still leave without arousing suspicion.

The building directly across from her had reflecting windows. Although at night she could see inside the rooms if their lights were on, she noticed a fair amount of reflection from the darkened offices in her own building. Counting up to her level, she checked if the windows reflected any lights on her floor. Not as far as she could tell. She put her ear to her door and listened. Nothing.

She opened her gym bag and changed into black lightweight cotton sweats and black running shoes. Hanging the flash drive around her neck on the lavaliere provided, she hung up her clothes for the next day. *Now what time is it? Nine fifteen. Damn. It's never going to be two a.m.! I've got to pee.*

Dressed in her stealth garb, she quietly opened the door to her office. Still silent. She crept through the main area that was a maze of cubicles where support staff worked. When she was almost to the bathroom door, it started to open, so she dropped like a rock and crouched behind a cubicle wall.

"Whoa. Where did everyone go? I guess I was in there too long. Who said morning sickness is just for morning? I'm going home."

Leigh recognized Jeanine Montero's voice. She had told everyone she was pregnant about a month ago and had been green ever since. Poor thing. Her boss was a real jerk and insisted she finish her work every day, no matter how long she was in the toilet.

Leigh stayed put until Jeanine left the office, the wait only increasing her need. *This is getting to be a really bad idea.* Finally, she walked into the bathroom and completed her chores with the help of her penlight. Before leaving, she inched the door open and listened for a moment, then made her way back to her office to wait.

Office door securely shut, she was bored. Perhaps lying on the floor would relax her. She tried to let her mind wander, but no matter where she started she kept coming back to one person. Conn. The rescue from that goon at the restaurant. Point Reyes. Her eyes. Her nose. Her lips. Her lips. How the sun caught the fire in her auburn curls, her strong body, her body, her lips, her eyes.

She replayed every moment, savored every touch, every smile, every kiss. Not that there were that many. The woman was driving her crazy. Sometimes sweet, sometimes remote. *Would the real Constantina Stryker please stand up?*

A part of her had to admit that she wasn't trying to copy Peter's hard drive as a way to end her connection to Conn. She was trying to be noticed, trying to get Conn to react. Probably not the smartest thing she had ever done either. But another part of her felt responsible to help solve a problem she had helped create. She owed her clients more than just fading away into the shadows. Her mind kept going around until she fell into a light doze.

Suddenly the overhead lights were blazing, and she sat up with a gasp, disoriented and confused. When she tried to get up, she ran into a human leg. Fear shot through her and she scrabbled back, gazing up into somewhat familiar almond-shaped eyes. Ling's mother was watching her. Leigh almost let out a hysterical cackle. *God, Leigh, get a grip. Some spy chick you are.*

She quickly stood, now towering over the diminutive woman. From her lessons with Mr. Odo she had learned to bow the Japanese way to show respect. Without thinking she bowed, then momentarily hoped she hadn't somehow insulted the woman, since she was Chinese, not Japanese. Mrs. Fong regarded her and nodded slightly. Then she was all business.

"Where?"

Leigh had to hesitate a moment to translate.

"What? Oh! Down the far hall. I'll show you." She realized that the entire floor was lit. *There must be a master switch for the floor that the cleaning people throw while they do their jobs.* It belatedly occurred to her that she would have been better off in jeans and a sweatshirt than black sweats.

They walked quickly to Peter's office. Mrs. Fong had probably guessed it was his office to which she wanted access. It was the only one that required a special key card to enter, and she didn't hesitate to swipe the card. Leigh was in.

Going directly to his computer, Leigh turned it on, counting on Peter's carelessness and lack of techno-knowledge. She knew his passwords, and sure enough he hadn't changed them since their breakup. She sighed in relief when she got in, then inserted the flash drive into a USB port. After she had copied the contents of the hard drive, she searched his office for anything else she might copy. Mrs. Fong had left the room, but came back in and busied herself emptying wastebaskets, dusting, and vacuuming. That done, she worked in Georgia's office.

As Leigh searched, she also tried Georgia's office. She was probably in this up to her evil little eyebrows. The day after Leigh and Conn had put on the kissing show for the van, Peter was just his usual arrogant self, but she had caught Georgia studying her appraisingly.

All of the drawers in Georgia's office were locked tight, so Leigh shrugged and returned to Peter's computer. He had shown her a hiding place when he was drunk one night. Bragging that no one could find it, he had popped a false bottom in a desk drawer.

After opening the same drawer, she emptied the contents carefully. *Now, how did he open it?* He had done it easily, and he was smashed. She pressed the board at the corners, and in one place she could slide her finger under and lift it. One CD-ROM. *Okay. Let's copy that, too.*

Mrs. Fong came to the door with a question on her face, and Leigh held up two fingers to indicate she needed a bit more time. Mrs. Fong frowned but continued cleaning in the outer office.

After copying the disk, Leigh removed the flash drive, clicked it back on the lavaliere, and erased her tracks, finally closing down Peter's computer. She replaced everything as she had found it, then checked around the desk as she stood to leave.

Abruptly, Mrs. Fong appeared at the door and motioned for her to get down. Leigh heard a man's voice and silently dropped, scrambling under the desk. She wanted to yank the desk chair close to her but was afraid the movement might be noticed. She thanked the stars that Peter didn't like all-glass furniture.

The man and Mrs. Fong sounded like they were speaking the same language, and Leigh hoped he was another worker. They seemed to be arguing about something. Then Mrs. Fong said, "Okay, okay," and the door closed and locked.

Leigh heard the lock and let out her breath slowly. At least they were gone. She stayed where she was for a few more minutes, then crawled out from under the desk. Keeping low to the ground, she tried to listen at the door and heard conversation between Mrs. Fong and the man and the continued sounds of cleaning. She leaned against the door and sat. After fifteen more minutes the lights went out. *Shitfuck.* Silence.

Leigh sat motionless, trying not to panic. She worried that if the door was locked from the outside, then opening it from the inside would either set off some kind of alarm or be impossible without a key card. *Maybe it's like a hotel door. Anyone on the inside can open it.*

She turned her flashlight on and examined the lock. Unfortunately, this one had a place for the key card to be swiped. She sat back heavily on the floor.

As she tried to think up a plausible excuse for being found, in black sweats, in Peter's office, none popped to mind. Her thoughts raced through every horrible scenario before she almost physically slapped herself to calm down. Reasoning that Mrs. Fong was very aware she was there and would be back for her, she settled down to wait. *Just be patient. I have to go to the bathroom. Don't think about it.* She sat down in one of the plush chairs and waited. Forever.

Another thirty minutes, and she was ready to strangle a tall redhead. "This is all your fault, Conn Stryker! If you had more than the emotional availability of a sea slug, we'd be together now. Dancing to a slow samba." Her harsh muttering echoed off the dark walls of the office, and she fell silent. *What if Peter's office is bugged like my apartment? What was I thinking? How did I get into this mess? I was too vulnerable to even consider being in a relationship so soon after the Peter debacle. Why couldn't I have just done the mature thing and walked away from Conn and her program, and even the sniff of danger?* That's what her parents would have advised. But nooo, she had to go and develop a huge crush on a woman who obviously wasn't interested. Based on what? A dance?

Those thoughts made her heart ache. Conn made her feel more than Peter or any man ever had. Though Conn was beautiful and exuded confidence and power, it was the vulnerable Conn that made Leigh's heart flip, her temperature rise. She was fascinated by everything that was Conn. And she'd thought she'd seen something in those beautiful eyes that matched her emotions. Perhaps it was all an illusion. But this, this was no solution. This was childish acting out that could get her into serious trouble.

By three a.m. Leigh had run through so many scenarios, her head was pounding. What kept cycling back to her was that she'd volunteered for a lot of reasons, all of them hers. She alone had decided to be where she was at the moment. And she alone would have to get out and leave the rest to fate.

In the moonlight she spotted an award that Peter had received and kept on his desk for all to see. She picked it up and hefted it in one hand. Slipping out of the chair, she felt her way to sit behind the door, clutching the heavy object. If anyone but Mrs. Fong came through that door, they were in for a surprise. She waited.

At four thirty she jerked upright, momentarily disoriented. The service elevator clanked open and someone got out, along with something that was probably a heavy cart. She stood behind the door and prayed. The footsteps abandoned the cart, and she heard voices: Mrs. Fong and the man. Then more talk and Mrs. Fong's voice, loud and jovial. She could hear her coming closer.

The lights went on and she blinked, trying to adjust just as the door opened. Mrs. Fong came in, still loudly talking to the man in the main room. She glanced appraisingly at Leigh, the clear Lucite trophy held in a striking position above her head, and motioned for her to follow and be quiet. As the door swung shut slowly, Leigh flew to the desk to put the weapon back and exited to crouch next to the sofa in the waiting room. She watched as Mrs. Fong held up a bottle of cleaner like a prized possession she had lost and found. She and the man were laughing as they got in the elevator and left.

Leigh thought she might faint with relief. She bolted for the bathroom, where she promptly threw up. The adrenaline was pumping so hard she was shaking. She used the toilet, washed her hands and face, and rinsed out her mouth. Just before she left the bathroom, she used some paper towels to wipe down the counter, needing action to counter the rush.

At seven o'clock all the elevators came on, and the stair doors unlocked automatically. A freshly changed, if somewhat bedraggled, Leigh took the elevator to the second floor, then the stairs to the parking garage. She stowed her gym bag and briefcase in her car. Taking the UPS envelope and the note for Mrs. Fong, she strode out through the auto entrance.

It was a crisp fall morning. She was breathing all sorts of bus fumes but couldn't have cared less. Being outside was glorious. She walked into Ling's shop.

Ling made Leigh her usual, but a double, in a very tall cup. She must have looked like she could use it. After Leigh gave her the card and note for her mother, she walked down the street to the UPS store and dropped off the envelope. Then she took herself out to a big breakfast. She was starved.

When she came back, Mary was there and nothing seemed out of place. No sideways glances, no thugs waiting in her office.

She sat down at her computer and wrote her letter of resignation. After that, she removed the hard drive from her computer and replaced it with a new one she had purchased the day before. As predicted, by the end of the day she was officially unemployed.

Late the next day, Conn's receptionist, Yasue, sorted through the contents of the president's mailbox. Recognizing a handwritten note as probably personal, she put it in her boss's in-box without opening it. Its security stamp indicated it was one of two items delivered that morning. The handwritten envelope had already been x-rayed and tested for any unknown pathogens, and the second item had been routed to analysis, so it was probably some sort of software.

She had worked there a year and never seen a personal note delivered to her employer. She realized it must have missed the morning delivery.

Her curiosity was piqued. Too bad Dr. Stryker had already left for the weekend.

Chapter Twenty-One

Conn had left early on Friday for a meeting with Maggie, and the news was not good. Dieter and company were for hire and apparently had ties to some of the most dangerous terrorist organizations in the world.

To top it all off, Jen was probably in Paris by now enjoying her time with Marina, and Leigh wasn't speaking to her. She couldn't remember the last time she had slept for more than two hours. She had spent the weekend resisting calling Leigh and trying to wring more information out of the program Leigh had installed. Monday promised more of the same.

Having arrived at her office before anyone else, Conn brewed a pot of coffee and began booting the computers.

Two hours later Yasue stuck her head in to say good morning and deliver the morning mail. Conn barely acknowledged her as Yasue silently came in and busied herself with arranging the mail. Taking the envelope from the previous Friday, Yasue placed it on top and cleared her throat.

Conn finally looked at her, feeling the fatigue of the past weeks. "Good morning, Yasue. How can I help you?"

"I, ah, was wondering if you had read your mail yet. I know you're quite busy, but several of the pieces might need your attention. I'm caught up on my work and could help once you decide how to disseminate the information."

Conn's eyes drifted back to the computer screen. She rarely paid attention to snail mail.

"There's even a handwritten card for you."

Conn paused over the keyboard and pinned Yasue with her gaze. "What?"

"A handwritten note. For you." Yasue placed it in front of her.

"For me. Oh." Conn picked up the note. Addressed to Constantina Stryker, Ph.D., no address. Personal. Must have come in something else. She flipped it and found the log number. Friday, a UPS letter, the second of two pieces in the envelope. Reading the front, she recognized the feminine handwriting. Leigh.

Yasue had taken Conn's cup and placed it on the sideboard. "I'll prepare your latte. Will there be anything else?"

"Huh? Oh. No. Thank you, Yasue." Her gaze returned to the envelope as Yasue left.

Conn sat with the note for a few more seconds before opening it. She read, "'Hope this helps. Regards, Leigh.'"

"What the hell?"

Conn called the mailroom and asked about the items in the envelope. Flash drive. Sent to be analyzed, standard procedure at the company on computers not linked to the company network, in case of viruses or worms. No exceptions.

Her next call was to research and analysis. Yes, they had received it; no, it had not been examined. Wasn't scheduled until Wednesday. Yes, right now, priority one. Priority one meant that Hema Dutt, the chief analyst with the highest security clearance, would take care of it.

She reread the note. "'Regards.' Crap."

Conn was uneasy. She called the department back and told them she wanted the complete report by noon, in her office.

Her next call was to Leigh, and the phone rang four times before someone answered.

"Um, hello?" Leigh's voice was husky from sleep. She sounded wonderful.

Conn cleared her throat. "Did you send that flash drive?" She knew her tone was accusatory, but she couldn't help it.

"Wha—oh. Yeah, I did."

"What's on it?"

"Good morning to you, too, Conn. I'm fine, thanks for asking. It's five a.m. out here, you know."

"Oh. Well, um, good morning." Conn waited, jumpy with anxiety.

"So, let me see, what was the question? Oh, haven't you opened it yet?" There was definitely anticipation in her voice, fogged by sleep as it was. Conn got even more nervous.

"It's in analysis now. I won't have the report for several more hours. I didn't notice the note until a few minutes ago. What's on it?"

"Pictures of me dancing naked, trying to get your attention. Why do you ask?" The silence that followed was deafening.

Leigh let out a sigh. "A copy of Peter's hard drive. And a copy of a disk I found in a secret drawer he probably doesn't think I remembered. I got them before I quit. I thought it might help." Her voice was listless.

Conn was stunned and speechless. The few times she and Jen had talked, Jen avoided any mention of Leigh. Leigh was obviously upset with her, but all of this was new information. Conn hadn't realized that Leigh had finally quit her job. Her morning coffee was eating a hole in her stomach.

"How did you get the copy?" She tried not to sound upset.

"I have my ways. Actually, I spent the night in my office, and one of the cleaning workers let me into his. It was dicey for a while, but you have the information and I'm still here, so…I guess it worked." A hint of satisfaction was in her voice.

"Where is 'here'?"

"Where do you think?" Silence. Leigh's voice took on a decided edge. "I'm out in Bolinas. I finished over the weekend. By the time I got home Thursday, the van was gone. I guess it was a perk of the job I didn't know about. I got Ted and some of the rugby boys to help put my furniture in storage and was out here in time to help Jen pack and get her on the plane. Now it's just me and Tippy."

Conn felt like she was processing the information underwater. She had snapped at Leigh, and Leigh had snapped back. Their harsh exchange tore at a place deep inside and was making her normally controlled persona disappear. She struggled not to lose her temper because this was frightening her. When she was frightened, she got angry. She took a breath and slowly exhaled. She didn't want this call to be a battle. "I'm glad to hear you're out there. Are you sure you were undetected?"

"I went in, plugged in, copied, and left. I dropped the envelope on my way for coffee after the building opened at seven. End of story."

"I thought I had told you to not worry about it. It was too big a risk for you to take." Conn heard the harshness in her own voice and knew it came from her overwhelming fear.

"I'm the only one who could do it and not raise suspicion. I worked there, knew the routine. Why am I justifying myself to you? You're *welcome*."

The distance between them suddenly was more than just a continent.

Conn tried to calm herself. Leigh had done them a favor, right? She could have been caught, but she wasn't, right? But the only thing that stuck was the "could have been caught" part.

"I never, *never*, want to hear of you taking that kind of risk again! What if you had been discovered? You could have been killed! That's why I wanted you out at Jen's, so you would be safe! Don't you get it? These people are dangerous. If you pop up on their radar, they won't think twice about eliminating you. It was a stupid trick!"

Conn sat there staring at the dead phone in her hand. *She hung up on me.* She heard a knock on her door and saw Yasue's face, concerned, peeking in.

"Are you okay, Dr. Stryker?"

Conn slammed the phone down. "Of course. Just a business call. May I have that latte now?"

Yasue put it down on the desk and left without a word.

Conn tried to call Leigh again, and it rolled over to voicemail. She didn't leave a message but tried the home phone. That, too, rolled over. *Shit. Why do you always have to yell? She doesn't work for you. Hell, if she did, you never would have raised your voice.*

She slammed the phone back into its cradle and tried to return to her work, tried to let it go. Her private line lit up and she grabbed it, hoping it would be Leigh. Hema Dutt was on the line.

"Hi, Conn. How are you?" Her chief analyst's friendly voice barely cut through the haze Conn was in.

"Fine, Hema. And you?" Her tone must have discouraged small talk.

"Fine. Just called to give you a heads-up on the drive you wanted analyzed. I think it's some good stuff. Better than what we've been trying to dredge out of our remote program. You might want to call

Colonel Cunningham and Agent Frellen and have them at the meeting. I'll be there by noon."

After hanging up, Conn rang Yasue to have her contact the others. She tried to reach Leigh again, cursing when the phones still rolled over, and left terse messages to call her. When she hung up she noticed her hands were trembling.

"Food. You haven't eaten in a long time. You can't think and you're barking at everyone. Damn, you're even talking to yourself. Get some blood sugar." Forcing her eyes back to her computer, she could barely see the screen. Nothing to be done until the analysis was complete. The only thought that replayed in her mind was the silence after Leigh had disconnected and the feeling of dread in her chest.

Conn got up and snagged her bag as she strode out the door. She mumbled something to Yasue about breakfast and went in search of a private place to think. A few blocks away from her office was a restaurant that she frequented. When the hostess recognized Conn, she showed her to a corner booth where she sat, back to the wall, and studied her menu. After ordering eggs and pancakes and switching to tea, she stared out the window.

She desperately wanted to talk to Leigh, hear her voice, and apologize. After she had eaten, she paid and left the restaurant, calling as she walked back to her office. The phones were still rolling over, but this time she left messages to call, please, she had important news. *Maybe her curiosity will be stronger than her anger.*

Why had Leigh taken such a chance? Then Leigh's remark about dancing naked hit with an almost physical force.

"My God, she did it so I would notice. I've been so wrapped up in doing the right thing. How could I have been so blind?" *And so selfish. You didn't know what to do with your emotions, Conn. So you ignored what was right in front of you and refused to take a chance, refused to be out of control. You hid behind your stupid honor, but you turned out to be a coward. You've arranged your world in black and white according to you. How many times has it backfired and you haven't even realized it? But this is more important. Because it's Leigh.*

The truth of her words and thoughts blinded her, and she stopped short in the middle of the sidewalk, forcing others to detour around her. She yanked her phone from her pocket and dialed Leigh again. Voicemail.

"Leigh? It's Conn. I'm sorry. I just... Look. I'm coming out there. I'll be on my way in about three hours. By then I should have the analysis and we can decide what to do from that point. Preliminary report is really good. That's not important. What's important is that I'm sorry I've been so stupid. Until this evening, be careful."

Her next call was to the pilot of the company jet, instructing him to assemble the crew and be ready to take off for San Francisco by two p.m.

❖

Maggie and Jim were waiting for Conn when she returned at eleven forty-five. After exchanging greetings, they settled back, expectantly waiting for an explanation.

Conn briefly filled them in.

Maggie sat up straight. "Leigh Grove? The woman who contacted your aunt? She got the copy?"

Conn snapped, "Yes. Yes. Yes. Any other questions?"

She watched Maggie and Jim exchange a glance, knowing it was rare for them to see her flustered. *Flustered? Hell, I'm about to crawl out of my skin.*

"Conn, how did she get the information?" Jim seemed like he was trying to be as tactful as he could.

"She got it, and sent it, on her own. I spoke with her this morning, so she's still alive. I won't know more until Hema Dutt gets here with the analysis. I'm planning on leaving for the coast as soon as our meeting is over. The plane won't be ready sooner or I'd get it while in flight." The confusion on their faces prompted Conn to explain. "I, um, was pretty abrupt when I heard she had gone in by herself to get the information. I owe her an apology, and I plan to do it in person." She regarded them evenly.

Maggie was the first to say something. "Good. Good. Um, Jim and I can start the ball rolling from here, depending on the report. Right, Jim?"

Jim, whose mouth was hanging open, cleared his throat and said, "Oh, yes, of course. Get the ball rolling. Right."

Yasue buzzed to say that Dr. Dutt was waiting, and Conn got up to open the door herself.

Conn was relieved that both Maggie and Jim had put on their well-worn professional demeanor for the meeting. She didn't want to explain to anyone else about anything. Except Leigh. All turned their attention to the chief analyst of the company.

Though Hema Dutt was normally serious and quiet, Conn noticed a spark in her large brown eyes when she came in and sat down at the table where they had all gathered. She greeted them briefly before proceeding.

"Looks like we have a live one here. In fact, we might have hit the jackpot. We can show severe conflict of interest, stock manipulation, and outright fraud. Peter Cheney evidently is either not terribly computer literate or is downright lazy about deleting files, protecting them, or cleaning them up. Probably all of the above."

She was obviously elated at her find, her smooth olive skin glowing with excitement. "There's more. He evidently doesn't trust the people he's in league with and makes notes to himself about meetings. Sometimes he brags in the notes about the women he conquers, and sometimes he sounds afraid of his assistant, a woman named Georgia. He almost takes orders from her. Although he writes derisively about her, I got the impression he would never speak the words aloud. He thinks she is, and I must quote, 'fucking' his superior."

Conn was getting more anxious with each word.

Maggie was staring stonily at Hema Dutt. "Any identification on who's in charge?"

Here, Dutt consulted her notes. "Dieter. That's the only reference regarding a relationship. Anyway, Cheney resents her attitude, etc. In his most recent notes, he postulates that this Dieter is not the end of the food chain. He speculates that he is but a small part of a big organization, designed to use fraud to make millions in order to fund, and I quote, 'stuff I don't want to think about.' He seems worried about that." She paused.

After a few seconds Jim Frellen said, "What else?"

Explaining, Hema said, "There is evidently an IPO coming up that he has been pushing on his clients. He hopes that once they have artificially inflated the price and sold it off before it crashes, these people will go away. He even expresses regret he got involved with them. I can't have too much sympathy for him. He doesn't appear sorry for all the people he's cheating, just sorry because he fears for his life."

"Rightfully so. I'm sure they've set him up to take the blame." Maggie made the comment to no one in particular.

Conn spoke for the first time. Her jaw was so tight it ached.

"Anything else? Any mention of a woman named Leigh Grove?"

"Grove. Ah, yes. He refers to her giving him problems about her clients. Dismissive, like she just doesn't understand." Paper shuffling, back and forth. "Here. He mentions that he will have to get her out of the company. Says she told him someone threatened her." Checking a few more pages. "Here it is. 'I told Georgia to leave her alone and the bitch just smiled. Said they could find her whenever they wanted to.'" Hema sat back. "That's all."

Maggie asked, "Is there a way someone would know the hard drive has been copied?"

"Mr. Cheney probably wouldn't notice. If someone with technical expertise knew to examine, perhaps."

"Leigh was pretty sure she covered her tracks," said Conn. Her anxiety was popping as the report dragged on and the information got more incriminating.

Surprise in her tone, Dutt asked, "Leigh? As in Leigh Grove? What was she doing copying this information? I thought we had one of our people go in."

Conn felt ill. "I wasn't expecting this either. It came in the Friday mail. Ms. Grove obtained the copy and then tendered her resignation. She has moved to a safe house."

What Conn didn't say was that she was worried about Cheney's comment that Georgia Johnson and her boss would be able to find Leigh when they needed to. *How?* The answer was relatively simple. An expert could follow Leigh, or they could put a tracking device on her car without too much difficulty. If they found out who owned the house and put two and two together... She forced herself to sit.

Dr. Dutt appeared relieved. "Oh. Well, I'm glad she is in hiding. Because she has definitely compromised their operation. More than Cheney, she would be a detail they would have to eliminate."

Conn stood abruptly. "Maggie, ride with me to the airport. Jim, will you wrap up and call with a plan later?"

Jim nodded, reaching for his cell phone. "No problem. The first order of business will be to shut down that brokerage. I'll get the order."

"Meet you at the airport in forty-five minutes," said Maggie. "I'm going to California with you."

Conn barely heard her. She was on the phone moving up the departure time and giving a list of additional equipment needs.

❖

Dieter was displeased to see Georgia entering his office. They never met during regular working hours. And he didn't like her expression—a mix of anger and fear.

"What are you doing here?"

"I have something you should know about. We got the name of the owner of the house the Grove woman visits out in Bolinas. It's Jen Stryker."

"Stryker. Related to Constantina Stryker?"

"I haven't verified that yet. But I know that Constantina Stryker's biography lists an aunt. Constantina's physical description matches the one of the woman Hatch has run into. It could be coincidental. They seem to be lovers."

His mind was reeling with this new information. He *knew* something was wrong. "Get that idiot computer geek to check out her computer and Cheney's right away."

Georgia's eyes darted to the window behind Dieter.

"What is it?"

"Leigh Grove resigned Thursday. She's gone. I pulled the surveillance the same day. But our man is going over her computer and Peter's. He should have a report any time now."

Dieter stood and leaned over his desk. "*Gone?* What do you mean? Do we know where she is?"

Now Georgia visibly relaxed. "She's run out to Bolinas again. We can get her if we need her."

Her cell phone rang, and as she listened, the color drained from her face. "I'll call you back," she said, and hung up.

"Grove's computer has a new hard drive in it. And Peter's was a treasure trove of incriminating notes about meetings and our dealings. Names, dates, and places. It might have been copied. He'll know more in a few hours."

He turned his back to her. "Get Hatch. We need to take care of

Peter first, then the Grove woman. Tell him to not kill her. We might be able to use her to get to Stryker. She's the key."

He watched Georgia fight to not tremble as she punched in the number for Hatch. After she finished she stood, waiting for direction.

"Get out."

After she left he reached in his pocket for a cell phone he rarely used. He was not looking forward to the call.

CHAPTER TWENTY-TWO

D r. Stryker, Colonel Cunningham, please fasten your seat belts," announced the captain. "We will be on the ground shortly."

Conn called the steward over and gave instructions for off-loading the luggage bay. She had already changed into a black leather jumpsuit and stowed other gear in a small black canvas duffel.

Maggie had been watching her and finally said, "You remind me of a caged animal. A predator, coiled and waiting for the hapless keeper to open the cage to feed it, and I'm the keeper."

Her cell phone rang. After answering she listened for a few seconds, then disconnected. "That was Jess. They went to Cheney's office, and he and Georgia Johnson were missing. They're searching for them. They closed the place down and sent everyone home. Are you sure you don't want some backup out there?"

"No. I'll call again, though." She tried Leigh and got nothing. Then she noticed she had a message.

Accessing voicemail, she heard Leigh. *"I got your messages. Thanks. I can't wait to see you. I'm going for a hike, then I'll make dinner. I'll be careful. You too."* She sounded happy. Happy that Conn was coming. Happy to see her. Conn felt like someone was squeezing her heart. She shook off the sensation as the plane touched down. She needed to focus.

After taxiing for what felt like an hour, the plane stopped, and Conn was off as soon as they opened the hatch, supervising the unloading of a black motorcycle. She rechecked the gear stowed on the bike, along with the extra helmet mounted behind the seat, then faced Maggie. "Will you coordinate at this end with Jess?"

"My next phone call. Are you sure you don't want help? I could call the local police and have them wait for you."

"No. I'm afraid, much as I love those guys, they'd be one more thing to worry about. I can't risk it." Conn said grimly. "I can call Jen's friends Susan and Lisa if I need help. And there's Mr. Odo. Maybe these people haven't found her or they aren't interested in her. Let's hope so."

She put on her helmet, making sure her long curls were tucked away, nodded to the guard, and started the big bike. Lifting a hand to say good-bye to Maggie, she eased over to where the gate was opening and disappeared into the twilight.

Leigh carefully placed her hands on the jagged rocks above her and hoisted herself to the next level. "Now where the hell was that trail? That's what I get for not paying attention. Oh, it's over there. I should know it by heart soon."

She reached the steep trail at last and stood to take in the view. With hands on hips she took a deep, satisfied breath of clean ocean air.

"Yippee!" she yelled as loud as she could. *I mean, you'd think that having your perfect life disappear and damned near getting killed would cause you to feel something other than happy.* She grinned. *Nope.*

Gingerly easing her way over to the trail leading up to the property, she stole one more glance at the ocean and the orange streaks the sun was making on the water as it set. With seagulls dipping and soaring around her, she started up the path again, and her mind drifted to the events of the past few hours. What had started out as a miserable morning had become an afternoon of excitement and anticipation. *Life really does turn on a dime, doesn't it?*

"Ow!" She stumbled again and banged her thigh into a rock that was cropping out. *Pay attention! At least long enough to get to the top.*

She would have to hurry to finish her chores before it was completely dark. Conn was due in tonight. Her message had sounded urgent. *Until I see you, be careful.*

What was going on now? Since Jen had left for Paris, things were moving at a quickened pace. There seemed to be danger in the air. She only wanted Conn to arrive safely; they could deal with the rest together. But she knew the first thing she would do when she saw Conn. Well, maybe the second thing. First, she wanted to be in Conn's arms. But right after that she would apologize. Conn was right; copying Peter's hard drive was a stupid trick. But she seemed to have gotten away with it, and Conn would be here soon. She was excited.

Leigh boosted herself to the final part of the path. The climb was easier now. Just a few more feet, and she would be at the property edge. When she had started hiking down to the beach, it had seemed steep and forbidding. Familiarity and her improved physical conditioning made that a distant memory.

It was dusk, one of her favorite times of the day because of the flurry of activity in the yard. The hummers would be making their last swoops for the feeders to keep their tiny bellies full overnight, and she loved the way they usually dive-bombed around her.

She was halfway across the backyard before she stopped. Something was wrong. She stood still and opened her senses as Mr. Odo had taught. *Focus.*

Everything seemed in place. Quiet. Too quiet. What was missing?

The hummingbirds. Where were they?

The yard was still. No chittering, no hum of wings. Silence. The hairs on the back of her neck stood up. Suddenly she was completely alert. *Be careful.* Conn's words screamed in her mind.

She scanned the yard, forcing herself to breathe steadily and quietly so she could listen. The yard was mostly in shadow. She realized that she could be seen in silhouette because the ocean was the last place still in light. If anyone was there, she didn't want them to know she was on guard, so she ambled off to her left, toward some trees and tall shrubbery, pretending to pick up things as though she were putting tools away for the evening. Actually, she was searching for a weapon, and she was shaking. *Stop it, Leigh! Calm down and think. You can do this.* Her body remembered the last time she'd been threatened—and who had threatened her.

As soon as she was close to thicker foliage, she crouched down. If anyone was watching, she would have disappeared from view. She scuttled quickly along the perimeter of the yard, staying close to the ground, and worked her way to the house, where the kitchen light was the only one showing. The automatic lights set to go on in the yard and house at dusk were apparently not working.

When she reached the edge of the house, she stopped, deciding what to do. Just then she heard it. A footfall just behind her. She tried to run, but someone grabbed her from behind and heaved her upright, painfully twisting her arm behind her back and wrapping a huge hand around her neck, squeezing and lifting. Her feet left the ground, and still the man lifted, his foul breath next to her ear.

"I told you I'd see you again, cunt. This time I get to do whatever I want with you. And there's no one around, no Amazon bitch to save your hide."

He put her down enough to shove her toward the back deck, off the kitchen, where several shadows were moving inside. Leigh knew she couldn't go in the house; she'd never leave alive. She struggled, but his hold only tightened, and he twisted her arm higher behind her back. She was losing consciousness.

Then she saw a black-and-white shadow on the railing of the deck. *Tippy.* Leigh suddenly slumped in the man's arms, becoming dead weight. He swore as he loosened his grip slightly, allowing her head to fall forward just as Tippy leapt from the railing and landed on the man's head and shoulders, snarling and hissing.

The man screamed, releasing his grip on her, trying to separate the attacking feline from his face. Leigh fell to the ground and started crawling away as fast as she could. The snarling and spitting continued for a few seconds before she heard a loud thump as Tippy was thrown to the ground. She could barely make out his form skulking into the brush and disappearing.

Leigh managed to stand and back into the shadows as the man cursed and grabbed at his face. The door burst open and two other men spilled out, moving between her and the trail to the beach. The man was screaming about his eyes, and she could see something dark running down his hands and face.

Her arm and shoulder ached. Using her good hand to hold the injured arm tight against her, she crept across the yard and hesitated next to the cottage to watch the scene for a moment. They had taken the man into the house, but she knew it wouldn't be long before they came after her. Taking a few steps, she stumbled over a small garden shovel, about three feet long. She grabbed it and hefted the weight.

She planned to run directly across the yard and get to the trail, since they weren't familiar with it and she was. She'd have a better chance on the beach. She stood and ran. When she was about ten steps across the yard, the door banged opened and the men rushed out, flashlights blazing. She felt the lights land on her and heard shouts as her pursuers started running.

She zigzagged, jumping over the yellow jacket nest, picking up her pace. Just as she reached the edge of the trail, she felt someone almost on top of her. She stopped, planted her feet, and ducked. He flew over her, landing on the rocks several feet below, swearing and yelling. The other man was right behind him and had obviously seen what happened. He slowed, cursing at her, then started batting the air around him.

"What the fuck? Ow! Hey!" He kept swinging his arms, probably making the yellow jackets more aggressive, but still heading in her direction. She stepped aside just as he arrived and swung the shovel in his face, flattening him. He lay still, with furious buzzing around him. She ran to the trailhead and hurried down.

After a few minutes she slowed to listen. The man who had landed in the rocks was still struggling, but nothing was coming from the other one. She tested her arm and shoulder. Painful but working. She needed both hands to get down to the beach. She tried to get her breathing under control so her senses could work for her.

She was accustomed to the dark now, helped by the half-moon. The fog wouldn't be in for a while, so she needed to get moving before they regrouped. Quietly and cautiously she started down, calmed by how well she actually did know the trail. When she ran into something or stumbled, she never uttered a sound.

Suddenly she heard shouting and saw flashlight beams raking across the rocks. Crouching behind a boulder, she waited and listened to the crashing noises closer to the trailhead. Moving more quickly and yanking a few rocks out behind her to slow them down, she reached the bottom of the trail and started racing along the beach. It was so dark, so frighteningly dark, but she kept up her pace, urged on by the shouts and whistles behind her. The men seemed to be gaining on her, and they sounded pissed.

She tried to clear her mind. She was on the beach, heading for the outcropping of cliffs just below the bluff that the house sat on.

Dread started in her chest and began to work its way through her body, slowing her down. She was running into a dead end. What had seemed like a good idea on top…

"Oh, God! Where…where…where?" She picked up her pace. *I guess it's a good night for a swim.* But that would almost certainly kill her. It might be the Pacific Ocean, but it was the Northern Pacific, and even surfers wore wet suits. Add the waves crashing against the rocks, and visions of being shark chum suddenly seemed a real possibility. She stumbled and fell, almost screaming from the pain of jarring her shoulder and cutting her hands on the broken shells of the beach. Picking herself up, she headed for the cliffs, visualizing the large boulders she could hide behind.

The darkness seemed complete. The noise of the waves crashing on the beach behind her became fainter as she approached the cliffs. She had slowed to get her bearings when suddenly someone grabbed her and pulled her behind a boulder.

CHAPTER TWENTY-THREE

Leigh's assailant pinned her against the ground behind a rock. As she started to scream, she found her mouth covered by another, one that willed her to be still. She quieted, and the grip loosened; the lips on hers softened and...lingered.

Then those lips lifted and slid to her ear. "Hush. It's Conn. I won't hurt you. I'm going to release you so you can get your breath. Breathe into my shirt and neck so you don't make noise. They're close."

Leigh stayed that way for several minutes, listening to the search. She tried to breathe quietly, her nose and mouth buried in Conn's chest and breasts, and the smell of her skin and faint perfume had Leigh's thoughts drifting. *What are you doing? You're about to die and you're playing "Guess the fragrance"? Get a grip!*

The noises continued, once coming so close she froze. Then she heard someone shout, "Regroup! The dogs are here. Regroup now!" The footsteps faded.

After a minute, Leigh straightened up and stared at Conn, who broke eye contact first. "Um, sorry about the lip lock. I couldn't figure any other way to keep you from screaming."

Leigh stayed focused on Conn. "It's okay. You were right, I would have screamed. I think I should thank you...you know...for..." She cleared her throat quietly. "Sounds like they're going to sic dogs on me. And now you're involved. Conn, you have to stay and let me go. They seem to want me, always. You'll get hurt if we're together. I'll draw them away. Sit tight."

With that she tried to get up, but Conn grabbed her roughly and held her back. She winced and grabbed her shoulder.

"You're not going anywhere. What's wrong with your shoulder?"

"Not much. That goon from the restaurant was trying to tear my arm off, but Tippy landed on him and did some damage. That's how I got away. It'll be okay."

A brief smile crossed Conn's face, then she studied the water. "Are you a strong swimmer? How long can you hold your breath?"

Leigh followed her eyes to the frigid inlet. "I'm strong enough to hold my own, and over a minute if I'm not scared spitless. Which, by the way, I am. Scared spitless. On the other hand, I'm very motivated. Do you have a plan?"

Leigh felt the warmth of Conn's hands on her shoulders, and her breathing slowed. Even her damaged shoulder felt better at the touch. Conn's voice was calm, but urgent.

"The dogs will follow our scent no matter where we go unless we use the water to throw them off. If they catch us, it won't be a pretty picture for either one of us. I need you to trust me now. We'll go to the more protected inlet on the other side of the rocks. We enter the water here, swim straight out about thirty yards, then parallel to the beach until we're on the other side. Next, we dive and you follow me. You need to cut through the waves and tides and get out far enough so we can swim parallel without being thrown on the rocks. Can you do it? Will your shoulder hold?"

Actually, Leigh was thinking how a warm fire and a good book sounded just about then. Her thoughts drifted to the lovely low tones of Conn's voice. Then the reality of the words hit her. "You want me to *what*?"

Conn put her finger to her lips. After a few seconds Leigh heard voices and dogs barking and yipping. What moonlight there was shone on Conn's face. "Leigh, I won't leave you. If you can't do this, we'll try to find some other way. I just don't think any other way will work."

"Okay, okay…let's get the hell out of here. But don't get too far ahead of me. I don't know where I'm going, and I can't see anything. Please."

Conn grabbed Leigh's good hand and started toward the ocean. The only thing Leigh could think about was putting distance between them and the men pursuing them. She felt the sand becoming soggy with water. *Is it high tide? Low tide? Oh, sweet Jesus!*

As she ran straight into the ocean, the slap of the icy water made her gasp. She lost Conn's hand and started to flail in the water as a wave grabbed her. Her mouth filled with water and she spit it out, panic rising in her throat along with whatever remained in her stomach. She saw figures on the beach and lights flickering over the rocks and sand before another wave washed over her. Suddenly Conn was by her side, pulling her out to sea, through the waves to a place of relative calm offshore.

When Conn told her to kick off her shoes to prepare for the longer swim, it occurred to Leigh that she could very well drown. She pushed that thought away as she started to move on her own, keeping the dark figure in her sight as they paralleled the beach and swam to the other side of the jetty. There the water was much calmer, but the cliffs rose straight up from the sea. *Great. She didn't ask if I was an accomplished rock climber* or *if I had any phobias, like* heights. *I'm a dead woman.*

Treading water, Conn seemed to be orienting herself. Leigh wasn't sure how anyone could get their bearings at night, much less while treading water. It all looked the same out here. Conn started swimming again, heading toward the cliffs. Leigh spit out some salt water, took a breath, and followed, numb from the cold water. *I suppose that's good.* Running on adrenaline, she kept pace even though Conn had a longer stroke than hers.

As she got closer to the cliffs, the water became choppy and more difficult to negotiate. Still she swam. About fifty feet from where the water met the cliff, Leigh was so intent on her stroke that she almost swam past Conn, who was treading water again.

Conn put a hand on Leigh's chest to halt her progress. "This is it. Listen carefully. We're going to spend about one minute resting and filling our lungs with air. Then we dive. You let me guide you. Always be touching part of me—my belt, foot, shoulder. Don't lose contact! You'll need to hold your breath for at least fifty seconds. We'll go down, through a short tunnel, then up. As you start to come up you can exhale, but maintain control. Ready?"

"Tunnel? Underwater? Shit."

Conn continued to tread water. "Okay. Let's do it."

Leigh spent the next minute taking deep breaths to oxygenate her body, then Conn took Leigh's arm, squeezed it to signal ready, set, then shouted, "Go!"

She jackknifed down into the water and started kicking as soon as she was totally submerged. Leigh brushed her hand on Conn's belt, felt her going deeper and toward the cliffs. Still she dove and swam. Then she was level for a few seconds. Conn stopped Leigh, searching with her hands in front of her for something. An opening. Finally Conn squeezed her arm again to signal her to follow. *She also didn't ask about claustrophobia while frightened to death. If I live through this, we have to have a talk.*

The opening was narrow; only one person could fit through at a time with arms stretched in front and legs kicking in smaller arcs. Leigh's lungs burned, and she scraped against the sides of the tunnel. She exhaled for some relief, wanting to breathe in so badly. She was tired; it seemed she had been underwater forever. Then the opening widened, and Conn was heading up.

Leigh started to follow, the promise of air giving her new energy. Suddenly her progress stopped; her shirt had snagged on something. She tried to free herself from it but couldn't force her legs to kick anymore, couldn't focus, couldn't get away. The blackness of the water seeped into every pore. She stopped struggling, out of energy, and drifted.

Suddenly she was being yanked free of the snag, but she didn't care. She was aware of breaking the surface of the water, then being dragged onto something flat, rolled on her side, and pounded on her back. She coughed and sputtered and spit out copious amounts of salt water while gasping for air.

She lay there, panting, teeth chattering, in the dark. She heard a quiet snap and hiss; then a sickly green light cast a pale glow on the walls of a cave. She was being rolled again, this time onto her back. Conn appeared over her, a worried expression on her ethereal face, and started undressing Leigh, peeling her clothes off of her quickly. *What the hell?* Leigh was suddenly amused and started to laugh, but quickly began to cough uncontrollably. Her clothes were gone, and she was being maneuvered into something soft and warm.

Conn stood and stripped off her own wet clothes. She seemed to be shivering, too. Gently shoving Leigh over, Conn rolled her to face the other way. She wrapped her arms around Leigh, fit her body behind hers, and tucked the blanket and sleeping bag around them.

"This is the fastest way for both of us to warm up," whispered Conn. "I hope you don't mind."

Mind? Honey, I don't mind at all. Did I say that out loud? But Leigh had already drifted way beyond being able to analyze anything.

❖

Leigh stirred. She was warm and safe and so happy to have her favorite pillow to hug and…and…*This feels way better than a pillow. Where am I?*

She cracked open an eye, but it was pitch black. *How long have I been out?* She seemed to be draped over another body, her head burrowed into a shoulder. The other body was breathing evenly, distinctly female, and had her arms around her. She was pretty sure they were naked. *Nice. Am I dreaming?* Then the events before she slept started to filter into her conscious memory.

Was that real? Nah, you've got to stop watching those damned movies, Leigh! But what is this? If your memory is correct, you are in an underwater cave, having escaped armed thugs, and this body would be Conn, who came out of nowhere and saved your scrawny butt. Very dramatic, but real? I don't think so. But if that was a dream, what is all this?

She decided she needed a reality check; she would simply lick her skin to see if it was salty. Unfortunately the skin she licked was Conn's (salty), which got an instant reaction. Conn sat bolt upright. Again unfortunate because it decimated the rather cozy cocoon they had made for themselves. Cold air flooded in, and Leigh was an instant mass of goose bumps.

Conn was on guard, her muscles tense and ready.

Gently, Leigh touched her arm. "Conn, it was only me, Leigh. I didn't mean to lick you. I, uh…was trying to taste my own skin to see if it was salty. I guess I got the wrong body." Leigh was extremely grateful it was dark, because her fair skin was probably crimson at that moment.

"Oh. Oh. Salty? What for?" Conn seemed confused.

Leigh started to explain, but thought better of it. "Would you mind terribly settling back down while we discuss this? I'm freezing!"

Conn hesitated for a second before complying.

"Could you put your arms around me again? I just need to warm up a bit while we talk about this. I promise I won't lick you anymore." *Smooth, very smooth, you idiot.*

At that, Conn let out a sigh and settled down, seeming amused. The cocoon was warming again, and Leigh lay quietly next to Conn.

Conn started to speak, but Leigh interrupted. "Conn, I know we're in deep doo-doo here. And I know you can explain a lot about why and how. I want all of that information in time, but I have two questions I consider more important now. Will you answer them truthfully?"

Conn's body tensed again. Finally, she said, "Depends on the questions."

Leigh wasn't in the mood for anymore evasions. "Wrong answer. This involves you trusting me enough to tell me the truth. Trusting me like I had to trust you on the beach. Can you do that?" The challenge was there, and for a moment there was silence.

"Yes."

Leigh heard some anxiety in the answer, but forged ahead. "Okay. First, is there a way out of this cave without going out the way we came in?"

Leigh felt Conn's body relax slightly as she said, "Yes. It involves some climbing and crawling, but we can get out without having to swim out. What's the second question?"

Leigh was relieved, although the climbing and crawling part wasn't exactly good news. She took a breath.

"Did you mean that kiss last night? Not the first part, the last part. You know what I'm talking about." Leigh held her breath. *What do you want her to say? The truth.*

Now the silence was deafening.

Finally Conn shifted so that she was over Leigh, bent down, and slowly, softly, deeply kissed her lips. When they parted, she said, "I hope that's the answer you wanted."

Leigh slipped her arms around Conn's neck and and returned the kiss with a passion she'd never felt before. Every cell in her body was involved in that kiss. Her body was reacting, and when they finally separated she was panting…and speechless.

"What do you think?" Leigh waited.

Conn was next to her ear, and in a soft, low voice she said, "I think…wow."

They lay in each other's arms for a long while, not speaking. Leigh didn't want reality to rear its ugly head, but knew it was inevitable. Eventually, she stirred, but only in desperation.

"Um, Conn? Does this cave have a bathroom?"

Silence. Then Conn's body started shaking. At first Leigh was concerned because the shaking got worse. Then she heard a strangled gasp from Conn and realized she was laughing. Hard. She thought about being hurt by the obvious disregard for her physical comfort, but, well, it was sort of funny. Leigh poked her. "Hey, quit laughing!"

No luck. Then Leigh started laughing too and was sure she was going to really embarrass herself because she was *naked* and had to pee *now*. She sat up, struggling over Conn to scramble toward the water's edge. Conn took her hand, and they managed to make their way a short distance down from where they had slept.

"Here, just crouch over the water. I'll hold on to you so you don't fall in. Don't go modest on me now. I can't see you, and this is as good a bathroom as it gets until we're out of here."

Leigh gripped Conn's hands and hung precariously. "Hell, I'm so far beyond modest. Talk about getting to know someone quickly. Good thing it's pitch dark in here, for my sake." She heard Conn mumble something about night vision goggles, but chose to ignore the comment.

After that chore was complete, Leigh held Conn's hand and slowly felt her way back to the sleeping bag. From there, Conn produced another green light stick and used it to find other provisions: a lantern, clothes, energy bars. Leigh watched Conn work. She was quick and efficient and absolutely breathtaking. She didn't seem to notice her lack of clothing. Leigh's teeth were starting to chatter again, but Conn was oblivious to the cold.

As Conn located a long-sleeved shirt and fleece sweater and pants from the stash of provisions, Leigh struggled to not appear cold, but it was a losing effort. Conn knelt beside her and helped her into the warm clothes. Leigh's shoulder had stiffened up, and it was difficult to maneuver so she was grateful for the assistance. Then Conn sat her down on the sleeping bag, helped her into some thick socks, and stuffed her back into the bag.

She rummaged under a tarp and found and turned on a lantern, then found some clothes for herself. As she slipped a camisole over her head, Leigh watched her, mesmerized.

"What?" Conn had noticed.

"I was just thinking that I owe you so much, and I have no earthly idea how to repay you."

Conn shifted, looking uncomfortable. "Listen, about that, you don't—"

"I was also thinking that you're the most beautiful creature I've ever seen, and I can't get the thought of that kiss out of my mind. To top it all off, even though I know our situation is dangerous, the only words that come to mind are, 'Yes, please, may I have another?'"

Conn was halfway into a pair of jeans but had ceased any movement a few sentences before. She stepped out of them and, wearing only the black camisole, walked over to where Leigh was sitting up in the sleeping bag. Leigh wasn't sure but felt that her heart rate must be somewhere approaching liftoff. Her breath caught in her throat.

Conn knelt in front of her and gazed into her eyes for a long moment, then placed her hands on either side of Leigh's face and leaned in, and their lips met in a kiss that was so close to heaven Leigh thought she might faint.

Abruptly Conn broke away, put her hands in her lap, and dropped her gaze. In the dim light Leigh saw deep sadness on her face. She reached to comfort her, but Conn held her hand away and met her eyes.

"When I've explained everything to you, you might not think that way. I probably shouldn't have kissed you at all."

Leigh took both of Conn's hands in hers. Conn appeared cold and tired, as if suddenly resigned to her fate. Leigh took over, making her climb into the sleeping bag and lie down in her arms, covering them and wrapping her now-warm body around Conn. After Leigh kissed her forehead, she put butterfly kisses on her eyelids before claiming her lips gently.

"Listen to me. There's nothing you can tell me that we can't work out together." When Conn started to protest, Leigh snapped, "Don't, Conn. You always think you have to do things by yourself, that you can't trust anyone. You have to trust someone, sometime. Let me in, Conn. You know, I might surprise you at how resourceful I can be. Either way, whatever this is, I'm involved. You have no choice. So face it and get over it."

Conn looked at her with wide eyes, and Leigh ached at the innocence and vulnerability reflected there. She could tell Conn was trying to decide if she could risk her heart.

Leigh put a finger on Conn's lips. "Shh. You don't have to talk. I already have your answer. It was in your kiss. Let's rest for a while, then we'll figure out what's next."

Chapter Twenty-Four

When Conn opened her eyes, Leigh's arms were around her, holding her close. Conn castigated herself for selfishly bringing her into her dangerous and sometimes deadly world. No matter what Leigh said, she had no idea what she was involved in. Worse, Conn had allowed herself to care about her. *Oh, it's more than that. You're falling in love with her.*

As far as the outside world knew, Conn was unattached, so no one could be used as leverage against her. Even her relationship with Jen appeared to be remote and distant.

Now this. Well, she would just have to deal with it the way she always dealt with emotional issues. She would figure a way to get them out of this, then walk away. It was the only way Leigh would be safe. There, problem solved. End program.

But then the problem stirred and wrapped her arms more snugly around Conn. Conn felt a kiss on her head, then another. The problem stretched a bit and snuggled down in the sleeping bag until they were face-to-face. As the warm fleece slid against the naked parts of her body, Conn's pulse started drumming.

Perhaps this problem wasn't going to be as easily solved as she had thought.

The problem whispered in her ear, "Good morning, sunshine. How about some pancakes and eggs, with syrup, jam, and coffee? Fresh, hot coffee. You make it and I'll be here to eat it. Run along now, time's a-wastin'!" With that she gave Conn's ear a loud, wet, smacking kiss.

Conn squealed at the unexpected assault on her ear and deftly maneuvered the perpetrator so that she was looming over her. Then she growled, "Now, missy, you don't want to start something you can't finish, do you?"

Leigh suddenly developed what, to Conn's ears, was a rather poor rendition of a Southern accent. "Why, I have no idea what you're talkin' about. I simply stated my wishes and here you are, about to ravish me. You *are* about to ravish me, aren't you?"

Uh-oh. Danger. But Conn didn't feel prudent. "Madam, there aren't enough energy bars in the backpack for you to sufficiently recover after I ravish you. Therefore, there will be no ravishing for the moment." *Damn!*

There was an awkward silence.

Then Leigh quietly and seductively said, "Why, Captain, you do say the most intriguing things. I shall look forward to needing those bars at some time in the very near future. Thank you." With that, she kissed her well and thoroughly.

The kisses ignited Conn beyond the point of caring if they ever left the cave. Leigh's tongue had begun to explore Conn's mouth by the time she was able to wrench herself away and sit up to catch her breath.

"Leigh, ah, we're in a dangerous situation here. We probably have some very bad men searching for us, and we need to get away. We need to check the house and get some equipment and transportation. It's all risky, Leigh. I want you to stay here, and I'll come back for you when the area is secure. That's the plan."

Leigh was instantly in her face. "The plan? Am I just supposed to sit here and wonder what's going on? Wonder if you're even still alive? In the *dark*?"

Conn hadn't thought of that.

Adamantly, Leigh said, "Conn, I'm going with you. If something happens to you, I'm trapped down here like some goddamned helpless female, and I *won't* do it! It's my *life*. I need to help get myself out of this."

Stunned into silence, Conn was scrambling to regroup when Leigh said, "And, Conn? One more thing. You'd better get used to this, because I'm not leaving you."

Conn sat for a long time, and then Leigh kissed her cheek lightly. "You're finally back in my life, and I'm not leaving you. And I'm sure not letting you...leave me."

Conn nodded, vaguely aware that she might be losing control of this situation.

After a few moments Conn managed, "We'd…better get moving. There's a lot to do." Getting her breath had taken a lot of concentration.

Conn finished dressing and put on lightweight hiking boots, then dug out the only other pair of shoes she had, some old sneakers, and tossed them in Leigh's direction. Between the thick socks and tightened laces, they stayed on her feet well enough. Leigh was becoming a force to be reckoned with, and her points were well made.

She and Leigh drank some bottled water and ate stale energy bars. Then she took the skin-diving knife she had worn the night before and attached it to her leg and handed Leigh a Swiss Army knife.

"Conn, how did you find this cave and make it like this? All this stuff must have taken a while to assemble."

Conn grinned at the memory. "It did. Some of it has been here for years. When I was a kid I was, shall we say, inquisitive. I'd swim along the shore and climb and dive. After I got certified for scuba diving I explored underwater. When I found the cave I made it my fort. Over the years I added more to it, a little at a time. I guess I always thought if I had to, I'd have an escape hatch. What started as a kid's fantasy has finally come in handy."

"Does anyone else know about it? Jen?"

Conn sat back on her heels. "I think Jen suspected I had a secret place, since some of this used to be in her garage. But she never asked. You're the only one I've ever brought here."

She continued to stow the gear under the tarp in a corner of the cave. Finished, Conn switched off the lantern, replacing it with a small flashlight. "Follow me and the light. You know the drill. Keep me within touching distance."

"Do I ever get to do that when we're not in mortal danger?"

Conn started into the cave and muttered, "I sure as hell hope so."

They moved sideways through a narrow opening at the far end, their backs scraping against the wall for a short distance. They squeezed through more places, then walked bent over, angling upward a few degrees at a time. The flashlight bounced around, and Leigh made sporadic comments about the striations and formations of the cave. Anything to keep from thinking about where they were and how tight the quarters were. Then they stopped.

"Where to now?"

"I need the next tunnel. It's here somewhere, the last one before we come to the outside. According to my watch, it's almost dawn." Conn crouched down. "Here it is. Down here."

Leigh was musing that it was impossible only a few hours had passed. So much had happened. She dropped down, eager to get out of there. Then she realized that Conn was wiggling into a tunnel the size of which she was sure Tippy would have a hard time negotiating.

"Shitohdear."

Conn struggled to shine the light back in Leigh's direction. "It's the only way, Leigh. At least we're not underwater. A few more feet and we'll be out. Come on. I'm bigger than you and I fit. You can do it!"

There was humor in her voice, perhaps a challenge. Leigh let out a breath and took another. Almost like she was diving into water, she held it. She stuck her head in the tunnel, jerked it back out, put her arms in first with only a slight shoulder twinge, and started wriggling after Conn. Her shoulder continued to make itself known. *Now I know how snakes feel. Injured snakes.* She resisted the urge to whine out loud.

The tunnel seemed to get narrower, and soon she was sweating, even in the cold. There was barely enough room to inch along. The passageway went on forever, then widened a bit so she could use her elbows a bit more. After a year or two she could see some light ahead, beyond the body in front of her. Starting to let out a whoop, she heard a warning hiss.

"Hush! We don't know if they're out there. Let me go first. Stay back until I come for you. Please."

Leigh whispered, "Come for me. I like the sound of that."

Conn stumbled over a rock and almost fell out of the cave. Recovering, she peeked out, then quietly climbed over the last rock between them and the outside.

After a few moments, during which Leigh imagined Conn lying unconscious after being clubbed by those men, or killed before she could defend herself, Conn stuck her head inside the opening. "Leigh, come out quietly. Now."

Leigh crept to the opening and peeked out, then accepted the hand Conn extended until they were standing outside the cave. Scanning her surroundings, she could barely see two feet in front of her. Fog. Thick fog. It would hide them, but it could also hide their hunters.

"Great. *The Hound of the Baskervilles.* Where are we?"

A grin tugged at the corners of Conn's mouth. "About a hundred yards from the house. Stay close. We have a stop to make first."

Moving along, listening intently, Leigh was sure she was the only one making any noise as she walked. Conn seemed not to be touching the ground. She might have been making noise, but Leigh's own footsteps were reverberating in her head. At that moment the fog lifted a bit, and a small house became visible. Conn motioned for Leigh to stay put while she went forward.

An apparitional figure stood in the front yard of the house. Its movement was fluid, without effort, familiar. Conn stole up from behind, and the figure stilled, whirled to face Conn; then they bowed to each other. Mr. Odo.

He and Conn spoke quietly for a few moments, and as Conn motioned for Leigh to join them, the fog closed in again, making them disappear. Leigh froze in place, momentarily disoriented, the fog so complete she started to lose equilibrium. Within seconds Conn was by her side, taking her hand, her touch startling, then overwhelming Leigh with relief. She grabbed Conn in a fierce embrace, fighting back tears, and Conn held her tenderly until she calmed.

When they reached Mr. Odo, he bowed to Leigh and they entered his home. After pouring tea into a pot, he removed some warm scones from the oven, then provided jam and butter and told them to help themselves. Leigh realized she must have had a surprised expression on her face because he shrugged.

"Well, the tea is traditional. But I have been an American too long, and the bakeries around here are far too good, not to enjoy occasional scones in the morning. I hope you are not disappointed."

"I am delighted and honored," said Leigh. "Thank you very much."

She ate hungrily, grateful for the companionable silence. When the last scone disappeared, Mr. Odo spoke. "How may I be of assistance, my friends?"

"Leigh was chased by some men last night. I was able to intercept her and get her to safety, but we need to find out if they're still on the property. We need access to it and want to check on Tippy."

"I believe Tippy-san took care of himself." Mr. Odo rose and opened the door to the interior of the house, and Tippy stuck his head out and ran over to Conn, meowing the whole way. As Conn swooped him up in her arms and snuggled him, her throat tightened and she fought back tears.

"I found him at my door shortly after you left last night. He was upset and a little frightened, but some tuna and a warm bed seemed to assist his recovery."

Leigh turned to Conn. "After you left last night?"

"I came here first. Mr. Odo told me he had seen a lot of activity down on the beach, flashlights and such. I know a different route down. That's how I got to you before they did."

Mr. Odo nodded, and Tippy leapt down and ran over to Leigh, jumping into her lap and settling down. Leigh stroked his head and scratched his ears as he purred; glancing at Conn, she thought she saw her eyes shining again.

As she scratched Tippy's ears, Leigh said, "He might have saved my life last night. He jumped on the guy holding me and gave me the chance to run. He's my hero."

As if on cue, Tippy started purring louder, and Conn leaned over and tugged on his tail. "Thank you, Tippy. I owe you one."

At that moment, Leigh desperately wanted to kiss Conn. Instead, she caught Conn in a glance and watched as Conn blushed, which only made the urge more intense.

Mr. Odo cleared his throat, his eyes twinkling with excitement. "I suggest that I go in my pickup truck first. If anyone is there I will do my best 'humble gardener' act and check out the situation." He was obviously up to the task.

Conn tore her eyes away from Leigh. "Thank you, Odo-san. If the place is deserted, I'll still need to scan it for foreign monitoring devices. I've got my equipment in the duffel bag I left with you."

Within twenty minutes Mr. Odo backed out of his driveway and drove in the opposite direction of Jen's house, intending to take a more circuitous route and end up there within a few minutes. His old truck fit perfectly with the gardener ruse. Leigh and Conn had helped pile fertilizer, rakes and shovels, and other tools in the back.

If the coast was clear, he would press the button on a simple device Conn had quickly installed under his dashboard. If not, he would hopefully be told to go away.

Within fifteen minutes of his departure, the device was activated. Conn led the way, the duffel she had retrieved slung over her shoulder. She stopped Leigh just before they got to the property, and they crouched while she quietly opened the bag and produced a small device Leigh assumed was a scanner, and a gun.

Leigh said nothing while Conn stuck the weapon in her waistband with practiced ease and whispered, "Be right back."

Seeing Conn disappear into the fog yet again was wearing Leigh down. Though she tried to calm herself, the adrenaline rush was making her ears pound. She stayed rigidly in place.

After what must have been an eternity, Conn appeared in front of her. When Conn took her hand, helping her up, Leigh could barely stand on her own.

"Well, they're gone, but they put tracking devices on your BMW and the Audi. They might have tried to bug the phones or the house but gave up. Probably thought their stuff was defective because the house is too well jammed. They evidently didn't take enough time to find or disable the scrambling equipment."

Conn wrapped her arms around Leigh, and they clung to each other a moment before walking to the house, still holding hands.

Mr. Odo was checking the damage. The office had been trashed. The computer's hard drive was missing, and various machines lay in pieces on the floor. Someone had evidently picked them up and thrown them against the wall.

"Conn, they have your hard drive."

"Not too much of a problem," Conn said. "My laptop is safe, and that hard drive has only a limited amount of information on it. Even that will take a while to get to." After a moment's hesitation she added, "If they trace enough of the e-mail addresses, though, they'll really want to find us. We've definitely compromised their operation."

Leigh wasn't surprised, but couldn't care at that moment.

Then Conn led Leigh back to the guest bedroom where she had been staying, which had been tossed but not destroyed. Conn didn't say a word, but her eyes were dancing.

"What is it?" Leigh took a few steps to the full-length mirror and gasped. She was covered in cave dust, hair sticking straight out, clothes hanging on her, with clown shoes on. "Oh...my...gawwwd." She shot a comparison look at Conn. The long auburn hair was somewhat disheveled in a very sexy way, and she was a bit dusty, but still a showstopper. *Great.*

Conn rummaged in the closet and threw an empty backpack in her direction. "Everything you need for a week at least. In that backpack. We're going away where we can't be found." She winked at her and gave her a sexy smile. Leigh felt her body heat until Conn, suddenly somber, whispered, "Hurry," and retreated down the hall toward her own bedroom.

Left to ponder the many meanings of "hurry," Leigh closed the door, stripped down, and climbed into the shower. The hot fresh water felt wonderful, and she quickly scrubbed off the itchy salt water and tended to various scrapes. Then she gingerly dried herself and examined her shoulder in the mirror. Badly bruised. Her wrist showed the finger marks of her assailant.

"I'm getting sick of that sonofabitch."

As she stared at the mess of her bedroom, she realized what Conn had said. "Everything for a week in a *backpack*?" Shaking her head, she started pawing through her clothes.

A short while later she closed her backpack and put on underwear, jeans, warm socks, a camisole, turtleneck, and sweater, the color of which matched her eyes. When at last she put on her own hiking boots, she stood up and stomped around. Then she stared defiantly in the full-length mirror, crossing her arms over her chest, and growled, "You want a piece of this? Bring it on, asshole."

A polite cough came from the doorway, and Leigh glanced over to see Conn leaning against the door frame—dressed entirely in black leather, her blue eyes sparkling.

"Come on, Xena, let's rumble."

Chapter Twenty-Five

B oth cars have tracking devices on them," Conn explained to Mr. Odo and Leigh as they stood in front of the house. "Leigh and I are going to be traveling on an alternative vehicle while the cars do a little diversion driving. Eventually, we'll get the Audi back. I'll need the keys to the Beemer."

Leigh had found her fanny pack under a chair earlier and was searching for the keys when the front gate began to open. They ducked and scattered to get out of sight.

An old Jeep drove in and parked beside Mr. Odo's truck, and a tall, attractive woman about Jen's age got out, dressed in jeans and a white shirt. She had salt and pepper hair cut very short, rich dark brown eyes, and an athletic build. Conn and Mr. Odo stood as she was getting out of the car.

When she saw Conn she smiled and waved. They met halfway to greet each other with big hugs and kisses. Leigh had trailed Conn and watched shyly from inside the house.

When they separated, the woman waved and shook hands with Mr. Odo, and Leigh heard Conn call her name. "Thanks for coming, Susu."

Leigh slipped up beside her, and Conn took her hand. "Susan Renfrow, this is Leigh Grove. Leigh is, um, living with Jen now and is...my friend."

Conn was blushing furiously. Confused, Leigh glanced at the new arrival to find her beaming at Conn. The woman immediately stuck her hand out.

"Hi, I'm delighted to meet you. Jen told me you were moving in.

Welcome." Her eyes were warm and her handshake firm. She turned her attention to Conn and grinned again. "Gee, Conn, I've never met any of your friends before. Are they all this attractive?"

Conn was practically squirming. "Ah, no, I mean, I don't, well." She abruptly excused herself, mumbling something about getting the Audi keys and checking in with her office.

Susan chuckled and winked at Leigh as the two of them walked toward the house.

"What was that all about?"

Susan watched Conn's retreating figure. "Well, I was teasing her. I've known her since she's been coming to California, and in all that time, she's never brought a friend home. So she knows that *I* know how special you are."

Leigh felt her cheeks start to color and didn't even try to hide her pleasure.

When they walked through the door, Susan stopped and scanned the area, shoving her hands into her back pockets and rocking on her heels, her smile fading. Leigh followed her eyes to the fireplace. Someone must have taken an axe to the exquisite mantel, and the room was a mess.

"What the hell?" exclaimed Susan.

Leigh could see the fury building in her eyes. "It happened last night. Some men tried to, uh, grab me and, I…I ran down to the beach and…"

The words died on her lips as the enormity of the situation hit her like a brick. She felt the color drain from her face, and her knees gave out. Susan called for Conn, and suddenly strong arms spun her around and lifted, gently placing her on the sofa. She buried her face in Conn's neck and tried to collect herself, afraid she might be ill.

"Breathe. Just breathe. I've got you."

"She was starting to tell me what happened here."

At that moment, all Leigh wanted was for the world to go away and leave them alone. The familiar arms helped as Leigh tried to quiet her racing pulse, and she attempted to focus on the conversation instead of the terror of the previous night.

"Must have been some night. What can I do to help?"

Leigh looked at Susan, who seemed to be assessing the damage, grateful that she mercifully kept her eyes elsewhere. The tiny moment of privacy was welcome.

"We're going away for a while," said Conn. "Could you maybe get Lisa and put the place back together? When Jen and Marina get home I don't want them to have to see this. Sorry about the mantel. I know it took you a long time to create it. You could repair it or consider this a commission for a new one. A woman named Jess will be here soon with some others. Ask for her ID and let them worry about the office and security damage."

Susan merely nodded, eyes still on the mantel.

"Here's the big favor. I want you to take the BMW and drive south, maybe to San Luis or something. Leave the car in a parking lot at Cal Poly and either rent a car or have Lisa follow you. Mr. Odo is going to take the Audi and hand it off to someone who will drive to a truck stop and reattach the tracking device to a semi heading east. That ought to confuse the buggers for a while. Are you okay with this?"

"No problem. Lisa will get a kick out of it, and we'll start on the house when we get back. Will someone be watching the Beemer after I drop it off? We can, if you like. Just to see who's interested."

Susan's eyes were alive and focused. Leigh sensed the offer was not made lightly.

"No. Someone will be on it," said Conn. "Jess is on her way here and will give you a number to call to give its location. Most important is restoring the house and keeping an eye on it."

"Where's Jen?"

"In Paris with Marina. Thank heaven she wasn't around. But she'll be back in a few weeks."

"Don't worry, Conn. Lisa and I and the others will get the place in shape in no time. It'll be ready when she comes home. And, honey? If you need anything, *anything,* you let us know."

Conn nodded her thanks.

Then Susan came over and bent down to Leigh. "You two take care of each other, okay? Good luck." With that, she gave each of them a kiss on the cheek, collected the keys to the cars, and went to find Mr. Odo, leaving Conn and Leigh alone. Leigh sat close to Conn, unwilling to be separated from her.

Finally, Conn said, "We'd better go. Mr. Odo said that a storm's rolling through in a few hours."

"Conn, what you asked her to do might be dangerous. She agreed so readily. Why?"

"She and Lisa are ex-SFPD. They know how to handle themselves.

The only people in any danger will be anyone who tries to mess with them." Conn was grim. "They don't take their friends being threatened lightly."

"Who are the 'others' that Susan just mentioned?"

"Do you remember the picture on the mantel of Jen and a bunch of women sailing? You must have met some of them in town when you were out on the weekend."

Leigh nodded.

"Those are the others. It's a tight group of friends, some lesbian, some straight, but all very capable. They stick together. They'll have the place in shape in no time."

Conn stared at their entwined hands. "I called to give my superiors an update and tell them about the house. My…boss told me some bad news. The feds closed down Peter's office. At first they couldn't find him or Georgia Johnson. But when they were going over the place…"

Leigh didn't like the sound of this. "What is it? Tell me."

Meeting her eyes, Conn said, "They found Peter Cheney's body, stuffed in the closet in his office. He'd been shot."

"He's… dead?"

"Yes. I'm sorry."

"Oh, my God. Poor Peter."

They sat for a moment while Leigh absorbed the information. Suddenly, she focused on Conn. "Let's get the hell out of here!"

Conn put her arms around her and kissed her fiercely, then leaned back. "Let's go."

Leigh was breathless.

"Come on." Conn stood and pulled Leigh up with her. "Let's get over to Mr. Odo's and take a look at our transportation."

The wind had started to pick up as they arrived. While Leigh searched for Tippy to say good-bye, Conn went into the garage with the packs and her duffel. Opening the duffel, she extracted a small computer and booted it, tapped in some instructions, closed it down, and finished packing the bike.

Five minutes later she found Tippy sitting on Leigh's chest on the sofa in the living room, the two quietly communing with each other.

Leigh was scratching his ears and assuring him they would be back and the whole family would be together again soon. Conn's eyes became moist. *Family.*

Clearing her throat to get Leigh's attention, she said, "We have to go. We've got about a two-hour drive, and the storm will be here soon. I packed some rain gear for us, and we can stop to get food on the way. Ready?"

Leigh sat up, handing Tippy to Conn. "Give me two minutes," she said, walked into the small bathroom, and closed the door.

Conn flopped down on a chair and closed her eyes. She was tired and worried. She needed to get Leigh to safety, and it was a long ride.

"Are you all right?" Conn asked when Leigh came out of the bathroom.

Leigh walked over and knelt in front of Conn, sliding her arms around her neck. Her voice was steady as she said, "I found some aspirin and took three. My shoulder hurts like hell, I'm scared to death, and I could sleep for a week. But I'm alive, and I'm with you. Let's go, Tiger, the farther away the better." She kissed her soft lips lightly, then more deeply.

They broke away, breathless, and Leigh added, "Actually, sooner would be good."

Conn took Leigh by the hand and, as she opened the garage door, said, "I just hope you enjoy the ride." She indicated Leigh should go in first.

Inside, Leigh scanned the area; the only vehicle in the garage was a black Ducati 758 motorcycle.

"Is it already moving?"

Her eyes went to Conn, the cycle, then back to Conn. Conn couldn't suppress a grin.

"This is it? We're going on this? I've never been on a motorcycle. Well, Pat used to work at a shop, and he had me on one for a demo once. I mean, really?"

"Really. You'll have to wear one of the backpacks. I've stowed the other gear. Here's your helmet. Zip up your jacket and tighten everything you can. I also have a pair of riding gloves for you. All you really have to do is sit behind me, wrap your arms around my waist, and let me do the rest. Oh, and keep your feet up and on the footrests, never near the exhaust pipes. Got it?"

Conn hoped the small smile that crossed Leigh's lips had to do with the mention of wrapping her arms around Conn, but it quickly faded.

Sighing, Leigh started zipping and buttoning and tucking where she could, accepting help with the helmet and adjusting the backpack.

Conn walked the bike out of the garage with Leigh following, then pressed the ignition, and the big engine roared to life. She held out her hand and Leigh climbed on, adjusting herself for balance.

"My mother would croak!" Leigh shouted above the engine noise. Then they rolled out of the gravel driveway and started down the narrow, winding road.

By the time they got to town, it was apparent to Leigh that she might need some additional instruction if they were going to get up the coast in one piece. She was thinking too much, trying to counterbalance Conn on the curves, afraid they would tip over. She was pretty sure Conn got the idea, too.

When they arrived at a coffee shop, Conn stopped and got off, telling Leigh to wait. She sat on the back of the bike, watching, and the first thing she noticed was their reflection in the storefront window. *Whoa! Biker Babe and Biker Chick.* She had to chuckle at that one. Then she saw the appreciative glances the patrons sitting at the outside tables gave Conn.

She had dismounted the bike with feline grace and casually removed her helmet, shaking her auburn curls out as she did. Thowing her gloves into the helmet, she had put it on the seat in front of Leigh, winked at her, then strode into the store to place their order. Not many eyes missed her actions.

Except for one pair—a small man who seemed engrossed in his newspaper. Leigh noticed him because he was the only one who didn't ogle the amazing woman who passed by him. Something was odd. Her gut churned, and she started perspiring.

A few minutes later, Conn came out holding a brown paper bag and water bottles. She gave the water to Leigh and was stowing the bag when she must have seen Leigh's hands shaking and looked at her questioningly.

"That guy by the door behind the newspaper," Leigh whispered. "I think he was there last night. What if—"

Conn abruptly stood and put her gloves on. In a normal voice she said, "Okay, let's go."

She seemed in no hurry as she got on the bike, started it up, and entered the road. Two blocks away Conn suddenly whipped behind a stand of bushes and redwood trees and killed the engine. A few seconds later they spotted a green car driven by a little man with glasses, head swiveling from side to side, talking on a cell phone.

"That's him!" Leigh was sure.

Conn produced her phone from her jacket pocket and made a call, giving a description of the man, the car, and the license plate number, along with instructions to pick him up, then question and hold him.

"Someone will take care of him. We're going up the coast. In order for us to make it in one piece, you have to trust that I can get us there. Do you trust me?"

"With my life, you know that."

"Good. Now I want you to attach yourself to my back like wallpaper. If I lean, you lean. Be one with the machine and me. Don't think about anything but the road and being one with me. Got it?"

Leigh was relieved that Conn understood her trepidation and gave her a way to help overcome it. "One with you. No problem."

Conn patted her hand, then secured her helmet, and they headed for Highway 1. She drove slowly, allowing Leigh to get used to the idea of leaning with her around the curves. At first, Leigh squeezed her so tightly that Conn must have felt like a tube of toothpaste, but gradually Leigh relaxed into the rhythm of the cycle.

Conn challenged her by suddenly weaving or speeding up and slowing without warning, and they stopped one more time and quickly worked out some signals to communicate with. If Conn squeezed Leigh's hand once, it meant, "relax." Twice, "hold on." Three times, "brace yourself." If Leigh squeezed Conn's middle once, it meant "okay." Twice, "slow down," and three times, "stop."

After a short while, Leigh felt more confident. The signals gave her a small illusion of control, and she soon realized Conn was as capable on the bike as she was in the Audi. She readjusted her hands, and instead of clutching stiffly, she visualized the word "melt" and noticed how her body joined with Conn's. A very pleasant sensation. Very pleasant, indeed.

As her mind drifted to thoughts of dancing and sleeping and kissing, she was abruptly jolted back to the present when the bike suddenly swerved to avoid a cow that had meandered into the road. Her hands slipped because of her lack of attention, causing her to jerk. Conn was strong enough to compensate, but Leigh chastised herself for making Conn's job harder.

They rode for about an hour without incident, then a drop of rain hit Leigh's visor. The large, dark clouds she had been watching prowl closer were almost on them, and she felt a sense of anticipation as the wind picked up. The ocean had whitecaps as far as she could see, and the waves had grown in size and force.

Conn found a turnout and stopped the bike. Dismounting, she rummaged in Leigh's backpack for their rain gear, and they hurriedly climbed into lightweight jackets and pants and were on their way. When Conn had helped Leigh get into her jacket, the look they exchanged almost melted the plastic zipper.

The intensity of the rain and wind picked up, forcing Conn to slow the big bike down. After about thirty minutes they stopped at a roadside gas station and grocery store for something to drink and a few provisions.

Noticing Conn grab bread and cheese, Leigh asked, "Conn, where, exactly, are we going?"

Conn chose a bag of coffee. "I have a house up here."

"How far away?"

"Not far." She put the items on the counter.

Not far, Leigh glumly thought. She was tired. The clerk, a teenage boy, almost fell over a display trying to help them and encouraged them to stay out of the bad weather as long as they wanted. They stood inside the station. They gobbled down the sandwiches Conn had bought earlier, and Leigh took her turn in the funky bathroom while Conn paid and stowed as many supplies as they could carry.

Hearing the bathroom door open, Conn glanced at Leigh, so pale under her smile. She was by her side instantly, a supportive arm under her elbow. "Are you okay?"

"Hmm? I'm fine. I...just need the wind and rain in my face."

Conn grinned. "No problem."

Two miles later, the rain began in earnest. Conn squeezed Leigh's hand and received a response, then concentrated on the highway. A pickup truck some distance behind them seemed to be gaining, so she goosed the speed.

The going wasn't easy. Even when the rain let up, the roads were still slick, narrow, and winding, and they were gaining elevation. In some areas the fog seemed to swallow them, and Conn was careful not to make a wrong move. She knew just how far it was down to the rocks and water of the rugged Northern California coast.

The truck behind them sped closer and even took some of the curves at speeds that seemed reckless to Conn. Her gut tightened and her focus became acute. She squeezed Leigh's hand three times and felt her tighten her grip.

As she worked through a particularly treacherous part of the road, one with sharp switchbacks that weren't always banked well, Conn had no doubt that the truck was after them. At the crest of the hill and around yet another steep curve, when they were momentarily out of sight of the other vehicle, she slowed to cross a slippery metal cattle grate, then took a sudden right turn on a road leading away from the water, gunning the bike to get over a hill and disappear before the pickup rounded the bend.

Covering the hundred yards in record time, they became airborne for a second as they popped over the hill and started a slow slide around a curve. The big bike fought for purchase on the mud and gravel before grinding to a halt, nearly tipping over. Conn gained control and, still straddling the bike, walked them behind a nearby grove of trees and killed the engine.

She quickly set the stand, unlocked Leigh's death grip on her, and hopped off, running back to pick up the groceries that were scattered over the area. Then she climbed back on the cycle and got ready to take off if they were found. They waited. Five minutes passed. Nothing. A few more and they heard an engine rumble. A large silver truck went speeding past.

"They're after us, aren't they?" gasped Leigh. They watched as the truck slid around a curve, and Conn stared after it.

Taking Leigh's arms from around her waist, Conn tossed the groceries she had been carrying, hopped off the motorcycle again, and ran over to a larger rock on the ground, picking it up and smashing the bike's taillight with it.

Leigh stared at her. "What are you…"

Conn threw the rock down and climbed back on the bike. As the Ducati roared to life, she yelled, "Hold on," and they headed back to the highway just as the truck tore around the curve, retracing its steps. The rain and fog increased as Conn managed to keep a steady distance from the truck until they reached the main road and turned north.

Leigh was solid behind Conn as she leaned forward and worked through the winding, slick road, the road she had traveled since childhood.

Several times the truck was upon them, only to have to slow down to make a deep curve. They were gaining elevation again, and Conn noted that the dense fog was getting worse. Suddenly she heard a pop, and Leigh's helmet cracked forward into her own, forcing her eyes from the road for a split second. The bike wobbled and slipped, then righted, and Leigh hung on.

Conn shot forward into the fog, braked as hard as she dared, and, by memory and feel, leaned hard to the right. They drifted, then caught, and barely made it around the sharp curve. Conn tried to slow down but couldn't cut the speed fast enough, and the bike roared up the embankment and started to flip.

"Let go!" screamed Conn, and released her hold on the handlebars, allowing the centrifugal force to throw them free of the machine. Leigh's hands released, and Conn landed hard on her side. Gasping for air, she heard first the bike land and the engine die, then the truck engine. With no brake light on her bike to warn him, she prayed.

The engine revved as it got closer, then tires squealed as the truck started to slide toward the cliff. The fog momentarily shifted, and Conn watched as the driver frantically tried to control the vehicle. It lost traction and slid sideways off the road, disappearing from sight as the fog closed in again.

There was silence for a few second; then she heard a distant crash, coming from the bottom of the cliff, and collapsed on her back, gasping for air. *Thank you.*

Conn struggled to her knees and called, "Leigh? Leigh! Where are you?" She couldn't see a thing and had begun feeling around the area when her hand brushed against material. Conn ripped off her own helmet and knelt beside Leigh's inert body.

"Leigh! Oh God, Leigh, talk to me, sweetie! Say something, please!"

Leigh's helmet was gone. Conn gingerly felt legs and arms, torso, searching for odd angles or sticky substances. Finally, taking the still hand in her own, she sat back on her heels.

"Leigh? Please wake up. Don't leave me, I love you. I love you so much!" She stroked Leigh's listless hand. "Please."

The fog cleared momentarily, allowing better visibility.

"Love you, too."

Conn stared at Leigh's face. "What?"

A weak squeeze of her hand was the only response. "Am I dead?"

"Leigh? Can you open your eyes?"

"'Kay." After a few seconds her eyelids fluttered open, and she gazed at Conn and smiled.

"Did we get away?"

With eyes and nose running, Conn managed, "Yes. But the truck didn't do as well as we did on the last curve. It's at the bottom of the cliff."

"Good." Leigh tried to make sense of everything, tried to clear her head.

"Leigh? Can you move your feet for me? Just a little. Now your other hand. Squeeze. Now your head, *slowly*. Is anything numb?"

"No." Leigh finally tried to sit up. Conn was there to lean against.

"Where's the bike?"

Conn pointed to where it lay on its side on the shoulder of the road.

"You're a mess." Leigh studied Conn. "You okay?"

"I am now. Let's see if we can salvage anything. Stay here."

"No problem." Leigh leaned back on her elbows and watched as Conn slid down the hill to the bike. *She loves me. And I love her. I said it and I mean every letter of that word.* After a few moments she cast around and saw the backpack several yards away and her helmet a short distance beyond that. She crawled over to them and tried to inspect them.

Hearing Conn grunt and raise the bike upright, setting the stand, she whirled to face her. She was about to say something about her strength when she saw a large figure emerge from the mist, lumbering across the road, aiming for Conn. She screamed, "Behind you!" and the fog closed in front of her.

"Conn! Conn!" She heard sounds of a struggle and scrambled to get down the hill. Falling and running toward the melee, she saw Conn and the man from the truck circling each other. The man lunged for Conn, and her foot connected solidly with his gut, sending him sprawling. He rose again, and this time was able to land a fist to the side of her head. She went down and was still, and Leigh was at her side instantly.

Looking up, she screamed, "You bastard!"

He stopped, grinning at her. "Well, well, alone at last."

She stood and started backing away, him following. She needed to draw him away from Conn and buy some time. Able to put the bike between them, she danced back and forth to parry his lunges.

Blood poured down his face and chest from a gash on his head, but he seemed oblivious to anything but her.

"I...made a promise...to you. Come here."

He made a quick feint and grabbed her wrist as she tried to avoid him, grinning, his eyes fixed on his prize. She slapped him as hard as she could, then aimed for the gash and did it again. He howled but his grip got tighter. Suddenly he stopped, obviously surprised. His hold on Leigh loosened, and she tore free. Then he opened his mouth, lurched back a step, swayed, and slumped over the bike.

A skin-diving knife was lodged squarely between his shoulders, embedded to the hilt. Conn was behind him where she had fallen, on her hands and knees, staring.

Stumbling around the body, Leigh ran to Conn, helping her to her feet.

"Are you okay?" They said it at the same moment.

Conn wiped her face and stood up, arm around Leigh for support.

"I think he's dead." Leigh was afraid to touch him.

Taking her hand, Conn walked to the bike and ferociously yanked the man's head back while Leigh stared at the lifeless eyes.

"Yeah, he's dead. Help me get him off the bike," said Conn. They dropped him by the side of the motorcycle and dragged his body into a ditch a few feet away; then Conn slid the knife out of the body and wiped it on his clothes.

Breathing heavily, she said, "Where's your stuff? We need to call this in."

"What about your cell?"

"Don't know if he has friends. We have to get out of here."

After Leigh had located what she had found on the hillside, she walked over and stood beside Conn, feeling nothing but relief.

"How's the helmet?"

Leigh held it up and showed Conn the missing chunk.

"He took a shot. That was why your head banged into mine."

Leigh stared at it. "It saved my life." Then to Conn, "You saved my life."

Conn gazed at her for a long time before she said, "No, you saved *my* life. Come on."

As Conn mounted the bike, she crossed her fingers and held them up for Leigh to see. "Let's hope it starts." She pressed the ignition several times, with no response. After making some adjustments, she gave Leigh a sly grin. "Newer bikes have electronic ignitions. The problem is, if they die, that's it. I had a starter motor put in as a fail-safe. That way if this baby fails, I can still get 'er going. It pays to be prepared." Raising her body, she kick-started it on the first try.

"Okay! Let's make sure we have everything. We need to get out of here."

Leigh climbed behind Conn, and as they pulled away, she stared over her shoulder at the ditch where they had left the body.

They tracked along the two-lane road for another twenty minutes. The trees and occasional fields of grazing cattle amidst the background of the ocean were spectacular, but Conn suspected Leigh had to use all of her concentration to just hang on. As she turned away from the ocean and followed a narrow road disappearing into the trees, she noticed that the clouds were again getting heavier, but was relieved that she hadn't seen another car.

Leigh was quiet, almost sagging as Conn slowed the Ducati and drove into an asphalt driveway. When she pressed the button of the remote control she had zipped in her jacket, the garage door slid up, and she walked the bike into the garage and killed the engine. The door started down immediately, and the light from the automatic door cast a ghostly illumination around them.

Conn quickly dismounted and hit the button for the garage light. Unlocking the back door, she leaned around the doorway and checked the readout of a blinking box on the wall, tapped in numbers, and heard the hum of appliances working.

Back in the garage, she plopped down helmet and gloves on the wooden bench beside the inner wall and noticed Leigh struggling to get off the bike.

"Whoa! Easy there. Here, let me help."

Leigh almost fell into her arms.

After removing Leigh's gloves and unsnapping her damaged helmet, Conn helped Leigh take it off, sliding an arm around her waist to steer her to the bench so she could lean Leigh against it and relieve her of the soaked backpack. Next came the torn and muddy rain gear for both of them, left in a heap on the floor.

Conn replaced her arm around Leigh's waist and guided her inside. The house was warm, the furnace, water heater, and various appliances having kicked on when she'd sent instructions from her computer at Mr. Odo's house. They walked past a washer and dryer, up a few steps, and into a small kitchen.

Conn plopped Leigh in a kitchen chair and quickly got her boots and socks off. She had snagged a dry towel from the laundry room as they passed and wrapped it around and under Leigh's feet.

"We have got to stop meeting this way," Leigh muttered.

"I agree. Sit tight. Lean on the table if you need to." Conn put the teakettle on to boil, then disappeared through another doorway.

Conn was trying to talk to Leigh to keep her awake while she rummaged around in the bathroom, but when she came back into the kitchen, Leigh was barely upright.

Leigh sighed. "I tried to get up and help, but nothing happened. I'm a wimp." Her teeth were chattering.

"Leigh, you've been through a lot. But you hung on, and we're here and safe."

The kettle started whistling, and Conn rustled up some cups and tea bags and poured the water. After taking the cups to the table, she sat down next to Leigh. "Okay. The tub is about ready. You need a soak and some dry clothes, or you'll never warm up. Have a few sips of tea and let's get you in there. I'll find something dry for you to wear. Can you walk?"

"Did you call?" Conn knew Leigh was worried about the body back at the crash site.

"Yeah. I reported the…incident. Someone will handle it."

Leigh stood shakily, and Conn helped as they walked through a main room and into the master bedroom and large bath. The bathroom had windows that seemed to open to the woods and ocean beyond, and next to the window sat a deep tub full of steaming water. Leigh asked, "Is that a hot tub?"

"Japanese soaking tub. It will cure what ails you, trust me."

Leigh sniffed the air and seemed pleased. "Lavender?"

Conn nodded, suddenly nervous and shy. "I'll go get a fire going and give you some privacy. The tub is ready. Just climb up those steps and down on the bench inside the tub. Can you make it?"

"Yes. I can do this. Thank you, Conn. Thank you." Leigh wasn't very convincing, but Conn wasn't going to push it. It was probably better if she explained the whole situation to Leigh before they went any further in their relationship. It was only fair.

Conn left the room but didn't quite close the door, since she wasn't sure Leigh could manage on her own. She watched as Leigh struggled to take off her sweater and let it drop on the floor. Conn was torn, her conscience telling her to stay put, her gut in knots watching Leigh fight so hard not to need help. Leigh tried to remove her wet shirt, but her hands were shaking too hard. After fumbling with the snap on her jeans but failing to get any cooperation from the wet denim, she gave a quiet sob of frustration.

Conn couldn't stand it any longer and strode into the bathroom. "Let's just get these off and settle you in the tub. No arguments."

She tried to be businesslike and hide her own trembling as she peeled off the shirt. Then she knelt down and unfastened Leigh's jeans. When she pulled them down, Leigh's underwear came with them, and Conn stood abruptly, busying herself with the soaker in an effort to hide the intense blush she knew was on her face. *This is not the time to start lusting after Leigh. She's exhausted.*

"Conn, I need help." Leigh's voice was weak, and Conn briefly thought about just putting her under the covers and spooning her like in the cave, but she suspected it wasn't enough this time. Leigh was bone cold.

Conn gently helped her shed her camisole, then carefully supported her as she tried the steps, but Leigh was stuck and seemed about to break down in tears again. So Conn took her in her arms and hoisted her over the lip of the tub, lowering her slowly into the soaker. Leigh's groan of pleasure and gratitude for the heat melting around her body sent a spike of arousal through Conn's entire body.

Conn almost tripped over the wet clothes trying to get out of the bathroom. As Conn disappeared out the door, she heard Leigh mutter, "And I thought chivalry was dead. Pity." Leigh made more grateful noises as she settled into the tub. Those noises were almost Conn's undoing. She pushed off the wall where she had been leaning, just outside the bathroom. Time to get busy or "chivalry" would be dying a lustful death.

After Conn brought in wood and started a fire in the main room, she unpacked the bike, stripped out of her leather jacket, started a load of laundry, found an old set of her sweats for Leigh, and changed into some herself. She set the security system, studied the contents of the freezer and cupboards, then stood in the middle of the kitchen desperate for something else to do to occupy her mind. *A natural blonde. Oh yeah, you noticed. Calm down, sport. You're a wreck.*

She was so distracted it took her a while to register that no sound was coming from the bathroom. Walking to the door she knocked, then pushed it open when she got no response, and saw Leigh, asleep and almost submerged. In two strides she had a hold on the somnolent woman and was talking to her.

Leigh started, frightened eyes opened, and as soon as she recognized Conn she threw her arms around her neck. Conn held her, savoring the contact.

When Leigh finally released her, she managed, "You're a wonderful woman. Could I have a towel?"

The request made Conn grin in relief. Leigh was okay. She grabbed a soft white bath sheet out of a cupboard behind her and helped Leigh out of the soaker.

Leigh felt warm and cozy curled up on the sofa in front of the fire, wearing sweats and thick white socks that had materialized out of somewhere. *I might look like hell, but I am sooo comfortable.*

She heard Conn banging around in the kitchen and wanted to help, but before she could muster up the energy, Conn appeared, a little frazzled, with a tray laden with bowls of soup and something that resembled frozen sandwiches. She gingerly placed the tray down on the coffee table in front of Leigh and backed away, staring at the tray and wiping her hands on her sweatpants.

Leigh studied the food and glanced at Conn, then down to the food again. "Is it going to explode?"

"Wha...? Oh, no. I just don't, I mean I haven't cooked in...a while."

Leigh studied the tray. "Um, what kind of..."

"Well, I had some soup and tuna fish and frozen bread, so I made...that."

How bad could it be?

Soggy, cold, and a *lot* of mayo. She smiled brightly at Conn and took another bite, glad she was so hungry to begin with. *Maybe the soup will help.* Aware that Conn was watching her closely, she took a spoonful, holding the tepid bowl closer to her mouth. It smelled like chicken noodle, only slightly congealed and tasting like the can. She took another sip and put it down.

"How is it?"

"Oh, it's good, it's..."

Conn abruptly sat down, took the bowl from her and placed it on the tray, and took Leigh's hands in her own. She looked directly at her. "Remember, you've never lied to me."

Leigh took a breath. "Right. You know what? I am much better now, and I think I can improve it a little. Okay?"

Conn sighed in relief. "Deal."

Leigh got up and took the tray, nourished by the two bites of the mystery food. "You stoke the fire and relax. We'll eat soon."

Conn started working on her end of the bargain, while Leigh went into the kitchen.

When she returned the soup was steaming and the sandwiches edible.

"This is great! What did you do to make it taste so good?"

Leigh grinned. "Well, I heated the soup more and toasted the bread and added a bit more tuna." She was delighted at Conn's enthusiasm, but tried to keep in mind that she probably ate out or lived on cold cereal.

❖

Conn leaned back from the coffee table and sighed contentedly as she took a sip of chamomile tea and regarded her guest. After she'd stoked the fire, she'd set the table using some of her emergency candles to try to make it nicer, and Leigh was exquisite in the low light. Her eyes were indigo, and the angles of her cheeks, lips, and jaw cast shadows that heightened the effect. As exhausted as Leigh was, she was breathtaking.

Conn was happy just to share the same space with her. The outside world seemed far away.

Leigh was quiet, sitting on the floor with her head propped up by a hand, pushing her spoon around the bowl.

"Hey, I think you've hit the wall. Come on." As she took Leigh's hand and they headed toward the bedroom, Leigh protested that she absolutely wouldn't be able to sleep unless she had brushed her teeth, so Conn steered her through the bedroom and into the master bath.

"When you're ready for bed, climb into that one." She pointed to the king-size bed in the master bedroom. Feeling shy as she absorbed the look that Leigh gave her, Conn said, "I'm going to go clean up the kitchen, then take the couch."

Leigh started to protest, but Conn held up her hand. "Whatever's between us will be there tomorrow. We need to talk, because you need to know who I am. If we have something together, I want it to be because you walk into it, not back into it. Go brush your teeth, missy."

With that, she ruffled Leigh's hair and turned her around, aiming her toward the bathroom sink, and gently pushed.

Leigh fiddled with the Japanese soaker to fill it again with hot water, and while it filled she brushed her teeth. *There. Just right.* Next, she rummaged through some drawers and found the object of her search.

When she stuck her head out of the bedroom, she saw Conn sitting on the sofa, staring at the fire. *She is magnificent.* Her long, soft curls caught the reds and golds that the fire was throwing off, making the burnished color seem alive. Her eyes might have reflected the fatigue of the day, but no fear. *Lovely.*

Leigh tried a quiet cough and throat clearing to bring Conn out of her reverie. Finally after she smiled at her from the doorway and crooked her finger, Conn got up and walked over to her. "Do you need something?"

Something about the honesty in Conn's eyes touched Leigh's heart, and she took her hand and guided her into the bath. The lights were low and the tub was steaming.

"Now. You. In the tub. I found what I suspect is your sleeping attire. It's hanging on the back of the door. When you're through, you come and get into your bed. If you don't, I'll be on the sofa with you. Don't argue. Just do it."

"Right. Um, if you want to turn down the thermostat, it's down the hall on the right."

As Leigh left to address the thermostat, she heard Conn splash in the tub and groan in pleasure. After about twenty minutes the water was draining.

She smiled when she heard Conn say, "I really must be easy to read." *She must have found the T-shirt on the back of the door.*

Conn turned out the light, then tiptoed into the bedroom and quietly got into the bed.

"Come here." Leigh moved to make room for her on the warm side of the bed, tucked her body so that Conn was spooning her, and let out a big sigh.

After Leigh yawned and smacked a little, she took Conn's hand and placed it under her breast, bringing it to rest on her heart, with her hand on top of it. "Sleep tight."

Chapter Twenty-Six

Conn's eyes popped wide open, and she stayed perfectly still, trying to orient herself. Where? Her place in Gualala. Good. In her own bed. Check. Still dark outside. Okay. Beautiful woman half on top of her.

"I must be dreaming."

The sound of her voice made the dream stir. A small snort and it snuggled closer, an arm thrown carelessly over Conn's belly, a leg entwined with her own. Conn was perfectly still. She registered every molecule of her body that was in contact with the other form. Cotton on cotton. Skin on skin.

Sometime during the night, Leigh must have shed the bottoms of the sweats she was wearing, because the warmth Conn detected had no cloth around it. It tickled and was warm and moist.

That realization made a five-alarm fire run through her. She tried to just go back to sleep, but found it impossible. She wanted to let herself go and absolutely ravish this astonishing creature. *That's right, Conn. Now's the time to wax poetic and take advantage of her, when she's vulnerable and feels beholden to you. That's honest, that's fair. That'll last. Holy shit! Do you want it to last? What are you thinking?*

In a fraction of a minute Conn had just gone down a very slippery slope and arrived at a startling conclusion. She did want it to last. She wanted Leigh in every way. She was breaking every one of her own rules. She had to get out of that bed *now*.

Gently, she rolled Leigh over and tucked the warm blankets around her, hoping she hadn't left sweaty handprints. Then she quietly got up, sore and stifling a groan. Grabbing a fleece vest from the closet, she found some slippers and went to adjust the heater and stoke the fire. She put the kettle on and made some tea, then sat down on the sofa in front of the fire. The sun seemed to be about to sink into the ocean. They had slept a long time.

She picked her cell phone out of its charger, pressed a speed-dial number, and a familiar voice answered on the second ring.

"Hi, Maggie. I'm checking in. Anything new?"

"We sent a crew to the crash site. The truck was crushed. Mr. Hatch must have jumped out just in time, but didn't count on you and your knife. He was right where you left him. The crew thinks they were the first to arrive. Is Ms. Grove all right?"

"Yeah. She's asleep. What about Dieter and the Johnson woman? Have you found them?"

"We got a report that they slipped into Canada before we could stop them. They shouldn't be back, but there are plenty more like them around."

Conn let out a long sigh. "Do you think we're in the clear?"

"It appears that way, but you never know. The stock scam is shut down, and the people running it, at least in the States, are either dead or have skipped. You can come back, but you two better keep up your guard for a while, because we might not have all the players identified."

Conn sat staring at the fire, listening. *Maybe it's better this way.* Just then she heard a throat being cleared, and leaning against the bedroom door frame was Leigh, arms crossed in front of her, watching. Conn's eyes flicked down her body. The pants were back in place. *Maybe I was dreaming.*

Wondering how much Leigh had heard, Conn had the irrational urge to not tell her they could leave. But, of course, she had to.

"I'll call you back, Maggie, and let you know the plan. Thanks for the update." Flipping the phone off, she stayed seated, leaning forearms on thighs, hands tightly clasped together. Leigh came over and sat down close beside her, and Conn could smell the scent of the soaking salts she had put in the tub the night before, the scent she had enjoyed all night.

"Good news," Conn said half-heartedly, watching the fire. "They cleaned up the, uh, accident, and it appears no one else has seen it. They think Dieter and Georgia skipped across the border to Canada. We can go back."

Leigh was quiet for a moment. "No."

Conn's head whipped around. "What?"

"No."

"Why not?"

"You promised me a few days off. Alone."

"Really?"

Leigh looked around the room, cast in shadow. "What time is it? It seems late."

Conn absently found a wall clock. "It is. It's close to five o'clock."

Leigh jumped up and grabbed Conn's tea mug. "Let me make us some tea, and you call your friend to tell *her* we'll be back in a few days. Then we talk about our vacation."

The back of the woman heading into the kitchen was every bit as alluring as the front. Conn knew she had a stupid grin on her face but couldn't erase it. As she made the call, she was humming, and Maggie let her off the hook remarkably quickly.

Leigh busied herself making tea and toast. After she absently slapped frozen butter on the toast, she carried the tray out to the coffee table in front of the fireplace.

Sitting beside Conn she said to the fire, "Did you make the call?"

"Yes."

"Good. What'll we do for the next few days?" Leigh was rapidly tapping her fingers on her thigh.

Conn stared at her for a moment, then reached over and took the busy hand in her own and held it.

"Leigh, look at me. Please." When Leigh complied she held her gaze.

"Before we make any plans you need to hear me out." Leigh was silent.

Conn took a deep breath. "When you first discovered the crap going on at your—at Peter Cheney's firm, you were roughed up. That had everything to do with your ethics and honesty and being in the wrong place at the wrong time."

Leigh nodded, wondering where this was all going. Conn's eyes bore into her, beseeched her to listen and understand.

"But as you became involved with me, the disk, and trying to nab these guys, the stakes became much higher. I think they discovered what you had done and who I was, and they either needed you dead or in their control. As a bargaining chip. This group is far bigger than Peter or Georgia or even Dieter, for that matter. They mean business." She cut Leigh off before she could speak. "I know because I work for the people who are trying to stop them."

Confused, Leigh blurted, "But you own a huge company. You work for yourself."

"I also work for several government agencies. They paid for my graduate school and helped me set up my company. For that, I've developed security and forensic programs that the government uses. The versions that are sold publicly are watered down compared to what the agencies have."

Leigh squeezed Conn's hand tighter. "Okay. It's public knowledge that you have government contracts. And I can see why that would make those people nervous."

Conn leaned toward her. "That's not all. I've been involved in more than software development. I've been…in covert operations. I'm trained and have acted as an…agent, Leigh. I've done things you would never dream of doing. Things I'm not proud of. Few people know that, but if the people Dieter works for are among those few and have identified me…" She dropped her gaze to the hand that Leigh continued to hold.

Leigh let out a breath and was silent. "So you set me up? How? Did that man who broke into my apartment work for you?"

"Of course not!"

Leigh could see the pain her words had caused and gently squeezed Conn's hand again to encourage her to go on. She was confused and, more than that, terrified that her love for Conn was based on nothing but a lie.

"The truth is that your former fiancé had been on the screen for a while," said Conn. "The money that Jen used to invest in his firm was provided by the Treasury Department. Running into you at that restaurant was no coincidence. I planned the whole thing. Jen's friendship with you was deliberate in the beginning. We snared you and used you, even though we knew things might get dangerous. I've kicked myself a million times for getting you involved, but I believed in this mission. What was one casualty when we could defeat the bad guys?

I'm as bad as they are. And now you know." Conn sat back heavily on the sofa. She seemed defeated.

Leigh had removed her hand a few sentences before. She sat staring into the fire for a long while. Now things made sense. It wasn't what Leigh wanted to hear, but it was what she needed to hear. It was real. Just as real was her reaction to it. She knew that she had to make a choice. Not as the girl with a crush on a mysterious and unattainable woman, but as a woman who had control of her destiny. She could get up and leave; certainly her parents would tell her to get as far away from Conn Stryker as possible.

It was Leigh's life, and she knew, without a doubt, that Conn was in her future. But Conn had to answer more questions. Leigh wasn't willing to risk everything for a fling. She had never been and never would be someone who could treat a relationship casually. Especially with Conn.

"So, Jen just pretended to like me to get me to act on your behalf?" That part hurt a lot.

Conn shook her head vehemently. "Absolutely not! True, she was supposed to befriend you, but almost from the beginning she thought you weren't involved. The invitation to live at our place was not part of the plan and wasn't necessary. And my...my feelings for you were never supposed to happen." The last sentence was almost a whisper.

Although her heart leapt at Conn's admission, Leigh had to know everything. "Are you still an agent? The way you said it almost sounded like it was a thing of the past."

Conn hesitated. "I've have been thinking about giving up the covert part for a while. The truth is, I'm too recognizable these days. I used to be able to avoid publicity, but the pressure to be interviewed, give speeches and all, has increased with the size of the company."

"I can see why. Most CEOs are pudgy white men. You definitely don't fit into that category. The media must love you."

A wry smile crossed Conn's lips, and she rubbed her temples with her fingers, as if fighting a headache. "I'm not sure they would agree. I haven't exactly been cooperative in the past."

"Is that the only reason you've considered giving it up?"

Conn's eyes strayed to Leigh.

Leaning to within inches, Leigh demanded, "Tell the truth. Let me make my own decision."

Conn almost flinched, and Leigh saw fear and pain in her eyes."I'm tired of…that life. I actually wasn't aware the decision was made until you asked me. But when I met you, something changed. And when I thought I might have lost you…might still lose you because of this…"

Her voice caught, and Conn seemed surprised by her own tears. Leigh touched her thumb to capture one, then brushed her thumb over her own lips.

"Conn, that night we met, when you rescued me. If you hadn't been there, I don't know what would have happened. At your house with those terrible men, you were there for me. And now I'm here, and I'm fine, thanks to you." Leigh leaned in to softly graze her lips across those of the woman who had captured her heart.

Conn tried to resist. "You don't understand. I could have gotten you killed!"

"But you didn't."

"I don't want you to stay with me out of *gratitude*! That would be—"

Leigh, her heart aching for Conn, put a finger on Conn's lips and gently shushed her. "Something I would never do. I want to be with you. I want this time to get to know you. I can't explain it any more than that. I'm sure of one thing: I know what I want. Have wanted almost from the moment I met you. And I can assure you, gratitude is only a small part of it. Please."

"Leigh, have you ever even *been* with a woman before? Are you gay?"

"I always led the life my parents planned for me. I even tried to make you part of my fantasy."

Seeing Conn's confusion, she explained. "I was so taken with our dance, our kiss, our one night together trying not to touch, that I based every decision on trying to get you to play your role. With almost disastrous results. I owe you an apology."

Conn started to say something, but Leigh shook her head. She needed to get through this while she still had her wits about her, because unlike the highly ethical Conn, she had no intention of holding back one second if Conn would have her.

"Through my own blundering, you were forced to rescue me, yet *again*. But we escaped together, we ate stale granola bars together, and we dealt with that man together. What I learned is that I trust you. And, maybe more important, I trust *me*."

She brought Conn's hand to her lips, kissed it gently, and their eyes met. "You asked me if I've ever been with a woman and if I'm gay. The answers are no and I don't know. I've never thought about it. Please be content with those answers. I do know that I've never felt before what I feel for you. I'm not willing to let that go. If that means I'm gay, then that's the way it is. Mother will not approve."

Conn was silent for a moment, then snorted and started laughing. Leigh joined her and their laughter got louder, and soon they were gasping for breath, leaning on each other as they quieted down.

"Well, what would you like to do today…excuse me…this evening?"

"I would…hey, where the hell are we anyway?"

"In Gualala." A hint of amusement was in Conn's eyes.

"Say what?"

"Gua—we're not far from Mendocino. Have you ever been there?"

"No. But isn't that the town where they shot *Murder, She Wrote*? It was her home, Cabot something. I've always wanted to go there. I remember watching it on TV as a kid and hearing my parents grouse about using some California town instead of a real Cape Cod fishing village. When I got out here I never traveled except to Los Angeles. I hope they're not even remotely alike."

"They're not. It's more like Bolinas, but with great restaurants and wonderful shops. Though it hasn't lost its, shall I say, bohemian touch. It's the pot capital of Northern California. Want to go? We can pick up groceries on the way back."

"Do you want to know what I really want?" Her voice must have conveyed her desires because Conn gulped and her eyes got rounder.

"Of course I do."

"I want to stay here. With you. That's what I really want."

"Do you want to, uh, eat?"

"We just ate."

Leigh climbed on Conn's lap, straddling her, then leaned in and captured her lips for an unbelievably soft and sensuous kiss that left them both gasping.

❖

Standing, Leigh asked, "Do you have any wine?" and left the room. Conn sat for a moment, her body screaming, then stood and numbly took the dishes to the kitchen, absently plopping them in the sink. She found a bottle of wine, opened it, and stood staring out the kitchen window, her mind spinning. *Maybe I shouldn't...*

Conn was rescued from any more ethical dilemmas by warm arms slipping around her waist from behind. Turning, she was enveloped in a passionate kiss, one that she returned. Leigh was wearing one of Conn's old T-shirts and a pair of heavy socks. And apparently nothing else.

"Come on, I've gotten the soaker ready for us." Leigh picked up the wineglasses and walked toward the bathroom, her hips moving in a way that invited Conn to follow.

Conn flicked the dishtowel over her shoulder to land wherever, grabbed the bottle, and trailed after her.

When she stepped through the door, Leigh was waiting, surrounded by lit candles that Conn recognized as more of her emergency stash.

Leigh closed the door and gazed at Conn. "Undress."

"I'm not very—"

"Now."

Conn fumbled with the zipper on her vest, hands trembling. Having no success, she attempted to untie her sweatpants. *How can I possibly fail at getting out of a pair of sweatpants? Now, of all times!* Suddenly another pair of hands was there, helping, and Conn watched with amazement at Leigh's ability to perform simple motor tasks. The vest came off. Then Conn felt Leigh grasp the hem of the long-sleeved T-shirt. "Put your hands up."

She noticed with some relief that Leigh was now trembling as she tried unsuccessfully to raise the shirt over Conn's head. Conn covered her hands with her own, stilled them, and searched deeply into the teal eyes so close to her. "Are you sure?" Her voice came out husky with need.

When Leigh held her gaze and backed a few feet away, Conn stopped breathing. Gracefully removing her socks and very slowly peeling the T-shirt off, she dropped it on the floor. Conn was lightheaded. Allowing herself to gaze at Leigh's body through a lover's eyes, she found her incredible. Long, well-shaped legs, a small waist, and eye-poppingly beautiful breasts. Everything in proportion. She watched her walk to the tub and climb the few steps to get into it. Settling in, Leigh poured wine into both glasses.

"I'm sure."

Conn tore off her sleep shirt and threw it on the ground. She also made short work of the sweats, registering the cold tile on her feet as she walked to the soaker and climbed in, aware of Leigh's eyes following every move.

Leigh moaned, "God. Your body is so strong and so completely feminine. And you don't even know it. I've dreamt of seeing you, feasting on you with my eyes since that night at my apartment. The night you yanked me into the bathroom and were only wearing a towel."

"I had no idea."

As they sat in the tub together, sipping their wine, Conn couldn't believe she was here. Naked with this woman who had occupied so much of her thoughts and dreams.

"I want you to know how much I...I mean I haven't..." Conn lowered her eyes. "Damn. I've been shot at and never been this scared. This is hard."

Leigh studied the magnificent woman who suddenly was so open and vulnerable. Vulnerability that mirrored her own. Putting her glass down she reached for Conn and slid her arms around her neck.

"Conn, you're the most wonderful person I've ever met," breathed Leigh. "I can't stop thinking about you. You're my first thought in the morning and my last one at night. Just the touch of your hand makes me react in ways I didn't know existed. I may not have been with a woman before, but that doesn't mean I haven't thought of exactly how I want to be with you. Does that help?"

Conn searched the eyes so close to her and something shifted. Leigh knew from her smile that they would soon be lovers, and her heart rate doubled.

"I do believe you've been reading my mind. But I have to warn you."

Leigh frowned.

"What I was trying, unsuccessfully, to say earlier, was that I've never felt this way about anyone before. I don't want to rush it. If you only want to kiss, that's what we'll do. I don't want to make you afraid." Conn was blushing. "I want you—"

"Are you telling me you're afraid of your own passion?"

"I guess I am. I've spent my life being in control, and I don't feel that way around you. I don't know what's going to happen."

Leigh slid next to her, tucked an errant strand of auburn hair behind her ear, and whispered, "Let's find out."

❖

They kissed gently, tentatively exploring each other's lips and mouths. But the weeks apart and the need inside both of them dissolved their fears and focused their passion. Conn stood and held Leigh tightly in her arms, and for the first time they could feel their naked bodies touching.

"My God, Conn," Leigh gasped, "you're so soft." She moaned as she felt Conn's thigh slip between her legs and push upward, then reflexively tried to bear down to increase the pressure. Conn held her steady and placed gentle kisses on her jaw and neck, sucking and nipping here and there.

The warm water swirling around them and the unbelievably erotic sensation of their bodies touching made Leigh shift to wrap her legs around Conn's waist. "I want every part of me to connect with you. I can't get close enough."

After a moment Conn gasped, "I don't think I can stand much longer. Are you clean enough?" The last word barely came out.

"I'm clean. I just don't think I can move. C'mere." Leigh stood and kissed Conn deeply, passionately, a kiss that didn't end until they had to part to come up for air.

Panting, Conn grinned. "You know, if we don't get out of this tub soon, we're liable to drown here. You go on that side for a minute. Please. I need to collect myself."

Leigh floated away but found herself wanting desperately to be back in Conn's arms. They sat silently for about ten seconds.

"Okay, we're out of here." Leigh was closest to the steps and climbed out, grabbing a towel and starting to dry Conn as soon as she was out of the soaker. Conn nabbed the other towel and draped it around Leigh's shoulders. Leigh was so turned on, the drying was more fumbling than anything else. She dropped the towel and leaned into Conn.

"I can't do this now."

Conn looked stricken, but she choked out, "It's okay, it's okay. You don't have to do anything you aren't comfortable with. It was a bad idea. I apologize."

Leigh stared at her, trying to figure out what she was saying.

"No! Conn, I've never been more sure of anything in my life. I just can't *wait* while we dry each other off. I want you beside me, in bed, *now*. Come on!" She grabbed her hand, and they raced toward the bedroom, vying to see who could get there first.

By the time they had jumped on the bed, they were both giggling and wrestling, whapping each other with pillows. Finally, they lay side by side, staring up through the skylight at the stars above them. Conn rolled onto her side, supporting her head with her hand, and Leigh finally cooled down enough that her skin stood up in goose bumps and her nipples followed suit.

Quickly, Conn jerked the covers up and wrapped her arms around Leigh, warming her in a strong embrace. They lay that way for a few minutes, Leigh's head tucked under Conn's chin, their heartbeats the only sound. Leigh watched the rhythm of Conn's pulse and immersed herself in their nakedness.

With little thought Leigh put her lips on Conn's throat and kissed the skin above the pulse. When she heard a sharp intake of breath, she gently sucked on the same place, this time boldly moving her hand up the center of Conn's chest and over to cover one breast. The nipple hardened immediately as her fingers caressed it. Noticing the heat in her own body notch up, she carefully kissed her way down to claim the other nipple with her mouth, circling with her tongue, tasting what had to be her partner's arousal.

"Yes," gasped Conn.

Leigh continued her exploration of the amazing woman beneath her. With a sudden movement, Conn reversed their positions, and Leigh was gazing into her fathomless eyes.

"Let me, please. Let me," Conn murmured and gently covered Leigh with her body, causing both to moan with pleasure.

"You feel so good, Conn. So good."

Instinctively their bodies searched for places of mutual pleasure, the kisses becoming more heated, and Conn returned her thigh to the place Leigh had responded to in the tub.

Leigh was overwhelmed with every touch, her breath caught in her throat. "More, Conn, give me more now."

Conn slid to her side and captured a nipple with her tongue, teasing and sucking on it. Her hand traced down Leigh to rub her flat abdomen, causing Leigh to moan and arch into her. She released her thigh enough to slide her fingers into Leigh and moaned at the slick wetness Leigh knew she would find there.

Conn breathed, "I've dreamt of touching you so many times."

Leigh tried to control or at least register everything as Conn brushed her clitoris, hard and pulsing, and started stroking, gently at first, then with more urgency, keeping her thigh in place so Leigh could push against it.

"Conn, yes, harder, please. God, Conn, harder."

Conn increased the pressure and speed, Leigh flying higher with each stroke. She had no sense of time, only wanted it to never stop

Suddenly Leigh tensed and stopped moving, her body flooding with sensations that were new to her. She released Conn's leg and lay on the bed, opening up completely to her lover's hand. Conn increased her stroking, straddling one of Leigh's legs and moving against it.

Leigh's breath was ragged. Her body and mind exploded in a cascade of pleasures so raw and primal she didn't recognize them. A moan broke from her throat as first she shuddered, then bucked, reaching for Conn. Conn held tight as she continued to stroke her center, having slipped deep inside Leigh to heighten her release. Waves poured off Leigh as she responded to everything Conn did. Gradually she calmed, and Conn stayed inside her body, following its instructions, until Leigh was spent.

Conn started to slowly come out, causing a sharp intake of breath from Leigh.

"No. Not yet." They lay side by side.

Leigh let her hand drift down the exquisite body next to her, and Conn sighed. Slowly she kept touching until she found the treasure she was searching for between her lover's legs, wet and swollen and pulsing.

"You are so lovely," Leigh murmured. "So absolutely, breathtaking." Kissing Conn, she began to explore the folds beneath her fingers, her passion for her lover translating into movements that brought Conn to a strong climax within minutes. Leigh was amazed to find that she almost joined her in release. *God, this woman!*

"I'm sorry." Conn was panting. "I wanted to make it last, but I couldn't. You're so exciting when you tell me what you need. It was all I could do to hold it together then. As soon as you touched me I nearly exploded."

"Are you apologizing? You were wonderful. I almost—um, I enjoyed every minute of it. Trust me."

Conn reached down again. "You're wet." Her voice was husky.

Still sensitive, Leigh gasped when touched, then pushed into her lover's caress. "You must think I'm a sex addict or something. I've never had this happen before. I—" Before she could continue, she found her mouth covered in a deep kiss that only heightened her arousal.

"Hush." Conn breathed into her ear. "Just be with it. I want to taste you. You're so wondrous." She slid down Leigh's body, licking and sucking, seeming to pay particular attention to any place that made Leigh moan. Leigh couldn't have stopped; she didn't even recognize her own voice.

Conn slid her fingers inside Leigh and settled her body between her legs, her mouth covering, then her tongue finding the velvet tissue swollen by desire. She tasted, licked, tugged gently on Leigh's clit with her teeth, then flicked it with her tongue, until Leigh was sure she was going to die of passion before she could even orgasm. Conn found Leigh's rhythm and matched it perfectly. When Leigh came, she cried out Conn's name, and Conn continued to knead and suck and press until Leigh begged her to hold her.

Just hold her.

After she had recovered enough to speak, Leigh said, "My God. Is that what happens every time women make love to each other?"

"I don't know. I've never experienced that before."

"So…it might be us?"

"Uh-huh."

"Sign me up."

They nestled together under the covers, and Leigh was almost asleep when she heard Conn whisper, "I love you."

She waited a moment, then said, "Love you, too." She felt the corners of her mouth turn up, but kept her eyes closed.

They lay in each other's arms for a long time, savoring the sweat and salt and passion that they aroused in each other. Each time one would doze, the other's touch would bring them together again.

The dawn found them tangled under a pile of sheets and blankets. Two inches from Conn, Leigh watched her slowly awake.

Conn brushed her lips over Leigh's. "I love you, Leigh. But I might not be good for you."

Leigh felt fury in the gray light of dawn. "Don't ever say that again, Conn. What isn't good for me is being without you. Whatever happens, I want to face it together. Now close your eyes."

Conn's expression of pure joy and peace just before her eyelids fluttered shut imprinted on Leigh's heart for eternity. Leigh fussed with the sheet and blanket until they were under them, then pulled Conn closer and stroked her russet curls until she felt Conn's body loosen into slumber.

As Leigh watched her lover sleep, the day took on vibrant colors she'd never seen before. Conn said they were probably still in danger and would have to be very cautious, but Leigh was convinced that they were stronger with each other than without. And unquestionably she was in love with Conn Stryker. She would do anything to protect that love.

When Conn shifted and rolled Leigh on top of her, kissed her neck, and mumbled, "Love you. Sleep," Leigh burrowed into Conn's shoulder and closed her eyes, home at last.

About the Author

JLee Meyer utilizes her background in psychology and speech pathology in her work as an international communication consultant. Spending time in airports, planes, and hotel rooms allows her the opportunity to pursue two of her favorite passions: reading and writing lesbian fiction. Jlee's hobbies are photography, hiking, tennis, and skiing. JLee and her life partner split their time between Northern California and Manhattan.

Her romance *Forever Found* is available from Bold Strokes Books.

For news of upcoming releases and author appearances, visit JLee's website: www.jleemeyer.com

Books Available From Bold Strokes Books

Fresh Tracks by Georgia Beers. Seven women, seven days. A lot can happen when old friends, lovers, and a new girl in town get together in the mountains. (1-933110-63-5)

Empress and the Acolyte by Jane Fletcher. Jemeryl and Tevi fight to protect the very fabric of their world…time. Lyremouth Chronicles Book Three (1-933110-60-0)

First Instinct by JLee Meyer. When high-stakes security fraud leads to murder, one woman flees for her life while another risks her heart to protect her. (1-933110-59-7)

Erotic Interludes 4: Extreme Passions. Thirty of today's hottest erotica writers set the pages aflame with love, lust, and steamy liaisons. (1-933110-58-9)

Storms of Change by Radclyffe. In the continuing saga of the Provincetown Tales, duty and love are at odds as Reese and Tory face their greatest challenge. (1-933110-57-0)

Unexpected Ties by Gina L. Dartt. With death before dessert, Kate Shannon and Nikki Harris are swept up in another tale of danger and romance. (1-933110-56-2)

Sleep of Reason by Rose Beecham. Nothing is at it seems when Detective Jude Devine finds herself caught up in a small-town soap opera. And her rocky relationship with forensic pathologist Dr. Mercy Westmoreland just got a lot harder. (1-933110-53-8)

Passion's Bright Fury by Radclyffe. When a trauma surgeon and a filmmaker become reluctant allies on the battleground between life and death, passion strikes without warning. (1-933110-54-6)

Broken Wings by L-J Baker. When Rye Woods, a fairy, meets the beautiful dryad Flora Withe, her libido, as squashed and hidden as her wings, reawakens along with her heart. (1-933110-55-4)

Combust the Sun by Andrews & Austin. A Richfield and Rivers mystery set in L.A. Murder among the stars. (1-933110-52-X)

Of Drag Kings and the Wheel of Fate by Susan Smith. A blind date in a drag club leads to an unlikely romance. (1-933110-51-1)

Tristaine Rises by Cate Culpepper. Brenna, Jesstin, and the Amazons of Tristaine face their greatest challenge for survival. (1-933110-50-3)

Too Close to Touch by Georgia Beers. Kylie O'Brien believes in true love and is willing to wait for it. It doesn't matter one damn bit that Gretchen, her new and off-limits boss, has a voice as rich and smooth as melted chocolate. It absolutely doesn't... (1-933110-47-3)

100th Generation by Justine Saracen. Ancient curses, modern-day villains, and a most intriguing woman who keeps appearing when least expected lead archeologist Valerie Foret on the adventure of her life. (1-933110-48-1)

Battle for Tristaine by Cate Culpepper. While Brenna struggles to find her place in the clan and the love between her and Jess grows, Tristaine is threatened with destruction. Second in the Tristaine series. (1-933110-49-X)

The Traitor and the Chalice by Jane Fletcher. Without allies to help them, Tevi and Jemeryl will have to risk all in the race to uncover the traitor and retrieve the chalice. The Lyremouth Chronicles Book Two. (1-933110-43-0)

Promising Hearts by Radclyffe. Dr. Vance Phelps lost everything in the War Between the States and arrives in New Hope, Montana, with no hope of happiness and no desire for anything except forgetting—until she meets Mae, a frontier madam. (1-933110-44-9)

Carly's Sound by Ali Vali. Poppy Valente and Julia Johnson form a bond of friendship that lays the foundation for something more, until Poppy's past comes back to haunt her—literally. A poignant romance about love and renewal. (1-933110-45-7)

Unexpected Sparks by Gina L. Dartt. Falling in love is challenging enough without adding murder to the mix. Kate Shannon's growing feelings for much younger Nikki Harris are complicated enough without the mystery of a fatal fire that Kate can't ignore. (1-933110-46-5)

Whitewater Rendezvous by Kim Baldwin. Two women on a wilderness kayak adventure—Chaz Herrick, a laid-back outdoorswoman, and Megan Maxwell, a workaholic news executive—discover that true love may be nothing at all like they imagined. (1-933110-38-4)

Erotic Interludes 3: Lessons in Love ed. by Radclyffe and Stacia Seaman. Sign on for a class in love…the best lesbian erotica writers take us to "school." (1-9331100-39-2)

Punk Like Me by JD Glass. Twenty-one-year-old Nina writes lyrics and plays guitar in the rock band Adam's Rib, and she doesn't always play by the rules. And oh yeah—she has a way with the girls. (1-933110-40-6)

Coffee Sonata by Gun Brooke. Four women whose lives unexpectedly intersect in a small town by the sea share one thing in common—they all have secrets. (1-933110-41-4)

The Clinic: Tristaine Book One by Cate Culpepper. Brenna, a prison medic, finds herself deeply conflicted by her growing feelings for her patient, Jesstin, a wild and rebellious warrior reputed to be descended from ancient Amazons. (1-933110-42-2)

Forever Found by JLee Meyer. ·Can time, tragedy, and shattered trust destroy a love that seemed destined? When chance reunites two childhood friends separated by tragedy, the past resurfaces to determine the shape of their future. (1-933110-37-6)

Sword of the Guardian by Merry Shannon. Princess Shasta's bold new bodyguard has a secret that could change both of their lives. *He* is actually a *she*. A passionate romance filled with courtly intrigue, chivalry, and devotion. (1-933110-36-8)

Wild Abandon by Ronica Black. From their first tumultuous meeting, Dr. Chandler Brogan and Officer Sarah Monroe are drawn together by their common obsessions—sex, speed, and danger. (1-933110-35-X)

Turn Back Time by Radclyffe. Pearce Rifkin and Wynter Thompson have nothing in common but a shared passion for surgery. They clash at every opportunity, especially when matters of the heart are suddenly at stake. (1-933110-34-1)

Chance by Grace Lennox. At twenty-six, Chance Delaney decides her life isn't working so she swaps it for a different one. What follows is the sexy, funny, touching story of two women who, in finding themselves, also find one another. (1-933110-31-7)

The Exile and the Sorcerer by Jane Fletcher. First in the Lyremouth Chronicles. Tevi, wounded and adrift, arrives in the courtyard of a shy young sorcerer. Together they face monsters, magic, and the challenge of loving despite their differences. (1-933110-32-5)

A Matter of Trust by Radclyffe. JT Sloan is a cybersleuth who doesn't like attachments. Michael Lassiter is leaving her husband, and she needs Sloan's expertise to safeguard her company. It should just be business—but it turns into much more. (1-933110-33-3)

Sweet Creek by Lee Lynch. A celebration of the enduring nature of love, friendship, and community in the quirky, heart-warming lesbian community of Waterfall Falls. (1-933110-29-5)

The Devil Inside by Ali Vali. Derby Cain Casey, head of a New Orleans crime organization, runs the family business with guts and grit, and no one crosses her. No one, that is, until Emma Verde claims her heart and turns her world upside down. (1-933110-30-9)

Grave Silence by Rose Beecham. Detective Jude Devine's investigation of a series of ritual murders is complicated by her torrid affair with the golden girl of Southwestern forensic pathology, Dr. Mercy Westmoreland. (1-933110-25-2)

Honor Reclaimed by Radclyffe. In the aftermath of 9/11, Secret Service Agent Cameron Roberts and Blair Powell close ranks with a trusted few to find the would-be assassins who nearly claimed Blair's life. (1-933110-18-X)

Honor Bound by Radclyffe. Secret Service Agent Cameron Roberts and Blair Powell face political intrigue, a clandestine threat to Blair's safety, and the seemingly irreconcilable personal differences that force them ever farther apart. (1-933110-20-1)

Innocent Hearts by Radclyffe. In a wild and unforgiving land, two women learn about love, passion, and the wonders of the heart. (1-933110-21-X)

The Temple at Landfall by Jane Fletcher. An imprinter, one of Celaeno's most revered servants of the Goddess, is also a prisoner to the faith—until a Ranger frees her by claiming her heart. The Celaeno series. (1-933110-27-9)

Protector of the Realm: Supreme Constellations Book One by Gun Brooke. A space adventure filled with suspense and a daring intergalactic romance featuring Commodore Rae Jacelon and the stunning, but decidedly lethal, Kellen O'Dal. (1-933110-26-0)

Force of Nature by Kim Baldwin. From tornados to forest fires, the forces of nature conspire to bring Gable McCoy and Erin Richards close to danger, and closer to each other. (1-933110-23-6)

In Too Deep by Ronica Black. Undercover homicide cop Erin McKenzie tracks a femme fatale who just might be a real killer…with love and danger hot on her heels. (1-933110-17-1)

Stolen Moments: Erotic Interludes 2 by Stacia Seaman and Radclyffe, eds. Love on the run, in the office, in the shadows…Fast, furious, and almost too hot to handle. (1-933110-16-3)

Course of Action by Gun Brooke. Actress Carolyn Black desperately wants the starring role in an upcoming film produced by Annelie Peterson. Just how far will she go for the dream part of a lifetime? (1-933110-22-8)

Rangers at Roadsend by Jane Fletcher. Sergeant Chip Coppelli has learned to spot trouble coming, and that is exactly what she sees in her new recruit, Katryn Nagata. The Celaeno series. (1-933110-28-7)

Justice Served by Radclyffe. Lieutenant Rebecca Frye and her lover, Dr. Catherine Rawlings, embark on a deadly game of hide-and-seek with an underworld kingpin who traffics in human souls. (1-933110-15-5)

Distant Shores, Silent Thunder by Radclyffe. Dr. Tory King—along with the women who love her—is forced to examine the boundaries of love, friendship, and the ties that transcend time. (1-933110-08-2)

Hunter's Pursuit by Kim Baldwin. A raging blizzard, a mountain hideaway, and a killer-for-hire set a scene for disaster—or desire—when Katarzyna Demetrious rescues a beautiful stranger. (1-933110-09-0)

The Walls of Westernfort by Jane Fletcher. All Temple Guard Natasha Ionadis wants is to serve the Goddess—until she falls in love with one of the rebels she is sworn to destroy. The Celaeno series. (1-933110-24-4)

Change Of Pace: *Erotic Interludes* by Radclyffe. Twenty-five hot-wired encounters guaranteed to spark more than just your imagination. Erotica as you've always dreamed of it. (1-933110-07-4)

Honor Guards by Radclyffe. In a wild flight for their lives, the president's daughter and those who are sworn to protect her wage a desperate struggle for survival. (1-933110-01-5)

Fated Love by Radclyffe. Amidst the chaos and drama of a busy emergency room, two women must contend not only with the fragile nature of life, but also with the irresistible forces of fate. (1-933110-05-8)

Justice in the Shadows by Radclyffe. In a shadow world of secrets and lies, Detective Sergeant Rebecca Frye and her lover, Dr. Catherine Rawlings, join forces in the elusive search for justice. (1-933110-03-1)

shadowland by Radclyffe. In a world on the far edge of desire, two women are drawn together by power, passion, and dark pleasures. An erotic romance. (1-933110-11-2)

Love's Masquerade by Radclyffe. Plunged into the indistinguishable realms of fiction, fantasy, and hidden desires, Auden Frost is forced to question all she believes about the nature of love. (1-933110-14-7)

Love & Honor by Radclyffe. The president's daughter and her lover are faced with difficult choices as they battle a tangled web of Washington intrigue for...love and honor. (1-933110-10-4)

Beyond the Breakwater by Radclyffe. One Provincetown summer, three women learn the true meaning of love, friendship, and family. (1-933110-06-6)

Tomorrow's Promise by Radclyffe. One timeless summer, two very different women discover the power of passion to heal and the promise of hope that only love can bestow. (1-933110-12-0)

Love's Tender Warriors by Radclyffe. Two women who have accepted loneliness as a way of life learn that love is worth fighting for and a battle they cannot afford to lose. (1-933110-02-3)

Love's Melody Lost by Radclyffe. A secretive artist with a haunted past and a young woman escaping a life that has proved to be a lie find their destinies entwined. (1-933110-00-7)

Safe Harbor by Radclyffe. A mysterious newcomer, a reclusive doctor, and a troubled gay teenager learn about love, friendship, and trust during one tumultuous summer in Provincetown. (1-933110-13-9)

Above All, Honor by Radclyffe. Secret Service Agent Cameron Roberts fights her desire for the one woman she can't have—Blair Powell, the daughter of the president of the United States. (1-933110-04-X)